SUMMER ON
A SUNNY ISLAND

Sue Moorcroft writes award-winning contemporary fiction of life and love. *The Little Village Christmas* and *A Christmas Gift* were *Sunday Times* bestsellers and *The Christmas Promise* went to #1 in the Kindle chart. She also writes short stories, serials, articles, columns, courses and writing 'how to'.

An army child, Sue was born in Germany then lived in Cyprus, Malta and the UK and still loves to travel. Her other loves include writing (the best job in the world), reading, watching Formula 1 on TV and hanging out with friends, dancing, yoga, wine and chocolate.

If you're interested in being part of #TeamSueMoorcroft you can find more information at www.suemoorcroft.com/ street-team. If you prefer to sign up to receive news of Sue and her books, go to www.suemoorcroft.com and click on 'Newsletter'. You can follow @SueMoorcroft on Twitter, @SueMoorcroftAuthor on Instagram, or Facebook.com/ sue.moorcroft.3 and Facebook.com/SueMoorcroftAuthor.

Summer on a Sunny Island

Sue Moorcroft

MIX
Paper from
responsible sources

FSC
FSC C007454

This book is produced from independently certified FSC™
to ensure responsible forest management

For more information visit: www.harpercollins.co.uk/green

avon.

Published by AVON
A division of HarperCollins*Publishers* Ltd
1 London Bridge Street
London SE1 9GF

www.harpercollins.co.uk

A Paperback Original 2020

1

First published in Great Britain by
HarperCollins*Publishers* 2020

A catalogue copy of this book is
available from the British Library.

ISBN: 978-0-00-832182-6

This novel is entirely a work of fiction.
The names, characters and incidents portrayed in it are
the work of the author's imagination. Any resemblance to
actual persons, living or dead, events or localities is
entirely coincidental.

Typeset in Sabon LT Std by Palimpsest Book Production Limited,
Falkirk, Stirlingshire

Printed and bound in UK by CPI Group (UK) Ltd, Croydon CR0 4YY

Acknowledgements

I'm going to start this round of acknowledgements by thanking you, my readers. Without you, my books wouldn't be published. I feel privileged every time one of you gets in touch via my website or social media or turns up at an event to chat. Some of the most supportive readers form my street team, Team Sue Moorcroft, and they deserve a special round of thanks for loving my books and sharing my posts. I hope we carry on together for many more happy years.

Summer on a Sunny Island was sparked by attending a reunion for service kids in Malta, when Trevor, Kevan and Suzanne Moorcroft – my brothers, my sister-in-law – and I managed to convert one lunch into a ten-day holiday. My early life in Malta and my willingness to return there whenever possible made my research a) a joy b) a reason to write part of this book in Malta c) often a matter of searching my memory banks and chatting to my brothers.

However, I'm also indebted to:

My wonderful son Paul Matthews for everything related to education and data.

Trevor Moorcroft, who now conducts a lot of my

research. His retirement is his employer's loss and my gain as he finds factual answers to many of my questions. Through Trevor, Ron Leeman, who lives in Thailand was able to advise on the position of British people living and working there.

My nephew Ryan Moorcroft for answering questions on having Maltese family and the passport situation.

My friends Tom, Ian and Ivana Restall for filling in gaps in my knowledge of Malta, especially in terms of daily life.

Katy Beskow, the vegan food writer, who helped me enormously with Dory's career. Katy didn't even know me when she agreed to help, so special thanks to her.

Fellow author Lisbeth Foye for information on HR and rheumatoid arthritis.

Mark Lacey, retired Det Supt and independent member of the parole board, who answered my law-related questions.

Keith Martin for information on mortgage providers and their requirements and protocols. (It's a long time since I worked in a bank.)

As with almost every book I've written, I thank writer of chillers and thrillers Mark West for beta-reading *Summer on a Sunny Island* and making his pithy observations.

I'm a very lucky author to:

- be represented by the wonderful Juliet Pickering, and I thank her and every member of the Blake Friedmann Literary, TV and Film Agency for their enormous contributions to my career.
- be published by the team at Avon Books UK (HarperCollins) with enthusiasm, professionalism, creativity, great editing, and gorgeous covers via artist Carrie May. Thank you.

I hope you enjoy reading *Summer on a Sunny Island* and see a little of why Malta is always in my heart.

For The Romantic Novelists' Association
in its Diamond Anniversary year

I've been a member of this amazing organisation for
two of its six decades, during which it has given me:
a 'can do' attitude,
massive support,
industry knowledge,
career opportunities,
and an army of fantastic friends.

Chapter One

Rosa twirled her wine glass, trying to choose her words over the chatter and clatter of Gino's pavement café and the rumble of traffic along the seafront road. Here in the busy area of Sliema, new buildings outnumbered the old and the promenade was filled with people selling harbour cruises to tourists. Rosa preferred Ta' Xbiex, where she was staying, about a mile along the coast, with its traditional stone villas. Sliema's air was punctuated by the sound of car horns but in Ta' Xbiex you could sometimes catch the mellow sound of church bells rising into the blue sky above the boats bobbing on the sparkling sea.

The Maltese sun was setting in a blaze of lilac and pink. In the sea creek, a row of red and blue ferries bobbed at their moorings. Over the buzzing traffic Rosa could see their lights coming on. Beyond them, the skyline of the capital city, Valletta, on the other side of Marsamxett Harbour, was becoming a silhouette of ramparts and domes and spires.

Across the table, Zach Bentley watched her. His short dark hair was silky, eyes brown, skin golden. When he'd been working shirtless in the garden near the apartment she was sharing with her mum, Rosa had seen a tattoo of upswept wings across his shoulders. Now she could see ink above his wrist, too – a Maltese cross from which dangled a birdcage, its door swinging open.

She spoke in a rush. 'I'm afraid I'm not exactly dating. Mum thinks I need a "summer romance" to get over my last relationship. And with her being there when you asked if I was doing anything this evening and her having been to school with your dad Steve here in Malta . . .' She shrugged, silently cursing her warm and welcoming mother, Dory Hammond. 'She trotted out "How nice! Now Rosa won't be bored while I Skype Andy," as if I can't amuse myself while she chats to her boyfriend.' It had been hard for Rosa to do anything but accept Zach's invitation. Now, instead of brooding about Marcus, back in England, she was having to get to know this man.

Zach sipped his beer and she thought she saw amusement flicker in his eyes. 'I understand.' The slightest hint of Cornwall in his voice contrasted with her own short Yorkshire vowels. Then his grin flashed and he leaned forward conspiratorially. 'To be truthful . . . my sister Marci and her little girl Paige are staying with me at the family apartment. As Marci's pretty new here and you've just arrived, what I was actually intending to suggest was that you and Marci go out while I babysat Paige.'

'Oh!' Rosa almost choked on her next sip of wine, mortified heat flooding her face. 'And Mum shoved me at you instead!'

'Don't think I minded,' he assured her, eyes still dancing. 'But not-dating me is probably a good choice.' He seemed to have no trouble both enjoying the joke and gently turning it against himself.

2

Reluctantly, she gave a small laugh though she said wrathfully, 'My flipping mother!'

He sobered. 'Marci seems to think she has to hang around the apartment once Paige has gone to bed. She swims or explores with Paige during the day but I think it would be great for her to have an evening out now and then.' He paused. Then, 'I don't think Marci would mind me telling you – she's off work with stress. Her new boss expects a level of commitment to short-notice overtime that doesn't work for a single parent with child care to consider.'

The nearby cars had formed themselves into a traffic jam and Rosa lifted her voice over a hooting of horns. 'Hopefully Marci and I will get on when we meet. Mum told me she was here when I spotted Paige with you in the garden and asked who she was. Mum always knows everything about everyone.' Dory, who'd been in Malta since the beginning of May, had also been able to inform Rosa that Zach and Marci had a younger sister called Electra, presently travelling elsewhere.

Zach seemed to realise Rosa might not be any keener on Zach fixing up a girls' night for her than she had been on her mum wangling her a date, and returned to treating their not-date as a joke. 'I could drive you straight home, if you want, but it might make your mum think I pounced on you or was too boring to bear. And I've kind of got my mind on spaghetti rizzi.'

Glad to fall in with his mild teasing, she took up the menu. 'Let's eat. Mum doesn't need more excuses to get involved.'

A lithe, blonde waitress halted at their table, pen poised over her notepad. 'You are ready to order?'

The menu was printed in English as well as Maltese.

3

Rosa saw rizzi were sea urchins. Deciding she'd have plenty of opportunity to taste unfamiliar food with her mum, she said, 'Penne chicken and another glass of white wine, please.'

Zach gave his order then turned back to Rosa as the waitress whisked away. 'Does your mum often arrange your dates?'

Rosa managed a smile. 'Only when she's encouraging me to forget my ex.'

Over Zach's shoulder a cheer went up from a group watching football on a TV suspended from the canopy. The clientele at the close-packed tables was divided between those glued to the screens and others socialising all the louder over them.

Zach's gaze softened and he let his joking drop. 'In my experience you find your own pace with these things.'

Though he got points for both apparently understanding what she hadn't said and refraining from swivelling in his seat to see whether a goal had been scored, Rosa searched for another subject. 'If your dad was an army kid like Mum, how did your family get to own Ta' Xbiex Terrace House?' Her wine arrived. She thanked the waitress and took the first sip while it was still cold. Though she'd arrived on the island only two days ago, she'd already discovered cold drinks didn't stay cold on hot June evenings.

He settled into his chair, the breeze disarranging his hair, which had begun the evening combed diagonally back. 'My grandfather was here with the army, like yours. Grandad Harry met and married grandmother Rebekah, who's Maltese. Nanna and my great-aunt Giusi inherited the property from their parents. When they were children the road was called Ta' Xbiex Terrace rather than Ir-Rampa

4

– "The Ramp".' His pronunciation of 'Ta' Xbiex' was subtly different to Rosa's 'Tash Beesh' – his 'sh' holding something of a soft 'j' that made Rosa aware of her own limitations with Maltese pronunciation. Lucky for her that English was an official language of the island.

'"Terrace" is a good description,' she put in. 'I love the way it's like an upper deck to the more ordinary road below.'

Zach nodded. 'The house was too big to rent easily so Nanna and Aunt Giusi decided to convert it into four apartments, owning two each. After the structural work was complete they offered me the job of fitting them out.'

An image of the bathroom where she'd stood naked a few hours ago flashed through Rosa's mind. It was odd to think Zach had tiled the turquoise and white walls. 'Mum was delighted to find our apartment through your dad Steve on the Barracks Brats Facebook group. It's lovely. You've done a great job.'

He looked almost surprised at the compliment. 'I hope you'll enjoy your summer there.'

She shrugged. 'It feels odd at the moment because I've only lived in three homes – two with Mum and one with my ex, Marcus, all in our home town of Liggers Moor. Have you lived here long?' Their waitress approached, threading her way through the tables to set their meals before them. Rosa shook out her napkin.

He picked up his fork and loaded it with spaghetti. 'I was brought up in the UK too but I love Malta. I suppose I'll have to go back eventually but I haven't finished Aunt Giusi's lower apartment yet. She hasn't chosen a kitchen or bathroom because she's tempted to sell her house in Lija and move in herself. Also, I do some of my own work and help out at a cousin's place.'

'Is your dad coming over for the Service Kids' Malta reunion next week?' Rosa had begun to enjoy herself. Her penne chicken was delicious and Zach was proving easy company.

He shook his head. 'He's just begun a new job and Mum has severe rheumatoid arthritis, which makes travel tricky. He's asked Marci to go to the reunion for him.' He paused, eyebrows lifting. 'How would you feel about Marci going along with you and Dory?'

Rosa nodded, thinking a group situation would make it easier to get to know Marci and decide whether they might like one another. 'Of course, if she'd like to. Aren't you going?'

'I think Dad and Marci have it sorted out.' Zach laid down his knife and fork. 'Dory tells me she hasn't been back to Malta since she was a child.'

The next table was full of noisy tourists. Rosa had to lean in to be heard. 'Till this summer,' she agreed. 'Dad wasn't around much after I was born so money's been an issue. She's thrilled to be here until October. I was able to take unpaid leave from my job to be her assistant for the summer and Mum sorted out the residency permits.'

Zach's eyes had darkened as lights came on and the last of the short dusk faded into dark night. 'She seems to be doing OK as a cookbook writer. What's your job normally?'

'Events and sponsorship.' Rosa made her reply brief, not particularly wanting to go into the whole sorry story of how she and Marcus splitting up had impacted on her career. 'Were you in construction in the UK?'

He paused while they gave orders to the blonde waitress for iced coffee for Rosa and espresso for Zach before he answered. 'My last job was in data and report writing for a multi-academy trust.' He grinned at what she knew must

6

be a blank expression. 'You don't have to pretend to know what that is. I collected data from the different schools in the trust, consolidating and presenting it to the trustees, managers, staff, students, parents and OFSTED.'

'Not much like fitting out apartments,' she observed.

He glanced away from the chattering population of the pavement café and across the seafront road to where a large tourist boat was backing up to the quay, its passengers jostling to disembark. 'When I first left home I used to work weekends for a small building company, so I picked up some skills. I'm doing some freelance report writing for income to live on.' The iced coffee and espresso arrived and Zach dropped sugar into his cup.

Rosa sipped her drink, cold and creamy, glancing around at the people milling from café to café, Maltese and English mingling with other languages, palm trees rising up over nearby cars. 'This must have been a cool place for our parents to be brought up.'

Zach shifted and his knee brushed hers briefly beneath the table. 'I'd have loved it. It's as if I've only just become fully conscious of my double connection to Malta, with my Maltese grandmother and my grandfather being stationed here with the British Army. I used to sigh when we came on family holidays, visiting relatives or trudging around old barracks when I would have liked to have been snorkelling.' His smile flashed but it sounded as if his words came from the heart.

'Is your grandfather coming out to stay with you?' Rosa went on. 'Grandpa won't. Grandma died three years ago and he doesn't want to come without her.' She felt a pang as she pictured her beloved grandparents, Lance and Bette McCoy. The loss of Bette was now reflected in the distant expression she often saw in Lance's eyes.

'Afraid not.' Zach's shoulders moved as if he sighed. Around them people laughed and chattered, answered phone calls and called to waiters but Zach stared pensively towards the sea as if her questions had triggered a change in his mood.

Then he snapped back into focus and changed the subject. 'Paceville's the place to go if you want to get your party on. As well as the shopping area at The Point in Tigné, there's plenty in and around Sliema. The ferry to Valletta goes from over there, where Sliema Creek becomes Marsamxett Harbour.' He nodded in the direction of the boats. 'The buildings in Valletta are amazing and so's the view of Grand Harbour on the other side of the city. And don't miss Mdina . . .'

Rosa blinked as Zach went on about Malta's attractions. It was as if he'd flipped a switch that turned him into a tour guide. 'Thanks,' she answered, at last. 'I'm helping Mum, starting tomorrow. She's here to write a new book so I guess sightseeing will have to fit around that.'

He acted as if her words were a prompt. 'I'll ask for the bill.'

When it arrived Rosa put down enough euros to pay her half.

A corner of Zach's mouth quirked. 'Ah. The etiquette of not-really-dating.' But his smile was no longer natural. He pulled out his keys and Rosa took it that he was ready to take her home.

In the car, as he reversed into the stream of headlights with the air of one who knew the other vehicles would stop, she wondered, for the mental exercise, how the evening would have ended if they *had* been on a date.

That sudden change of mood would have been a proper bummer.

Chapter Two

Zach drove Rosa back to Ta' Xbiex along the seafront road. Two lanes of cars teemed in each direction. On their right, lights flared and music blared from bars. To the left, lights between the palm trees reflected in squiggles on the black surface of Sliema Creek. The Maltese harbours and creeks swarmed with boats: motor yachts, sailing yachts and catamarans, rowing boats, inflatable boats, ferries, cruise liners, party boats, harbour cruisers and water taxis. They, and the sea in all its seasons, were as much a part of the scenery as the golden stone of which the island was built.

When he reached The Ramp he parked outside Ta' Xbiex Terrace House. Everything in its three storeys was stone: walls, balconies and elegantly ornate balustrades. At street level stood the garages and basement. The lower apartment and terrace – presently rented to Dory and Rosa – were on the floor above and reached via a flight of graceful stone steps. The garden next to the terrace, where spiky agaves and shady palms grew behind elegant black railings, the upper apartment and the roof terrace were all reserved for the use of the Bentley family.

Rosa climbed from the car and Zach walked her up to her front door, not because he thought she needed protecting but because he felt he'd been boorish enough when, at the end of the meal, his thoughts had slithered off into the grey lands of unhappiness he knew so well. Her gaze had become wary and she'd said little on the journey home.

He hadn't wanted to explain that neither his dad nor grandfather would be visiting him in Malta. Zach and his dad had barely spoken for the last couple of years and Grandad Harry's dementia would transform the sunlit island he'd once loved to a frighteningly unfamiliar place. Nanna looked after Grandad so she wouldn't come either.

Now, Rosa turned with a polite smile. 'Thanks for driving me home.' She put her hand on the door.

'My pleasure,' he returned equally courteously. 'See you around, no doubt.' He thought about adding, 'Hope it was OK for a fake date,' but decided the moment for jokes had passed.

When she'd gone inside he turned not towards the next flight of stairs leading up to the family apartment but the one back down to the street. Once on the pavement he pulled up a cab app on his phone and booked a car to carry him to the bars of Paceville.

At a small sound behind him he turned.

And there was Rosa, hesitating on the stairs.

They gazed at each other. 'Oh,' she said. 'I thought you'd gone.'

'I thought you'd be in your apartment.' He watched her hover.

She took a few more steps. 'It's early. I thought I'd go and sample the nightlife you told me about.'

10

'In Paceville?' He hesitated. 'That's where I'm going. I'm waiting for a cab.'

'Oh.' She laughed uncertainly. 'Could we share? I don't expect you to hang out with me or anything. I fancy getting my bearings.'

'OK. Of course . . . Look, you'll get a cab home again, won't you? Malta's a pretty safe place but—'

She jumped more decisively down the last two steps. 'Thanks. I'll do that.' They waited in silence except for the sound of traffic on the road below The Ramp.

Zach thought about the woman beside him: delicately made with freckles on her high cheekbones and light brown eyes that sparkled in sunlight. He'd seen her from the roof terrace yesterday afternoon and stopped to watch her tangly, toffee-coloured bob bounce around her head with every quick movement as she chattered to Dory. When she'd laughed, her eyes had crinkled to slits.

He'd watched her finely drawn mouth and experienced strong sexual attraction.

Being sexually attracted to someone was great. It became fantastic if the person you were attracted to was attracted to you too. Though judging by the way she'd been at pains to tell him their evening together was not a date, this time that wasn't the case.

That was OK. One thing he knew about sexual attraction was that though it heightened your senses and prickled your skin you didn't have to act on it. It was like gazing at an expensive painting he liked in the art gallery in Sliema: *Boats at anchor in Spinola Bay, early morning*. He'd never own it but that didn't stop him enjoying the sight of it. Beautiful things were good to look at – though a painting might not provoke the same tingling eddy of arousal that Rosa did.

His thoughts were given a new direction when headlights cut through the night and a black saloon halted at the kerb. He opened the nearest door for Rosa then went to the other side to climb in beside her. 'Paceville?' the driver said and grinned as if to say, 'Clubbing, huh? With *her*? Wow.' Zach sat back as the car cruised around the bend and smoothly down the slope, leaving the rarefied neighbourhood of The Ramp for the seafront road, then striking inland to cut past Sliema and most of St Julian's Bay. The road swarmed with headlights and taillights, the journey stop-start. Rosa gazed out of the window, her expression one of serene interest.

The ironic thing about this evening, Zach thought, swaying with the movement of the cab as the driver raced a red light, was that he would have loved to date Rosa but they were living in too close proximity for anything casual and he wasn't available for more. He was wary of relationships. Twice he'd been unceremoniously dumped and once he'd been accused of callously breaking a heart. He'd hated that.

It would be better if Rosa and Marci became friends. Anxiety had his sister in its slimy grey grip and he hated to see her so listless that even responding to Paige was an effort.

As if picking up his thoughts Rosa said, 'So you really don't mind babysitting your niece?'

'Any time,' Zach responded. 'Paige is a big favourite with me. Maybe it's not cool to be entertained by a four-year-old but I love her.'

It occurred to him that he and Rosa were now not-dating for the second time in one evening. It made him want to laugh out loud, which at least lightened his mood.

Not convinced Rosa would see the joke if he shared it,

he turned his mind towards the booming clubs and neon-lit bars that tumbled over each other down Triq Santa Rita – or St Rita Street. Formed of a giant flight of stairs and open twenty-four/seven, Triq Santa Rita came alive at night.

For many female tourists it was Holiday Hook-Upsville and he was happy to be part of that. Sex stopped him thinking about everything that had gone wrong in the past couple of years. Everything he'd done wrong.

But now he had Rosa along. He hesitated, then said, 'Paceville can be a walk on the wild side. Maybe you should take my phone number?'

He got the impression that she smothered a sigh, but they did exchange numbers. When the driver pulled over in Paceville Pjazza she jumped out of the cab and meticulously split the fare with a quick, 'Thanks!' and took off through the crowds of holidaymakers as if to emphasise that she didn't expect to tag along with him.

After watching her head for Triq San Ġorġ, which was, at least, less crazy than Triq Santa Rita, Zach threaded his way through the crowds and past the incongruously situated Arkadia supermarket. In moments he was plunging into the heated air beneath a jumble of neon signage advertising bars and clubs, the uneven steps familiar beneath his feet. Halfway down was a bar called Spirit, its name in blue neon over big glass doors set in a matte black frontage. Shisha bars stood either side and a 'gentlemen's club' above. Zach liked Spirit because its clientele was made up of thirty-somethings and alcohol prices weren't as inflated as in some of the Paceville bars. Once he'd been inside to buy a couple of pints of Cisk – one for each hand – he claimed an elbow-height table outside to lean on.

Up and down the steps nightlife lovers jostled beneath the welter of multicoloured lights, crossing from bar to club and back again. Promotion staff dished out cards that promised money off entry fees, drinks or specialised entertainment. Competing sound systems boomed from doorways.

At a nearby table, four women sipped cocktails. They looked Zach's type. Bright, happy but not drunk, pretty but not obvious, ring fingers unadorned. When no men had arrived to join the group after a few minutes, one of the four – a cool blonde – let her gaze tangle with his, and Zach moved closer. She gave her name as Elsa and said she lived in Edinburgh. She asked him about restaurants in the Bay Street complex across the road. 'I'm not taken by this street,' she explained. 'It's seedy.'

'That's what I like about it,' he told her solemnly. Her hair was long enough to blow against him and he enjoyed its silky tickle on his bare arm as she leaned closer to laugh. Her friends glanced at her and smiled but then returned to their own conversation.

Elsa had just begun telling him about her holiday when he glanced down the steps and caught sight of a group of young men. A profile illuminated by a flashing light distracted him. He shifted slightly to try and single out the face again.

There.

Luccio.

Twenty-year-old Luccio, a Sicilian, triggered protective feelings in Zach, who hated to see him in his present company, a group led by a little shit he seemed in awe of – Beppe. Zach hadn't formed bonds with many people in Malta but he felt almost brotherly towards Luccio, who was on a youth support worker apprenticeship with Zach's

14

cousin Joseph at Nicholas Centre. Zach volunteered at the centre, a community youth facility, and Luccio was the staff member he was most often paired with to supervise games between the teenagers who came to the centre to hang out. Luccio didn't seem much removed from the older children and he was always happy to carry on past his scheduled hours if a fun activity was in progress. Many of the kids came from less-moneyed homes and identified with Luccio. His parents had died when he was only sixteen and he'd had to leave Sicily for Malta when his aunt Teresa, who'd married a Maltese man, offered him a home in Sliema.

Still very young, he could definitely do with good people around him. Unfortunately, in the last year Luccio's friend-ship group outside Nicholas Centre had changed and to Zach, who saw them hanging around Paceville, Beppe and his buddies didn't look like good people. Beppe was the oldest and hardest; Luccio the youngest and most eager to please. Zach understood exactly how that combination could lead to manipulation.

Luccio's aunt Teresa was concerned, Joseph had confided in Zach. Luccio had become reluctant to discuss his activ-ities or hear criticism of his friends and seemed to be viewing her home like a hotel that never presented its bill. The more she tried to talk to him the more uncommu-nicative he became. Zach, who'd often worked with Luccio over the past eighteen months, could see the young man's mood and attitude had changed.

Only half in the conversation with Elsa now, Zach finished his first pint and began on the second as he moni-tored the group fifteen or so steps below him. All of them were significantly younger than Zach's thirty-two years. Beppe might be in his mid-twenties, he supposed, and the

15

rest all younger. He noted the 'friendly' wrestling that was too rough to be friendly, despite accompanying laughter, plus the occasional ugly look from Beppe that turned Luccio's expression apprehensive.

The ringleader.

The easily led youth.

It was uncomfortably familiar because, back in the day, Laine Fitzmaurice or 'Fitzmo' had been the ringleader and Zach the easily led youth. He could almost have written the script as he watched Beppe begin to bestow smiles and Luccio blossom in response, then Beppe grasped Luccio's arm and murmured in his ear. Luccio, though he looked wide-eyed and unsure, eventually nodded.

Shit. Luccio was being put up to something.

Zach started forward, remembered Elsa and swung back long enough to mutter, 'Sorry, I've seen someone I have to talk to.' Elsa's eyes widened in obvious affront but, with another apology, he turned away.

Still grasping his beer, Zach took the steps casually, glancing about with a show of aimlessness. Then he let his gaze fasten on his young friend and changed direction to clap him on the shoulder. 'Hey, Luccio.'

Luccio jumped. 'Oh. Hey, Zach.'

Zach turned to the group as if he was their friend of old. 'I'm glad to see you guys. I've been feeling like Billy-no-mates tonight.' He shook Beppe's hand, knowing the value of paying lots of attention to the big shot. 'Want a drink?'

From the scornful glances Beppe gave his buddies he obviously interpreted the offer as an attempt to ingratiate himself. He bent his gaze on Luccio then indicated Zach. 'Maybe you should stay with your friend.' He said 'friend' as if he meant 'loser'. Beppe turned and headed inside and the rest of his group herded along.

'But—' Luccio gazed after his departing buddies.

Zach put his arm around Luccio's shoulders. 'We need something to soak up the beer. Let's eat.' Using 'we' was persuasive and inclusive language, Joseph had taught Zach.

Luccio frowned uneasily but he let Zach usher him up the steps towards Triq San Ġorġ and Paceville Pjazza. Bellowing over the sounds rocking out of bars, Zach tried to keep Luccio's attention. 'Think the teams promoted from the Championship will make it in the Premier League next year?'

Luccio, though usually an avid fan of British football, just shrugged.

Then, when they'd nearly reached the top of the steps, Zach caught sight of Rosa again. Oddly, as he was pretty sure those she knew in Malta was limited to the occupants of Ta' Xbiex Terrace House, she seemed to be leading five or six laughing women in a dance along one of the steps, singing along as she wiggled and clapped. Then a swaying man, grinning foolishly, grabbed Rosa's arm and said something with a leer. 'Piss off!' she snarled, glaring into his eyes. 'Women make their own decisions about who they sleep with.'

'Yeah!' chorused a couple of the dancing women and one yanked Rosa's arm from his grip.

Was it his night for rescuing people? Zach had almost forgotten Rosa while he interfered in whatever Beppe had had in mind for Luccio but he couldn't stand by while some guy gave Rosa trouble. Hoping it wouldn't get him into a ruckus that might catch the attention of the police, he changed course so he could loop an arm loosely around her, feeling her slight body recoil but then relax when she realised who he was. In a voice filled with bonhomie and beer he created a scenario she could easily fall in with. 'Look, I've found my friend Luccio. We're going to get something to eat. Why don't you come along?'

After a last narrowing of her eyes at the swaying man, Rosa muttered, 'OK,' called a casual goodbye to the women she'd been dancing with and allowed herself to be steered away. Zach glanced back and saw the man make an obscene gesture in the direction of Rosa's rear view. Luckily, Rosa didn't see it and Zach thought the wisest course was to pretend he hadn't either. He made the introductions and Luccio brightened enough to grin at Rosa. 'You told him off.'

'He deserved it.' Rosa fell in beside the two men, her expression still stormy. 'I appreciate your help there, Zach, but women shouldn't need protection. *Children* need protection. Men need to understand when to back off and when they don't it's up to women to speak up.'

'Completely agree,' Zach put in peaceably as he led the party through the piazza and down to Spinola Bay where the restaurants were of the calm and civilised variety, pleased when Rosa went along. If she wished to continue to wander around late at night it was none of his business, yet he'd rather she didn't. He agreed that women *shouldn't* need protecting but as the elder brother of two sisters he was aware that her desire that certain men learn when to back off might prove optimistic.

Intuiting that Luccio wouldn't appreciate the seafront restaurants bulging with middle-aged tourists he chose a small bar up Triq San Ġuzepp, another stepped street – though smaller and quieter – where a mainly Maltese clientele enjoyed the evening air. He grabbed the last empty table and, remembering he'd fibbed to Luccio that he needed to soak up beer, instructed his belly to forget it had already eaten this evening. He ordered a platter of flatbreads with dips. Rosa chose a chocolate cake and a glass of wine. Luccio ordered a burger and chips with a pint of Cisk. Zach ordered a pint too. He'd drunk enough alcohol but switching to lemonade didn't seem the way to bond with Luccio.

While they ate Zach questioned his motives in separating Luccio from his mates. He'd felt compelled to do so but had it changed anything? Luccio was almost silent and Zach suspected he hadn't endeared himself to his young friend.

Zach heaved a sigh. Who was he trying to save here? Luccio? Or himself?

Luccio's phone alerted him to message after message and in between scoffing chips he tapped out replies, the downturned corners of his mouth suggesting that nothing he read made him happy. Then the phone rang and he surged to his feet, stepping away to take the call. His side of the conversation consisted of, 'Yes, yes,' and the occasional half-begun sentence.

When he'd finished he shoved his phone in his pocket, scowling, and returned to the table. 'I must go.'

'Must?' queried Zach, softly. He ached to show Luccio that being sucked into the wrong crowd could end badly. He'd decided a while ago that he'd share his story with his young Sicilian friend when the time seemed right but he hadn't bargained on having Rosa in the audience. 'Luccio,' he said before he could talk himself out of it, 'I came out here because I got in trouble.'

Luccio's gaze flew to Zach's face. Zach didn't look at Rosa to see how she took his pronouncement but ploughed on, encouraged that Luccio – wide-eyed – resumed his seat. 'When I was eighteen my best mate moved away. I started hanging around with a guy called Laine Fitzmaurice – Fitzmo – who'd been two years ahead of me at school. He wasn't a good influence. I didn't see it, of course. I thought he and his friends were cool and we drank a lot. Dad's attention was on coping with my mum because she was developing rheumatoid arthritis and as the eldest of the kids I was sort of catapulted into adult status. It went to my head and I acted like a twat.'

Luccio looked interested despite himself. 'What did you do?'

Zach hoped he was going about things the right way. 'I didn't do much myself but I was there when the other guys did. Vandalism. Petty theft. Once, Fitzmo took a car and I piled in the back with the others. I kidded myself that it wasn't a crime because I hadn't stolen the car but that didn't make it true.' He took a moment to gather his thoughts. 'We all felt it was important to please Fitzmo. When he wanted somewhere we could hang out and drink I was proud when I was the one to find a place. It was an empty building behind a shopping centre. We trashed it, smashing light fittings and stuff. It seemed like high spirits rather than actual crime.'

Luccio frowned but Zach was pretty sure it was with the effort of translating unfamiliar phrases like 'high spirits' more than judgement of Zach's juvenile misdemeanours.

Zach pushed aside his beer and asked the waiter for coffee. Whether it was the alcohol or the story, he felt sick. 'The youngest of our group was called Stuart,' he continued. 'Most of us were eighteen, Fitzmo was twenty, but Stuart was only sixteen and he hero-worshipped Fitzmo. One Saturday afternoon we were hanging out and drinking. Stuart had way too much and Fitzmo bullied him into punching a window to smash it. Stuart tried. But he was

20

small and had to jump up to punch the glass. It smashed but a shard of it—' he drew a long pointed shape in the air in case Luccio hadn't before encountered the word *shard* '—caught him on the way down. Sliced into him. There was blood everywhere, spurting from Stuart's wrist.'

His nausea threatened to choke him as he remembered the blood splattering on the concrete floor, Stuart clutching himself and slurring, 'I'm hurt!' in tones of almost comical surprise.

He had to swallow and when his coffee arrived he found he didn't want it. 'The others ran off,' he explained. 'Every one of them, including Fitzmo. Even fourteen years later I can't believe they did that. Stuart was squirting blood and they left him. So I grabbed his arm—' hot and slippery with blood '—and I dragged him out of the building and up the alley to the shopping centre where there was a pharmacy. The pharmacist got a tourniquet on Stuart to slow the bleeding while her assistant called the ambulance.'

Luccio's brown eyes were wide and disbelieving. 'You saved your friend's life.'

Zach gave an angry snort of laughter. 'That part wasn't emphasised. The police arrived with the ambulance and they followed the trail of blood back to the building and found it all smashed up. Stuart and I admitted to being involved in causing the damage. I was eighteen so I got a fine and community service and it caused a tremendous row with my dad. Stuart got a supervision order. Fitzmo and our "friends" told me I was stupid for sticking around. They said, I should have rung the ambulance and run. When I asked why they hadn't bothered with the ambulance part, just run, they tried to joke it off.'

He sipped his coffee because his throat was closing around the ball of emotion that had lodged there. 'I saw

21

Fitzmo and the others for what they were. So I cut them off.'

Luccio took a gulp from his beer. 'But you were eighteen? That was a long time ago. You came out here early last year, no?'

'I got in trouble again.' Wearily, Zach rubbed his hand over his face, conscious of Rosa, having demolished her dessert, sitting statue-still. 'Stuart was permanently affected by the accident. He had a couple of operations but his hand never worked properly and became a withered mess. He doesn't have a job. He's into alcohol and suffers mental illness. He hangs around town, looking so defeated. I tried to help but . . .' He let his voice trail off. 'Stuart took the money or clothes I gave him and swapped them for cider.'

He took a deep breath. Luccio seemed to be listening and maybe Zach's excoriating confession was doing some good, even if Rosa's silence felt like judgement. If there was any chance he could stop his young friend Luccio turning out like Stuart – or even like Zach himself – then it was worth exposing his messy past. 'A couple of years ago I was in a pub in the centre of Redruth with some mates on a Friday night. I saw Fitzmo about six feet away and I should have left but I didn't want a loser like him to have any impact on me. I'd kept my nose clean since the trouble twelve years earlier. I thought I could ignore him. But I'd had a few beers.' His gaze fell on the almost untouched pint in front of him. 'Stuart was there too. It was noisy but I could hear Fitzmo ridiculing him. Stuart kept trying to smile as if it was just teasing. Then Fitzmo grabbed Stuart's bad hand, twisting it. He was hurting Stuart . . . and I saw red. I marched over and smacked Fitzmo right in his horrible, toxic mouth. I really lost it. Broke two of his teeth.'

22

Zach found himself flexing his hand as if he could once again feel the pain involved while Luccio gaped as if Zach had sprouted horns. 'At first I thought Fitzmo would murder me,' Zach continued. 'He'd been brought up hard. He'd also spent a few years in jail and had come out even harder. Then his expression changed and he began cowering, pleading with me not to hit him again, clutching his face and groaning. And why? Because he'd seen police officers walk into the pub and they were on their way over to check out the disturbance. They collared me. Fitzmo knew how to construct a compensation claim and insisted the attack was unprovoked. He said to Stuart, "He hit me for no reason, didn't he?"'

Luccio's black eyebrows almost disappeared into his hair. 'And . . . ?'

Zach held his gaze. 'Stuart said, "Yes," and I was arrested. Fitzmo got a kick out of the whole thing, especially when I was charged, got community service and had to pay him a small amount of compensation.'

He paused, longing suddenly for his bed. Soul baring was exhausting.

'So why come to Malta?' Luccio was obviously engaged in the story. His hair caught the light from a nearby bar, threading his dark curls with red.

Zach groaned. 'I hadn't intended to advertise my problems to my family but Dad saw me collecting litter at the side of a main road with "Community Service" written on my back and nearly had a stroke. It soured our already difficult relationship. My grandmother suggested I come here to get me out of the firing line because Mum wasn't coping with the animosity. She's in constant physical pain and doesn't deserve a war zone around her.'

Mentally, he compared the phone conversations he

enjoyed with his mum, hearing about the little bit that happened in her life, her sweet, familiar voice telling him about his little sister Electra's last call home from Thailand where she taught English or talking about Marci and Paige.

His dad? They texted. *Hope all's well with you. Tenants you got are working out well. Interesting to hear Dory talking about the same army primary school you went to.* He didn't make the effort to ring Steve and Steve didn't ring him either.

He forced himself to complete his story, though it felt as if each word was being hacked out of him. 'Fitzmo sent me a message that I didn't hit as hard as his mum. When I didn't react he sent another saying Stuart felt so bad about what had happened he'd taken an overdose and had to get pumped out. I went looking for Stuart in town and he was fine so Fitzmo was obviously trying to goad me, manipulate me. I realised I could be sucked in to dangerous situations again and decided to accept my grandmother's offer.'

He could hardly look at Rosa. She must be thinking she'd been on a not-a-date with a hooligan but he couldn't let that deter him from getting his point across. 'Luccio, that guy Beppe, he's as toxic as Fitzmo. I recognise his type. He's a coward who controls and uses people.'

Luccio recoiled, glancing around as if worried someone would hear.

Zach leaned closer. 'Just cut him off,' he urged. 'Avoid him. Find new friends. Believe me, when things go wrong you'll turn around to look for him and he'll have vanished.'

Luccio seemed to have no reply, gazing into the distance as he drank his beer. After a while, Zach used his app to book a cab. Luccio got in the back, though Zach had more than half-expected him to head back to Paceville. Zach joined him, leaving the front seat for Rosa. When they arrived at Luccio's aunt's house in Sliema, Luccio got out and Zach said, 'You know where I am if you want me.'

Then, drained, he sat in the car for the final few minutes to Ta' Xbiex Terrace House.

Once again he walked Rosa to her door. Insects danced in the yellow halos of light around the terrace lamps. 'I'm sorry,' he said. 'I wouldn't have spilled all that crap in front of you but I'm trying to help Luccio. He's a good kid, a youth support worker at the centre where I volunteer and I hate to see him being lured off-track. You don't have to worry that there's a madman living upstairs. I just—' He halted, defeated by the task of justifying himself; that he'd first been a young fool and then let himself be goaded into fury when he'd thought himself older and wiser.

She gazed at him, eyes solemn. 'A saying Grandpa's fond of is that someone is "more sinned against than sinning". I think he'd say that about you. You saved your friend's life when everyone else abandoned him and you stuck up for an underdog when you didn't need to get involved. I think it was brave to try and let Luccio benefit from your bad experiences.' A quick smile, then she was gone, into her apartment.

Zach was shocked how relieved he felt that Rosa wasn't disappointed in him.

Chapter Three

In the morning, Rosa was surprised but pleased Dory didn't question her about going out with Zach. Maybe she realised she'd been a little too busy on Rosa's behalf?

Or maybe she was too focused on jumping into her little white car and driving Rosa to a fish restaurant in Marsaxlokk in the south of the island. Her career as a food writer had fallen into her lap after a reality TV show featured the school where she was cook and brought on its heels 'The Cafeteria Cook' books. Dory's attention was firmly on being the best food writer she could be. 'Being here for the summer is an ideal opportunity to gain a broad view of menus and the use of ingredients,' she enthused as she cautiously sidled onto a teeming round-about. 'The resto we're trying today looks authentically Maltese but Marsaxlokk draws a lot of tourists so the menu's bound to reflect their tastes. Perhaps you can go online later and search out places off the tourist track?'

'Sure,' agreed Rosa, wincing as Dory put in a skull-jar-ring emergency stop to avoid a lorry lumbering out from a junction. She was glad when they hit quieter roads after a place called Paola, leaving built-up areas behind in favour of terraced farm fields separated by uneven dry stone walls. She pointed to cacti tumbling over the walls. 'They look like a spiky green Mickey Mouse ears.'

Dory laughed. 'Prickly pear. Ooh – idea! Can you grab my laptop from my bag and make a note to include a section in the new book on foraging for wild-growing foods like prickly pear, capers and wild asparagus?'

Note made, Rosa settled back to enjoy the ride, reading road signs for places like Zejtun and Ghaxaq and trying to say them aloud.

Dory tried to be helpful. 'J's sound like British y's, gh's are silent and x makes a sh or ch sound. I'm never sure about q's. A Maltese man once told me they were "halfway between a k and a vomit". But sometimes they seem to go silent altogether.'

At the restaurant, they ate outside gazing out at the pretty harbour of Marsaxlokk. Compact, high-prowed fishing boats, bluer than the sea and piped with red, green, brown, white and yellow, bobbed beside a quayside scattered with nets. Most of the boats had eyes painted or engraved on the prow. 'Those traditionally guard the fishermen from evil,' Dory explained, before moving on to what was preoccupying her – work on her new book *The Cafeteria Cook Does the Mediterranean*.

'The traditional Mediterranean diet's heavy on plant-based foods. Next comes fish, then chicken, and last and least of all, red meat and sweets. If you follow the right proportions you'll be healthy and avoid weight gain. You find most touristy places serve British chips and Italian pasta more than Maltese food, though.'

The sunlight danced on the rippling waves between the fishing boats sheltered by the broad sweep of the bay.

Tourists strolled between cafés or browsed shop windows and the sun relaxed Rosa's shoulders as she let her mum chatter happily about her twin favourite topics of food and Malta.

A beautiful Maltese teenage girl brought menus and Dory pored over hers, discussing with the waitress whether the swordfish was farmed or wild. As it was wild she ordered it, followed by grilled, stuffed squid – *klamari* – with green herb sauce.

Before Rosa could open her mouth Dory continued. 'Rosa, you don't mind if I order for you, as it's for research and a business expense? It gives me twice as many things to taste and I won't order anything you don't like.' She returned to the waitress. 'Parmigiana of aubergine with nut pesto and shrimp ravioli. Wine, Rosa? White? And still water, please.'

Rosa wasn't sure whether to be annoyed or resigned. Her mother had offered her a job as her personal assistant and kitchen porter for the recipe trials to be conducted at the apartment and was paying her pin money as well as covering her expenses. Her *mum* hadn't stepped in and ordered her lunch. Her *employer* had, and for a purpose.

Though her meal wasn't what she'd have selected, it was delicious. And it was fun, tasting each other's meals and discussing the ingredients. 'Mm, isn't the orange with the swordfish unusual?' Dory mused. 'I wonder how it would be with blood orange? I love Maltese blood oranges.'

'Would readers be able to buy them in the UK?' Rosa took another forkful, this time without sauce to get the flavour of the fish.

'Not sure. Can you check British supermarkets online?'

By the end of the meal, Rosa had documents open on the laptop on the tasting, jobs to-do and research to carry out.

She was on her second glass of wine before her mum – sneakily – got in the enquiry Rosa had expected earlier. 'How did the date with Zach go?'

'We ate together and then he showed me the nightlife in Paceville. It wasn't a date and I told him it wasn't.' Rosa watched tourists meandering by the sea while she batted flies away from her face. She didn't tell her mother about Zach's troubles because he was entitled to choose with whom he shared his secrets. Rosa had lain awake last night thinking about the story he'd told Luccio to show him what could come of getting in with the wrong crowd and concluded he was too hard on himself. Most people who got in scrapes would try to forget them and hope everyone else did too. 'There look to be a few market stalls further up the road. Shall we have a look?'

'I want to get back and experiment in the kitchen,' returned Dory impatiently. Then, refusing to accept the change of subject: 'Zach seems a nice man. And handsome!' She took Rosa's hand, wearing an earnest expression. 'Don't you think a lovely summer romance will cheer you up?'

'Do you mean an affair?' Rosa grinned.

'I said "romance",' Dory protested, though with a distinct twinkle. 'A nice man can really take your mind off an old flame.'

Although she knew Dory wasn't purposely being dismissive, Rosa felt she had to say, 'When a five-year relationship goes wrong, even if it's my fault, it's OK for me to be upset. Saying I'll get over my "old flame" with a "lovely summer romance" and a "nice man" is optimistic.'

Marcus's face swam into her mind's eye. His anger when she'd wrongly accused him. What he'd done next . . .

Dory looked contrite. 'You're right. I'm sorry if I sounded flip.'

Any tension forgotten, they drove home chatting about the flat-roofed buildings around them and spiky vegetation at the roadside, an open-topped tourist bus, the domes and cupolas of distant churches, the elegance of palm trees, a small horse trotting smartly before a cart – in fact anything but Rosa's personal life. Presently, Rosa let Dory do the talking. She'd forgotten her sunglasses and her head was aching. The sky was so blue, the sun beating on the square-cut limestone houses and dazzling her. The car's air conditioning was inadequate and seemed to emit dust that she could taste. She was about to suggest that when they got home they swim off the rocks in the beautiful turquoise sea across the road from their apartment when Dory broke in, 'We'll try that nut pesto sauce when we get back while the flavour's fresh in my memory.'

Oh, yes, she was still at work. Rosa closed her eyes, regretting the second glass of wine.

Once home, she took two paracetamol, changed out of the summer dress she'd worn for lunch and into shorts, washed her hands and opened her laptop, creating a document for the recipe trial while Dory went out onto the terrace to pick handfuls of basil and parsley that somehow seemed to smell of sunshine.

'We'll make four batches,' Dory said, returning briskly. 'One with walnuts, one with pine nuts, one with a combination of the two and one without nuts for comparison purposes.'

Rosa, who'd grown up cooking with Dory, washed the herbs and patted them dry while Dory toasted the walnuts and garlic. Then, Rosa gazed through the window at the terrace and the towering wall behind it. If she craned her neck she could see, probably twenty feet above, another large house. Maltese builders definitely understood how to work with the contours of the island but even the stone cut into big blocks instead of the red bricks of Liggers Moor in Yorkshire felt alien to Rosa.

Dory might have slipped back into her childhood home like a favourite pair of slippers but Rosa hadn't lived anywhere but England. As amazing as Malta was, she hadn't expected to feel homesick. She wiped her forehead – still aching – and switched on the air conditioning. Malta was hot. There were lots of insects, too many cars and endless construction going on. Maybe she'd been rash saying she'd stay till October.

At least the nightlife seemed vibrant. OK, discovering Zach at street level when he'd already escorted her back to the apartment had been awkward but sharing a cab with him had turned out to be a good stepping stone to discovering what kind of thing she'd do with herself in this tiny country for months on end. She already missed her friends in dance class at the gym and the pubs and clubs of her home town . . . though not her one-time friend Chellice.

'Can you grate the parmesan?' called Dory, interrupting Rosa's thoughts.

'Coming right up.' Rosa found the grater and as her arm made the mechanical movements she chided herself for her low spirits. *Hardly been in Malta two minutes and homesick?* For England or for . . . Marcus? She did miss Marcus, even if he'd changed from the steady, smiling man she'd once known to a disillusioned, discontented thirty-something with a problem.

She didn't want to miss him, because too much trust had been lost for their relationship to ever recover – even leaving aside the question of whether Chellice had maintained Rosa's friendship only so she could draw Marcus into her web like a sultry, curvaceous spider with a fly. Marcus denied it, of course. Rosa had met Chellice first at someone's hen night, he pointed out. They'd become friends. It was coincidence that when Rosa invited Chellice for dinner Marcus had discovered they'd had crafting in common. Marcus turned and carved wood while Chellice practised Kintsugi, the art of repairing broken pottery using lacquer dusted with powdered gold or silver to create shiny veins.

Later, they joined forces to form a part-time business, Spun Gold, which now had a website and shops on Etsy and Notonthehighstreet. But Rosa had come to believe that though Marcus's ambition for Spun Gold might genuinely have been to make it successful enough to let him quit his hated day job . . . Chellice used the business as a reason to spend time with Marcus.

Rosa also missed her job at Blackthorn's youth centre. She'd begun her leave of absence less than two weeks ago but she missed the role, her colleagues – especially her boss Georgine – and the kids. She missed weekend raft races or camping trips and schmoozing companies to donate equipment like mountain bikes then creating a Blackthorn's cycling event.

When Rosa had taken over improving Blackthorn's social media channels, social-media savvy Chellice had seemed happy to coach her. Had it been to keep Rosa occupied while Marcus devoted time to Spun Gold? The thought made her sick. She'd thought their friendship real.

Now, like a child touching a candle to see if it was hot,

in a break between taking notes, loading the dishwasher and whizzing things in the food processor, Rosa peeked at Chellice's blog and Instagram. Both proved to be full of Kintsugi and woodcraft for sale.

The blog, Chellice Reviews Life, demonstrated the sardonic humour her audience lapped up. She reviewed her journey to work, her own performance on a YouTube vid or the day's weather. Instagram got a one-star review because it didn't allow links in posts and Brexit minus one. Marcus got five stars for being 'the best biz-buddy in the universe and doing all the driving to fairs and markets. Read my review of Marcus's radio interview here.'

A sweat of anger broke out on Rosa's brow. Her memory of Marcus's local radio appearance was fresh and raw. At a craft fair he'd made the connection with a radio presenter, eagerly taking up an invitation to join her on her chat show. His motivation might have been to grab opportunities to mention Spun Gold but instead he'd kicked around more shit than a dung beetle, all of it rolling in Rosa's direction with devastating effect.

Dory's voice came from behind her, sympathetic but still making Rosa jump. 'Oh, Rosa, are you trying to get news of Marcus? I've trivialised your feelings about him, haven't I?' She dropped two dishes of pesto on the counter with a clatter and her arms, warm and soft, gave Rosa a big hug.

Rosa tried to laugh. 'I know you were glad to see the back of him.' She returned the hug as if she were a little girl again.

'I'm sorry. You know I'm prone to expecting the worst of men.' Dory's eyes were guilty.

Rosa felt guilty in her turn. Dory was the best of

mothers. Rosa had had a settled childhood only because Dory had been self-sufficient and able to give Rosa a double dose of love to make up for the shortcomings of Rosa's dad, Glenn. He'd contributed little, financially or emotionally. When Rosa had been old enough to understand, Dory had explained how she'd been ambushed by Glenn's complete lack of engagement with his child. 'They'd call it Attachment Disorder now but at the time we called him a crap dad.'

And Rosa had long ago overheard Dory telling a friend that Glenn had been revolted by Dory's pregnant body, disgusted by the process of birth and frightened by Dory's post-birth bodily functions and what he referred to as 'a shitty baby'. It had stuck with her.

She scarcely saw Glenn now but Rosa remembered all too well him dismissing opportunities to attend school plays as 'not my thing' and never taking Rosa out. When he'd visited her at home a couple of times a year she'd treated him like one of her mother's friends, someone who asked vague but polite questions to which she gave vague but polite answers. By the age of seven, Rosa had realised her dad was not like most other dads and when she reached her mid-teens his visits had faded away along with even infrequent attempts at paying child support.

His parents had barely seemed to notice her either, apart from small cheques for birthdays and Christmases, so maybe his lack of parental instinct was learned.

Luckily, Rosa had had Dory's parents living in Liggers Moor to shower her with love and also, living only an hour away in south Lincolnshire, Dory's sister – Aunt Lizzy – with her husband – Uncle Eddie – and three boisterous sons.

Straightforward, capable, jolly, hardworking Dory had fulfilled all other roles.

What Rosa and Dory had learned from Glenn was not to rely on men. Probably that's why Marcus's increasing self-orientation had eventually got to Rosa. It had all begun with online gambling and his losses affecting their disposable income. He'd changed. Rosa had been judgy. She admitted it. She'd had experience of an unreliable man from which to judge. So Marcus had promised never to gamble again . . .

'Are you homesick?' Dory asked suddenly, jolting Rosa back to the conversation.

She answered unguardedly. 'A bit.'

I'll pay your fare back to England if I you want to go.' Dory's voice shook. 'I thought it was such a fantastic way of solving a few issues for you that I didn't stop to consider that it was *my* dream to have an extended stay here, not yours.'

She sounded so woeful that Rosa's heart gave a huge squeeze. Dory had been generous and Rosa hadn't given Malta a chance. 'I know it's paradise to you but it seems strange at the moment. Maybe when I know it better—'

'I've scarcely given you a moment to enjoy it,' Dory declared, looking ever guiltier. 'Let's clear up and then we'll have a few days off so I can show you more of this gorgeous island. We'll wander by the sea, eat in cafés, take a boat into Grand Harbour, go to Valletta – be touristy.'

'That sounds great. And I'd love to swim. The sea looks glorious.' Rosa beamed, feeling better immediately. 'But we haven't done the tasting of the pesto.'

At that second a knock fell on the apartment door and a woman's voice called, 'Hello?'

Dory snatched the door open. 'Hello, Marci. And hello,

Paige! This is lovely. Come in and meet my daughter, Rosa.'

'Hello,' echoed Rosa, welcoming their visitors in. Marci was a rounded woman with similar dark glossy hair to Zach but worn in a long bob. Four-year-old Paige, who shouted, 'Hello, hello!' and beamed happily, was much more chestnutty.

'Can you spare a few minutes?' Dory demanded, not giving Marci a chance to say why she and Paige had called. 'We were just going to do a pesto tasting. And,' she added, seeing Paige looking unimpressed, 'I made *pudina* last night, so we can taste that too.'

Marci looked uncertain. 'Are you sure—'

'Pudina is cake! I had it in Valletta with Uncle Zach.' Paige bounced on her toes, the end of her French plait bouncing with her. 'Yes, please.'

'Then let's sit on the terrace.' Dory ushered them all outside. 'Oh, look, there's Zach working in the garden.' She raised her voice. 'Zach! We're going to taste pesto and pudina.'

Zach's voice floated back. 'In the same mouthful?'

Dory laughed. 'Not unless you want to. Rosa, if you can take the pesto and get people drinks then I'll slice bread and get the pudina from the fridge.'

Soon the five were gathered around the patio table, the adults sampling different batches of pesto on flat bread while Paige went straight for pudina on the grounds that pesto was green and looked yucky. The pesto with walnuts was pronounced the favourite of Zach, Rosa and Dory but Marci liked the mix of walnut and pine nut.

Zach seemed relaxed and apart from murmuring to Rosa, 'Don't think Dory's trying to fix us up this time,' didn't refer to yesterday evening.

Rosa laughed and turned to Marci, intending to draw her out in view of what Zach had said about his sister not having made friends on the island. Marci was a bit reserved but Rosa warmed to her when she rolled her eyes in the direction of her brother and said, 'The pesto's lovely but I actually came to apologise that Zach has tried to stick you with me for the reunion on Sunday.'

Rosa answered frankly. 'I'd be glad to have someone to talk to when Mum's yakking on to the other army kids about the good old days.'

'Are we all going together? That will be lovely! And I shall be swapping fascinating stories about my childhood, not yakking on,' Dory put in with mock indignation, cutting pudina into bite-sized squares. Paige was taking the pudina tasting ultra-seriously, carefully nibbling the traditional one with mixed dried fruit and glacé cherries, then the one with fresh figs and finally the one made with fresh dates.

'So, what's in pudina?' queried Zach, trying a piece. 'I've eaten it in Caffe Cordina in Valletta. Is it a very Maltese cake?'

'I've only come across it on Maltese recipe sites.' Dory made sure everybody had pudina from each batch. 'It's like bread pudding with a chocolate topping. It contains traditional cake ingredients like fruit, sugar, chocolate and milk but instead of flour it has bread. I'm experimenting to find the healthiest version with less sugar and different fruit.'

Under cover of this conversation Rosa said to Marci quietly, 'If you're not comfortable coming to the reunion with us, don't feel you have to.' She thought from a twitch of Zach's head that he was listening in, but he didn't interrupt.

Marci wrinkled her nose. 'I promised Dad I'd go but I feel . . . odd.'

Though she nodded as if she understood, Rosa rolled the word around in her mind. Odd as in unfamiliar? Odd as in panic attack pending? The odd one out? Asking might be awkward.

Zach turned to regard his sister, his dark eyes serious. 'Would you prefer me to go instead, Marci? I could, if that's what you want. But Dad asked you and I'd be happy to babysit Paige.'

Marci made a face. 'That's just Dad being Dad. I assumed you were staying away because he didn't ask you.'

Zach gave a grin that suggested he wasn't going to argue with that conclusion. 'If you'd like me to go instead, I will. I'll take pics to send back to him and chat to a few people and then it'll be done.'

Marci mulled that over. 'Can't we all go? It's a buffet lunch in a restaurant garden in Mdina so Paige wouldn't have to sit still for hours.'

Paige cried, 'Yay! I want to go to lunch. Will there be cake? Can I wear my best dress?'

At the same time, Dory chimed in. 'That's a great idea. I'll message the organisers with the new numbers.' She commandeered Rosa's laptop to log onto the Barracks Brats Facebook group.

Marci, looking over her shoulder, became interested in photos posted on the group of grinning school kids of the Fifties, Sixties and Seventies. Winter uniforms were trousers for boys and gymslips for girls, worn with shirts and ties. In summer boys wore shorts and open-necked shirts, the girls summer dresses, all sand coloured and looking slightly military. Backdrops of prickly pears, palm trees, spiky agaves and flat-roofed buildings were recognisably Malta, though today's towns had become very high-rise and crowded in comparison.

Paige, presumably seeing her mother otherwise occupied, backed up to Zach, shoving her hair out of her eyes. 'My plait's coming down, Uncle Zach. Can you do it, please?'

Rosa felt her eyebrows shoot up. 'You can do a French plait?'

Zach grinned lazily. 'Is that disbelief I hear in your voice?'

'Watching with interest,' she responded affably.

'He can,' Paige assured her, holding still while Zach pulled the elastic out of the bottom of the plait and teased it apart before combing it with his fingers. Beginning with three locks from the top of the small head before him, he pulled in sections from each side in turn to weave deftly until he got to Paige's downy little neck, then he plaited normally to the bottom, between her shoulder blades. 'Marci taught me,' he informed Rosa smugly.

'Impressive. But can you do Dutch?' she asked. Then flushed because 'can you do Dutch' sounded like something from an erotic novel.

Judging by the gleam that sprang into Zach's eyes his mind must have run along a similar track, though he answered gravely. 'I don't know what that is. Maybe you could show me?'

'What's Dutch?' Paige demanded.

Rosa gave the little girl her attention so she didn't have to look at Zach. 'It's similar to a French plait but the plait's raised up.'

'I want one!' Paige switched allegiance and presented her back to Rosa.

Rosa quickly unravelled Zach's handiwork and began the plait anew. 'All you do is weave each strand under instead of over. Then the braid stands proud.'

'I'll have to practise,' he said solemnly, and took a photo of the back of Paige's head so his niece could inspect the result.

Under cover of Paige clamouring for Marci and Dory to pause their conversation and admire her Dutch plait, Zach tilted his head closer to Rosa's. 'I hope you don't mind me joining you at the reunion lunch?' He gave the ghost of a smile. 'It's not as if it's a date.'

She found herself laughing. 'Let's hope my mother understands that! Of course I'm happy for us all to go together. It's nice to have friends here in Malta.'

Then Marci joined the conversation with the perennial 'What will you wear?' As Rosa talked summer dresses with Marci, she could hear Zach chatting to Dory about Malta's post-World War II history and the tunnels under Valletta.

Marci, obviously hearing too, nodded in Zach's direction, stretched out in his chair. 'He's developed a big interest in Maltese history. I think it's his way of trying to find himself.'

Zach caught the comment and shrugged. 'Maybe I'm the only one looking.'

Rosa laughed, though, after hearing his story last night, she wondered if there was a spark of snark in his answer. 'Maybe I'll start trying to find myself too,' she said. It would be better than feeling lost.

Chapter Four

Over the next four days, Dory devoted herself to encouraging Rosa to fall in love with Malta.

They ambled to Sliema along what Dory referred to as The Strand, though it said Triq ix-Xatt on the map – the seafront road, dotted with graceful palm trees. They strolled the hilly streets of narrow pavements and busy roads, browsed the shops and ate in bustling pavement cafés. Rosa got her head around Sliema being situated on a promontory so having a coastline that on one side looked over the calm waters of Marsamxett Harbour, past Manoel Island to the ramparts, golden buildings, balconies, domes, spires, lookouts and towers that was the capital city Valletta. On the other it faced the open ocean and she could gaze along towards the towers and hotels of St Julian's Bay, which encompassed Paceville.

They crossed Marsamxett Harbour to Valletta on the tubby white catamaran ferry, a journey of a few minutes over the sparkling blue sea, yachts, tourist boats and ferries manoeuvring around each other and leaving behind them a cat's cradle of white wakes. After queuing with a hundred others to leave the ferry they puffed towards the centre of the city up streets so steep that Sliema's seemed gentle in comparison. The narrow pavements, in the Maltese way, occasionally turned into stairs and, in fact, so did whole streets. Most of the buildings were traditional limestone that glowed in the heat of the day, many heavily carved into graceful ornamentation around windows or coats of arms on parapets. The enclosed balconies known as 'galleriji' were painted in green and red. Rosa craned to inspect a frontage towering several storeys above. 'A *gallerija* is like a cross between a balcony and a bay window.' Dignified statues met them on street corners. The air was filled with the sounds of engines in low gear, chattering voices and church bells.

Some streets were broad, others narrow, many opened into squares set with open-air cafés, parasols in cream, green or burgundy hoisted against the sun. When they reached the part of Republic Street that was both pedestrianised and fairly level, they paused to catch their breath. Dory panted, 'Let's begin with me showing you my favourite view in all the world.' They crossed the little city in a few minutes, some streets offering shade but others only dazzling sunlight and Dory steered Rosa to the Upper Barrakka Gardens. Entering through a gated arch, Rosa paused. 'It's beautiful!'

A simple but graceful fountain danced in the centre, circled by flowerbeds and benches. Following one of the geometrically laid-out paths they passed through two rows of graceful arches.

Then they stepped onto a terrace so high above a harbour that they were actually looking down on massive moored cruise ships.

'Wow,' Rosa breathed, trying to drink in the vista before

her. The afternoon sun bounced on the cerulean sea upon which boats of every size drew white criss-cross wakes: industrial-looking vessels with battered red hulls and grey deck cranes, tiny motor boats, blue freighters and bobbing tug boats. From tankers to cruise ships, water taxis to ferries, Grand Harbour teemed with nautical life from the breakwater and lighthouse at the mouth of the harbour to an expansive dockyard area in a creek opposite where they stood.

'This is Grand Harbour,' Dory announced impressively. 'Valletta's built on a peninsula, like Sliema, with Manoel Island between. On a map they look like arms curving around a fish. Over the other side—' she gestured towards the area across Grand Harbour '—are the Three Cities, also known as the Cottonera area.'

'Wow,' Rosa repeated inadequately. The harbour was magnificent. Vibrant. Surrounded by reminders of Valletta's history. On a saluting battery below them stood a row of cannons; watchtowers hung from the massive sloping curtain walls protecting the city, tunnels disappearing into them here and there. Dory went into tourist guide mode, pointing to a soaring modern silver structure. 'There's the Upper Barrakka Lift, which carries passengers between these gardens and Valletta Waterfront, where the big ships moor.' She pointed across the harbour. 'That's Fort St Angelo, there's Fort St Michael, and the naval museum that was Bighi Hospital when I was a kid. I went there when I broke my nose, and Aunt Lizzy had to go when she trod on a harpoon someone had left out.' She went on, spouting far too much information for Rosa to absorb, though she recognised some of the places Dory and Zach had talked about: the War HQ Tunnels, Lascaris War Rooms, Fort Rinella.

When Dory finally wound down they stopped for morning coffee in the garden café, overseen by a flock of pigeons and a couple of curious cats, then wandered further into the city, almost entirely laid out in a grid. 'Mum was once told the streets were "bisexual" rather than "bisectional".' Dory grinned. 'Her face must have been a picture. Somewhere here there's a place called Strait Street – it's full of lovely bistros now but was the red-light district in the day.'

'You seriously remember that?' Rosa challenged, brushing back her hair, feeling sweaty and damp as the sunshine poured down on them. 'You were a child!'

Dory laughed, stepping further back on the pavement to let a small horse-drawn carriage, a *karozzin*, clip-clop past, its domed roof well above the driver's head, a couple of pink-looking tourists perched inside. 'Of course I don't remember it! I talk to Dad about Malta and there's a lot of reminiscing on the Barracks Brats Facebook group. My own memories concern things like the old-fashioned school bus and the term when the bus drivers went on strike and we went to school in three-ton trucks with soldiers for bus orderlies. Summers when we went to school in the morning and swam at the lido in the afternoons. Leaving the camp to sneak off to out-of-bounds areas like the docks.' She waved vaguely over her shoulder.

Rosa wasn't sure whether she was indicating the past or an actual place behind them. It was weird seeing the present Malta through her own eyes and simultaneously, like a benevolent ghost floating along with them, Sixties Malta through her mother's reminiscences. This café was where her parents used to take Dory and Lizzy for Fanta and a slush-like treat called granita. Several centuries ago, that enormous building was the lodging of the Knights of

Castile and Lyon, now the offices of the prime minister, but important to Dory for being British Army Headquarters, where her father Lance McCoy's military duties had taken him every day. 'Sometimes we used to sit on those cannons to wait for Dad to finish work. They were as shiny and black as they are now. That archway opposite, with the steps up to it, that was the way to the NAAFI. If I'd walked that far without whinging Mum used to buy me a lollipop from a kiosk halfway up the steps.'

On one level, Rosa had always known perfectly well that Grandpa had been a career soldier, Grandma an army wife, her mum and aunt army kids, but now she began to really understand that for several years this hot, rocky island in the middle of the Mediterranean had been her mother's home in the same way that the Yorkshire market town of Liggers Moor had been home to Rosa. Parade grounds had been where Dory had played rounders or ridden her bike; that turquoise sea had been where she'd learned to swim. Rosa felt that, till now, she'd let a vital part of her mother's make-up wash over her.

As well as the sightseeing, Dory made sure she gave Rosa time to herself. In the cool peacefulness of her room Rosa created a playlist of Zumba videos on YouTube so she could play them on her iPad and dance. Something about the sensuous moves and throbbing rhythms brought her back to herself. It wasn't the same as attending classes at the gym with the girls she danced with regularly – Emily, Brenna, Zoë and a dozen others – but in her room here she could do it naked and in bare feet.

On Saturday, Dory took Rosa to a dive shack and they bought snorkels, masks and fins, then hurried home to change. Across The Ramp and the seafront road were a small rocky beach and a swimming area. Rusty old cannons had been cemented upside down into the rock as moorings. A lady fished and teenagers shrieked as they swam and splashed. Beyond the swimming area there were boats. Blue harbour cruisers full of tourists beat past, the muffled commentary stealing across the water. Pleasure craft rocked peaceably at anchor and towering motor yachts were moored on the opposite shore, Manoel Island. Sailing dinghies, looking hardly big enough to sit in, skimmed the waves, their sailors parking their bums on the high side when the wind heeled them over.

On the beach, young women wore brief costumes, Rosa noticed, but none were topless. She laughed to watch the antics of a black pug dog in what looked like a life jacket rolling on people's beach towels to dry off between dips, to the irritation of the towel owners.

Rosa breathed in the briny air, feeling a beaming smile take charge of her face. 'Look how many shades of blue and green make up the colour of the sea. I can't wait to try snorkelling.' Although she was a strong swimmer, opportunities to snorkel had never come Rosa's way, maybe because Marcus didn't care for the sea so their few holidays had been more about hill walking or city breaks. She let Dory show her how to swill her mask with seawater to help with fogging then position it over eyes and nose, waiting until she was at the edge of the rocks before wrestling on her fins, which snapped over her feet like bizarre slippers and felt a size too small.

'You'll be fine once you're in!' Dory grinned, held her mask in place and took a giant stride straight into the sea, bobbing up after a moment with an exuberant 'Whoo-hoo!' before positioning the snorkel in her mouth.

When Rosa copied her she realised the 'Whoo-hoo!' was prompted by the rippling turquoise water being *cold*.

46

It was also magical, once she'd made herself believe she could breathe through the snorkel and, safely protected by the mask, open her eyes in salty water.

Below her she discovered a place she'd only seen on David Attenborough TV programmes, an azure world of slow motion, where all you could hear was water in your ears and your own breathing, where fish nibbled unconcernedly at rocks studded with spiky black sea urchins. Sun filtered through the water to glint off fish scales, silver, grey-green or, her favourites, those like shimmering, swimming rainbows.

Dory led the way, pointing out crabs hunkered down beside rocky crevices they could scuttle into, the pink rubbery tentacles of sea anemones stirred slowly by the current that shrank into themselves when touched. There was even a patch of mottled grey that Dory spat out her snorkel to tell her was an octopus in its hole. The water flowed over Rosa's body like a caress, pushing her to and fro, bobbing her around in the wake of passing boats.

When they finally clambered out via a metal ladder set into the rock to dry themselves they found Marci and Paige poking around in nearby rock pools.

'Hey Rosa, hey Dory!' Paige cried, running over. 'In a minute we're going to the café. Wanna come?'

'If your mum doesn't mind.' Rosa smiled at Marci, shaking her head to get the water out of her ears before wrapping her towel around herself.

'It would be great,' Marci said and they packed up their things and clambered over the rocks to the café that stood nearby, claiming a table under a yellow parasol and ordering drinks and gelato.

'Mm.' Paige flicked her ponytail back to keep it clear of her strawberry ice cream. 'I love Malta.'

'Me, too,' chorused Dory and Marci promptly.

Rosa was barely a beat behind when she said, 'It's growing on me.' She was rewarded by a delighted grin from her mum.

Sunday was the day of the Barracks Brats Reunion lunch in Mdina, 'the Silent City', once the capital of Malta. Zach, looking continental in linen trousers, flip-flops and a short-sleeved shirt, had ordered a large cab. Rosa and Dory climbed in with him, Marci and Paige and enjoyed the journey through the narrow streets of residential Sliema crammed with cars before they headed out into the countryside where white or vivid pink oleander and twisty, dusty pine trees decorated the roadside. They passed brown scrub growing through cracks and prickly pear lolling over the dry stone walls that marked out small farm fields until the taxi dropped them at the city gate.

They crossed a stone bridge over formal gardens into the beautiful, compact walled city that was Mdina, looking as if it hadn't changed in centuries. It rose up, its slopes clothed in farmed terraces and olive groves, its honey-coloured buildings wearing wrought iron over their windows, arches beside statues, beautiful ornamentation carved from living stone. Balconies were everywhere, open ones of wood, stone, wrought iron, or the enclosed *galleriji*. In the narrow streets where doors were set into walls Zach said, 'I've read the streets were curved so archers could lie in wait at windows behind the wrought iron and enemies coming up the street wouldn't see them until it was too late. Malta's always been of great strategic importance. People were queuing up to conquer it and the Maltese fought back.'

'Grisly,' Rosa commented as they wandered a street so

cramped she could stretch and touch the walls on each side. Most streets were too small for cars, and even the horse-drawn carriages, the *karozzini,* could only use the broadest of the thoroughfares. Streets opened into squares and guides herded tourists.

As they reached a flaming mass of cerise bougainvillea clinging to a towering wall, Zach glanced at the map app on his phone. 'If we turn left here we should be at the restaurant.'

They entered the venue through a pair of tall glass doors set into a wall and stepped down into a cool double-height area set with snowy tablecloths and gleaming silverware. Rosa gazed up at the vaulted ceiling and curving stone arches. 'I feel as if I'm always looking at something in Malta and saying, "Wow!"'

'I know what you mean.' Marci took Paige's hand to prevent her from getting too close to an ancient suit of armour.

A smiling Maltese woman greeted them. 'You are here for the reunion? Good afternoon, I am Claudette.' She led them down more stone stairs and between the tables before taking a flight of stone steps up again. A hum of conversation grew louder as they reached a pretty function room open to a garden. The hum became a babble, punctuated with bursts of laughter.

Claudette stood aside. 'Here is your party. Lunch will be served presently. Please order drinks from the bar and enjoy!'

A woman with long wavy hair stepped forward. 'Hello! I'm Lesley, one of the hosts of the Barracks Brats Reunion. Let me show you the name badge table. We have sixty-eight attending – isn't that amazing?'

From behind a long table a portly bald man in

well-pressed cream shorts and a blue open-necked shirt handed out name badges on lanyards.

'Blimey, Dory's name badge is almost military.' Marci gave a rare giggle. And, indeed, Dory's badge, edged with khaki to denote her status as a barracks brat, said:

Dory McCoy Hammond
School: Tigné Barracks Infant and Junior
Lived (67–70): Royal Court, Ta' Xbiex and St Francis Ravelin, Floriana

'That's the last we'll see of Mum for a while.' Rosa watched Dory vanish into the nearest group of people with khaki-edged name badges, her mouth set on 'nineteen-to-the-dozen'. Zach fell into conversation with a guy called Trent about the history of Mdina and Rosa followed Marci and Paige out into the garden, helping themselves to drinks as they passed the bar.

What looked like the wall of the garden proved to be part of one of the curtain walls that formed the fortifications, at least twelve feet thick with a sloping top that led to a scary drop. While Paige counted the resident goldfish in an ornamental pond with a fountain Marci asked Rosa, 'Has your mum subjected you to the "Here's where we lived" and "here's where I went to school" tours yet?'

Rosa laughed. 'She's shown me where the school's stone arches and clock tower have been incorporated into the high rises that obliterated Tigné Barracks.'

Marci nodded. 'Dad says Tigné looks like a mini Miami now.'

'Zach told me you have a Maltese grandmother.' Rosa watched Paige dipping her fingers in the water and the flash of goldfish flipping their tails and shooting away.

Marci settled on the coping of the pond and tilted her face to the sun. She wore a loose black linen dress and her dark hair swept down onto it in a silken sheet. 'Grandad and Nanna met at a dance in Valletta in the Fifties. His army career took them back to the UK long enough for my dad and his two brothers to arrive, then to Cyprus. They were posted back here 1966 to 69, which would be when your family was in Malta. Grandad was in 235 Signal Squadron. After the army, Nanna and Grandad settled in Cornwall. Redruth. Not one of the craggy or pretty bits.'

Rosa wrinkled her forehead. 'Grandpa Lance was in the Ordnance Corps. Something to do with supplies.'

'The Royal Army Ordnance Corps went wherever there was British infantry.' It was Zach who provided this information as he strolled up to join them, looking relaxed and cool despite the heat.

'You sound better informed than I am,' Rosa confessed. 'I know National Servicemen only did a couple of years in the forces rather than the twenty-one years Grandpa served, but that's about it. Mum natters to Grandpa about the posts and pictures on the Barracks Brats Facebook group but I don't find it as fascinating as they do.'

'Zach's interested too,' Marci said. 'He'll swap Maltese history with anyone. Dad read out some bits from the Barracks Brats about your mum's success, by the way. How did she get to be a famous cook?'

Rosa settled on the coping alongside Marci. Paige was still trying to count fish, sighing in exasperation because they wouldn't keep still. 'That career exploded out of nowhere a few years ago after a reality TV crew came to the school where Mum was the cook.' Rosa was used to telling the story but it still felt as if it were something that had happened to another family. 'Her big personality came over well on camera and she became the character who stole the show. When she waxed enthusiastic about her initiative of "stealthy eating" – getting good food into the kids by disguising it, like putting beetroot in brownies – the director lapped it up and it went down a storm on social media.' She paused, remembering that it didn't always feel good to be talked about on social media. She shoved the thought away. 'I helped her start a blog and various social media channels. The production company invited her onto a Christmas special, increasing the buzz. Then a literary agent contacted her saying she thought she could get her a deal with a major publisher.'

'*The Cafeteria Cook Does Stealthy Eating*,' Zach supplied, easing Paige back before she toppled in the water. 'Dad bought Nanna the book.'

'Mum will be delighted.' Rosa fanned herself with her hand. The afternoon seemed to be getting warmer. 'The book took off.' Then she laughed. 'Gross understatement! It was a number one *Sunday Times* bestseller and at the top of the Amazon charts. It's still selling steadily. The follow-up, *The Cafeteria Cook Does Stealthy Weight Loss*, did just as well and sold around the world. Mum does guest spots in food magazines, on blogs, on radio, TV and video channels. She left her school and now she's writing *The Cafeteria Cook Does the Mediterranean*.'

Marci sighed. 'That's fantastic. I wish life had been so kind to our mum. She keeps surprisingly cheerful but she's in constant pain. We Skyped her this morning and she couldn't wait to hear everything we're doing.'

Zach joined in. 'She's more or less housebound or I bet she'd have been out here for this reunion.'

A man joined them, middle-aged and florid despite his olive skin. His name was Jim, he told them, and – like Zach and Marci's dad – he had a British Army father and Maltese mother. 'Dad was with the Anglians 66 to 68.'

As Zach chatted to Jim, Rosa gazed over the wall at the panorama of buildings, domes large and small and a tower on a nearby rise. Terraces followed the contours of the land like the lines on an ordnance survey map and the rich chime of church bells carried distantly on the air.

Jim drew her back into the conversation by pointing out a few features of the landscape. 'That's the hospital at Mtarfa where I and many children of servicemen were born. See that clock tower and the buildings beside it? That's Mtarfa Barracks.'

'Another barracks?' she asked. 'How many were there on Malta?'

The man blew out his cheeks contemplatively. 'Depends on period. Pembroke, St George's, St Andrew's, Tigné, Lintorn I remember from when I was a kid. Then there was the navy and RAF.' When Rosa stood up to take a photo he gallantly held her drink. She smiled when she'd finished, taking back the glass with murmured thanks.

Jim was evidently feeling jocular. 'Always happy to help a lady. Some men refer to women as "the weaker sex", y'know, but I think the phrase "the fairer sex" will get me in less trouble.' He let out a guffaw.

Always irritated by condescension towards her gender Rosa gazed at the distant view.

Unfortunately, Jim persisted. 'What? Not offended, are you? I said women are *not* the weaker sex.' He guffawed again.

Slowly, Rosa turned to him. 'Of course they aren't. It's men who carry their most sensitive organs outside of their bodies where they can be so easily hurt.'

Jim halted mid-guffaw and stared at Rosa. 'Erm, quite,' he muttered and drifted away to invade someone else's conversation.

Zach grinned. 'I think he's worried he's just been threatened.'

She sniffed. 'I'm afraid Mum taught me to speak up for
myself. Maybe it's because we didn't have any of "the
stronger sex" around to do it for us.' Her tone was so
dry that Zach burst out laughing.

Other than the encounter with Jim, the event was hugely
more enjoyable than Rosa had dared hope. Everyone had
Malta in common in some way and more than one person
had to wipe their eyes at a shared memory. Even as the
grandchild of a soldier, Rosa began to feel she was mixing
with her tribe as she heard snatches of conversation about
the Royal Anglian Regiment, REME, RAOC, the Lancs
and the Paras. Dory introduced her to Janice from Robb
Lido and Carol from Tigné School. A delicious lunch of
meats, salads, fruits, pastry and cakes went beautifully
with Marsovin wine or Cisk beer. Paige tried a local soft
drink called Kinnie but said it was 'too pepper'. Dory
drank it for her because Kinnie had been a treat '. . . when
I was a kid in Malta' Rosa finished for her.

Dory looked abashed. 'Sorry. I'll try and stop saying
that. It's the first of these reunions I've managed and
they're usually a few years apart.'

Rosa gave her a hug. 'I'm only teasing, Mum. I'm happy
you're happy.'

Dory plunged off to exchange reminiscences with a new
group of people. Paige began to play with two boys a year
or two older than her and Rosa wandered over to an old
lichened bench right at the end of the garden to watch,
soaking in the statues, paths and the golden walls of all
the buildings around while the sun baked her.

Zach appeared with wine that glowed like a glassful of
pink jewels in the afternoon sun. 'I thought you might

like to try this as it's called Santa Rosa rosé.' He joined her on the carved stone bench, leaning in to add in a theatrical whisper, 'Marci's talking to *a man* so I said I'd come and check on Paige.'

Rosa thanked him for the wine. 'Doesn't Marci usually talk to men?'

He pulled a face. 'Paige's dad vanished while Marci was pregnant, and then the next guy cheated on her.' He sipped his wine and licked his lips. 'She's overdue a positive interaction, even if it's just chatting about favourite books at a party.'

'Brotherly of you to look out for Paige,' Rosa commented with real approval.

He shrugged. Then he grinned disarmingly. 'Also, Dory asked me to keep you company in case you're getting fed up with her talking Malta all afternoon.'

'Oh, dear, I'm afraid I've made her feel like that.' Rosa shielded her eyes to gaze at where Dory was still trying for the world record in cramming the most conversations into one party. 'She's having a fantastic time and I'm glad. I came here with a negative mindset but I am actually in Malta for her.'

'Her version is she put you off the island, bossing you about her kitchen like Gordon Ramsay,' he said. 'I can't see your mum as him though.'

'She can do the swearing!' Rosa laughed and they looked at each other and chorused, 'Army kid.'

Zach watched Paige driving toy cars through the dust at the edge of the path. 'She says the job at home is in a youth centre and you're missing it.'

Rosa stiffened, wondering whether Dory had given any details of what had led up to her taking leave. 'Yes.'

He glanced at her. 'My cousin Joseph Zammit heads up

a drop-in centre in Gżira and I think I mentioned that I help out there. We're doing a sea clean tomorrow afternoon, if you fancy getting involved as a volunteer. It's on a public beach in Sliema – a load of teens clearing out bottles and stuff.'

Instantly, Rosa's heart lifted at the idea of being involved with something that involved young people. 'I'd love to. As long as Mum doesn't need me then.'

'Let me know,' he said easily. 'You'd have to be ready at three tomorrow afternoon with your snorkelling gear.'

He told her more about Nicholas Centre, named after Joseph's great-uncle Nicholas who had left the property to him. 'It's tucked away in a little street in Gżira. There's not much outdoor space,' he said, 'but a room for arts and crafts, a function room, a small gym and a computer room. It's open to thirteen- to eighteen-year-olds. Some of the kids come from less wealthy backgrounds because there's plenty to do that's free.'

'I'd love to see it. It sounds as if it operates in a similar area to Blackthorn's, where I organise events and sponsorship,' she responded. 'It was set up by JJ Blacker, the drummer from the band The Hungry Years. My branch is in my home town of Liggers Moor in Yorkshire but the first was on the Shetland Estate in Cambridgeshire where he was brought up. He doesn't want today's kids to feel like he did – trapped by low incomes and low expectations, nowhere to go, nothing to do but fall in with the wrong crowd.' She halted, remembering the story he'd told her and Luccio in the restaurant in Spinola a few nights ago. 'Sorry! I wasn't having a dig at you.'

'Don't apologise.' He'd finished his wine and was twirling the glass between his fingers. 'I'm the first to worry about negative peer pressure.'

Before Rosa could answer, her phone burbled. Her stomach shifted to recognise Marcus's ringtone. Though they had things to sort out regarding the transfer of their house to Marcus's name it was the first time he'd called since she'd come to Malta. She pulled the phone from her bag and saw he wanted to FaceTime. She hesitated, apprehension wriggling through her in place of the thrill she would have felt a couple of years ago. 'Do you mind if I take it?'

'Of course not,' Zach replied politely.

Rosa took a few steps away to accept the call. Marcus's image flashed onto the screen, his hair looking as if he'd rummaged through it. 'Hi.' Then, evidently getting a glimpse of her exotic surroundings, 'You look as if you're somewhere nice.'

Rosa didn't mind that he looked slightly envious. She even extended her arm so he could see more. 'What's up?' She debated telling him she'd call him back but didn't want to wait to know why he'd called.

'Who's that bloke?' Marcus asked suddenly. 'He's looking at your arse.'

Rosa could see Zach on screen behind her but not where his gaze lay. She could have snapped at Marcus that just because he'd rejected her didn't mean other men weren't interested but she chose instead to keep the conversation neutral, not least because Zach might hear. 'Why did you call?'

Marcus forgot Zach and became breezy. 'Just a formality to do with the mortgage.'

'Go on,' she said, politely.

He cleared his throat. 'There's another piece of paper for you to sign. You know what solicitors are like – every box ticked, even the irrelevant ones.'

'Oh?' Her arm was getting tired of holding her phone in the air and she probably looked as if she were trying to present herself at a flattering angle. She sat back down on the coping around the pond, propping the phone on her lap.

Marcus's gaze became guarded. 'I probably shouldn't even have told my solicitor because it doesn't actually matter.'

Rosa's senses prickled. She'd known Marcus for too long not to recognise the signs of him trying to misdirect her attention. Her mind began to work. The only way money still connected them was via the mortgage. Her heart sank. If he was unable to meet a payment then she'd have to do it instead because the formalities of transferring it into his name alone were incomplete. 'You haven't run through all your money *already*?' She didn't have her usual salary right now and, thanks to Marcus, she'd come out of their relationship with precious few reserves.

Marcus's expression froze. 'Your faith in me is touching, as always. My bank balance is still healthy, thanks.' There was a touch of smugness in his words.

Rosa was losing patience. 'So what's the problem?'

Marcus cleared his throat again. 'I didn't want my money to vanish while trying to make a go of Spun Gold full-time so I took a lodger to help pay the mortgage. In the bloody backwards way solicitors do things, they've mentioned it to the mortgage provider, who says they need your formal consent before switching the mortgage into my name. I should have got their OK before taking in a lodger, apparently, so I have to cross their T's and dot their I's retrospectively.'

Rosa just about followed this. 'So it doesn't really affect me? I sign a consent and everything goes through?'

Marcus smiled. 'Exactly.' The smile remained pinned to his lips. 'Something else I should probably tell you because it will be on the paperwork. The lodger is Chellice.'

'*Chellice*?' Rosa broke in. 'The same Chellice you absolutely swore you weren't having a thing with?'

'She's a lodger,' he snapped, smile switching off. 'It makes sense because it's cheaper than her last place and means she can put more into Spun Gold.'

Rosa heard her voice rising. 'Either you're a gullible idiot for believing that's all there is to it or you think I am. Either way, it doesn't matter. Email me the details of how I go about signing so we can end this. But I just want to say, MARCUS, YOU'RE A SHITTY BASTARD!' With shaking fingers she ended the call.

Slowly, she came back to herself, realising she was still at a party. At the shady end of the garden she saw several people swiftly turn their gazes away. Great. Her outburst had been heard.

Zach had obviously caught it too as he uncoiled himself and left the bench to perch on the coping beside her. 'More sticking up for yourself. Love it.' But there was so much sympathy in his voice that Rosa's eyes boiled for a moment. 'Are you OK?' he added softly.

'Yes, it's just . . . men.' She gave a watery smile.

'Yeah. Shitty bastards,' he agreed contemplatively.

Shakily, she laughed. 'Possibly not all of you.'

He patted her arm. 'How about you keep an eye on Paige for a minute while I go get us more wine?'

'Plan,' she agreed, grateful to have a few moments to herself.

The event began to draw to a close at about six, which Rosa didn't think was bad going for 'lunch'. As the afternoon had grown hotter and hotter, Dory, Zach, Rosa and

Paige waited in the shady function room for Marci. When she finally joined them she looked a bit pink. 'I've been talking to this guy, Jake.'

'Really? Hadn't noticed,' Zach said, deadpan. 'It's only been about three hours.'

Marci flushed still pinker. 'He's invited me for lunch on Wednesday . . . if I can get a babysitter.' Her eyes sparkled hopefully at her brother.

'I'll have Paige for lunch,' Zach agreed easily.

Paige's ponytail swung as she whipped round to regard her uncle with a winning smile. 'On the pirate ship?'

Marci's eyebrows shot up. 'We use the word "please" when we ask for big favours, Paige, don't we? Even if you can wind your uncle round your finger? Restaurants cost money.'

'Sorry,' said Paige, not sounding particularly so. 'Please, Uncle Zachary, would you take me to the pirate ship for lunch, please, please?'

Zach smiled down at her with such affection that Rosa's heart expanded. 'Wellllll . . .' he mused.

Paige all but batted her eyelashes.

'OK,' he agreed.

'Yay!' She bounced on the spot, clapping her small hands. 'Can Dory and Rosa come too? *Please?*'

'I was about to suggest the very same.' Zach gave his sister a wink before she could butt in with more parental objections.

'The pirate ship is pretty cool,' Dory said, 'so thank you. I'd love to join you.'

Rosa felt a stirring of misgiving. A ship? 'Can I wait and see if the sea's still calm? I get seasick.'

Paige giggled. 'It's a pirate ship on the *ground*.'

'Firmly on the shore,' Zach confirmed.

'Oh! In that case, thank you. I've never eaten on a pirate ship.' Rosa smiled at Paige's beaming delight.

As the group finally made their way downstairs Zach fell back to where Rosa brought up the rear of the party. 'About lunch,' he growled theatrically out of the corner of his mouth. 'I'm not dating at the moment.'

She stifled a giggle. 'I'll tell my mum we're just good friends.' Then, before he could make a joke of that too added, 'I could do with a friend out here.'

The merriment in his eyes faded away. 'I'm your man,' he said, which left Rosa with a surprising case of the warm and fuzzies. She kept seeing Zach being kind to people and it was heart-warming to find herself included.

Chapter Five

On Monday morning, Rosa was happy to return to her role as kitchen porter. Dory was working on several versions of *bigilla*, the dip made of beans and garlic popular in Malta, but she was content for Rosa to join the sea clean later. Rosa texted Zach to tell him.

He arrived at their door at three p.m., jingling his car keys. 'Do you have ID to show Joseph? I don't want to put him in an awkward spot if he doesn't identify you and you turn out to be a criminal.'

'I'm not!' she returned shortly, then realised that, unless Dory had been spilling beans, he wouldn't know the ups and down – mainly downs – of why she and Marcus had split up and she flashed a smile to offset her terseness. 'Give me a second to grab my UK driving licence.'

After they'd driven along the seafront road, Zach had shoehorned his car into a spot in a side road in Sliema. The public beach on Tigné seafront had a breathtaking view across Marsamxett Harbour to where Valletta shimmered in the heat haze. Rosa managed to get down onto the rocks without dropping fins, mask, snorkel or towel and was introduced to Joseph, who, in the mixed-culture way of Malta, had an English mother. 'Joseph's dad was a cousin of Nanna's,' Zach explained. 'We say we're cousins because the exact relationship takes too much working out.'

'Pleased to meet you.' Joseph was a stocky man with a waistline that suggested he didn't totally adhere to the healthy part of the Mediterranean diet. He introduced his wife, Maria, who when she'd kissed Zach on each cheek, shook hands with Rosa and eyed Rosa's snorkel gear with a smile. 'I think you wish to be in the water rather than on the shore to give out snacks and drinks?' She indicated two coolers of drinks and a cardboard box containing crisps and fruit.

Rosa felt sympathetic, remembering the times she'd drawn an uninteresting task at Blackthorn's events. 'I could do some of each,' she offered.

Maria laughed and patted Rosa's arm. 'You swim. It's good to clean the water. I have Luccio to help me.'

Rosa hadn't noticed Luccio nearby but now he sent a grin her way. 'Let her give out drinks, Maria. Then I can cool off in the sea this hot afternoon,' he teased and kissed Rosa on both cheeks.

'Great to see you again.' Rosa had forgotten Zach had mentioned that Luccio worked at Nicholas Centre. He looked much younger than when she'd seen him last time, happier and cleaner cut, although his outfit of T-shirt, flip-flops and skinny shorts that showed the tattoos on his legs was much the same. It was 'the look' for young men on the island. Older men tended to wear roomier shorts and – usually – no tattoos.

Teenagers began to arrive as Rosa chatted to Luccio about how he liked working as a youth support worker.

They approached Joseph to sign in to the sea clean project, collecting bottles of water or soft drinks from Maria, pulling off shorts and T-shirts to reveal swimming gear beneath.

Rosa was introduced to the other adults present: Peter, Axel and Malin. Peter was Maltese and Malin was a pretty Swedish blonde woman who was in Malta for the scuba diving which, she explained, she funded by working at Nicholas Centre and casual work in bars. Axel, a German in his early forties, had lived in Malta for years and was the assistant manager at Nicholas Centre.

Joseph gave a 'housekeeping' talk to the teens while cool drinks were consumed. 'You will each be assigned to a group. Zach will lead one group with his friend Rosa; Peter and Malin will lead the other.' Each of the teens was given a rubber sash and belt combination, blue for Zach's group and red for Peter's. The sash part could be seen from above the water and the belt from below. 'I will be on shore to check Zach's group is safe and Axel will provide surface cover for Peter's.'

Zach and Peter took over, assembling their respective groups of eight. They'd work in pairs, one diving for debris and the other loading it into floating baskets. Zach made sure he had the attention of everyone in his group. 'This is our area and you'll see it includes the cave. You'll stay away from that,' he declared in a no-nonsense tone. He pointed at the crevice – which was like a gaping, triangular mouth in the rocks – in case anyone had any doubt what he was talking about. The cave narrowed sharply, tumbling every wave that entered and boiling it white before spitting it back out to sea. 'We all know it's fun to let the waves take us in but I can't save you all at once.'

The teens laughed, nudging one another.

'And,' Zach emphasised, 'if anyone does go into the cave, even if they pretend the sea took them, I'll set Rosa on them and she's very fierce.'

Familiar with this kind of 'instructing under the guise of joking', Rosa bared her teeth and pulled her eyebrows into a grotesque frown. The teens laughed again.

'Seriously, if you get too near the cave I'm afraid you'll have to get out of the water,' Zach finished with more gravity.

Rosa, fully aware that if you took young people to a public place you actually had very little leverage over them other than to bar offenders from activities or premises, nodded emphatically, which encouraged the teens to nod back.

Before long they were all in the water, pumping their feet energetically while they made adjustments to masks and snorkels and gathered baskets from those on the shore. Zach and Rosa supervised four kids each, putting their faces in the water to spot bottles or cans.

Zach tried not to get distracted by the sight of Rosa's body underwater. A swimming costume, even one-piece and plain purple, left little to the imagination and one glance told him she had an hourglass figure. In the green-blue marine world he observed several of the lads in his team risk quick glances at her too. Boys would be boys but he wasn't going to have her made uncomfortable. He tapped the arm of the nearest lad and pointed at a yellow Cisk can between two rocks. It was more than six feet down so the effort of retrieval would give him something else to focus on.

He did have to keep glancing at Rosa because she was on his team and so he needed to know how strongly she swam and whether to bring Luccio in to relieve her. She seemed at home in the water, even if, as she informed him, she'd only recently snorkelled for the first time.

They took a break after an hour. Most of the Maltese kids swam as naturally as walking but there was no harm in taking a breather, drinking a bottle of water and eating an orange. He sat down next to Rosa on a towel because the rock was hot.

'Is your name really Zachary?' she demanded, peeling her orange with her thumbnail.

He blinked. 'Yes. Why, what did you think?'

'I don't know. I heard Paige call you Zachary yesterday. I suppose I hadn't thought Zach was short for anything, maybe because people often think Rosa is short for Rosalind or Rosamund and in my case it's not.'

He shrugged. 'Some Zachs are Zachariah or just Zach. Our parents are Steve and Amanda and as they grew up always knowing about five others with the same name they called each of us something less usual. Marci is Marceline and our little sister is Electra.'

She'd put on sunglasses but her face was turned towards his. 'Electra's a great name. Is she coming over this summer?'

'She's in Thailand, teaching English.' He felt the hollow-ness that often accompanied thoughts of Electra and found himself explaining, 'Truth is, it's not just me who's not getting on with Dad – she doesn't either. He's had a rough few years, trapped in a cycle of being made redundant, taking a less prestigious job then being made redun-dant again and so on. Mum's rheumatoid arthritis prevents her from working so the financial burden falls on him and his age of retirement has moved further away.'

Silently, Rosa's hand settled gently on his on the towel

between them. Surprise tingled through him but he wasn't about to object to the friendly gesture.

Zach went on. 'Because he can't control the big things, Dad's trying to control the small ones or those that are, frankly, not his business. Electra went home two years ago and Dad told her he expected her to get a proper bloody job and stop gallivanting.'

'So she went straight off again?' Rosa guessed.

He nodded. 'He's turned very "my way or the highway" and one by one his family members are choosing the highway. Marci only came out here for a month or so but she's begun finding out about residency and schools.'

'Really?' He heard the surprise in her voice. Marci probably didn't seem that adventurous to her.

Zach grimaced. 'I don't know if she'll follow through but I wouldn't be completely shocked. When she got pregnant with Paige it wasn't planned. Dad went all Victorian and tried to make her move in with him and Mum because no doubt she'd expect help with "the child" and he "couldn't do everything for everyone". He managed to alienate both Marci and Mum in one go and when Paige arrived, though he loved her to bits, he'd already built a wall between them because Marci was adamant she'd never look to our parents for child care.' Nearby teenagers chattered loudly, sometimes in Maltese and sometimes in English. One even spoke Italian with Luccio, who, apparently, spoke it along with Sicilian and English. Peter, Axel, Malin, Joseph and Maria all joined in in one language or another.

Zach carried on. 'My latest bout of trouble was the catalyst for Dad really losing it. He and I squared up to each other at one point before Nanna stepped in.' He sipped from his bottle of water. 'She's the one Dad really talks to and she probably makes more allowances for him than the rest of us.'

'She's his mum.' Rosa moved closer.

He nodded and swallowed painfully. 'Grandad Harry has slithered into dementia and Nanna needs help with him but she offered me the work at the apartments and said she wanted me to take it. I said she'd have less help with Grandad if I did that but she wouldn't take that into consideration. She said Dad and I needed time apart. I checked with Mum whether she minded and she said no. Mum's always the understanding, gentle one. Dad over-heard and said he could look after his own wife. As she's the one he's capable of showing love to, I took her at her word and left.'

'I'm sorry things have been so tough.' Rosa removed her hand from his as if realising it was there and began to part the flesh of her orange. 'I scarcely know my dad because he found fatherhood didn't suit him. He's a distant stranger who visited, rarely, and gave Mum money toward my keep, also rarely. Still, you have my sympathy.'

He struggled to find a reply, shocked by her casual statement. 'And you have mine.'

'You can't miss what you never had.' She licked orange juice from her hand and he watched the quick movement of her tongue.

Then Luccio arrived to gather empty bottles and orange peel and they moved on into the second part of the sea clean.

Joseph declared the sea clean over at the end of the second hour. The last of the drinks, fruit and crisps were handed out and some of the teens moved further up the beach to throw themselves and each other off the rocks with a lot of good-natured shrieking. Others packed up and drifted off. The adults gathered the equipment belonging to Nicholas Centre and stowed it in the boot of a people carrier.

'Rosa works in a youth centre in the UK,' he said to Joseph.

Rosa nodded. 'My title is Development Officer. I don't have the right qualifications to be a youth worker but I'm good at organising events and getting publicity and funding for them.'

'Funding?' Joseph pounced on the word. 'Tell me how you do it in the UK because in Malta we're always looking.'

'In the UK too,' Rosa admitted. 'One of my favourite tricks is to work with firms who like to organise team-building exercises. For example, we got them to design and build gym bars at our centre, Blackthorn's. A local joiner donated his time to oversee the project but the company paid for the materials and its employees did the work. I, obviously, have a whole pitch about team building in terms of better communication and group strategising. Then I do all the attendant PR, which makes their budget work twice as hard.'

Zach looked at her with new respect. 'They go for that?'

Rosa grinned. 'Often enough for me to keep doing it.' She asked Joseph about Nicholas Centre and Zach zoned out, familiar as he was with the story of how Joseph's great-uncle Nicholas had always helped kids with less-than-ideal backgrounds so Joseph had begun the centre in his name. He found himself watching the way Rosa's hair jiggled around her face as the breeze dried it. Gold streaks shimmered in her drying locks and gold flecks glittered in her eyes. It was as if she had some special relationship with the sun: it loved her best. She took his breath away.

He tuned back into the conversation when he heard Joseph say, 'Will you visit us? We're always pleased to have guests at Nicholas Centre.' His eyes crinkled. 'And we can talk more about fundraising when I have a pad and pen to take notes.'

Rosa's eyes lit up. 'That would be great! Maybe I could bring Mum? She's been to Blackthorn's to put on cookery demonstrations, like how easily kids can make a healthy stir-fry rather than buying takeaway. She could do the same for you. Our kids loved it because she's been on TV but I'm sure she'd bring a book with her so they can see her face on the cover.'

'That sounds fantastic,' Zach and Joseph said together. Joseph and Rosa exchanged phone numbers so they could make plans after Rosa had spoken to Dory.

Eventually, Joseph and Maria drove off. Zach stretched. 'Right, this is when I have to get all that crap out of the cave.'

'But you said it was dangerous,' Rosa objected, frowning.

'Dangerous for the kids,' he amended. 'But I can bear a scratch or two if I get washed against the side. I've done it before. The cave's a natural collection point for whatever blows into the water.' He ferreted in his backpack and pulled out a thin, lightweight netting bag.

'Nice to know you're in favour of saving the ocean. I'll hang back and take the debris from you.' Rosa settled the bag crosswise on her body and reached for her snorkelling gear.

Once again they made the transition from the hot rocks to the cold salty ocean then finned up to the cave, avoiding an area where young men hurled themselves into the sea from the rocks with howls of glee. Zach checked Rosa appeared to be dealing with the choppy foam of the inlet

70

then got her to tread water while he swam into the shallow cave, judging the waves, sculling backwards when they tried to fling him against the rocky sides, grabbing floating bottles and tossing them to Rosa. Soon the bag floated in front of her, buoyed by the mass of plastic bottles.

When it was full and cumbersome he swam back to her. 'Let's get rid of that lot on shore.'

At the ladder, he paused to ease off his fins and toss them onto the rocks before climbing out, a technique he'd learned from scuba-crazy Malin. Once on dry land he took the bag from Rosa. She copied his action in removing her fins before exiting.

Taking a bin bag from his backpack he emptied the bottles into it and they headed back over the rocks to the sea. He fell in behind Rosa, from which position he couldn't help noticing her rear view. Quickly, he wrenched his gaze away. Maybe that was where the convention of men allowing women to go first had arisen from – not good manners but the instinct to check women out unobserved. However, after witnessing the pithy way she dealt with the Paceville guy who'd crossed her boundaries and Jim at the reunion who'd offended her sense of respect, he didn't intend to get caught 'noticing'. It was possible to enjoy her directness when it was focused on others, without particularly wanting to draw fire himself.

When the bag was once again full he towed it back to the ladder. 'We've cleared it for now.' He let her go first again but made an effort not to watch her female charms this time. There would be no cold water to hide any reaction once he was out of the water.

After resting on the sun-heated rocks to dry, Zach offered to buy Rosa a beer and an ice cream and they pulled their clothes on top of their swim things, stowed in Zach's car their snorkelling gear and the sacks of flotsam to be recycled, then headed down the road towards the row of outdoor cafés, one of which was where they'd eaten on their accidental date, and found a table not too close to the road.

It was only when he tried to pay for two pints of Cisk and two ice creams that Zach's stomach dropped to the floor. Something was missing. 'The cash has gone from my wallet!' Automatically, he patted his pockets, although he knew the notes couldn't have leapt out of his wallet and into another place.

Rosa's hand flew to her mouth. 'Oh, no! You *left* your wallet on the beach while you swam?'

'Yeah. It sounds stupid when you say it like that but Malta's usually safe,' he explained, feeling both angry and foolish. 'It was only after the others had gone that there was no one on shore with it. I'll have to buy one of those waterproof belts for when I'm in the water.'

She unzipped her backpack. 'I have thirty euros in a hidden pocket, so I can get the bill.'

'It's OK,' he muttered. 'My credit cards are still there.'

What he didn't tell her because he didn't want to even think it let alone say it out loud was that this was the third time he'd lost money recently. Joseph had lost some too.

And each time Luccio had been around.

Chapter Six

Zach debated. He could brush the theft aside and go with Rosa's assumption that the notes – about eighty euros – had been snatched by an opportunist thief while they'd been doing their bit for the ocean. But was that the best course of action?

His ice cream arrived and he ate slowly, never enjoying salted caramel gelato less in his life.

Rosa's eyes were sympathetic but her voice tentative. 'Was it a lot of money? I could probably help you out—'

'No.' He cleared his throat. 'Thank you, but it's not the money. Well, obviously, nobody wants eighty euros to vanish but it hasn't left me destitute.' He thought he detected a flash of relief in her expression and wondered. Maybe she'd felt compelled to offer but was short of money herself? He managed a smile. 'Would you mind if I made a phone call to Joseph? It's not the first sum that's gone missing. I need to let him know.'

'Oh, dear. Of course not.' Rosa shook her head.

Joseph picked up the phone on the third ring. 'You're missing me already?'

Zach gave a short laugh. 'I wish that was all. My wallet's been emptied this afternoon.' He sketched in the details.

Down the line, Joseph gave a heavy sigh. 'Shit. Luccio was there again.'

'But I did go back into the sea with Rosa after you'd left so that's when it could have happened.' He switched his gaze to Rosa, who'd taken out her phone and was stabbing at the screen. Her jaw was set, her brows almost meeting over the bridge of her freckled nose. He wondered whether her frown came from concentration or irritation.

'OK.' Joseph paused for several seconds. 'I've spent too long hoping this will blow over. I think you should report it to the police. We'll make the police involvement public at Nicholas Centre and it might discourage the thief. People should know what's going on so they can be careful. Luckily, none of the children has reported a theft.'

After a few words of agreement Zach ended the call. 'Joseph's suggested I make a police report. I'd better go now. Would you like me to run you home first?'

She shrugged. 'No need, if you don't mind me tagging along.'

He had to check the way to the police station on Google Maps because the one-way systems of Sliema often defeated him but they were able to park fairly near the porticoed stone building. Once through the weighty door of wood and bevelled glass they found a few people already in line for their turn at the polished counter so took a seat.

While they waited, Rosa received a text from Dory, which she showed to Zach with a laugh:

Would you be able to do social media stuff for me tomorrow? You know how I hate that shit. x

He grinned. 'I really like your mum. She's a lot more

laid-back than Dad. I always wondered whether his need to try and rule his kids came from having an army father. Grandad was no soft touch and Dad used to say it was the Regimental Sergeant Major in him. Maybe your grandfather's easier going?'

She shrugged. 'On the surface, maybe, but Mum says he never flinches from conflict. Maybe that's where she and I get it from.'

The desk sergeant called the next person over. 'I've already spotted that quality in you,' Zach murmured. Somehow he and Rosa had moved close enough that their shoulders were touching. It was fairly cool in the police station but her skin was still warm from the sun.

Finally they were called to the desk and Zach made his report to the desk sergeant so he could get a crime number to bandy about at Nicholas Centre. The sergeant performed his duty meticulously but his expression said that if you left a wallet full of money unattended on a public beach it was not to be wondered at if it disappeared.

By the time they were going down the steps outside the police station the quick Maltese dusk was almost over and stars were beginning to appear in a violet sky. Rosa rubbed her stomach and glanced around until her gaze lit on a nearby restaurant. 'Do you fancy something to eat?'

'As long as you know I'm not really dating,' he said gravely.

'Glad I don't have to disappoint you,' she teased as she swung off towards the restaurant. It looked small at the front but went back into the depths of the building.

Once they'd taken leather chairs at a rustic wooden table she ordered pork with vegetables and he went for *bragioli*, a Maltese dish of beef stuffed with bacon, egg and bread, always a treat in a proper Maltese establishment.

Then Rosa's phone rang and she glanced at the screen, groaned and declined the call.

'Don't mind me. Take it,' he said, remembering her stabbing at her phone earlier and wondering if she was wrestling with some ongoing issue.

'Don't want to, not really.' Immediately, her phone pinged. She read the message on the lock screen and turned the phone to silent before dropping it in her bag. 'Ex-boyfriend being a pain,' she explained.

His brows shot up. 'From everything I've seen and heard of you, I'm surprised if you're worried by him.'

'Oh, no. Not worried. Annoyed. It was him I swore at yesterday in Mdina.'

'Right.' He could have left the subject alone but he had his share of human curiosity. 'I'm sorry you were upset.'

The waiter arrived with their drinks and she lifted her beer and clinked glasses – water for him as he was driving. 'I was when the relationship ended but he's making it easier and easier to get over him.'

Zach waited, in case she wanted to tell him anything else. The room was dim and cool and everyone else there was speaking Maltese. The waiter had addressed him in Maltese at first, then switched to English. Zach looked pretty Mediterranean and he probably ought to learn more Maltese than he had. Street signs, menus and a few swear words were currently his limit.

'Mum says Marcus and I drifted together,' Rosa said suddenly. 'I prefer "got closer over time" but it's true that we were friends before we were anything else. We had trysts at parties when neither of us was with someone else.'

'"Trysts",' he repeated appreciatively. 'Like the description. I'm seeing smooching and kissing.'

She looked as if she might have blushed but it was hard to tell in such low light. 'More or less. We moved on to friends-with-benefits when I visited him at uni. I didn't go to uni myself.'

'I didn't either,' he put in. 'I'd had my first fall-out with Dad and didn't want to be dependent on him. I did my degree via employment.' He sat back so the waiter could place his steaming meal before him. It smelled deliciously herby.

'I didn't want the student loan,' she admitted frankly. 'I've done whatever training came my way, especially when I was doing admin jobs.' She smiled at the waiter when he set her pasta down and he gave her a big, appreciative smile back. 'Marcus got a good degree and set off in the world of finance. A couple of years after he finished uni we got together full-time and eventually bought a house together. He was nicer then, more easy-going and fun. Unfortunately, when I landed a role I loved at Blackthorn's, he got jealous because he'd discovered he hated his job. He began to resent my job satisfaction, saying he was an artisan at heart and wanted to make his hobby of wood turning and carving into a business. Making that kind of financial jump's hard. I didn't earn enough to support him and I didn't see why I should.' She ate silently for several moments, the golden wall light above her casting a halo about her hair. Finally, she added flatly, 'He resented that too but he'd developed a problem with gambling.'

Zach felt shock shimmer through him.

She took a sip of her drink. 'Online, that is. I don't think he's got the chops to hang out at an actual casino. He got addicted to a virtual roulette wheel. You've seen those ads about getting a ten quid stake if you sign up to a certain site? He signed up to them all. Said it was a stress reliever from his terrible job. Obviously, he lost more than he won. We began to argue over money because I had to cover bills that were his responsibility but I think the real issue was that I'd spent my childhood watching my mum making up for the shortcomings of a feckless partner. It pushed my buttons. So he promised he'd stop.'

'Tricky,' he commented.

'Yep. Another tension was Chellice. She began as my friend but she was into craft stuff. Next thing I knew they'd begun a side business together. I'd help load up their stuff in Chellice's van then they'd shoot off to a craft fair leaving me behind because the van had only two seats and nobody suggested I follow by car. I felt taken for granted, especially as any money he made on his products vanished either into his ever-expanding tool collection or online casinos. The crunch came a couple of months before I came here when I overheard him talking to Chellice outside our house. The window was open.' She took a sip from her beer. 'He was talking about "tens of thousands" and "couldn't believe it". He sounded as if he'd been hit by a truck. Chellice kept saying, "Oh, Marcus. Oh, my God!" equally shocked.'

'Ouch.' Zach flinched. 'So you got involved in bailing him out of a big gambling debt?'

For a second he thought she was going to cry but she laughed instead, though her mouth trembled. 'That's what I thought. I ran out and shrieked at him in the street that he'd promised to stop gambling . . . how could he let me down? Betray my trust? What were we going to do? Then he told me he'd *won* money, won huge, nearly a hundred thousand pounds!' She stopped and wiped her eyes on a napkin. 'He didn't appreciate my fury. I didn't appreciate his deceit.'

'Crap. I guess it didn't end well?'

'He broke up with me then and there. I was shocked. Hurt.' Quickly, she drank the rest of her beer. 'Mum says now it was obvious the relationship would end sometime. I don't think she thought it would be me who made the fatal error though.' She turned back to her meal.

He frowned at her so easily shouldering the blame. He'd caught Marcus's tone if not his words yesterday and he'd sounded self-important and brusque. 'So he gambled, which you hated and cost you money; he spent his spare time in a way that excluded you; he even gave the news of his win to Chellice before telling you, the woman he was living with – yet *you're* the one responsible for the relationship's demise? Bit of a reorganisation of the truth! If the relationship was coming to an end as Dory thinks, he obviously didn't want to share all that dosh. Was there anything between him and Chellice?'

She pushed her plate away, meal half eaten, eyes troubled. 'I suspected so. Marcus denied it but the "shitty bastard" argument was because he's taken her in as a "lodger" so they can funnel everything into the business. I moved in with Mum temporarily when we split up and Marcus is taking over the mortgage on our house. It's not a good time to sell because there's a big road being built behind our estate, making prices plummet. He used his winnings to fund leaving his day job.'

'He does sound a shitty bastard,' he owned.

'And you don't even know the whole story yet.'

'There's more? Let me get a cup of coffee to see me through the next instalment.' He signalled to the waiter.

Rosa continued her tale as they waited for the coffee to arrive. 'Marcus threw in his job and cranked up his involvement in Spun Gold. He met a local radio presenter doing an outside broadcast at a fair and she invited him onto her Friday lunchtime chat show. The subject that week was people who turned to crime.'

'Crime?' Zach repeated, looking confused.

Absently, she picked up a sugar sachet and fiddled with it. 'One of the other guests told a story about an old schoolmate who grew up to be a gangster. Marcus chimed in that a girl in his school year was accused of stealing an expensive watch. It was found in her things and she was excluded from school. The police were involved. He described his feelings of shock.' She drew in a short, hard breath almost like a sob. 'That girl was me. He even gave my first name.' The coffee arrived and she became absorbed in stirring in sugar and cream before adding, 'He *completely* omitted that the real culprit had panicked and stuffed the watch in my bag; that she confessed and I was exonerated. He made it sound like the Covent Garden jewellery heist rather than a storm in a teacup.'

'The shitbag,' he breathed.

She smiled but it was watery. 'Chellice has this really popular blog and, in all innocence – she said – blogged about Marcus and the radio appearance. Then "someone" used that blog post as a platform from which to rehash the story he told on the show and leak my full name. Social media accounts purporting to provide local news sprang up and began a wave of shares. It all got dragged up on the school Facebook page and I was embarrassed.'

'Chellice?' he said heavily, placing his hand over hers, offering comfort just as she'd done for him on the beach.

She laughed bitterly. 'She strenuously denied she was behind it but to me it was her attempt to increase tension between Marcus and me. Maybe she thought there was a risk of us getting back together. Anyway—' she paused to

80

take a gulp of her coffee '—it didn't matter that the watch story was never *true*, some of those awful tweets mentioned where I worked – and with young people. My friend Georgine is the director of Blackthorn's and she understood it was all malicious but then Mum offered me the job here and I was so upset with the way everything was piling up that I asked Georgine for leave of absence so I could take it.'

'What did Marcus say?' He could hardly get the words out for the anger pulsing through him.

'He apologised, adamant he'd intended to explain that the girl had been falsely accused but the news announcer dashed in to report some political storm and suddenly Marcus was being ushered out of the studio. He refused to believe Chellice was to blame for the social media crap.

Over the table, he watched her face work as she tried not to cry. He found himself on his feet, rounding the table, holding out his hands. 'Rosa—'

With a sob, she launched herself into his arms. He held her tightly. Despite how much he enjoyed looking at her, despite how much he was getting to like her, all he wanted to do at that moment was hold her until her body stopped shaking with sobs.

Chapter Seven

In the morning, Rosa awoke to text messages from Marcus.

Presume you declined my call but it's important.

Then:

But nothing to get your panties in a bunch about. Please pick up the phone when I ring!

Later:

Please return the call as soon as followed by a grumpy face emoticon.

'OK,' she muttered to herself. 'I will.' She accidentally-on-purpose forgot that Malta was an hour ahead of the UK and it would be six thirty a.m. there.

'You woke me up,' Marcus complained blearily when the international call tone had burred several times.

Rosa wondered suddenly if he was in bed with Chellice. The thought made her feel vaguely sick.

'But now you've woken me up let's talk,' he added in a rush. He took a breath. 'Sorry, Rosa. Let's start this call again. May I have your address in Malta? My solicitor wants to send you the consent form to sign. It has to be witnessed by a non-family member. Do you know someone out there who would?'

'Yes, no prob.' She was sure Zach or Marci would perform that small service.

Marcus hesitated as if expecting her to tell him who. When she didn't, he sounded unsure. 'Well. OK. Right, that's great then. Thank you.'

'You're welcome. I want the mortgage formalities completed as much as you do. But don't send me angry emoji because I don't answer your calls if it doesn't suit me. I'm sure you could have handled this by email,' she added. They ended on that prickly note without even asking how the other was doing. It made her feel sad after being together on and off since school but . . . they were over. Marcus had made that clear from the moment she'd screamed at him about gambling again – or the moment he'd won big and didn't want to share, if you fancied Zach's version – and now Rosa was moving on. Marcus had proved himself not the right man for her.

Dory, she found, once they were both up and dressed, had her own ideas for the day and soon they were strolling along the seafront road towards Sliema before it got too hot. 'I want you to choose something for the apartment, something we'll see every day, so you'll feel more at home,' Dory said, squeezing her arm.

'I'm OK, you don't need to let me nest-build,' Rosa protested.

Dory cocked her head and raised one eyebrow. 'I'm your mum. Do you think I didn't notice your red eyes when you came in last night? You scurried off to your room and I lay awake fretting you'd been hiding out somewhere having a good cry.'

Rosa didn't put Dory right about the tears because the

heat of a blush was creeping up her cheeks. After her stout rejection of Dory's summer romance idea it would only excite comment to admit she'd been 'hiding out' in Zach's arms as she cried for the hurt caused by Marcus and Chellice. She'd felt embarrassed afterwards – the waiter had brought her a box of tissues for goodness' sake! – but also cleansed.

Maybe her tears had been a farewell to Marcus?

Whatever it had been, Zach had taken the whole scene in his stride. He had sisters so perhaps he'd been called upon to provide a shoulder to cry on in the past. He'd brushed away her thanks with a smile and driven back to the apartments. Then they'd crossed both roads to the rocky beach. Zach had talked about how they were more or less at the meeting point of three sea creeks – Lazaretto, Msida and Pietà – and they watched the lights from all the shores around them shimmer silver and gold on the black water, wavering and stretching as the surface rippled. The rigging on bobbing yachts sounded like wind chimes on the still night air and the sea slip-slopped softly on their hulls.

The idea had been to allow plenty of time for Dory to go to bed but, instead, when Rosa finally said goodnight to Zach and made her way yawning into the apartment, she'd found her mum curled up in a chair reading from the light of her Kindle. Dory had burst out, 'This book's amazing! I can't stop reading. It's set here in Malta—' Then she'd halted as she'd turned on the lamp beside her and seen Rosa's face. Rosa, not feeling equal to facing concerned questions, had said a hurried goodnight and made a head-down escape to her room.

Now, as they negotiated the uneven pavements past the Manoel Island bridge on one side and cafés, shops and banks on the other, she distracted Dory by telling her about Marcus's 'lodger' and the form he'd asked her to sign. 'There's no reason to refuse,' she wound up. 'I need him to take over the mortgage while I get on with my own life. Moving Chellice in is a tad rude but doesn't change anything.'

Dory tutted in irritation. 'He's acting like a knob but I agree you've done the right thing and I'm proud.' She paused thoughtfully. 'I could help you get on with your own life. There wasn't much spare cash when I was a school cook and had to scrimp to send you on a school trip or take you camping in France, but things are different now.'

Rosa gurgled a laugh. 'Do you remember that interminable coach trip to Brittany when it rained so much the roads were flooded and we had to go at thirty miles an hour the entire way? You clipped coupons from the newspaper for that.' Honestly, she added, 'I could have done more travelling as an adult but travel's expensive and then Marcus—'

Dory stopped to cup Rosa's face, her hands too hot for comfort but full of love. 'Marcus bitched and moaned if he got in a queue for a taxi, let alone suffered a flight delay. But now you can leave all that behind. If you want to go backpacking or get a degree or start up a business, I could help you. I would *love* to help you.'

Heart burning with love, Rosa gazed into her mother's face, regardless of the narrowness of the pavement or the other people trying to get along it. 'Thank you, Mum,' she said hoarsely. 'You're already helping me by inviting me here for the summer and if I've been ungracious about that, I'm sorry.'

Dory laughed, her voice a little wobbly. 'But you're working your passage and because I was used to moving all the time I forgot I brought you up in one town. Just promise me you'll give real thought to my offer.'

Moved by the sincerity in her mum's eyes, Rosa smiled. 'I'll use the summer to decide. Being here will broaden my horizons.' Turning, she changed the subject, pointing to a nearby shop. 'And what I choose for the apartment is flowers for the terrace, to go along with your herbs.'

They spent an enjoyable half hour choosing red geraniums and a peach and yellow lantana, green and red capsicum and white impatiens. Dory paid for it all, along with compost and terracotta pots, and arranged to call later with the car.

'Let's go back and do your social media now,' Rosa said firmly. 'I can add to my CV "Personal assistant and kitchen porter to bestselling food writer. Aided in recipe development; redesigned blog and website; maintained social media channels; created graphics and other digital media". Chellice taught me how to use Canva and I don't see why I shouldn't profit from it. We can get one of those halo lights and a tripod to help take good pictures on my iPhone, then I can add "photography and flat lays for social media". I can feel a whole new LinkedIn profile coming on.'

'I'd employ you,' said Dory solemnly, allowing herself to be turned around outside the shop. 'You're perfect.'

Once home, they reviewed Dory's online presence together then Rosa settled at the kitchen counter and got so immersed in a redesign of the Cafeteria Cook blog that she only paused to choose the halo light and tripod from the website of a shop in Sliema. Dory drove off to pick up the equipment and the plants they'd paid for earlier. Rosa had plenty of pictures of food they'd already taken, not too flawed by being hand-held. Then she drew up a schedule of posts. Some Dory could dictate to her about what she was doing for the new book. Occasionally they could give a free recipe or a video of a chopping technique. Backlist titles had to be mentioned to keep sales going. Post notifications would automatically appear on the Cafeteria Cook social media channels.

Immersed in her work, she didn't waste time and emotional effort in checking out Chellice's blog or the social media channels of Spun Gold and only paused when Dory returned in order to help her carry the plants and pots up from street level.

'Work's over for the day,' Dory declared, shutting the laptop before Rosa could return to it. 'Let's rearrange our terrace.'

A lovely couple of hours followed. The adjacent garden might be reserved for the use of the Bentley family but its palm trees shared their dappled shade in the late afternoon. They trowelled the compost into the apricot-coloured terracotta pots, laughing at the black crescents that formed at the ends of their nails. 'It's like being a kid again.' Rosa remembered the tiny strip of land behind the terraced house they'd lived in. 'You grew beans and peas, courgettes, lettuce and carrots. I wanted you to buy from the super-market like other mums. I didn't think it was cool to "grow your own" but, of course, it was cheap and healthy.'

'Kind of my mantra,' Dory agreed. 'Where shall we put this big pot?'

They were sweeping up the spilled compost when Marci and Paige came up the steps and paused on the way to their apartment.

'That looks gorgeous,' Marci said admiringly, while Paige told them about their afternoon swim at the top of her voice. Marci gave Paige's wet hair an affectionate tousle. 'We're worn out, aren't we?' She turned her dark gaze to Dory and Rosa, saying shyly, 'Come up to our roof terrace? I'll bet your tubs will look gorgeous from up there and I think we all need a cool drink.'

Rosa thought it was nice that Marci evidently felt she now knew them well enough to make the suggestion and Dory didn't need a second invitation – although she got one in the form of Paige yelling, 'Yes, yes, yes!' and bobbing excitedly. They put away the broom and followed them up the stone steps, past the door to the Bentley apartment and up the final flight.

'This is beautiful,' Rosa breathed as they reached the top. The flat roof was walled around by a parapet and looked over the lower terrace and the Bentley garden at the back, and provided a breathtaking view of the sea at the front. 'I can see Manoel Island, Valletta, Gzira, part of Sliema . . . it's gorgeous.' She gazed at the view until she heard Paige cry out, 'Heyyyyyy, Zachary!'

'Heyyyyy, Paige,' answered a deep voice and Rosa turned to see that Zach was seated at a table under a canopy, a laptop open on a small table. He wore only shorts, his torso bared to the sun. His chest was sprinkled with hair but there were no tattoos to go with those she'd seen on his back and arm.

'We're interrupting,' Rosa apologised, raising her eyes to his face. 'We wanted to see how the new planters look from here and had no idea it was your office this afternoon.'

His smile was warm, hair ruffled by the breeze. 'The terrace looks great. I've been watching you work. I tend to sit on this side of the roof because it's under shade. The view's not normally so distracting. Thank you for giving me something lovely to look at.'

There was something about the solemn way he said it

that made Rosa wonder whether he was actually referring to the flowers. Her shorts were pretty short and she'd been bending over without a thought that someone might have a good view. 'I hope you enjoyed the show,' she said ironically and narrowed her gaze at him when his eyes gleamed with laughter.

Paige arrived at his side with a bounce that sent her damp ponytail flipping. 'Dory and Rosa have come up here for a drink with us. Shall we give them some of your wine?'

'That sounds like a good idea.' He closed his laptop then dipped to give Paige a kiss on her forehead.

The casual affection warmed Rosa but she demurred, 'You're working. We can easily come another time.'

'It wasn't going very well anyway.' He slid the laptop into the bag on the floor beside him. Marci and Paige crossed to a small structure that looked like a mini stone house, opened the door and vanished inside.

'Working on reports?' she asked sympathetically. His explanation of what he did hadn't sounded fun: gathering data from people and writing about it.

'Side project,' he answered economically.

At the same moment Dory said, 'He's writing a book.'

He actually blushed, shooting Rosa a look from under his brows. 'I'm a bit bashful about it but I'm trying to write a novel set on the island. I've mentioned it to your mum.'

Dory leaned in and gave him a hug. 'We authors must stick together.'

'I call myself a wannabe rather than an author,' Zach returned ruefully. He directed his explanation at Rosa. 'My interest is from the Fifties to the Eighties. In that period my grandparents met here, Grandad was stationed here, Dad and my uncles lived here. It was a changeable period politically. My novel – all six chapters of it – is action adventure and I'm enjoying writing it rather than actually knowing what I'm doing.'

'And he's going to get an agent and be a great success,' Dory supplemented.

Zach tried to frown her down. 'More likely it's going to languish half-finished on my computer forever.'

The shutters at the front of the small stone building opened with a rattle and Marci and Paige were visible behind the counter of a bar. 'Orders, please!' called Paige, beaming. Two drinks fridges stood behind her, one stocked with wine and beer the other with soft drinks. Marci was emptying a pack of ice cubes into an ice bucket.

Dory approached the bar with alacrity. 'A glass of white wine, please, bartender.'

Paige passed the order back to her staff, Marci, and looked expectantly at Rosa. 'Rosé for me, please.'

Paige giggled, almost overbalancing from the step she was standing on in order to see over the counter. 'Rosé is like Rosa! Heyyyyy, Rosé.'

Zach chose rosé too, and Marci red. Marci gave Paige elderflower pressé in a wine glass so it looked like Dory's chardonnay and also opened a large bottle of cold water for people to help themselves.

When Dory's phone began to ring she glanced at the screen and gave a quiet exclamation. 'Oh!' Then she got up and moved away, answering as she went, 'Yes, of course I remember.' And then, after a pause, 'It would be lovely. No, I'll meet you there.' When she returned to her seat she said to Rosa, 'I'm going out for dinner this evening. That was Lesley who I met at the reunion asking if I'd like to join a few people who came for it and haven't gone home yet. We'll eat at Valletta Waterfront.'

'Sounds great.' Rosa thought of the woman who'd been one of the hosts of the reunion. She'd seemed as mad on Malta as Dory. They'd have tons to talk about. Rosa could enjoy a solitary dinner on the terrace, maybe dance to her Zumba playlist then watch a DVD or read. She could even ponder Dory's touching offer to fund her through whatever she decided to do next. She didn't think she'd had a *jus' chillin'* evening since she'd arrived.

That evening, Zach prowled about the Bentley apartment, unable to settle. Rosa being around and looking edible wasn't keeping his mind off his libido at all.

It was ten p.m – only nine in the UK. He took out his phone and FaceTimed his mum, Amanda. She answered with a big smile, her blonde hair fluffed about her round face.

'Hello, darling! How are you? Are you still enjoying Malta? Have you finished the last apartment? Are Marci and Paige OK?' The questions kept coming and he grinned as he answered, knowing that she wouldn't have much to contribute on her own account. Her life consisted of the house and health matters.

'Have you heard from Electra?' he asked, when he got a chance.

'She sent me a great long email.' Amanda's ready smile flashed. 'I haven't had a call for a while. She's busy and the time difference gets in the way.'

'And how's Dad?' It would have been pointed not to ask. He wondered whether his father was in the room and hadn't even shouted a hello.

But Amanda said, 'Bed already, because he has a regional sales meeting in the centre of Birmingham at nine and has an early start. He's OK.'

'Tell him I asked after him,' Zach said. It disguised the fact that if Steve had been available he and Zach would have had difficulty finding anything to talk about. Chat between them was a thing of the past.

Not so with his mother, thankfully. She began talking about Marci's upcoming lunch date with Jake, who she'd met at the reunion – Marci had told her about him, apparently – and then they reminisced about past family holidays to Malta when Amanda had been more mobile, until the end of the call.

Their conversation had made him think of Electra but it would be after five a.m. in Thailand. He left her an email via his phone. *How's everything? Still enjoying Thailand? We should schedule a chat when our different time zones allow.* He caught her up on his doings on Malta in a couple of sentences.

Then he returned to feeling restless. Earlier he'd met Flaviu, a Romanian guy who worked in a bar in one of the arches beneath The Ramp. They occasionally hung out together. Zach picked up his phone and texted him. *What are you up to?*

Flaviu replied. *In the kiosk near Manoel Island bridge. Coming?*

Quickly, Zach texted back that he would. Marci was watching TV in the sitting room at the same time as painting her nails pale pink, maybe for the benefit of the guy she was having lunch with tomorrow. Zach was glad she was coming out of her shell enough to go on a date. Paige was already in bed, no doubt exhausted by the energy it took to be four years old all day.

He was on his way to shower and change when his phone rang. *Joseph* popped onto the screen. 'Hey,' Zach answered, entering his room and flopping onto his bed.

The nights were hot enough that he used only sheets on the bed and they felt cool beneath his bare arms and legs.

Joseph got straight to the point. 'Axel thinks he has lost money now. You're down to come to the centre tomorrow afternoon so I wish to give a talk then about these thefts to put people on their guard and warn the guilty person that his – or her – actions are noted.' He sounded tired and tense. Nicholas Centre was Joseph's life and difficulties such as these bruised his heart.

Zach agreed straight away. 'What do you want me to do? Bandy my crime number about and complain bitterly about having to go to a police station? Say how embarrassed I was to order a drink and then find I had no money? That I'm broke for the rest of the week?' He wasn't, but the thief wouldn't know he wasn't paying rent to Nanna because her apartment was open to all the family. He'd received money from Aunt Giusi for the work he'd done for her and what he earned freelancing kept his bank balance healthy. But that wasn't the point.

'All those things,' Joseph agreed crisply. 'Crimes have victims and we need to make that clear.'

When the call was over Zach jumped in the shower, enjoying the water sluicing over him, then wandered into his bedroom as he dried himself. From the window he could see Rosa on the terrace below, reading in the cool of the evening by the light of the terrace lamps and surrounded by her newly planted pots. Her shorts rode up her legs.

Irritated with himself, he turned away. There was admiring beauty and there was being a creep. He generally got women interested in him with an open approach but he hadn't made that approach to Rosa. Everyone knew you didn't 'do it on your own doorstep' – let alone get so fascinated with your grandmother's tenant that you spied on her.

Zach had just finished dressing when he heard Rosa scream.

It wasn't an 'eek' as some people might emit at the sight of a gecko. It was a full-blooded, full-throated, terrified scream.

Zach turned and sprinted up the hall.

Marci appeared, nail varnish in hand. 'Was that Rosa?'

Zach saved his breath for his flight out of the front door and down the stone steps, taking them three at a time. He saw a male shape on the edge of the lower terrace in the light thrown by the lamps, chest heaving for breath.

Then the man lifted his hands up placatingly. 'Sorry, sorry. I didn't mean to scare you.'

Luccio.

Zach jumped down the final three steps and halted, his heart thundering. 'What the hell happened?'

Luccio turned to face him, sweat running at his temples. 'I didn't know she would be there.'

Rosa was standing at the side of her lounger, a hand to her heart. 'I was reading and suddenly there was a man. I didn't see it was Luccio. Sorry if I disturbed everyone.'

'You've got nothing to apologise for,' Zach told her shortly and glared at Luccio. At that moment, shouting came from the street. Men's voices, bellowing and angry. Luccio backed rapidly away from the stairs and cast around as if looking for somewhere to hide. Zach didn't understand the shouted words, wasn't even certain what language they were in, but he understood the tone of voice.

It was a threat.

'Someone chasing you, Luccio?' he asked, some of his anger draining.

Luccio gave an unconvincing laugh. 'No, nobody. I'm sorry, Rosa. I did not know you'd be here outside. I come to see Zach only.'

Although the look he threw Zach was pleading, Zach didn't buy the story. He thought he heard scuffling and whispering at the foot of the stone steps and the hair on the back of his neck stood up. As well as Rosa, still looking jumpy and uncertain, his sister and niece were upstairs.

He thought fast.

Yanking out his phone he brought up the smart home control app and turned on several lights in the apartment next door, the one he was still working on. Deliberately edging towards the stairs that led down to the street he raised his voice. 'You can't frighten people like this! I'm afraid one of the neighbours has just texted to say they've called the police because they heard the screaming.'

'The *police*?' gasped Luccio, sounding satisfactorily horrified.

Zach held up his hands in a silent gesture for Luccio to remain where he was, though he was pretty sure that Luccio had no wish to run back down the stairs and into the arms of whoever was down there.

Right on cue, Marci came halfway down from the upper apartment. 'The police? What's happened? Is Rosa OK?'

'Just shaken.' Zach still talked loudly, wanting to be heard. 'One of my friends from Nicholas Centre turned up and gave her a start. Don't worry. Stay upstairs and I'll deal with the police.' This last for the benefit of those lurking in the street.

'I'm fine,' Rosa called too, though her voice wavered.

'If you're sure everyone's OK I'll stay near Paige.' Marcie ran back up the stairs and Zach heard the door close.

Then came a man's voice from the house behind, the one further up the slope. 'All OK?'

'Yes, thank you,' Zach called back, thinking that the more audible the reaction to Rosa's scream the more likely it was that whoever was below would be scared off. 'Someone was frightened by one of my friends, that's all.'

'OK.' The disembodied voice sounded relieved and a door slammed.

There was no more shouting from the street. Zach listened for a long minute then moved away from the head of the stairs, waving Luccio in front of him, murmuring to Rosa, 'Can we step into your apartment? I don't want to disturb Paige again.' Her eyes were huge but she nodded and led the way.

Once they were indoors he slid shut the terrace door and pulled the blinds. Then he rang Marci. 'The police aren't really coming. It was Luccio who surprised Rosa into a scream. It looks as if he's attracted unwelcome attention. Lock the doors as a precaution.'

Marci gave a tiny gasp. 'You won't get involved, will you?'

'You don't have to worry,' he said reassuringly. He was grateful that his sister, despite her anxious moments, rarely lost control.

'Sorry I screamed,' Rosa said as he came off the phone. She was pale but she opened the fridge with perfect composure and took out chilled bottles of water for each of them. Luccio grabbed his, twisted off the top and gulped it down. His breathing had steadied, but if he'd been running as hard as he looked to have been, his throat probably felt like sandpaper.

Zach took his bottle with a word of thanks. 'Hopefully my amateur dramatics about the police will scare off whoever was outside.' He hadn't turned the lights off next door yet. If a few lit windows gave the impression of people having been disturbed enough to remain out of bed, that was fine with him. 'Luccio, we need to talk.'

Luccio glanced at the terrace doors as if considering whether he had a better option.

'Please, stay where you are and let me see what I can do to help,' Zach said softly. He dialled Flaviu's phone, explaining the situation. 'I won't come to the bar,' he said, 'but if you fancy coming here for a few beers . . .'

'I come,' Flaviu said instantly. 'I bring some friends.'

Zach felt a wave of relief. 'Thanks, mate.' Then he called Axel and Malin from Nicholas Centre and soon they too were en route, along with Malin's boyfriend, James. The more the merrier so far as Zach was concerned.

Rosa perched on the edge of the sofa. Her gaze flicked to Luccio as she sipped her water. Zach didn't think her hand was entirely steady. He sat beside her. 'Are you OK?'

She gave him a nearly convincing smile. 'It's not like me to make a fuss. Just a man appeared, in the shadows, gasping. It was scary.'

'I'm sure. Now you know it's Luccio, are you happy for us to be here? Sorry I invited people to your mum's apartment but Paige is asleep upstairs.'

'It's fine. I can't imagine anyone undesirable hanging around if it looks as if there's a party going on,' she responded promptly.

Zach turned to Luccio. 'Who was chasing you?'

Luccio shrugged. 'Nobody.'

Zach's brow lowered. He'd thought he'd established a rapport with the younger man as they worked together at Nicholas Centre and was disappointed at this evasiveness. 'Who was chasing you?' he repeated evenly.

Luccio's gaze shifted back to the terrace doors. 'I don' know. Probably they think I'm someone else.'

Zach sighed. 'I want to help you, Luccio, but you don't make it easy.' Was it Luccio's own group, led by the unlovely Beppe, who'd been hunting him down? Or someone else? He hated to think of either. Observing the way Luccio's gaze darted about, his heart went out to him. He was only twenty, not much older than Zach had been when he'd been briefly sucked into Fitzmo's orbit. Fitzmo and Beppe had obviously taken the same Ringleader 101 course to learn how to manipulate others. 'I want to help you, Luccio,' he repeated, though with slight emphasis on the word 'want' this time as if he doubted whether he could.

Luccio regarded him with apprehension but there was something else there too. A hint of hope? Did some small part of him want to co-operate? Zach knew from Joseph that sometimes a small crack in someone's shell could be prised open by the right person.

Zach really wanted to be that person and made his smile open and easy. 'When my friends come round we'll have a couple of beers and then all leave together. I'm sure the numbers will be off-putting *if* there's anyone lurking outside.' He moved to the chair, closer to Luccio, maintaining eye contact. 'I'd much prefer to keep my sister, niece and Rosa clear of any possibility of trouble but I understand that you might have felt desperate. I understand if you were seeking safety. *I understand*, Luccio, because I know about being sucked in and frightened. I'm available if you want to talk. Ever.'

Almost imperceptibly, Luccio nodded.

Then guests started arriving and Zach found himself helping Rosa host as if they were together. She'd already met Axel and Malin. Malin's boyfriend, James, was a jovial

Maltese dive master who'd met Malin in one of the scuba bars. Flaviu attached himself to Rosa as if she were the only one in the room – smooth bastard, Zach thought.

Zach fetched beers from the bar on the roof, calling in at the apartment to check Marci was OK. She was just going to bed to watch a film on the TV in her room. She seemed composed and waved away his apology that there was a party going on without her. 'Paige is in bed so I couldn't come,' she said. It was true but he guessed the coming date with Jake was enough on her social calendar anyway. She wasn't going to develop a raging social life overnight. He took the opportunity to peek through her shutters, as her room overlooked the street, and he could see nothing to worry him.

An hour later, after checking Rosa felt OK to be alone till Dory came home, Axel, Flaviu, Malin, James, Luccio and Zach clattered down to the street, Luccio wearing a baseball hat back to front to hide his curls.

Zach put him in his car and drove him to the small house where he lived with his aunt in Sliema. He gave his parting advice before he pulled up so that Luccio couldn't avoid listening. 'Change who you hang out with, Luccio. Or even head off back to Sicily.' Then, when Luccio didn't answer, he sighed. 'Don't let anyone use you, mate.'

Luccio stared stonily out of the passenger window. When the car finally stopped, he jumped out with a careless, 'Thanks, Zach,' as if he'd already forgotten turning up at Ta' Xbiex Terrace House with every appearance of the hounds of hell being on his heels.

Zach drove home unsettled.

A bad feeling about Luccio lay like a stone in his gut.

Chapter Eight

Rosa awoke with the sun, which was before seven in Malta in June. She lay thinking about last night, about Luccio storming the stairs, gasping and whooping for breath. When he'd halted in the shadows her heart had rebounded off her lungs and somehow forced her scream out into the evening.

She remembered him gabbling 'Sorry' and 'It's OK', the words falling over one another. His voice had been hoarse, the words heaved out between breaths, and it hadn't been until Zach said urgently, 'Luccio?' that she'd realised who it was. Her fear had drained away, though adrenalin had continued to pump her heart and lungs.

In retrospect, the scream made her feel slightly stupid but she didn't wish it undone. It had brought Zach, alerted Marci, created fuss. If Luccio had continued up the next staircase to Zach's whoever had been chasing him might have arrived on the terrace where Rosa was or got as far as the upper apartment, where Paige had been lying asleep.

She shivered as she got up and made herself coffee,

mentally excusing an extra spoon of sugar for yesterday evening's shock. She'd seen kids from Blackthorn's get in trouble. A couple had ended up in jail at eighteen. It was obvious why Zach was trying to help Luccio, of course – he saw himself in the young Sicilian and was, anyway, protective by nature. It had been protecting Stuart that had got him in trouble with the law and she'd have to be blind not to notice his concern for Marci and the way he was with Paige.

She opened the French doors and wandered onto the terrace, seating herself quietly at the table to drink her coffee and admire the red geraniums. The early morning air was fresh and cool with a hint of brine. Traffic was already grumbling along on the nearby seafront road and a couple of distant voices called to each other. An insect swooped past her ear with a *ZZZ-zirrrr*.

And then a movement caught her eye. She turned her head sharply, remembering last night. This time, though, it was only Dory hovering at the top of the steps from the street, wearing last night's clothes, a serious case of bedhead flattening her hair on one side as she placed her feet carefully on the paving as if not wishing to be heard.

Rosa waited until she'd taken another four steps and then said, 'Hello, Mum.'

Dory jumped, clutching her chest, puffing in surprise. 'Rosa,' she gasped. 'What are you doing out here?'

'Drinking a cuppa.' She lifted her coffee. 'And how about you?'

Dory drifted closer. 'I stayed at my friend's overnight.' Her eyes sparkled.

Rosa caught on. 'I don't wish to pry but that friend – is their name spelled L-E-S-L-E-Y or L-E-S-L-I-E?'

A wicked grin split Dory's cheeks. 'The male variation.

He was at the reunion and we got along well and . . .'
Her hands came up in a 'why not?' expression.

'Oh, my,' Rosa breathed. 'My mother is wilder than I
am. What about Andy?'

Dory assumed a rueful expression, raking her fingers
through her hair in a belated attempt to neaten it.
'Now I'm out here he says I'm taking the long-distance-
relationship thing too far. I agreed and we parted friends.'

'When did this happen? Are you OK about it?' It was
no surprise to Rosa. All Dory's relationships fizzled out
sooner or later. She avoided commitment. No shared life,
no shared property, no ownership, no promises and, as
Dory was fond of pointing out, no doing someone else's
laundry. She liked men, but not full-time.

Dory screwed up her nose. 'Yesterday and I'm fine
because he's right.'

Rosa rose to give her mum a hug. 'Marriage with Dad
certainly had a lasting effect on you.' She and Dory had
talked frankly about this often so she knew she wasn't
jumping on her mother's corns.

Dory sighed, hugging Rosa back. 'It showed me what
I didn't want. I got something good out of it though.' She
planted a smacking kiss on Rosa's cheek to indicate that
the 'something good' was her.

This time, though she smiled in response, Rosa took
the conversation up a road she hadn't really explored
before. 'Is that why you're glad Marcus and I ended? So
you don't have to worry that he'll hurt me? Would you
rather I skated over the surface of relationships?'

Dory pulled back, her shocked gaze boring into Rosa's.
'No! I didn't believe Marcus was the one for you and I
think events proved me right. I want you to be happy. If
that involves a man, great; if it doesn't involve a man,

that's great too. Man, woman, career, travel, pet dog, singing canary – I want you to do what's right for you!' Then her customary smile broke over her face. 'Now, what will make me happy is a little more sleep. We're going out with Zach and Paige at twelve so I'll set my alarm for eleven.' She slipped away to her own room leaving Rosa to think – really think – about everything her mum had said.

At noon, when Marci tapped on the terrace door, Rosa was seated at the kitchen island browsing blogs written by mature students. She jumped up and opened the door. 'You look fantastic,' she said, beckoning her new friend in.

Marci wore a fitted maxi dress with ribbon lacing one side. The sea-green fabric went beautifully with her golden skin and glossy dark hair. 'Do I look OK?' she asked hesitantly, as if nervous about asking advice. 'Zach said, "Great" without really looking up and Paige said, "Yes, but not like a princess."'

Rosa giggled. 'That's a tough yardstick to measure against. You look gorgeous. Jake isn't going to know what hit him.'

Marci looked half gratified and half anxious. 'This dress doesn't say "Up for it" does it?' She ran her fingers over the lacing where tiny glimpses of her skin could be seen and then the neckline, which was low enough to allow the tops of her breasts to say hi to the sunshine.

'It says, "I'm a classy lady and you're lucky I'm letting you take me out to lunch,"' Rosa promised, wanting to encourage this tentative, friendly conversation.

'While you get the pirate ship with my brother and little girl.' Marci flashed a grin, which turned to a flash of panic when her phone beeped on a text. 'Jake's here, outside.'

Rosa gave her a hug. 'Have a fantastic time.'

'Going to try,' Marci said wryly, holding up crossed fingers.

Almost as soon as she vanished, Paige's piping voice could be heard on the outside stairs, Zach's deeper voice quieter and more controlled. Dory appeared from her room wearing palazzo pants of rust and cream with a floaty top, her hair freshly blow-dried.

'We're going to the pirate ship!' Paige bellowed as soon as they made the lower terrace, swinging on Zach's hand like a yo-yo. 'It truly is a pirate ship, Rosa.'

'Shall we remember our manners?' Zach suggested. 'Morning, ladies.' He kissed first Dory's cheek and then Rosa's. His proximity, the brush of his lips, the shower-fresh smell of him . . . Rosa was surprised by a shiver. Zach looked at her thoughtfully, as if he'd caught it.

Paige held up her face for kisses too, obviously comfortable with this sign of growing friendship. Then she towed Zach towards the stairs. 'Pirate ship, pirate ship!'

Rosa was astonished to discover that their journey was only a hundred yards along the seafront road to the right, a direction she hadn't taken until now, before they turned a corner and . . . 'It *is* a pirate ship!' she breathed, halting to admire the black wooden hulk, its masts rising up into the blue sky. *The Black Pearl* had somehow been parked on the shore, benches and tables around it shaded with red parasols.

'It used to belong to Popeye the Sailor Man,' Paige told her, eyes shining.

Still marvelling, Rosa followed the others up a set of wooden stairs to the interior of the ship, now a beautiful restaurant of polished wood. A table was ready for them by a window with a view of the sea.

'It's thought to have been the yacht belonging to the

movie star Errol Flynn,' Zach said, as Rosa continued to gaze around. 'Someone restored it and it was used on the *Popeye* movie, as Paige said. I doubt it would float now.'

'It's amazing.' Rosa patted Paige's shoulder. 'Thank you for inviting me to your special place.'

Paige beamed.

It was a cool place to have lunch – in both senses of the word 'cool' – and Rosa enjoyed watching yachts bobbing on the startling blue of the sea, some moving majestically on or off their moorings. Although she listened to Paige's chatter about the colours of sails, big yachts, small yachts and boats with engines, she also listened to Dory talking to Zach about her childhood in Malta. 'Your dad was in my sister Lizzy's year but I had a bit of a crush on him.'

'Really?' Zach sounded incredulous.

Dory laughed. 'I suppose I thought all the boys two years older than I was were heroes.'

Zach didn't share any thoughts he might have on his father's likely heroism. 'I've found a fascinating document online about the troops from Australia and New Zealand who were stationed here in World War II. Someone from Oz has traced his father's movements and written a blog about it.'

'The Anzacs,' Dory supplemented. 'There's an Anzac Hall at Pembroke – a broken-down place these days, I'm afraid. I played recorder there in a concert and it was put out on British Forces Radio. We could hear my dad say, "Yesss!" like we were Leeds United.' She laughed at the memory.

Rosa turned away from yacht spotting. 'I can imagine Grandma shushing him. Was Aunt Lizzy in the concert too?'

Dory nodded. 'Of course. She played piano melodica.'

'What's that?' Rosa and Zach asked in unison.

'You blew into it and it had keys like a piano – probably a museum piece now.' Dory rolled her eyes and laughed.

'Do you speak Maltese?' Zach asked next.

Dory shrugged. 'Only a handful of words: "yes", "no", "please", "thank you", that kind of thing. As English is an official language and we travelled with the British Army, it wasn't considered essential.'

Rosa began reading the names of yachts for Paige and let Dory tell Zach her Malta anecdotes. His interest was obviously genuine – even in Lizzy putting a gecko in Dory's hair and Dory, in revenge, collecting black beetles in a tin and tipping them out in Lizzy's den in the garden. Dory breezed from story to story. 'The British Forces Radio studio was in our camp in Floriana. It was out of bounds so, of course, fascinating. I went in once with a friend to ask for a record to be played and the presenter said on air, "Playing this for the two girls who have just come in here on roller skates . . ." and there we were, skating away from the studio. We were kept indoors to help our mums as a punishment.' Dory had pushed her glasses up on top of her hair. 'That camp, St Francis Ravelin, is home to the planning authority now.'

'Can you still get in?' Zach asked.

Dory looked pleased. 'If you ask the man at the gate nicely.'

Rosa's conscience gave a twang, knowing she could have shown more interest in Dory's past on this island.

By the time their lunch arrived Dory had moved on to talking about her school days. 'In summer we only worked in the mornings. I think we might have been at school by

106

seven and went home about one. Maybe we had two lunches, one at school and one at home. I'll ask on the Facebook group and see if anyone remembers.'

'You can't have been at school by seven,' Rosa objected, tucking into the quinoa salad she'd ordered. 'What on earth time would you have had to get up?'

Dory shrugged. 'The days were adapted. It's the same in all hot countries. The shops shut for siesta between noon and four.'

Rosa had to acknowledge that many shops still observed siesta, despite the advent of air conditioning.

Lunch passed comfortably, the conversation returning to the Malta of the present and whether the UK could match Malta for espresso.

'Mummy doesn't like expresso,' Paige said, finding a way to join the conversation. 'She likes tea. Mummy's gone to lunch with a friend.'

Zach smiled at her. 'And I told her not to hurry back so you've got me for a while.'

Paige beamed and offered him a high five. 'Heyyyyy, Zachary.'

'Heyyyyy,' he said, returning the salute. 'You act and sound like an America teenager since you got an American working at your nursery.'

'Nathanial,' she said. 'But I'm going to proper school in September.' Then she high-fived Rosa and Dory with more enthusiastic 'Heyyyyys'.

It was almost three by the time lunch was over. Zach was negotiating with Paige what they might do next when a flustered-looking Marci flew in, her sea-green dress billowing.

'Mummy! Yay!' Paige hurled herself at her mother's legs. Then she stepped back, making a connection between her mum's return and a change to her afternoon's plans. 'I was going to go swimming with Uncle Zach and I still want to.'

'Well—' Marci began, hooking her hair behind her ears and looking doubtful.

'We could all go – you, me and Mummy,' Zach suggested. He threw his sister an appraising look. 'But if Mummy wants to sit on the rocks and read while we swim then that's fine too.'

'Well—' Marci said again.

Dory held a hand out to Paige. 'I think Mummy and Uncle Zach want to talk about it. Would you be able to show me where the toilets are?'

'Yes! I know, I know!' Paige towed Dory off. Rosa would have followed but Marci plumped down in Dory's seat, blocking Rosa in.

'That tosser,' Marci hissed as soon as her daughter was out of earshot.

Zach's brows clanged down. 'Did he try something on? Hurt you?' he demanded.

'No.' She grabbed a napkin from the table and used it to wipe smudged mascara from beneath her eyes. 'He was just a dick. We were getting on OK. Nicely, in fact. He'd suggested we might go on a dinner date soon. Then—' she sucked in a long breath and blew it out again '—I explained I'd been off work with stress and he said our grandfathers would have told me to "grow some backbone".' She made air quotes with her fingers, her bottom lip wobbling. 'I began to explain how I felt but I got choked up so I threw some money on the table and said I'd walk home. He followed me, apologising, but it made me feel worse.' She made a fluttering motion in front of her chest as if to brush the offending Jake away.

'Classy of him,' Zach said, in a low, angry voice. He gave his sister's arm a pat. 'Here, have a drink of water. Or maybe a glass of wine?'

'Dessert?' Rosa offered, deciding she might as well contribute. 'It's my go-to when I'm upset. I ate half a family-sized tiramisu when Marcus and I first broke up.'

Marci managed a strangled laugh and sipped from the glass of water her brother poured for her. 'Thanks, but I no longer have an appetite.'

When Paige and Dory had returned and the bill was settled they all left the restaurant, taking the wooden steps to the garden. When they passed under the arch to the street they found Jake hovering on the pavement outside, looking red-faced as if he'd been standing there in the sun too long.

'Marci,' he began tentatively. 'I'm sorry if I sounded insensitive. *I* wasn't saying that thing about backbone. My grandfather was in the army like yours and it was one of his favourite sayings. I actually meant times had changed since then.'

Zach stepped closer to his sister as Marci halted, taking a deep breath. 'Thank you for clarifying.' She didn't sound as if she'd bought his explanation.

Jake looked dismayed at her chilliness. 'Sorry,' he muttered again as Marci brushed by.

Zach gave his sister another pat but Rosa could see Marci trembling. Perhaps that was why she stepped out onto the service road to Msida Marina without checking for traffic. A small green car swinging in off the main road blared its horn as it screeched to a halt.

The man shouted something at Marci, who clutched her chest and stammered an apology.

Dory, though, was more assertive. 'Perhaps if you used

109

your indicators?' she suggested to the driver with steely politeness.

The man shouted something that didn't sound very polite at all and Dory snapped something back in outraged accents. The man halted in mid-flow and gaped.

'What did you say?' Rosa demanded in a whisper.

Dory tossed her head. 'It was just some more Maltese I remembered.' She fell into step with Paige and Marci, who were preparing to cross the road hand-in-hand.

Watching her mother march off, Rosa became aware of Zach smothering convulsions of laughter. 'Oh, I do love your mother,' he gasped. 'Her essential Maltese vocabulary is "yes", "no", "please", "thank you" and "motherfucker".'

Chapter Nine

In the awful, sneaky way of deadlines, a Thursday 9th July target date for a freelance job had crept up on Zach and he'd spent much of the past two weeks chained to his laptop. Even slaving on an airy roof terrace with panoramic views of Malta rather than in an airless office in Bell's Park, Redruth, wasn't adequate recompense for the pain of writing suitability reports on a grammar school's management information system and 'providing technical advice on appropriate data reporting and extraction techniques suitable for a diverse academic team'.

Just about the only break he'd taken was to visit Nicholas Centre last weekend. Joseph's lecture about missing money had been and gone and there had been no further problems. Zach had made a point of keeping in touch with Luccio even before he joined him in working with a group of teens honing soccer skills. An English boy, Oliver, a fresh face at the centre, set a new Nicholas Centre record at keepy-uppy. 'Forty-one!' All the kids had cheered. Neither Luccio nor Zach had been able to better it. When Zach had practised later on the roof terrace the ball had shot over the parapet and bounced next to Dory on the lower terrace where she was picking herbs, which earned him a comment pithy enough to make him laugh.

He filed the report a couple of hours ahead of the midnight deadline with a melting feeling of relief. He had to get out of this business. The boredom and drudgery was killing him from the neck up. Sending in his invoice for a chunk of money, he felt able to notify the agency he wouldn't now be available till well into August. Aunt Giusi had almost decided on a kitchen and bathroom for the apartment next door and he was to fit them. Apart from that and Nicholas Centre, he wanted space in his schedule for himself.

An email had come in from Electra though. *Dead busy getting students ready for exams. Thailand is hot and beautiful, as always. I can stay pretty much as long as I like as long as I'm teaching English.* She described a restaurant she'd been to with students and other teachers and a long weekend spent in Koh Samui, a resort. She ended with, *Yes, must Skype or something.* But she didn't give any ideas when. Zach grinned. Electra was a very free spirit.

Laptop firmly closed, he looked over the roof terrace parapet and saw Rosa on the lower terrace, tucking her keys away in her bag.

'Rosa,' he called softly.

She turned to look up at him and smiled. 'Hiya! I'm going to "Partyville".'

It wasn't that Zach thought there was anything wrong with a woman seeking nightlife on her own but he instantly saw that a trip to Paceville was exactly what he needed after being crouched over his laptop for so long. 'Can you give me two minutes to shower and change so I can come along?'

Soon he was sitting in the passenger seat as Rosa drove Dory's little white car. 'So,' she said brightly as they turned off the seafront road, 'you looking for a lady to spend time with?'

'Who, me?' he asked enigmatically, considering the idea. He actually wasn't sure of the etiquette of tagging along on a night out then going separate ways.

Rosa, it seemed, had no expectations of him. He introduced her to Spirit but after a while she drifted into conversation with a woman she'd apparently never met before but who knew the best clubs for dancing. When there seemed to be no need for his escort he found himself talking to a couple of girls who were telegraphing their interest in him. One had a tattoo on her upper thigh of a garter with a dagger through it and she drew his attention to it several times.

Then he looked up and saw Rosa kissing a bloke across the darkness of the bar.

He stopped listening to the girl with the tattoo, feeling winded. OK, Rosa had told him she wasn't dating but a) a kiss wasn't a date, b) that had been more than three weeks ago and c) he supposed, she might have been letting Zach down lightly.

Nevertheless, his feet, without consulting his brain, carried him closer. Rosa was wearing a summer dress with a deep V at the back and the guy had placed his hand on her skin. Zach didn't identify what emotion swept through him at the sight of the guy touching her smooth, naked flesh but it stirred his breathing up.

Two more steps and he arrived behind Rosa as she broke free from the man with a brief and breathless, 'I hope you enjoy the rest of your time here. It's an amazing country.'

The man, tall with fair curly hair, looked baffled. Then annoyed. 'Have I done something wrong, babe?' He reached for her again.

With a quick step to evade his hand, she shook her head. 'I'd better be going.'

His frown deepened into two thick furrows above his eyes. 'So I've been wasting my time?'

Rosa just smiled and turned away from his sullen stare, halting when she almost piled into Zach. She narrowed her eyes. 'You didn't think I needed rescuing from the man I was kissing?' she demanded.

He pasted on his best blank look. 'Were you kissing someone?' He kept one eye on the guy over her shoulder who, now Zach was on the scene, was turning away with a last resentful look at Rosa.

There was a combatant note in her voice as, together, they turned and threaded between people's shoulders. 'It's so long since I kissed anyone but Marcus that I decided to try it.'

He shrugged. 'If you were willing then there would be no need for rescue.' He didn't actually say he definitely would rescue her, if it were necessary. Or even if unnecessary, possibly. Electra had once complained he had an 'I'm watching you' stare that put men off approaching her when they were together.

They made it out of the overly warm air indoors and into the barely less warm air outside. Rosa fanned herself. 'I'm thinking about heading home. Are you coming or will you get a cab later?'

The weather had turned thundery and gusty. Although Malta was a hot, dry country Zach had witnessed a few spectacular storms here and wasn't keen on being caught in one. 'I'll come now.'

As they made their way up the overpopulated stairs of Triq Santa Rita Rosa confided, 'I didn't like the kiss very much. He seemed to think it was super sexy to suck my upper lip but it made me feel like I was making duck faces. Did you meet anyone?' She edged aside as a group of women in short skirts and high heels bulldozed by, one of them holding aloft a cocktail with a luminous swizzle stick.

'Got talking to some people,' he answered casually.

She sounded equally casual. 'Any of the "people" women?'

'All of them.' He waited, but she asked no more and when they'd travelled home together she called goodnight on the lower terrace and went indoors.

The next day Zach enjoyed a lazy morning but it was Friday and he was taking Rosa and Dory to Nicholas Centre after lunch. Notices had been up for a couple of weeks about the cookery demonstration from 'The Cafeteria Cook'. There would be a full complement of volunteers as well as youth workers. A few friends of Maria and Joseph's had given donations in order to attend too.

Rosa had talked the event through with Joseph and also discussed repeating it on a larger scale at an external venue so Rosa could show him how she worked regarding sponsorship. Joseph was already pretty good at getting funding but was always keen to pick up tips.

They took Zach's car, driving through the streets under an unusually grey sky. Zach hoped the thundery showers forecast would materialise to wash away the dust.

When they arrived at Nicholas Centre it amused him to show Rosa and Dory through the unassuming green door in the wall in Triq Bonnard with its small black plaque:

'Ic-Centru Nicholas' and, underneath, *Nicholas Centre*. He led them across the courtyard, up the steps to the double doors and into a hall with archways to other rooms, enjoying the surprise on their faces as they stepped into what had been a grand house in Great-Uncle Nicholas's day. The rooms were lofty, ornately moulded plasterwork on the ceilings and wrought iron on the outsides of the windows. Joseph met them in the hall. 'Welcome to Nicholas Centre,' he said, in his accented but fluent English. 'Let me show you around.'

They peeked into his office with its eclectic collection of chairs then into the games room with table tennis and table football and an area given over to battered gym equipment. Zach fell back to watch while Rosa and Joseph inspected the small collection of weights and talked about equipment, funding, insurance and more funding.

Rosa looked relaxed in a white T-shirt with washed-out cut-off jeans and flip-flops. Her gaze remained on Joseph as she nodded along to his commentary. Peter and a couple of volunteers were leading events in the room. Zach noticed them checking Rosa out. Then one of the teenaged girls realised who Dory was and asked what it was like to be on TV as others began to cluster around her. The reality TV series that had changed Dory's life hadn't aired in Malta but Zach knew they'd checked her out on YouTube. The tour progressed upstairs with an entourage whispering and chattering in Dory's train, those who were more able in English translating for others.

That Dory had worked in a school was obvious in the easy way she engaged with the teenagers, smiling and laughing, saying 'Wow!' at the faded grandeur of the big salon, admiring art projects and looking suitably impressed by the computer room, though its contents were a rag-tag collection of cast-offs.

Finally, they returned downstairs and arrived in the kitchen where the tables had been stacked up to allow three rows of chairs to be set up for the kids while Dory and Rosa took up station between sink and hob. The chatter rose to new heights. Zach brought Dory's box in from the boot of his car then hung up his jacket and got involved in putting out an extra row of chairs to accommodate the crowd. Joseph and Maria's friends, two middle-aged couples, seated themselves to one side.

Everyone loved Dory's friendly banter, craning to watch as she unpacked a chopping board, peeler and knife, explaining she was going to create a healthy, cheap stir-fry in fifteen minutes: 'So you have no excuse to eat junk!' After washing her hands she used a table as her workbench with the sink behind her and the hob to her right. Rosa hovered on the sidelines and Maria propped the back door to the street ajar to let in air that was, thanks to the arrival of the first of the showers, fairly fresh.

Dory had begun her spiel. 'Lots of people like meat, fish or chicken in a stir-fry but today I'm going to cook with vegetables. And an easy way to eat vegetables healthily is to eat the rainbow.' As she spoke she peeled carrots in a blur of movement. 'These carrots are orange. So now I need red.'

'Tomatoes!' someone shouted.

'Peppers!' another.

Dory nodded approvingly at the girl who'd said 'peppers'. 'Tomatoes are lovely and good for your heart – we call that "heart food" – but they go sludgy in a stir-fry. Peppers fry well.' She held up two red peppers then proceeded to nimbly core them and chop them into sticks. She halted as if struck by a thought. 'What about blue?'

The room fell silent. Zach smiled. He could almost hear the racking of brains.

'There are no blue vegetables.' Dory laughed and the kids laughed with her. 'Let's move on to green.'

'Cabbage!' someone suggested.

Dory grinned. 'Great minds think alike. I've brought the beautiful, crinkly Savoy cabbage. I washed the leaves at home to save time. Now I'm going to shred them with my knife.' Dory paused again, looking around to hold everybody's gaze. 'You need to stay safe when you use a knife. Curl the fingers of the hand holding the food inward.' She demonstrated. 'Then there's a lot less likelihood of you cutting your finger along with the cabbage.' She demonstrated slowly and then let her movements become quick and sure. Out of her box came a large wok and a big pan that Rosa filled with water for the noodles. Dory chattered on, making the kids laugh while Rosa drifted silently to the back of the room to take photos – by arrangement, only over the children's heads – while her mum explained a few safety rules when it came to using a hob.

The phone Rosa held gave a double beep and Zach watched her glance at the screen then slip out through the door to the hall.

He turned back to the cookery demonstration as the air began to fill with the appetising smell of food frying. When he made a stir-fry he bought a bag of prepared veg and threw it in a pan with oil and sauce. Dory's way was much more entertaining.

In the hall, Rosa reread the message she'd just seen on her phone from Georgine Blackthorn:

Hey, you, how are you doing? Is it possible for us to chat, please? xx

Her stomach lurched. She'd begun to put missing Blackthorn's to the back of her mind but the message brought it sharply to the front again. Her mum wouldn't need her for the next few minutes and it would be great to talk to Georgine. She made the call.

'Hi, Rosa!' Georgine answered immediately. 'How's life in the sun? We're all missing you.' They chatted for several minutes before Georgine got to the point. 'Kiley's leaving Blackthorn's in October and she's been covering most of your job. I know you said you'd be away until October but I wondered what the chances were of you returning in September to ensure a smooth transition.'

'Kiley's leaving?' Rosa said, to give herself time to think as she visualised the long, low building that was Blackthorn's Liggers Moor, an English, more modern and better funded version of the centre she was standing in. Georgine was based in Cambridgeshire but travelled regularly between the three Blackthorn's centres. Rosa had hit it off with her the moment she'd met and they often went out when Georgine was in Yorkshire.

'But if you can't come back until October then we'll work around it,' Georgine added. 'I know your mum's rented the place in Malta until then so I understand if you want to stick to your original plan.'

'October, yes,' Rosa echoed. It was the oddest thing but she was having trouble imagining herself back at Blackthorn's, conjuring up events, making posters, working out costings, hitting up companies for sponsorship. She actually shook her head to clear it.

Georgine suddenly sounded wary. 'You are coming back. Aren't you?'

Asked the direct question, Rosa had to reply, 'I don't know.'

It was Georgine's turn to say, 'Oh!' But then sympathy flooded her voice. 'Look, don't let Marcus's crap drive you out of a job you love, Rosa. You chose to take a leave of absence until Twitter moved on to its next victim but so far as I'm concerned, you can come back tomorrow. Today!'

Rosa's mind whirled. 'It wasn't just Marcus's radio stunt. The opportunity with Mum arose . . .' What was wrong with her? Why wasn't she making a decision? Talking options over with Georgine?

'No, I know. Sorry, I shouldn't put pressure on you,' Georgine said contritely in Rosa's ear. 'We agreed you'd come back in October and I don't blame you for wanting to spend your summer in the sun. It's an amazing opportunity. I was being hopeful.' She laughed.

Rosa tried to laugh along with her but it sounded uncertain.

Silence. Then, in a shocked tone, Georgine asked, 'Were you serious that you don't know if you're coming back?'

'I—' Rosa began. Then stopped, because she had no real idea what was about to come out of her mouth. After a moment she gathered her wits and told Georgine about Dory's offer to fund her if she'd like to make a change to her life.

'That's . . . awesome,' said Georgine. But sounded winded.

'It's not that I don't love Blackthorn's,' Rosa hurried to reassure her, leaning her back against the cool wall. 'But now Mum's made this offer I owe it to her to think about it. And to myself.'

'To yourself particularly,' Georgine said slowly. Then, honestly, 'But this conversation wasn't what I expected when I agreed to you going off for the summer. I thought

120

I was working hard to keep you and had succeeded.' She sounded hurt as well as shocked.

'I'm sorry.' Rosa's heart beat heavily. 'I didn't expect this either. I need to think things through.' A burst of laughter came out of the nearby kitchen, reminding her Dory might be looking for her to do something.

'That's your right,' Georgine agreed quietly. She hesitated. 'It sounds as if people are having a good time where you are.'

'Mum's doing a cookery demonstration.' Then, because she didn't want to lie, even by omission: 'At a youth centre. The manager's connected to the family who own our apartment. We got talking and Mum said she'd do a demo for the kids.'

A pause. Rosa tensed as she almost heard Georgine's mind working. 'I know you're drawn to working with young people,' Georgine said steadily but Rosa heard questions in her voice that were business, not friendship.

With a sense of things veering out of her control Rosa answered defensively. 'I had a conversation with Joseph about fundraising but I'm working for Mum, not the centre.'

'Right.' Georgine's voice was so quiet that Rosa could hardly hear it. 'Rosa . . . if I need to replace you then I need to know sooner rather than later.'

'Please don't think I've jumped ship,' Rosa said, unhappy to hear the disappointment in her friend's voice. But Georgine said she must get on with her work and ended the call without her usual cheery affability.

The screen on Rosa's phone returned to its lock-screen image of a Blackthorn's team in a raft race. She stared at it, feeling as if she'd let Georgine down, even though, logically, she knew she was perfectly entitled to change

121

her job. On unpaid leave of absence she was entitled to act as her mum's assistant and visit a youth centre too . . . It was just that she hadn't wanted to upset Georgine. She loved Georgine and the way she ran Blackthorn's with energy and good humour.

Sighing unhappily, she returned her phone to her pocket and slipped back into the capacious Nicholas Centre kitchen where Dory was draining noodles in a cloud of steam. Rosa would be just in time to set out rows of small tasting dishes on the table and share out the noodles and stir-fry for the teens to try.

But she hesitated, her attention caught by Luccio. His back was to her as he apparently watched Dory along with everyone else, but his right hand was busy with a jacket hanging on a hook on the wall.

It was Zach's jacket.

Dumbfounded, Rosa stared as Luccio unbuttoned the top pocket flap and stuffed in a small roll of euros. Then, without closing the flap, he edged away.

Rosa's mouth went dry. Was Luccio trying to temporarily stash money he'd stolen? Get rid of evidence? Then, with a rush of relief, she realised. *Luccio might be replacing the money he stole from Zach.*

Wanting to think his conscience had driven him, she drew on her experience of working at Blackthorn's and decided her responsibility was to convey what she saw to Joseph and Zach after the demonstration and leave the situation to them.

She hurried up the room to put out the tasting dishes and, as Dory used a spoon and fork to slither a small portion of noodles into each bowl, Rosa followed behind with stir-fried veg. Youngsters lined up, Joseph and Peter handed out forks and a hubbub broke out as the teens wolfed down their sample-sized portions. Dory took a moment to chat to Joseph and Maria's friends and Rosa put the pans in the sink.

Then Luccio's voice rose above the clamour. 'My money has gone!' As all heads swung his way he patted himself down, making a show of checking the inside pocket of his thin grey jacket. 'All my money has been stolen!' Ferociously, he scowled around.

The noise died down, forks pausing on the way to astonished faces.

'But—' began Rosa hotly.

However, Luccio was evidently actioning a plan. He grabbed Zach's jacket from its hook and tossed it wildly to him. 'You'd better check yours too.' The fold of euros he'd tucked in Zach's pocket tumbled onto the floor.

Luccio turned big accusing eyes on Zach. 'You!' he breathed. Even Joseph's jaw dropped.

Zach's face flooded with angry colour. 'That's my jacket but I don't know how the money got there.' He sounded fairly composed but even across the room Rosa could see the horror in his eyes.

She jumped forward and grabbed Joseph's arm. 'I watched Luccio putting that money in Zach's pocket when I came back into the room from taking a phone call,' she said loudly and firmly, knowing she should offer only facts. Embroidering them with opinion or speculation only invited debate.

Joseph twisted to look at her, his eyebrows shooting up.

Luccio looked wrong-footed. 'Is a lie! She is his friend so she says that. Zach is in trouble with the police in his own country, often.'

'I watched you do it, Luccio, and was going to tell

123

Joseph and Zach after the demonstration,' Rosa said steadily, choosing to gloss over the point about the police. She was no stranger to this kind of situation. Possessions 'walked', fingers pointed, stories were told, old sins raked up.

The colour drained from Zach's face as he stared at Luccio, the young man he'd tried to help and who was returning the favour by setting him up. 'I saw him do it,' Rosa repeated, gazing steadfastly at Joseph. She hadn't had time or the forethought to whip out her phone to video Luccio's activities but that didn't alter what she'd seen.

Joseph gave a decisive nod. 'We will continue this discussion in my office. Luccio, Zach, Rosa, would you be kind enough to come with me?'

'I tell you, she is his friend! Probably more, I don' know!' But Luccio's voice was thin and shaky now, his gaze darting from Zach to Joseph to Rosa and then around all the pairs of eyes fixed on him.

Then, with a convulsive movement, he broke through the rank of teenagers and sprinted for the back door, still standing ajar, and vanished through it. Joseph hurried after him. 'Luccio, please!'

A buzz of exclamations erupted in the room while the teens polished off any remaining stir-fry. One of the youth workers, Axel, moved to the front. 'Let's sit down and ask whether Dory will kindly answer some questions about food,' he called, his German accent making the words flowing yet precise. Dory moved up to stand beside him, beaming expectantly at her audience. Rosa busied herself with collecting empty dishes as the kids took their seats again.

The euros lay untouched on the floor where they'd fallen, waiting for Joseph to return.

Zach, still clutching his jacket, stood frozen at the side of the room, his gaze on the door through which Luccio had disappeared.

Rosa wanted to go to him but was reluctant to lend even a whiff of support to Luccio's accusation of their being 'probably more' than friends. It had made her feel surprisingly defensive, though she'd done nothing to defend.

Joseph returned without Luccio, breathing heavily and wearing a furrowed frown. With as little fuss as possible he picked up the money by its edges and indicated with small movements of his head that Zach and Rosa should go with him. In his office, Rosa took a worn green chair and Joseph closed the door before seating himself behind his battered desk but Zach stood, one hand in his pocket, his jacket tossed over his shoulder.

Rosa recounted what she'd seen of Luccio sliding the money into Zach's pocket. 'I hoped he was returning what he'd stolen so I decided to speak quietly to you both as soon as the demonstration was over.'

Zach stirred. 'The pockets were empty when I hung my jacket up.' He kept his eyes fixed on Joseph and didn't look Rosa's way. 'I'm not responsible for any of the thefts. Luccio brought up my police record but that's nothing to do with stealing—'

Joseph drummed his fingers on the desk. 'I'm not accusing you, Zach. You've been transparent about the issues you've had and I have complete faith in you, though I'm glad Rosa saw Luccio plant the money for your sake. I'm afraid Luccio losing his nerve and making a run for it rather confirmed his guilt.'

With a jerky nod at the euros lying on Joseph's desk, Zach asked, 'Are you going to call the police? Get that lot fingerprinted?'

Joseph's smile was wintry. 'Luccio's fingerprints will be present because he will say it's his money.' A knock sounded at the office door and Joseph called, 'Come in!'

It was one of Joseph's friends who entered, looking abashed. 'It is me, Tonio. I think the money is mine. I left my jacket on a chair. It was foolish. I had sixty-five euros and now the pocket, it is empty.'

Using the end of a pen, Joseph spread the notes on the desk. Two twenties, a ten and three fives. He nodded. Zach let out a long breath as if he'd been holding it. Rosa turned her head to give him a reassuring look and this time he met her gaze, though briefly.

'Do you wish to involve the police?' Joseph asked Tonio.

Tonio shrugged. 'Not unless you think it best.'

Joseph stared at the notes contemplatively. 'The evidence against Luccio is circumstantial. As manager, I have discretion. I will report to the trustees the situation and my decision not to involve the police at this stage and send Luccio an official request to attend an interview.'

Tonio was obviously embarrassed by providing temptation to young people of limited means. 'I don't ask for the money, Joseph.' He made a shooing motion with his hands. 'You keep. If, in some months, there is no better explanation, it is a donation to Nicholas Centre.'

This course of action agreed upon, Tonio let himself out of the room. Joseph stared at Zach unhappily. 'Luccio must be desperate to deflect attention from his own activities if he'd implicate you.'

Zach slumped, his whole demeanour one of misery. 'Or he didn't care who he made the patsy.'

'Sometimes,' Rosa put in tentatively, 'it can be a sign that the person thinks you care about them enough that your caring is unconditional.'

Rising, Joseph came around the desk and clapped Zach's shoulder. 'Do not despair of our young friends. When they behave at their worst, they are most in need of our help.'

Zach didn't reply to either comment but his expression grew no less bleak.

Chapter Ten

Sunday. The storms that had threatened had hit the island on Saturday with bouncing, diagonal rain and lancing lightning then rumbled off, leaving a beautiful twenty-eight degrees of sunshine behind. A light breeze carried the scent of the sea to Zach as he sat on the rooftop terrace.

Marci and Paige had gone off in his car to spend the day at the Popeye Village in Anchor Bay at the north end of the island and he was lounging in the shade of the canopy, with several peaceful hours in which to write his book. So far today he'd written:

Chapter Seven

Then he'd gone over and over the Luccio situation in his head, writing not a word more.

Why had Luccio chosen him to plant stolen money on? Did he bear some grudge? Or was it as Rosa had suggested, that because Zach had tried to help, sheltering Luccio when he'd stormed Ta' Xbiex Terrace House in a panic, that he thought he somehow wouldn't mind taking a fall?

What about Joseph's theory of a cry for help? *Look how bad things are that I'd do this to you . . .*

The other thing stopping him from writing – apart from a blank screen and zero idea of how to take the story on – was Rosa draped over a sun lounger on the lower terrace. He'd avoided her since Friday afternoon when, he knew, he'd been morose or what Marci and Electra had always called 'growly'. He was rock-bottom mortified not only at being publicly accused of stealing but his police record being proclaimed to all and sundry, and felt as if he were one giant cringe.

Now he was wondering what Rosa was doing. A big pad lay open over her legs and she seemed to be having more success than him at getting words down. Her page had been divided into columns and, so far as he could make out at this distance, she was scribbling paragraphs in each. Occasionally, she'd cross something out or draw arrows. Then, as he watched, with an abrupt movement she tossed the pad on the floor.

It allowed him to see that her rust-coloured shorts were shorter than she usually wore.

Rising, he propped his elbows on the parapet and called down to her. 'Need a beer?'

She twisted around, shading her eyes and grinning. 'I think I do.' She levered herself off the lounger and moved out of sight. A few moments later she appeared at the head of the stone steps, her legs and feet bare, her summer top clinging. He could have looked at her all day. Instead, he turned to the rooftop bar, open already because he'd killed two bottles of Cisk while he'd been up here not-writing.

'Mum's gone off to try a new restaurant in Mosta with Leslie, the guy she met at the reunion.' Rosa's breathing had been barely affected by the run up the stairs. She smelled of sunscreen and shampoo and her eyes were all different golden browns.

He rounded the counter and took two beer bottles from the fridge, opening them and pouring. 'Marci and Paige are out too. What is it you've been doing so industriously down there? I have to admit to being curious.'

She took the beer he handed her, her throat working daintily as she slaked her thirst before answering. She licked the moisture from her lips. 'I'm planning the rest of my life. Are you writing?' Using her beer to gesture towards his laptop, she added, 'If someone wrote a book of my life till now it would be boring.'

'Boredom's underrated. Parts of my life have been exciting but not in a good way.' He pulled two wicker chairs from the stack behind the bar and set them at the front of the roof terrace so they could sit down and look at the sea, its restlessness a reminder of the recent storms. Manoel Island and its ruined buildings formed one shore and the area of ramparts and buildings called Sa Maison the other, leading the eye up Lazaretto Creek to Valletta. He loved Valletta, its stone bastions, the *galleriji* balconies, the Carmelite Dome and the spire of the Anglican cathedral known as 'the British Church'. He liked to imagine the Knights Hospitallers treading its narrow streets, nineteenth-century British soldiers firing cannons from the ramparts, the Mediterranean Fleet being controlled from the underground war rooms during World War II.

'I don't know what I want, that's the problem.' Rosa propped her small bare feet on the parapet. Her legs weren't very brown – she didn't have easy-tan skin like him – but they were smooth and shapely.

He trained his gaze back on Valletta. 'I suppose with

what happened with your ex, your future doesn't look as you'd expected.'

She laced her hands behind her head and squinted at the sunlight glittering on the sea. 'True. No Marcus, no home, no more friendship from Chellice – though that was an unreliable thing anyway – and when I go back I have to find a new home. My old job's still there if I want it.'

'Don't you?' he asked, made curious. 'I thought you liked your job.'

A frown curled her eyebrows. 'I did, but now Mum says that if I want to get a degree or start a business or travel, she'll fund me. I don't know what to do with all that choice.'

He studied her, noting the frown, the tension in her shoulders. 'Have you ever tried solution-oriented coaching? I've done it at work. The coach helps the colleague progress a challenge. It's more concerned with what happens next than how the situation arose.' He thought Rosa needed someone to talk to and liked the idea that it could be him.

Rosa turned an enquiring gaze his way. 'Looking forward rather than back sounds healthy. Go on then. Coach me.'

He laughed. 'At work, I had someone coaching me through it and was given tools like a wheel of life diagram and stuff but I'll do my best.' He paused to gather his thoughts. 'The aim is to ask you open questions. There's no point me asking, "Do you want your old job back?" because there's probably not a yes/no answer.'

'And I've already asked myself that about a hundred times and I don't know,' she put in.

'So establishing your goal is about examining your options.'

She nodded. 'Uni, travel, business, back to my old job.'

He almost said, 'Or stay here?' but she'd never mentioned that so there was no reason for it to pop into his mind. 'If you were to go back to uni, what would you want to study? Which university? What would be your goal at the end of it? Would your degree open doors to you that are closed at the moment?'

Instead of attempting to answer any of these questions she added more. 'What's holding me back? Do I want more than one thing? Can two options be woven together? I'm at a crossroads but I don't seem to want one route more than the other.'

He drained his beer and joked gently, 'And if I'm looking to change my career then it probably shouldn't be to life coaching.' He swung himself to his feet and fetched two more beers, welcoming the cool air that fell out of the fridge when he opened it. The afternoon was getting hotter and a jump to thirty-four degrees was forecast tomorrow.

'Are you looking to change your career too?' she asked when he returned.

'I hated my job in the UK,' he acknowledged. 'When I worked on the apartments I could see the fruits of my labours, something that would exist for years. When I'm at Nicholas Centre—' he paused because his stomach lurched as he remembered the horrible episode on Friday '—I can see the pleasure on the face of a kid playing a game of football or enjoying a craft project. Either's more satisfying than constantly gathering and interpreting data.'

One feathery fine eyebrow dipped as she regarded him thoughtfully. 'Your job didn't make a contribution to education?'

'Of course! Everything from leadership teams to trustees' meetings demand data. And OFSTED bothers you

132

less the more proof of success you can shove at them . . . stuff like safeguarding, e-safety, learning outside the class-room, literacy across the curriculum, cross-curricular topics, trips and visits.' He sucked the froth from his beer. 'What's difficult to present as data is the whole child rather than their academic success. How do you reflect the emotion a kid feels to have access to a musical instrument, for example? What attracts me to Nicholas Centre is kids doing things they want to do for the hell of it.'

'Do you hate freelancing too?' Now her gaze was fixed on him rather than the vista of sea, shore and boats.

He answered honestly. 'Pretty much. And it's not even advancing the career I had.'

She considered this for a few moments. 'So we're both at a crossroads but the difference between our situations is that I like my job. Why did you go into data analysis if you dislike it?'

Because he'd been young and furious. 'At the height of the conflict after the first Fitzmo trouble I told Dad I didn't want anything from him. That meant no three-year stay at uni because I didn't qualify for the full loan and would have needed his financial support. So I took a job with a big enough salary to allow me to leave home. The company dealt in logistics for software and they put me through a business degree. My move into education came later but was still based in data analysis.'

'I can't imagine wanting to leave home that much.' Sympathy lurked in her eyes.

He grunted. 'Dad and I argued all the time once I'd been given community service, the public evidence that I'd shamed him. Till then, we got on OK. He taught me to garden and decorate. I grew tall early and enjoyed flexing my manly muscles and feeling useful.' He narrowed his eyes against the sun, remembering life before he'd disappointed his father. 'I got scant praise but I don't suppose I noticed. Some teachers are the same, aren't they? Designed to annoy teenagers. Dad was particularly good at it.' A laugh escaped him.

The breeze blew her hair into her face and she hooked it impatiently behind her ears. 'The silver lining for us both is that at least we're able to make changes.'

He was struck by that. 'Like, I don't have a relationship or kids so I'm free?'

She giggled, her eyes dancing. 'Not everyone sees no relationship or kids as such a positive, but yes.'

'Here's to the future.' He lifted his beer and they clinked glasses. On his fourth pint now he was feeling pleasantly relaxed.

'What about your book?' she asked. 'Maybe you'll have success, like Mum, and that will be your new career. It's *so* transformed her life.'

'Only if it becomes fashionable for books to have six chapters and no particular story,' he admitted. 'Belatedly, I've read a novel-writing guide and discovered I've begun in the wrong place and run out of steam. My idea is hackneyed and trite. Language laborious, characters like cardboard, no dialogue, nothing happening.'

'Oh dear,' she said, smothering a grin. Then, more bracingly, 'Probably every writer thinks that.'

'Lots of them will be right.' With a sigh, he fell to watching young sailors under instruction in little white-sailed boats on the choppy blue sea, envying them their apparent sense of purpose.

Rosa turned to gaze out to sea too, wiggling her bare toes. 'I suppose either of us might get a new relationship and that would affect other decisions.'

He shuffled down in his chair. 'Do you have one on your horizon?'

Her nose wrinkled. 'No. When we split up, Marcus said I have trust issues and had been waiting for him to fail me.'

'Which is what he did.' He was comfortable enough with her now to call a spade a spade.

She waved her beer. 'True.' She glanced at him and away. 'We haven't talked about your relationships.'

He flinched. 'We don't need to. I have trust issues too.'

'OK.' She put down her glass, folded her hands on her stomach and gazed at the view. A couple of insects whirred past them, sounding lazy in the heat. The traffic below rumbled and a staccato beat was provided by a construction site nearby. 'But,' she added, 'I told you about mine.'

It wasn't necessary to answer, he told himself. Why drag up his failures? 'Three major relationships,' he heard himself saying, dragging them up anyway. 'At eighteen, it was Kelly. She was my girlfriend the first time I got in trouble.' He gestured with his nearly empty beer glass. 'She was no happier when I got community service than Dad. Said her parents weren't keen on her being involved with "a boy like that".'

Rosa waved away his words. 'Perhaps they could have thought of you as "a boy who saves his friend's life".'

He paused to consider. His mum and sisters had voiced that view of him and so had his grandfather – 'never knowingly leave a man behind!' – but their voices had seemed faint compared to his dad's and Kelly's. The police hadn't put much emphasis on his loyalty to a friend either. 'Anyway, I was dumped; she felt virtuous.'

'And you felt betrayed,' Rosa put in. She crossed her

legs at the ankles. He was pretty sure she didn't have an ounce of fat on them. Not a dimple or a ripple.

He concentrated on answering. 'Yes. But nobody seemed to see that. In my early twenties I got another girlfriend. Mel. At first I really liked her but, man, she was manipulative! It took me a while to notice because I was deeply in lust.' He toyed with the idea of getting another beer but decided if he got much more 'relaxed' he might shoot his mouth off more than he already was. 'And she liked sex.'

She snorted a laugh. 'A sure-fire attraction to many men.'

He shrugged, a grin twisting his lips. 'Undeniably. But then she started trying to spin a web around me. Make me her possession. I decided to get out of the relationship. I tried to be gentle but got a storm of tears and what more or less amounted to a stalking, and then she began telling lies about me. According to her, I either couldn't—' he scrabbled for a polite term '—perform, or sex was over before it began.'

'Cheap shot,' Rosa observed but there was sympathy in her eyes.

'Next, she began threatening to harm herself if I didn't resume the relationship,' he went on. 'I took the pragmatic attitude that it wasn't my responsibility.' He paused, no longer allowing even ironic amusement in his voice. 'I got back to my shoebox of an apartment one night to find her on my doorstep. She'd slashed her arms.'

Shock flitted over Rosa's face. 'Hell.'

'It was. All that blood,' he said. 'It was everywhere. I had a flashback to Stuart's artery being severed and began to panic. She kept shouting about it being my fault and people appeared from other flats and demanded to know what I'd

136

done. It was horrible. I felt guilty, which is what she wanted, of course. Then I realised . . . she was watching me carefully, examining my reaction. Her shrieking and splashing blood around was calculated. It shocked me into functioning again and I remembered what the pharmacy assistant had done with Stuart. I took out my phone and dialled 999 and asked for the ambulance. I told the operator my ex had cut herself. I said it looked deep but not dangerous. There was no pumping blood – unlike Stuart – but she was hysterical and maybe she was on something. She stopped shrieking and glared daggers. I suppose she began to see I wasn't going to be played.' He exhaled sharply as he remembered the way his heart had beat out of his chest.

Rosa was very still, waiting for him to continue.

'I supplied her name and my address. The ambulance turned up and I waited solicitously while she was cleaned and taped up. I answered questions candidly. Eventually the paramedics agreed I should return to my flat and leave Mel to them. They carted her off and when we met after that she pretended I didn't exist, which was a relief.'

'Wow. So did Kelly and Mel put you off women for life?' Rosa sounded sympathetic rather than sarcastic. It was refreshing. Usually only his mum and sisters thought he'd been hard done by. Dad had shaken his head as if Zach had brought the whole Mel debacle down on himself.

'I definitely felt girls could be tricky,' he admitted. 'Mum had taught me to play fair with women, but I wasn't convinced anyone had taught women to play fair with me. I had my share of casual encounters.'

'Hook-ups?'

He nodded. 'Then, a couple of years ago, I met Amelia. I thought that might work out. I like my space but she did too so that was OK.'

She waggled her eyebrows 'Showing your maturity?'

He gave a modest shrug. 'I thought so.' Joking made it easier to talk about. He wondered whether she knew that and was giving him a lead. 'We even kept stuff at each other's houses. But when I had the second run-in with Fitzmo she was distinctly unimpressed by "grown men brawling" and said, "I don't want a boyfriend I have to make excuses for." I said I could see that but it was an aberration. I was goaded into the fight and then Fitzmo used me as a money-making scheme because the courts awarded a nominal compensation of £70 so he shot off instantly to one of those "no win, no fee" bloodsucking solicitors – not that he got anywhere with that in the end. Maaaaybe I deserved a teeny bit of understanding and support?'

'Did you get any?' Rosa's beer was empty now too.

'No,' he sighed. 'We were in a restaurant. I saw in her face that she had detached herself from me and my situation. I called the waiter over and cancelled our order, leaving enough money to cover it. I said to Amelia, "Let's get the exchange of possessions over with now while it's dark and nobody has to see you with me."'

'Ouch. Pointed.' She winced.

'When I left her place an hour later with my end-of-relationship bin bag of stuff she called after me that I'd made her feel in the wrong. I kept walking. Lots of women would have done what she did. A boyfriend with a record isn't a good career move.'

She pulled herself more upright in her chair. 'You say "record" as if you were a murderer or armed robber. You got in a punch-up because someone pushed you into it.'

He tipped his head back and closed his eyes. The sun moving lower and the cessation of the yammer from the construction site suggested the afternoon was nearly over.

138

'And when the good guys do that in the movies they manage to stay the good guys but it's never worked for me. I got an interview with HR to be given "words of advice" and told another incident would get me an official warning. Dad got all sad and bitter.' He assumed a reproving voice. '"Why are you still fighting this battle, Zachary? You can't even say someone's life was in danger this time." Mum was more understanding but you know: violence, police. It pisses people off. I wasn't so much reaping what I sewed as spreading the toxic crop about the gardens of those I care about, like my sisters, because they weighed in on my side and it caused issues between them and Dad.'

She fidgeted. 'But what should you do? Just let bullies bully, unchallenged?'

'I'm probably not the person to ask.' He sighed.

After a minute Rosa asked, 'How are you feeling about what Luccio did on Friday?'

'Seeing a pattern.' He shifted in his seat. 'I tried to help Stuart and he turned on me; I tried to help Luccio and ditto. I presume you're seeing the same pattern for you to raise the subject at this moment.' He glanced at her and saw confirmation in her eyes. 'I feel upset and hurt. Worried about what's going to happen next. Joseph advises me to go on as before at Nicholas Centre and let him deal with Luccio, if Luccio ever returns. Easier said than done though.'

Hesitantly, she said, 'You've only ever tried to be kind to Stuart and Luccio. Don't let unexpected consequences change who you are.'

'I'm not sure being who I am is working particularly well. Maybe on some level I thought that because helping Stuart didn't go to plan I'd try again with Luccio? Or if

I can help Luccio in whatever situation he's found himself I'm somehow rewriting my own unsatisfactory history?'

Did he want to be the person he'd just described? Until this moment he hadn't really examined what was behind his concern for Luccio, although he'd accepted a long time ago he despised his younger self for being so easily led and knew that, in retrospect, it could have been avoided by simply changing his friendship group. And the second lot of bother: he'd allowed Fitzmo to turn the tables on him with such contemptuous ease that maybe he deserved the 'Idiot!' his dad Steve had thrown at him. He drew in a breath on another thought. 'Maybe I'm trying to get revenge on Fitzmo by robbing Beppe of Luccio? Revenge against the ringleader-type rather than an individual?'

'Or maybe you're a decent guy who tries to help,' she said gently.

Harbour cruise boats made their ponderous way across the water, dipping and rolling on the choppy water. Zach grew more and more aware of the woman beside him. Her hair flipping in the breeze. Her bare legs. The way she'd talked about his situation without being judgy. Stuart and Luccio faded from his mind and he went for a complete change of subject. 'You going to kiss any more men in the near future?'

She laughed. 'Don't know. The opportunity arose and I thought . . . you know. No boyfriend. Why not? I felt curious.'

He could feel himself falling prey to a similar curiosity. What would it be like to kiss her small and perfect mouth? To pull her curvy body against him? He tried to remind himself of the reasons that he'd decided only to admire her from afar. *Own doorstep. Nanna's tenant. Potential for embarrassment if it's a fling. If it's not, we don't even know if we'll end up in the same country.* But the whiff of intimacy in the conversation had made him feel connected to her and, maybe because of the four pints of beer, he couldn't resist gently pushing. 'Still curious?'

Her hair swung as she turned to look at him, the atmosphere suddenly prickling. 'Maybe.' Then he caught her eyes dropping to where his oversized vest had slipped aside, exposing much of his chest. As if she realised she'd been caught noticing, she blushed.

Now wasn't that interesting? She was aware of him.

Her laugh sounded forced. 'Maybe I ought to go back to Paceville and find a different bloke to kiss.'

Don't say it, Zach. Don't say . . . 'Or you could try me,' he said, ignoring the voice of good sense.

Her eyebrows almost vanished in her hair. Then mischief flashed in her eyes. 'You've been drinking. Are you in a fit state to give consent?'

His throat dried. 'Totally. To whatever.'

Those fine, sparkling eyes narrowed. 'A kiss.'

He hoped he could hear *for now* hanging unspoken on the air. 'Yeah, that.' He let his smile tell her he would consent to a whole lot more if she wanted, reaching out to stroke the back of her hand, enjoying the satin feel of her sun-warmed skin.

Slowly, slowly, she turned her hand over to take his. As if pulled by a string he rose and drew her gently to her feet, giving her plenty of opportunity to laugh and push him away as if it had been a joke all along. Instead, she tilted her face up, a searching look in her golden eyes as if asking, *What are we doing?* The wind blew her hair back from her face and he dipped his head and brushed his lips over hers.

141

Her mouth was soft. Heated.

He placed tiny kisses at the corners, then her cheek, lowered his head to nuzzle her neck. Returning to her mouth he covered it with his, feeling a tremor run through her. His eyes closed as she nestled against him. He rested his hands on the inward curve of her waist and deepened the kiss, almost losing the power to breathe when her mouth opened and she made a tiny noise of pleasure at the back of her throat.

Instant arousal.

She didn't pull away from his hardness so he ran his palms up her back, learning the shape of her, following the dip of her lower spine to her waist. He really had a thing about neat waists. Thumbs brushing her ribs, he leaned in closer.

He kissed her harder.

Then he realised her phone was ringing and she'd stopped kissing him back. He released her with a breathless, 'Sorry. Took me a moment there.' Probably because all his blood had deserted his brain cells.

Her cheeks were flushed, her eyes heavy-lidded. 'No, I'm sorry – I didn't mean to . . . but the phone kinda shocked . . . that ringtone—'

Her run of half-sentences told him little except she was going to answer the phone. He was still trying to get his head around the abrupt end to the kiss when he heard Marcus's voice.

'Hello, Rosa. I feel bad about this but I want you to hear it from me because—' Marcus's tone altered sharply. 'Oh! You have company again?'

Zach realised belatedly that it was a FaceTime call and he must be in shot. A shaft of irritation shot through him at Marcus's pissy tone, especially as he'd ruined a bone-melting moment between Zach and Rosa. He gave Marcus a smile and Marcus's eyes widened.

'My company's my business,' Rosa said. Her breathing was uneven, eyes bright. Zach wondered whether Marcus would realise he'd interrupted something or assume Rosa was feeling emotional at hearing from her ex.

He decided on the former, judging from the way Marcus began to snap. 'Obviously you're not pining but I thought you ought to hear this from me. Chellice and I are in a relationship. Now I'll leave you to your own . . . activities.' He managed to sound judgy and disapproving.

Marcus drew breath as if to say goodbye when Rosa said tightly, 'So now I've signed your form allowing Chellice to "lodge" at our house you're coming clean. I can't believe how cynically you kept it to yourself while the formalities were underway instead of showing me the respect I deserve by telling me the truth. You deserve each other.' She stabbed at the screen to end the call.

Rosa didn't cry. Instead she stared blankly at her phone as if silently blaming it for the treachery she'd encountered. Zach realised she was trembling.

He drew her into his arms but with none of the heat he'd felt only minutes before. 'Sorry,' he murmured. 'I feel partly responsible for the way that went down. When I realised he could see me I gave him a smug smile. That's when he spat that bad news at you. I wanted to piss him off because he'd hurt you but he just hurt you more.'

She leaned into him slightly. 'Don't worry. He seized on that because he doesn't like being in the wrong. He probably didn't really want to own up to me.' She pursued her mouth thoughtfully. 'So I wonder why he did.'

'Chellice wanted him to?' Zach guessed.

'Maybe.' She eased away from him to open Facebook.

Then Instagram. Grief flickered across her features. She turned the phone so he could see an image of Marcus, hair on end, eyes barely open, and a petite woman with spiky red hair, a sheet drawn up to her naked shoulders. The caption read: *Sunday delight with my awesome man* and then emoticons with heart eyes.

'Ah. He realised you might see the post so tried to get in first.'

'That would be my guess.' She sighed. 'Chellice lives her life on social media. If she wanted Marcus to tell me the truth and he was resisting this would be the obvious way of forcing the issue.'

'And she's a friend of yours?' Zach slid his arms around her again, feeling the Mediterranean breeze filtering over his skin and the sadness of the woman in his embrace filtering through it.

Her laugh held no humour. 'She *was* my friend,' she acknowledged. 'She goes after what she wants and I think she used me to get close to Marcus.' She sniffed. 'And to think the reason I jumped away from you when the call came in was because I recognised Marcus's ringtone and felt guilty.'

Then she eased away from him once more.

When Rosa stepped out of Zach's arms he made no move to keep her. He just smiled easily and dragged their chairs into the shade. Perhaps he realised that her emotions had been tumbled about by Marcus's FaceTime call and decided now was not the time for experimental kisses.

The breathless moment of heightened awareness had taken her by surprise. Hunger had churned inside her as he'd fitted her against him, pulse kicking and heart pounding. His mouth had felt delicious on hers.

The contrast between that and Marcus's callousness had been almost too much to cope with. She was the kind of person who needed time to process.

Marcus and Chellice. Betrayal. Pain.

Zach's kiss. What was *that*?

When she'd kissed the guy in Paceville she'd felt little. But Zach's kiss had played pinball with her insides.

He didn't mention the kiss as they sat down so she circled back to their earlier discussion about the crossroads they each felt they stood at. 'One change I'd like to make to my life in Malta is to find a dance exercise class,' she said. 'I danced a lot at home and I miss it. I think I saw a notice at Nicholas Centre that they're putting something on there.'

He accepted the return to polite conversation easily. 'That's right. Let me get the date for you.' He took out his phone and began scrolling. Then, 'Wednesday afternoon. "Dance is hot and cool". I'm sure Joseph would be happy for you to attend. Paige and Marci would probably be interested too.'

'Isn't it for the kids?' But her heart kicked up and she didn't even ask what kind of dance might be involved. Ballroom, street, Latin, anything would be fun. Maybe the instructor would be able to signpost her to local classes.

Zach gave her a boyish smile, squinting in the late-afternoon sun. 'He usually doesn't mind in return for a small donation.'

'Brilliant! There's a change to my life right there.' She managed a smile, though she felt sad that the changing-her-life thing was a result of being rejected. She drained her final inch of beer, though it tasted sour and flat now. 'Think I'll head off for a swim before the sun goes down.' She didn't invite Zach and he didn't invite himself, seeming to understand that she needed space.

'Enjoy,' he murmured. 'I'll text Joseph and check he's OK with us going on Wednesday.'

Us not *you* she noted, but she was still feeling too down to query it. 'Thanks.' She said goodbye and drifted downstairs to slip into her swimming costume. Before she left her phone in her room she did a very bad thing, foreign to her nature but cleansing for her soul.

She went back to Chellice's Instagram post depicting her and Marcus in bed and added in the comments: *#Leftovers.*

It would be the last time she looked at any of Chellice's social media channels.

Rosa was moving on.

She grabbed her beach towel and set off down the stairs, across the two roads to the rocks and was soon throwing herself into the briny turquoise depths. She swam slowly, soaking up the early evening sunlight on the waves, boats, golden buildings, domes and spires and mentally comparing it to the familiar, ordinary brick-built town of Liggers Moor. This was a wonderful place and she was going to enjoy the rest of a wonderful summer. It was hard to remember that she'd felt out of place on the island at first. Now she loved the glorious weather, the scenery, the things she was doing . . . and she was getting pretty fond of some of the people here too.

Maybe Zach could be her first post-relationship dalliance, she thought, turning over to float and admire the blue sky, paling as sunset approached. Had she ever felt sparks like that from a kiss before? Certainly Marcus had never made her feel as if her feet were hovering an inch from the ground.

She flipped onto her front and began a fast crawl, tasting the saltiness of the cool water. She and Zach each knew

146

how it felt to be judged and considered in the wrong. In fact, she reflected, as shouts of nearby children carried to her ears whenever she turned her head, Zach was defined by it. If all dads were as judgemental as his then she was glad hers never bothered with her.

Another thing she and Zach had in common: they were both single. She turned and swam back, a tight tingly ball of excitement forming in her stomach.

It was a long time since Marcus had caused feelings like that.

Chapter Eleven

They were part way through trialling tomato salads when her mum's phone rang. Rosa was making notes, clearing up and taking pictures for the Cafeteria Cook blog and Instagram to whet readers' appetites for *The Cafeteria Cook Does the Mediterranean*. The dishwasher was half full and there was enough chopped tomato and onion to supply a restaurant.

Dory's phone rang and she paused in spooning tomatoes to answer. 'Hello, Dad!'

Rosa noticed her voice contained the mixture of pleasure and apprehension with which she seemed to greet any unexpected call from Grandpa these days. Early in the year Lance had undergone a knee replacement. He'd treated the necessity with exasperation but it had been a reminder of advancing age. He'd felt the absence of Grandma keenly in his convalescence too, though he'd flatly refused to stay at Dory's house for more than two weeks after the op.

Dory continued, 'Rosa's here. I'll put you on speaker.' She moved aside a bottle of chilli oil and leaned her elbows on the worktop.

'Just thought I'd ring for a chat,' Lance's voice boomed from the phone. 'All's OK here. Getting two or three games a week in, just nine holes, you know. Rod and me take turns with the buggy so we walk a bit and rest a bit.'

'Good idea,' Rosa chimed in, closing her laptop and moving close enough to be heard. 'Hi, Grandpa. Glad you're enjoying your golf.'

'Rosa! Are you having a good time in Malta? What did you think about the reunion and meeting your mum's childhood schoolmates?'

Rosa suppressed the urge to say, 'But that was three weeks ago and we've told you about it already.' Lance's memory of conversations was becoming random. It made her sad but others of his age were worse off, like Zach's grandad, Harry. She simply repeated how Dory had hurled herself into the reunion with barely a backward glance and that the conversation had been littered with references to regiments, barracks and postings.

'Sounds excellent!' But Lance sounded wistful.

'You could still come over, Dad,' Dory chimed in. 'There's a room here waiting for you. I'd book your flights and a cab to Stansted Airport and pick you up at this end.'

Lance came back with his usual reply. 'It's not the same without your mum, Dory. We were so happy there. There would be too many memories, I think.'

'I understand,' Dory answered brightly but Rosa noticed her frown.

They talked on about Malta, how blue the sea, how hot the sun, how welcome the apartment's air conditioning. Lance told them about his neighbour moving into a retirement village and then hurried on as if he didn't want them to ask whether he was considering doing the same. Finally, he said cheerio. 'I'm going to walk to the corner shop for a newspaper now and then watch cricket on TV.'

'Bye, Grandpa,' Rosa said.

'Yes, bye, Dad. Love you.' But Dory was frowning more than ever as the call ended. 'Do you think I've been thoughtless coming here and inviting you too? It's kind of left Dad out on a limb. Perhaps he's lonely.'

Rosa halted halfway back to her laptop. 'I hadn't thought of it,' she said slowly, 'but I can see what you mean, especially if his neighbours are moving out. Poor Grandpa. I respect his reasons for not coming out to join us but it's a shame.'

Obviously troubled, Dory rinsed a handful of herbs and began chopping them. 'Could you fetch in more basil, please? Is the big blue bowl washed up?'

'I'll do it now. How about dividing this batch between the blue and the green bowls to see which photographs best?'

'Good plan,' Dory returned absently. Rosa fetched basil from the pot outside the back door, rinsed it and put it ready for Dory to rip. When the tomato salads were ready they tasted them, making notes, adding a shake of black pepper and tasting again. Next Rosa photographed the finished bowlfuls. She'd done a webinar on iPhone photography and was able to set up the tripod with confidence and creativity.

As a recipe for traditional rabbit stew was next, Rosa did the clean-down while her mum checked emails. Then, 'Oh no!' Dory cried.

Rosa halted in the act of taking out the non-veg chopping board. 'What?'

'Defne, my editor, says she wants me to stop work on this book and do a vegan one instead.'

150

'Why?' Rosa asked blankly. The title and contents of *The Cafeteria Cook Does the Mediterranean* had been agreed for ages.

'She says she'll have more information for me soon but feels it will "substantially increase the options". Nita, my agent, was copied in and has emailed asking whether I want to chat before responding to Defne. I'll reply that yes I bloody do, but I'll start the vegan book.' Dory's forehead was one big frown. 'She hasn't said whether *Mediterranean*'s to be dropped completely or just put back. I hope it won't affect the next contract.'

'Why should it?' Rosa frowned.

With a shrug, Dory began tapping at the laptop. 'If they're asking me to leave *Mediterranean* then there's something going on. Maybe they think it won't sell. Does that mean my other sales are dropping?'

A little out of her depth with the ways of the publishing world and not liking to say that it seemed to her as if her mum was looking for negatives, Rosa flicked through the tomato salad pictures. Absorbed, she hadn't even realised that Dory had stopped typing until she groaned instead. 'What now?' she demanded, looking up.

'I shouldn't read my Amazon reviews. I've got a horrible one.' Her shoulders drooped.

Rosa put down her phone to slide a comforting arm around her. 'Oh, no! Let me look.'

The one-star review was based on the colour coding of the margins of the pages in one of Dory's books. *Not for the colour-blind!* it began. The author of the review, apparently, couldn't tell blue from green.

'It's a publisher decision to have blue margins for fish and seafood and green for veggie stuff,' Dory protested glumly. 'If you struggle between those colours it could be

151

an irritation but really? A one-star review, though she acknowledges she loves the recipes? *Really*?' Despondently, she shut the laptop.

'Gin?' Rosa suggested sympathetically.

Dory did manage a smile at that. 'Maybe after I stop wielding a knife.'

Rosa got them cold water instead and closed the door so the air con would click in. 'I never used to give a thought to books having deadlines or attracting bad reviews. It's awesome that you have the money to come to Malta for the summer and—' she gave a wink '—offer to help your daughter but you certainly have to take the rough with the smooth.'

'And there's so much more smooth than rough that I have no business getting upset.' Dory stood still. 'But there's not much point trialling rabbit stew now, is there? Not exactly vegan.'

'Oh!' Rosa stared at Dory as it sunk in what the ramifications were of the editor wanting a different book. All those weeks of work down the drain or, at least, on hold.

Dispiritedly, Dory went out on the terrace, saying, 'I'm going to call Leslie to talk things over. I'd planned today's full day in the kitchen because he's going home on the 16th of July and I wanted to spend his last two days with him but now I feel as if we've wasted our time anyway.'

Dory had been seeing a lot of Leslie, Rosa reflected, moving the rabbit from fridge to freezer. He'd been divorced for years and his children were adults but he had a job to return to. She couldn't remember any other man in her mum's past being the first Dory turned to in a crisis.

Had Dory fallen for him?

She'd even brought him along to a meal on Manoel Island last weekend.

She grinned as she remembered. They'd got talking to the Brits on a nearby table whose 'have you visited Malta before?' had elicited the information that Dory and Leslie had lived on the island as army kids. The woman tourist had wrinkled her nose and dismissed military personnel with, 'I'm afraid I have no time for people who kill for a living.'

Dory had laughed genially. 'We do need people who run towards danger while civilians run away from it.'

The woman had flushed an ugly brick red.

Rosa had been embarrassed but Leslie had given Dory a hearty round of applause while the tourists had paid their bill and left.

Rosa had met Leslie three times since the reunion and liked him because happiness fairly radiated from Dory when she was with him. OK, he was brash and tended to take over the conversation but his eyes lit up when they rested on Dory. He lived in Norfolk and Rosa wondered whether Dory would carry on the relationship when she returned home to Yorkshire at the end of October.

Dory stepped back indoors. 'I talked to Nita after Leslie. She's going to email Defne to see if she can get any more information but I think I'll go home for a week. I can see if Dad's OK and Nita can try and set up a meeting with Defne so I can get a better feel for what's going on.'

Surprise washed over Rosa. 'You're that worried about Grandpa and your publishing contract?'

'Unsettled,' Dory admitted shortly.

Rosa wondered if Dory was glad of a reason to follow Leslie back to England too. 'Not to make it about me, but what do I do? Go back with you?' Rosa tried to decide how she felt about this.

'You'll have a week off,' Dory answered with her customary generosity. 'I'll soon be back to crack the whip.'

'If you're sure . . .' But Rosa could see little assistance she could render Dory on a trip home.

A knock fell on the door. Dory answered, pushing her curls out of her eyes with the back of her hand. 'Hello, Paige! Hello, Zach.' Rosa got a glimpse of Paige beaming up at Dory but it was Zach who spoke.

'Paige's Mummy's having a break today so Paige is taking me swimming. She wants to know whether Dory and Rosa would like to come too.'

'Yeah!' agreed Paige, bouncing on her toes.

Dory answered regretfully. 'I'll be going out when Rosa and I have finished in the kitchen, I'm afraid.'

'Awww,' mourned Paige, her beaming smile fading.

Rosa joined Dory at the door, conscious of Zach's gaze switching to her. 'I might be able to join you in an hour when we've finished.'

'Awww,' Paige complained again, but more loudly.

Zach glanced down at her. 'We could find something else to do for an hour until Rosa's ready.'

'Yeah!' Paige beamed at him, joggling with excitement. 'Or I could stay here and help while you go shopping.'

'That's a great idea,' said Dory, even while Zach was trying to say no. 'Rosa can fetch Uncle Zach when we're ready.'

Zach took an uncertain step back. 'Well . . . I could work in the garden on this level when I get back so I won't be far away.' He ruffled Paige's hair and reminded her to do everything Dory and Rosa told her before he turned away.

It seemed to cheer Dory up to have Paige around. Dory checked through their recipes so far for those that could be made vegan while Rosa updated the Instagram and Twitter feeds with pictures of tomato salad and unscheduled already scheduled posts about *The Cafeteria Cook Does the Mediterranean* as Paige gravely dried up things out of the dishwasher, apparently not noticing that they were dry already. Rosa was reminded sharply of her own childhood. Dory had always let her 'help' and had never run out of patience.

When Dory had helped Paige make home-made ice lollies that would be delicious tomorrow, she sent Rosa out to locate Zach.

Relishing the idea of plunging into cool, clear water, she let herself through the black iron garden gate between the garden and the terrace, enjoying the shade cast by palm trees and pines, kicking up brown pine needles at the edges of the path. She'd expected to see Zach placing stones over the dry, dusty soil to harbour moisture, a project he'd begun a couple of weeks ago. Instead, she saw that by 'working' he'd meant on his laptop. It stood open on a small table, a chair pushed out from beneath. Zach was nowhere to be seen.

He'd probably run up to get a drink, she thought. But as he could equally well have gone for a bathroom break and not appreciate her knocking at the apartment door, she decided to wait for him to reappear. She wandered along the paths, enjoying the peaceful hum of insects and the still, shadowy air under the palms and around the pink-flowered oleander bushes. When she reached the laptop she saw text on the screen.

Her eyes caught on the word *breasts*.

Her breasts were high, she read, without really thinking that she shouldn't be peeking at someone else's document. *Her waist was neat and firm and he couldn't take his eyes off the way her body moved. She was beautiful and in his bed. His heart banged against his ribs. Her naked legs wound around his and her smile was hot as she reached for . . .*

And then she realised that Zach was standing on the path. She hopped back from the computer as if it had bitten her. 'Um, sorry!' she began.

He looked rueful. 'I'm half embarrassed and half intrigued as to your reaction.'

'Um,' she bleated again, face on fire. Wow. That was what was in his head?

He took a couple of awkward steps. 'That's not the book I was writing. It's a . . . a scene that came into my mind.'

'I shouldn't have looked,' she stammered.

Slowly, he picked up the laptop and closed it. 'Are you ready to swim? I'll fetch mine and Paige's stuff.'

Rosa escaped back to the apartment to change and grab her snorkelling gear. She hoped the sea was cold because her cheeks were still scalding. Part of her was sorry he'd returned when he had though. She'd stopped reading at a real *What happens next?* moment.

When Zach arrived on the lower terrace, fins protruding from his backpack, a second bag in his hand, Rosa and Paige were ready and waiting. 'I've still got my cozzy 'neath my shorts,' Paige cried, beaming, ponytail swinging. 'I said bye-bye to Dory already an' she's gone in the shower. We can go.' She linked hands with Rosa to take the stairs down to The Ramp.

They crossed the seafront road to the beach and found themselves a spot. A lot of folk were there before them and the rocks reminded Rosa of the seal colonies she'd seen on nature programmes: some basking, others shifting around, swimming or calling to each other. Paige hurled off her T-shirt and shorts and rifled Zach's backpack for

156

her armbands. After he'd inflated them he gave her a smile. 'I bought you something.'

Paige froze in exaggerated anticipation, her eyes growing wide. 'What?' she whispered.

Zach stroked his chin. 'First we need to ask Rosa whether you were a good girl while you were helping in the kitchen.'

'I was,' Paige assured him earnestly. Then, to Rosa, nodding to encourage the right answer out of her. 'Wasn't I?'

'She was.' Rosa grinned. 'She helped a lot.'

'Then . . . ta daah! Snorkelling gear like Rosa and me.' Zach emptied his second bag on the rocks and a tiny green mask, snorkel and fins fell out.

'Shnorkelling! Yeah, yeah, thank you, thank you, thank you, Uncle Zach!' Paige shouted, almost bouncing out of her sandals.

Rosa laughed, not just at Paige's obvious joy but at the pleasure in Zach's eyes too. 'That's really nice of Uncle Zach.'

'Yeah!' Paige shouted again. Then she leaned forward to where Zach crouched over the bags and pressed a kiss on his cheek. Zach looked as if she'd given him a gift and he thanked her with a big hug. Then he pulled off his T-shirt and Rosa's eye was caught by the way the wings tattooed across his shoulders moved over his muscles as he assisted Paige.

Getting the little girl sorted out with her new snorkelling gear took several minutes as she wasn't very sure of what it was she was getting or how to use it but, once in the water, Paige proved herself fearless. As far as she was concerned, Uncle Zach had said it would be OK to breathe through a tube, so it would be OK. Soon she was bobbing on the waves, gazing into the turquoise depths at the fish and seaweed below, lifting her head every few seconds to spit out her snorkel and bellow a comment or a question. 'I can see black spiky balls. I don't like them! Can they get me?'

Patiently, Zach caught her hand to stop her being carried away on the swell. 'They're called sea urchins. The spikes are to protect them but they won't come after us. They barely move.'

''Kay.' And Paige put her face back in the water only to come up spluttering and laughing an instant later. 'I forgot my shnorkel. Urgh, the water's salty.' She let Zach help her get her snorkel back in her mouth and ducked her head again.

Rosa once again revelled in the peacefulness of shutting out the on-shore world. The water was cool but the sun warm. Fish of all shapes and sizes floated and flitted beneath her, some as dull as the proverbial dishwater, until they turned on their sides and flashed a brilliant silver.

Paige declared herself in love with the rainbow fish but eventually tired of watching them and wanted to jump off the rocks into the sea instead. Zach put everyone's snorkelling equipment out to dry and he and Rosa trod water ready to grab Paige when she jumped in to make sure her armbands brought her back to the surface.

Occasionally the wake from a passing boat tumbled the waves. Once, Rosa was swept against Zach and her wet flesh slid across his, the sensuous slither of it setting every inch of her body a-tingle.

'Sorry,' she gasped.

Zach's laugh was strained. 'Don't be.'

A gleeful shout of 'Catch me!' and a small body plummeting into the water with a salty splash saved Rosa from having to answer.

Paige took a lot of exhausting but, finally, she climbed out and yanked her water wings down her arms. 'Can I have a drink?'

After the obligatory request for the word 'please' Zach pulled a Little Mermaid insulated bottle from his backpack, telling Paige that if she'd stayed in the sea much longer she might have turned into a mermaid herself. Paige glanced back at the frothing water as if deciding whether it might work but then exchanged a conspiratorial 'OK, funny joke' look with her uncle and wandered a few feet away to examine salt-encrusted cracks in the rock.

Rosa and Zach had brought water and drank while they watched her crouching down with her bottom sticking out, prying at something with her fingertips. Zach spread out his towel for them to sit on. 'I'll give her time to dry off, then enter the sun cream battle.'

Rosa settled alongside him to let the seawater dry on her skin. 'You're great with her.'

'She's not hard to look after and Marci needed a break.' He didn't look happy.

Wondering, she asked, 'That was meant to be a compliment. Why the frown?'

Instantly, he smiled instead, using his fingers to rake back his hair. It was so thick and strong that it wouldn't lay completely flat even when damp. 'I could have helped Marci more than I have. Our sister Electra and I have been living our own lives while she did the single-parent thing and it took her coming close to meltdown for me to wake up to the pressure she was under. She doesn't accept much help from our parents, Mum having rheumatoid arthritis and Dad being so righteous when she was pregnant.'

Rosa protested, 'Paige is so at ease with you. You must've been in her life, even before now.'

'Some,' he acknowledged. Then, when Paige dropped her drink bottle so she could use both hands to perform whatever task was absorbing her he called, 'Paige, maybe you could bring me your bottle so it doesn't get lost.'

'In a minute,' she called back. 'There's something shiny.'

'Now would be good though,' he persisted and Rosa grinned as Paige heaved a great long-suffering sigh and brought the bottle, abandoning it in mid-air before Zach actually made contact with it. He picked it up from where it had fallen with a grin, murmuring to Rosa, 'She probably wouldn't mind losing it because she has her eye on a Warrior Princess one.'

Paige evidently caught his words as her head swivelled so she could regard him over one rounded shoulder. 'It's Mummy who's that. A worrier. Not me.'

Zach watched silently as Paige found a nearby lolly stick to use as a digging tool and became absorbed once more. 'I bet it's Dad who's said that in her hearing,' he said softly, pitching his voice so that Paige definitely couldn't hear this time.

It wasn't Rosa's place to comment and she wasn't a parent but it didn't sound like a supportive thing to say. Steve Bentley must really call it as he saw it.

A few minutes later, Zach called Paige over. 'Sun cream!'

His tone had suggested a treat but Paige wasn't fooled. 'In a minute.' She continued to winkle at the crack in the rock.

'Will you put some on my back, please?' Zach asked implacably.

Paige hesitated, then, bringing her lolly stick with her, ran to her uncle's side. 'Can I colour in the wings?' she asked, as if that were a condition.

160

'I'd appreciate it because they burn easily.' Zach got her to hold out her hand while he squirted cream into it.

Beginning with the upswept wings inked across his shoulder blades, the little girl slathered white cream over Zach's back. When she said, 'Finished!' he took the bottle from her and, discussing what they were going to eat this evening, coated her little body without her apparently noticing. Rosa had to admire his technique in both demonstrating that he thought sun protection a good thing and distracting her long enough for her to let him apply it.

It made Rosa realise she hadn't yet topped up her own protective layer so she fished out the bright yellow bottle from her backpack and began to smooth oil on her arms. Self-conscious as she covered the tops of her breasts where they showed above her costume she moved on to her legs, head bowed as she ensured that not a square centimetre was missed.

Of course, she couldn't reach her back. Dory had put the original layer on for her. Her skin was fair and she didn't want to burn. She'd opened her mouth to seek Paige's help when the little girl, evidently reaching the limits of her patience, broke away from Zach, reclaimed her lolly stick and ran back to whatever was fascinating her in the crack in the rocks.

Zach's rich voice was full of amusement as he watched Rosa try and reach her own back. 'May I?' Gently, he took the bottle.

His touch felt hotter than the sunshine. Her shoulder blades seemed to slide apart as if on their own private relaxation programme. Slowly, gently, his hand travelled over her, not taking a single liberty but stroking with his palm, his fingers, his whole hand, following her contours, finishing off with a slow sweep down her spine until he encountered the fabric of her swimsuit.

'Thanks,' she murmured, risking a glance at him and seeing his eyes on her in a way that sent heat ricocheting through her.

'Any time,' he said with slow emphasis.

He'd just raised his gaze to Rosa's face when Paige shouted triumphantly. 'I got it!' She flung down her lolly stick and scrambled back across the rocks, an expression of beaming triumph on her round face. 'Look!'

Reminded of his uncle duties, Zach held out his hand. 'What treasure have you found?' And Paige delivered into his palm a shining gold and diamond ring.

'Oh! This really is treasure.' He brought the ring closer to his face to examine it.

Paige crowded close, breathing hard. 'From a pirate ship? Or a mermaid?'

'I think it's most likely it's from a human but you never know.' Zach took Paige on his knee so they could examine it together.

Rosa leaned in. 'It's not costume?'

He squinted inside the band. 'Hallmarked.'

'Is the stone real?' Rosa could hardly believe it might be.

He shrugged and passed the ring to her, his fingertips brushing her palm. 'What do you think?'

The stone was as clear and bright as starlight. Rosa tipped water over it from her bottle and dried it on her towel. 'I'm not an expert. I've never owned a diamond but I certainly don't look at it and think "fake".'

'Same.'

'It's mine—' Paige snatched the sparkling ring from Rosa's hand but Zach gently relieved her of it.

'We're not sure yet, Sunshine. It's valuable and someone

162

will be very sad to have lost it. Even though you found it—'

Paige burst into sobs, yanking away from Zach's comforting arm and trying to grab the ring again. 'It's mine! It i-i-i-s, it I-I-I-S!' she bellowed.

They began drawing attention as Paige's yells rose on the breeze.

Rosa waited for Zach to speak sharply to her but instead he gave her a big hug. 'Whoa, you're like Bilbo Baggins! I know it's disappointing because you spent a lot of time getting it out of that crack in the rock but you have to think about if you lost your very best thing and someone found it but wouldn't give it back. You'd feel so, so, sad, wouldn't you?'

Paige nodded but didn't stop crying, her heart obviously broken. 'What's a Bilbo Baggins?'

Zach began to tell her the story of *The Hobbit* but Paige lost interest and began to cry again. As she refused to be comforted by offers of another snorkelling session they packed up their things. She did manage to calm herself enough to eat a strawberry ice cream Zach bought her from the café – asking at the same time if they knew of anyone who'd lost a ring on the rocks nearby – but then she was too sad to walk across the roads and up the steps, so Zach gave her a piggy back while Rosa carried the bags.

When they reached the lower terrace they found Dory about to leave, hair smartly blow-dried and wearing a floaty dress of cream and green. Her eyes widened when she saw Paige's tear-stained face. 'Are you hurt?'

Paige stopped licking her ice cream long enough to grizzle out her grievance and Dory listened sympathetically while Zach took the ring out of his pocket to show her.

Leaving Dory asking Zach what he was going to do with the ring, Rosa decided everyone would feel better for another cold drink and slipped into the kitchen, watching the ice rattle into three glasses and topping up with copious amounts of Sprite. Her phone, which she'd left on the worktop while she swam, beeped. She tilted her head to look at the lock screen. *Dad*.

Dad? It was the first text she'd had from him since *Merry Christmas* on Boxing Day, presumably in reply to her text saying *Christmas greetings!* the day before. Warm and cuddly their relationship wasn't.

Curiosity raging, she carefully put the glasses down and opened the text.

Hi rosa can you give me your mums number pls.

'Sheesh, don't you get all gooey on me,' she muttered sarcastically, stuck her phone in her shorts pocket and carried the glasses out.

As her mum was on the verge of going, Rosa told her about the message. Dory's brows almost vanished into her hair. 'You'd better give him my number, I suppose. Bloody typical that I'm not even in his contacts.'

'I'm sometimes surprised that I am.' Rosa invited Zach and Paige to sit on loungers and handed out the drinks then shared her mum's contact information with her dad. Taking a seat herself she prepared to try and cheer Paige up.

'See you later,' Dory said, waving. But even as she turned away, her phone began to ring. She sighed, checked the screen then hesitated. 'Does your dad's number end three, three seven? This is him already. I can't imagine what's so urgent.' She took the call. 'Hello, Glenn. This is an unexpected pleasure.' Her tone suggested she was only being polite.

As Paige slurped her drink, Rosa listened to the

one-sided conversation. It began, 'Yes. Yes, that's right.' Then Dory burst into laughter. She had a rich, loud laugh and it rang out as if she'd heard the best joke ever. 'Sorry,' she said, when she'd finished, 'but that won't be happening. Bye, Glenn.' Then, after listening a moment more, 'Get a lawyer and try it on. Be my guest.' She ended the call. Eyes agleam she told Rosa, 'He's asking for money! After shirking his responsibilities to us so badly, he thinks that as I've "made it big now" and I'm "a celeb" who is obviously "coining it", he's entitled to a share. Women do it all the time, he says; claim money when the husband has made some. He's only doing the same.'

Rosa's jaw dropped. 'I can hardly believe the cheek of it.' Unlike Dory, though, she struggled to find humour in the situation. Instead she was aware of a sick sadness that she was descended from such a human being.

Dory threw her arms around her. 'Don't look so blue, lovey. I'm not worried so you certainly don't have to be. Your dad'll never change. He's woken up to me as a possible gravy train but I don't think I've left him in any doubt what his reception will be if he persists. Now,' she went on, releasing Rosa and doing a twirl, 'do I look nice?'

Love for her unflappable mother pulsed through Rosa. 'Gorgeous. Leslie won't know what's hit him. Have a lovely time.'

'I will.' Dory winked. 'Don't wait up.' She sashayed over to the steps leading to the street and disappeared.

Though comforted by her mum's insouciance, Rosa sighed. Paige, without removing her face from her glass, had presented her back to Zach and he was untangling her ponytail with his fingers. He gave Rosa a reassuring smile. 'Thanks for the drink. Nice, isn't it, Paige?'

'Mm,' Paige mumbled into the glass.

Rosa smiled at their scene of family affection, then sighed. 'The stupid thing is that if Dad had simply said to Mum, "I'm down on my luck, is there any chance of you helping me?" she probably would have, no matter how weak a reed he's been. Hitting her with his sense of grievance and entitlement after abandoning her with a small baby, that's a mickey take.' Rosa shook her head. 'Only my dad could think *Mum* owes *him*.'

The conversation moved on to easier topics and then Zach took Paige off for a bath before dinner, agreeing solemnly with her request that he brush her hair with 'ditioner so it didn't hurt.

Rosa listened to their voices disappearing up the stairs, smiling when she heard Zach reassuring his niece that he would use the whole bottle of 'ditioner if necessary. He was so sweet an uncle that she had to remind herself he was the same man who'd written the erotic scene she'd managed to read so little of.

But she did catch herself wondering where the scene would have gone next if she'd carried on.

Chapter Twelve

Paige had been in bed for a couple of hours – after another go at getting Zach to let her keep the ring she'd found. Now she was finally asleep, Zach, still on babysitting duty, lay on the sofa in front of a TV action movie but his mind was on Rosa. When he'd entered the shady garden this afternoon shock had juddered through him to see her staring at his laptop. He'd known what was on the screen.

His mortification would have been greater if Rosa hadn't looked so caught up in what she was reading. He'd forgotten to move as he watched her lips part, colour delicately flushing her cheeks, her eyes moving over the lines. She'd looked so guilty when she'd realised she was being observed. He wondered how far she'd read.

And, oh, her body sliding over his when they'd gently collided in the sea . . .

He was still trying to concentrate on the car chase on the TV when his sister came home. He looked up. 'Hi.'

Marci's hair, which had been whisked up in a clasp behind her head when she'd left, now tumbled dark and loose around her shoulders. She half-smiled. 'Hi. Has Paige been OK?' She dropped into an armchair and turned her face towards the TV.

Zach didn't like her lack of animation. Lately she'd regained a little of the sparkle she used to have and losing it again wasn't a positive thing. Rather than ask questions, he told her about the ring Paige found. 'I haven't done anything about it because you're Paige's mother and she found the ring so I think it's your decision.'

'But what do you think?' she asked tonelessly.

It seemed straightforward to him. 'That we should hand it in to the police. It looks valuable and someone may be heartbroken at losing it. Maybe local jewellers might have ideas of the worth then we could get a receipt from the police. I read online that it's a good idea to have proof of exactly what you're handing in. Flaviu says there's a Ta' Xbiex Facebook group where we could post a lost property notice too.'

'Good.' She nodded. 'Thanks. That would be perfect.' Her eyes strayed to the TV screen where a young cop was shooting baddies with his handgun while baddies armed with much bigger weapons were failing woefully to shoot him.

Zach hadn't actually thought he'd take the lead on dealing with the 'treasure' but he didn't mind doing so. He'd been the one with Paige when it was found. 'Paige is narked at not being allowed to keep the ring.' He repeated his Bilbo Baggins remark. Marci smiled faintly and nodded.

Concerned at her lifelessness he asked casually, 'What have you been up to?'

'I've had a shag,' she said, equally casually. 'It was . . .' She made a "so-so" movement of her hand.

A small shockwave rippled through Zach. He didn't ever remember having a conversation with Marci about her sex life other than as it pertained to getting accidentally pregnant and she was definitely not wearing the glow that followed a wonderful encounter. 'Someone you just met?' he asked carefully, feeling that if Marci was telling him then she was telling him for a reason.

'Jake.'

'From the reunion? The man you went out to lunch with and he offended you?' he clarified, astonished.

She hunched a shoulder defensively. 'He rang to apologise again about the backbone comment. I realised I'd overreacted. He invited me out and I went.' She paused to watch a car slide sideways beneath a lorry on TV, then added, 'We went back to his hotel.'

'Right.' Alarm bells were ringing in Zach's head. OK, Marci had been wilting since her new boss arrived and proved totally unsympathetic to the strains associated with being a working single parent but this listlessness was worrying.

'Seeing him again?' he asked conversationally.

'Doubt it,' she replied in the same colourless voice. 'He leaves the island tomorrow. He was here working with a bank for six months, which is what allowed him to attend the reunion with his dad. Now the system he came to implement is up and running he's returning to the UK.'

'How do you feel about that?' he asked.

She shrugged.

While Marci watched cars exploding, putting paid to the baddies inside while the good guy managed to scrape through the carnage on his motorbike with barely a beautiful lock of hair out of place, Zach wrestled with his thoughts.

He'd read about casual sex being a sign of low self-esteem in women and thought it had indicated a shocking imbalance in perceptions. Surely adult females had as much right as males to feel horny and satisfy their horniness, even if they weren't in a committed relationship? But studying Marci's empty expression now and observing her over the past year, the self-esteem theory could definitely be applied tonight. He wanted to ask whether this was usual behaviour for her but knew he'd brush her off like a mosquito if their positions were reversed and she questioned his sex life.

Instead, he asked tentatively, 'How are you doing, Marci? Over the last year I feel as if I've missed something vital. Is there more going on than I know about?'

Marci stared at the TV, her dark eyes big and blank. Then, slowly, her face began to sag, her lip to tremble. Her hand flew to her mouth but it wasn't enough to suppress a big, wrenching sob.

'Marci?' Zach scrambled from the sofa to crouch beside her chair. 'What's wrong? What can I do?'

'N-nothing,' she wailed. 'Nobody can do anything. I'm just unhap-happy.'

Worry slithering like a snake in his guts he slid an arm along her shoulders. 'Want to tell me?' A horrible thought assailed him and he realised he had to voice it. 'Jake – it was consensual, right?'

She nodded, sniffing, burrowing in her bag for a tissue. 'Of course. In fact, it was my idea.' She began to cry harder and suddenly a story burst out of her in snatches and gasps. 'Last year I had an affair with a colleague. I didn't tell anybody because he was married. It was so all-encompassing that I ignored the moral issue. I felt that if his wife couldn't keep such a wonderful man she must be an awful woman.' She gulped, blowing her nose for the tenth time. 'That wasn't true, of course. She was perfectly nice. On his birthday, she turned up at work to surprise him with dinner out and tickets to a show he'd wanted to see. Her face! It glowed with love for him as she chattered about who was babysitting so she could give him this treat.'

Marci snorted into her tissue, heaving in the breath she needed to carry on. 'I could see he was trying to hurry her off. I *hated* myself. We'd been talking about a future. I was so stupidly infatuated that I'd tried not to think of his family.'

Wordlessly, thoughts spinning, Zach got up and fetched her a glass of cold water from the kitchen and watched her gulp thirstily. Marci embarking on a wild affair with someone else's husband? She hadn't had good luck with men but he would never before have put that down to her, the calmer and more staid of his sisters, choosing behaviour likely to invite disaster.

Finally, she gathered herself. 'It was Niall, my old boss.' Her breathing steadied as she sipped the water, clutching the soggy tissue in her other hand. 'Then he gave in his notice. I'd been going to tell him I was pregnant,' she confessed dully.

Zach heard a noise come out of his throat: a combined gasp of shock and groan of dismay.

'Yeah.' She pulled a wry face. 'I never told him. Didn't have to, because I miscarried. I lost our child. I felt as if wa-was judgement on m-me.' Her mouth squared off on a new sob. 'I never told you or Electra because I didn't want you to f-feel you had to k-keep my secret. Obviously, I didn't want Dad to know. Be judged by him again. And I was ashamed.'

Aching for her, Zach gave her a hug. 'So the depression and anxiety wasn't about your new boss's unsympathetic management style at all?'

171

She shook her head. 'The old one's faithlessness. I took a week's holiday after the miscarriage, stayed with a friend. You know Mallory from uni? She was on maternity leave so she looked after Paige while I rested.' She gave a long drawn-out sniff. 'Everyone could see I didn't get on with my new boss so it was assumed he was the source of my anxiety. HR was good about me being off with stress but when I came here I had to take it as holiday.'

'Holiday?' Zach tried to count up in his head. 'But you've been here about six weeks. How much holiday do you get?'

'Four,' she admitted dolefully. 'HR rang when I didn't turn up back to work and I said I hadn't been able to face booking a flight home. They asked me to see a doctor here so I did, and got a new sick note. I'm back on paid sick leave. Occupational Health has rung too and we've talked through how they can help me and I've agreed to keep them informed. The lady was super-nice and obviously wanted to help but I couldn't wait to get her off the phone because the only way my company can help me is by continuing to pay me for an admin job I'm not doing. That can't last forever.' She laughed a bitter, brittle laugh.

'I'm sorry you went through all that.' Zach's heart ached, remembering how Marci had been pursuing a job as a travel rep until she fell pregnant with Paige. She'd wanted to leave behind the routine nine-to-five and work in different countries, undeterred by the long, unsociable hours involved. Once pregnant, frowns had become her most common accessory to her business suits as, post maternity leave, she prioritised a safe job with hours that worked best with parental responsibilities. Maybe because her adoration of Paige was so evident he hadn't given

172

much thought to how she'd felt about sacrificing her early dreams. He wished he'd thought more about Marci the person than Marci the mum.

Then she said what he'd been half-expecting since he'd realised she'd scoped out schools. 'I might stay here.'

He made his voice as soft as possible. 'But what would you do for money?'

'If Nanna's OK with me staying without paying rent for a bit I can live on my savings and child support in the short term.' She waved a tired hand and shut her eyes. 'Then get another job. Stay. Like you.'

'Sure,' he said automatically, thinking through possible snags. Their grandmother had decreed the apartment was 'for the family' but she couldn't be expected to stand all the costs while they were there rent-free. He'd been covering the utilities without demanding a contribution from his sister and in the short term could continue to do so but it wasn't a long-term solution. He thought about the crossroads of life he and Rosa had talked about. His had just got a whole lot hazier. 'There aren't many jobs in winter.'

'I'll cross that bridge when I come to it.'

He thought harder. 'Who will look after Paige? I can help sometimes but I have to work too.' He didn't add: 'And I want the freedom to leave.'

'Got to be childminders and nurseries here same as anywhere.' Wearily, Marci rested her head on her hand. 'I've browsed jobsinmalta.com a couple of times but I really haven't made any decisions,' she added, as if her uncertainty wasn't already abundantly clear.

They lapsed into silence. Finally, Zach asked, 'How much sick leave do you get?'

'Three months full pay, three months half.'

173

'Generous package.' He tried not to let his relief show that she was OK for now. 'Paige has a place in a school at home, doesn't she? If you decide to get her in a school here in September, how—'

'I've got her a provisional place here too,' she interrupted. 'She'd learn Maltese as well as English but she wouldn't be as at sea with Maltese as I'd expected because there are a lot of Maltese children in this area who learn English first and Maltese only from the age of five.'

'You've done this without telling anyone?' He could hear astonishment in his voice.

'Seems so.' Marci didn't sound as if she took any satisfaction from having covered her bases. 'Funny how all of us are floating about not achieving much,' she mused. 'I'm off sick. You're freelancing at a job you hate. Electra's treading water teaching English in Bangkok.' She sighed. 'That makes me sound like Dad but we are all underachieving.'

Zach had returned to the sofa now but perched on the edge as if ready to jump up and combat the next chunk of negative news that came along. 'Regardless of your career situation, I think you're doing a good job as a lone parent under difficult circumstances. Paige is a happy little girl – unless she finds a diamond ring and you won't let her keep it – and Electra and I don't need to be scaling corporate ladders to be living productive lives. I've had more satisfaction out of painting Nanna's walls and fitting the kitchens and bathrooms than I ever did out of crunching numbers. The paycheque was the main pleasure in my job.'

'Maybe,' Marci said, looking a degree less desolate. 'Have you heard much from Electra recently?'

'We've chatted by text and email but she claims to have

been too busy to schedule actual conversation.' He took out his phone and opened his messages. 'I'll suggest it again now. I don't want to ring her because of her classes.' Zach pictured his little sister with her short hair and endless energy as he texted. *How's everything with you? Marci and I want to find a time to chat on phone. Can we do it soon?* Bangkok was five hours ahead of Malta so it would be past two in the morning. He half-thought energetic, free-spirited Electra might still be up, but she didn't reply.

'Has Mum mentioned her to you recently?' he asked Marci as he pocketed his phone.

'Only the usual stuff: wondering if she'll ever go back to the UK.' She smiled faintly.

Zach rubbed his chin. 'Maybe we should feel guilty that none of us is currently living in Cornwall near Mum and Dad.'

Marci's head tipped back tiredly. 'It's not that we don't want to be near Mum . . .'

'No.' Zach didn't need reminding. 'I think she gets how we find Dad difficult.' Zach made a mental note to have a FaceTime session with his mum tomorrow. He stretched and yawned. 'It's nearly two years since I've seen Electra. Maybe I ought to go to Thailand for a couple of weeks and check all's OK in her world. Or, if you wanted to go,' he added tentatively, 'I could keep Paige here. It would give you a nice period of time to yourself.'

Marci closed her eyes and groaned. 'I couldn't face the journey. But thank you. You're a good brother.' She tried to smile. 'Maybe I need to up my pills. The Maltese doctor renewed my prescription for mild antidepressants.'

'Maybe,' he agreed. A happier life would be a better cure, in his opinion, but he didn't know where to get the prescription for that.

When Marci had blown her fast-reddening nose a couple more times she said she was going to look in on Paige and then read in bed. He gave her a quick hug.

The TV film had ended and the next programme was a British sitcom he had no trouble turning off. It was past ten o'clock. He thought about going on the Nicholas Centre staff WhatsApp group to see if anyone fancied a drink. Or he could text Rosa to suggest a glass of wine. They could go to the jazz bar under the arches where Flaviu worked. He imagined laughing and chatting with her, listening to the music on the warm air. Maybe repeating that kiss, despite its potential for complications.

But he wasn't comfortable leaving the apartment tonight. If Marci got upset again he'd rather be around. He lay on the sofa and stared at the smooth white ceiling he'd painted himself, thinking. He had every sympathy with Marci shying away from going home to Redruth and having their dad point out her deficiencies: going nowhere and no significant other. They were the comments Steve made about him too.

Bringing up Paige might be the best and most important job there was but he was pretty sure Marci was lonely as hell. He wished the last person she'd fallen for hadn't been a git-faced married man. Would things have been better or worse if she hadn't miscarried the married man's child?

He could've had another niece or nephew by now. Marci would have had another child. No wonder she was grieving.

Chapter Thirteen

Rosa began Wednesday morning in a good mood, reading over breakfast on the terrace in her most comfortable shorts. Dory hadn't come home last night, as she'd hinted might be the case, and Rosa couldn't deny she enjoyed having the apartment to herself. If Dory really did return to the UK for a week then Rosa could look forward to more of this guilt-free liberty and this afternoon there was the dance session at Nicholas Centre to look forward to.

After breakfast, she put on her headphones and listened to music while she deadheaded and watered the nodding red geraniums on the terrace. As she worked, 'The Shape of You' came on and she began to dance her way around the terracotta pots.

Carried away by the sensuous moves, she twisted on the spot and zigzagged her hands down her torso.

Delighted giggles burst onto the air behind her.

Rosa snatched off her headphones and whirled around to find Paige laughing and clapping. 'You were dancing! You were good.'

Zach, standing behind Paige, wore a broad grin and a

decided gleam in his eyes. 'Most . . . arresting,' he confirmed.

'I want to dance too! Please can we?' Paige jumped on her tippy toes.

'I could teach you an easy one, but maybe it wouldn't work with Uncle Zach's plans.' Rosa tried to sound as if she wasn't discomposed by being found grinding to an Ed Sheeran song.

'Mummy's got a headache and Uncle Zach's looking after me,' Paige declared, as if that settled matters.

Zach met Rosa's eyes over Paige's head. 'Maybe for five minutes?' Then, to his niece, 'We do have stuff to do this morning, Sunshine.'

Paige nodded absently, focused on Rosa disconnecting her headphones so the music poured from her iPad.

'OK,' she said, taking Paige's hand. 'We're going to go side-side to the right – no, this way's right – then side-side, left. And we're going to clap. Side-side, clap! Side-side, clap! Then forward, back, forward, back, while we wiggle our shoulders. Let's try that.'

The strings and piano introduction to a Celine Dion number began. Rosa nodded along, trying to concentrate on where she was meant to come in rather than on Zach's interested gaze as he stood back to watch. She suddenly had a better idea. 'I think Uncle Zach ought to dance too, don't you?'

'YEAH!' Paige shouted, jumping up and down.

'Not me.' Zach folded his arms.

'Aw, c'mon, Zachary!' Paige cried, running over to him and trying to pull him along by his belt loops. 'It'll be fun.'

Zach pulled a long-suffering face but, uncrossing his arms, took up station so that Rosa was in the middle. She started the music again. 'Ready?' She tried not to react to

Zach being so close but his warmth felt as if it was all over her. 'Aaand . . . step-step, clap. Step-step – no, other way – step-step, clap, step-step, clap. Yes, you've got it! Well done, Paige.'

'I've got it too,' Zach pointed out, pretending to pout at not getting his praise.

'Well done, Zachary,' she said solemnly. As he step-stepped he managed to edge up so he could slide an arm around her waist, his body moving with hers. He'd obviously not been born with two left feet.

Breathless that he was touching her Rosa said, 'Now wiggle-wiggle, clap-clap and forward, back, forward, back – wiggle-wiggle, clap-clap and other foot forward, back, forward, back.'

Paige didn't get her change of direction but Zach did, though his wiggling was more like thrusting.

'That's not right,' Paige told him loftily. 'Your bum should go side-side not front-back.'

They performed the dance right through twice, giggling and wiggling, then Zach glanced at his watch and stepped out of the chorus line. 'Sorry, ladies. Paige and I have to call a halt there.'

'Awwww . . .' Paige began, her small, finely marked eyebrows curling ominously over her snub nose.

''Fraid so.' Zach was evidently unmoved by stormy expressions from a four-year-old. 'We came down to ask Rosa a favour and then we're going to talk to Granny on Skype, aren't we?'

'Yeah!' Paige's face cleared. 'Rosa, we're going to talk to Granny on Zachary's computer. We're going to tell her everything we're doing here in Malta.'

She was so obviously repeating what she'd already been told, complete with the intonation of an adult telling a child she was in for a treat, that Rosa felt like picking Paige up and hugging her. 'Sounds fantastic,' she said, stroking Paige's hair, hot from the sun. 'So, what's the favour?'

Zach pushed back his hair, disarranged by the dancing. 'You talked once about taking photos on an iPhone. I'd like to take some of the ring Paige found, including the hallmark, before I take it into the police this afternoon and post pics on the local Facebook group but I can't work out how to do the extreme close-ups without blurring. I follow the instructions I found online but it doesn't work.'

'I don't want to take it to the police.' Paige pouted.

Zach smiled down at her. 'I know. But it's the right thing to do.'

Rosa took out her phone. 'Of course. There's a macro function.' She showed him the setting. 'My halo gives an even light that's great for detail.' She led them into the kitchen and quickly affixed the light to the tripod. 'The dark worktop gives a nice plain background.'

Rosa demonstrated how to get the image in focus then tap on it so it locked and they could close in on the target. They got good images of the hallmark and ring itself, their heads close together as they viewed the phone screen. Zach smelled of shower gel and sunshine.

Pleased, he enlarged the image to check the detail. 'I was hoping to take it to a jeweller this morning to get it documented before handing it over to the police but I'm not sure I'll have time. I hadn't expected to have Paige with me.'

Rosa tried to help. 'I could keep Paige with me, if that works.'

'No!' Paige shouted, not very politely. 'I want to speak to Granny!'

'Hey, hey,' said Zach, mildly but reprovingly. 'That's not how we talk to each other, is it?'

Paige looked down at her feet so Rosa came up with a new offer. 'How about I get the ring valued? I'm going to Sliema for groceries. I could pop into a jeweller's shop.'

His expression lightened. 'If you don't mind, that would be great. And thanks for the other offer, too.' He lowered his voice to not much more than a breath, moving in close so she could catch his words, the fresh shower-gel smell making the back of her neck prickle. 'Marci's feeling down and I think Paige is picking up on it. When Marci asked me to look after Paige this morning Paige looked so sad. She said to me, "Sometimes my tummy wizzles." I'm not sure how a wizzling tummy feels but I'm guessing it's a nervous thing.' He looked abashed. 'Sorry, you didn't ask to hear all that.'

She instinctively put her hand on his arm. 'Don't apologise. It's great that you're there for your sister and niece.' She only realised that her hand was stroking his forearm when he glanced down at it.

Before she could put a little more distance between them Paige demanded, 'Why are you touching? Are you going to kiss?'

Zach laughed and asked, 'Do you think we should?' The light in his eyes chased away the sombreness of a moment ago.

'Yuck, no,' said Paige. 'Can we talk to Granny now? I want to show her my shnorkel.'

So Zach and Paige headed for their own apartment and Rosa drove into Sliema and approached a jeweller's shop. There were several in Bisazza Street and she chose one at random. The jeweller, when he came out from the cool recesses of the small, traditional-looking shop, was interested in Paige's find, studying the ring carefully through his eyepiece. Rosa explained that it had to be handed in to the police and she needed a valuation for receipt purposes.

The jeweller made a disappointed shape with his mouth. 'To give you a proper valuation I would like to keep the ring and do some research. If you take it away today I can be only approximate.'

'Approximate's fine,' Rosa assured him. And what the man told her made her breathing pause, before placing the ring very carefully back in her bag and taking care to zip the compartment right up before heading for the supermarket.

Dory still wasn't back when Rosa arrived home. She only took the time to put the frozen food away before taking the stairs to the upper apartment. The front door stood open to the breeze so she knocked on it and shouted, 'Hello?'

Zach popped his head into the hall. 'We're in the kitchen. Come on in.'

She followed him. The apartment was the same layout to the one downstairs but with marble floor tiles and ornate light fittings. Once she stepped into the kitchen, she found Paige seated at the table, swinging her feet, eating toast fingers and watching a children's TV programme. 'I was hungry,' she said, shooting Rosa a quick smile and then returning her attention to the screen.

'I wanted to give you this straight back.' Rosa fished the ring out of her bag and placed it firmly in Zach's hand. 'The jeweller says it's a fine piece, Italian, and someone is probably unhappy to have lost it. It's had very little wear and he feels it was purchased in the last ten years.' She paused for breath. 'He thinks it would have cost seven to ten thousand euros and should be insured for ten.'

182

Zach's gaze flicked to her eyes, making her realise he'd been watching her mouth. *'Ten thousand euros?'* he repeated.

'It's a lovely diamond, apparently. It's quite large, isn't it? I can't imagine anyone wearing a rock like that but I'm sure the jeweller knows his stuff.'

'I'll take it to the police after we've been to Nicholas Centre this afternoon.' Zach took out his wallet and slipped the ring into a small compartment.

Rosa took a step towards the door. 'I'll see you at two, shall I, ready for the dance session at Nicholas Centre?'

'That will give us plenty of time,' he confirmed. 'Thanks for getting the valuation, even if it almost stunned me into silence.' He touched her arm and she went back downstairs with her skin tingling.

While she put away the rest of the shopping and prepared her lunch her mind strayed back to Zach. His focused gaze, the squareness of his jaw, the softness of his lips when they'd shared that kiss on the roof. Searching, exploring, sensuous lips that had left her wanting more. She was sure he'd thought about kissing her again, just now. His gaze had been fixed so hungrily on her and she'd swear he'd begun to sway towards her.

It had left her with a funny feeling. Maybe she had 'wizzles' in her tummy like Paige.

She ate lunch on the terrace – she was definitely into the outdoor dining thing in Malta – when her phone, which she'd left in the kitchen, began to ring. It was the ringtone she'd assigned to Marcus.

Groaning aloud, she went in and answered.

'Hello!' Marcus sounded more cheerful and friendly than he had for some time. 'How are you? How's Malta treating you? Is your mum OK? I bet she's enjoying it too.'

'Fine thanks and we like it here,' she said politely, glancing at the clock on the cooker. 'Is there a problem? Only I'm going out at two and I have to get ready so it's not a good time for a long call.'

He laughed, as if she'd said something funny, and her antennae went up. Sometimes when Marcus had a tricky conversation ahead he assumed a false bonhomie as if inviting you to share a rueful joke at the way things had turned out. 'Won't be long,' he said, still with the faux joviality setting on 'high'.

Silently, Rosa waited.

Marcus cleared his throat. 'Have you had a notice from the mortgage company?'

She was puzzled. 'What kind of notice? All the paperwork's been done for you taking over the mortgage, hasn't it? Unless you mean notice that the process is complete and I'm off the mortgage? No, I haven't had that.'

'No.' The laughter left Marcus's voice. 'I'm afraid there's a blip.'

A sigh came to Rosa's lips. She'd forgotten how annoying Marcus could be when he didn't want to tell you something, as if the problem would go away if he strung out the explanation long enough. 'What blip?'

Silence. Then he said, 'I didn't make this month's mortgage payment.'

A longer silence, while Rosa struggled to digest this. Finally, she managed, 'Why not?'

This time the silence went on so long that Rosa began to think he'd ended the call. Then his voice came again, stiffly apologetic. 'It's as you suspected once before.'

Bewildered, she snapped, 'I want to put my arm down the telephone and drag the truth out of you. What are you talking about?'

184

A sigh. 'I don't have the money. It's gone.'

Realisation dawned with a sick certainty. 'You've gambled it away again.' Her voice came out dead and dull.

'Yes.'

'And the mortgage formalities aren't complete.'

'No.'

Her breath actually hurt her throat when she drew it in. 'So they can come to me for the payment.'

'I thought if you paid this last one then it would allow the changeover to go through. If not—' he sounded as if he were swallowing hard '—we're both in default.'

'You fucker,' she said quietly. Then, as he seemed to have no reply to that, 'Ask Chellice to cover it.'

'She says her name's not on the mortgage. She's paid her rent and . . .' He tailed off, clearing his throat.

'And you've gambled that away too?' Rage filled Rosa, so hot she shook. 'I'll have to contact my solicitor for advice and come back to you.' She ended the call with shaking fingers. Marcus should have had tens of thousands left of his big win. How could he have lost so much? Did he gamble night and day now? Though she'd been hurt when their relationship ended she was glad it had. He'd grumbled about what he called her trust issues but look how untrustworthy he'd become.

It took her half an hour of trying to find someone at her solicitor's office who was not at lunch and had some idea of what she was talking about. When she got through to a woman called Jeanine she explained Marcus's call.

'Hmmph,' said Jeanine. 'That's not very helpful of him, is it?' Then she talked Rosa through the situation, which was as she'd thought. She'd have to make the payment or she would, indeed, be in default. The liability was 'joint

185

and several', which meant each individual was liable for the whole. The mortgage provider had no interest in Marcus having promised Rosa he'd take over payments. The mortgage was not yet in his sole name.

'Question mark over how he's going to make next month's payment?' Jeanine asked with what Rosa considered a little too much brisk efficiency.

'I'd guess so.' Rosa had to sit down on one of the kitchen stools. Her knees had turned to water.

'Let me see if I can get the remortgage formalities through before the next payment's due then,' Jeanine suggested, lifting herself considerably in Rosa's estimation.

'Oh, yes, please!' Rosa breathed, feeling better.

'Leave it with me,' said Jeanine.

Although she felt a rising sense of injustice, Rosa had little choice but to make the payment online. Then she scarcely had time to jump into the shower and into a summer dress, blue with a swirly hem, before Zach and Paige were at her door, Paige going into 'report' mode the instant she saw Rosa. 'Mummy's got to talk to a lady on the phone so she's going to meet us there. Is Dory coming?'

'I think she's out with her friend Leslie,' Rosa said, trying to hide her worries with a smile.

'Then can we go in your car so Mummy can use Zachary's car, please?' Paige asked, doing her boinging-about-on-her-toes thing as if Rosa's reply was of the utmost importance.

Zach gave Rosa a smile. 'What she said.'

'Of course. It would be a long walk to Nicholas Centre for your little legs, Paige.' Rosa picked up her mum's car keys, hoping Dory wouldn't turn up and want them, and they clattered down the stairs to the street. Zach moved the child seat from his car to Dory's, then, when he'd got

Paige strapped in, eased himself into the passenger seat, having to duck his head in order to accommodate his height.

The movement gave Rosa a good look at his rear view, neatly encased in a pair of cream shorts. His T-shirt was grey-blue. She was glad she'd scraped time for a shower even if bloody Marcus had screwed up time for make-up.

Zach sat beside her, relaxed, reminding her that their best route was along the seafront road and then left into the heart of the residential area of Gzira. 'You OK? You seem tense,' he murmured, once they'd set off.

She managed a smile but whispered, 'Marcus is playing silly beggars about the mortgage. It wound me up.'

He nodded and frowned but didn't enquire further.

They arrived in time to help set out the seating in the centre's big room upstairs, leaving half the floor free. The dance instructor, Victor, was a small, neat man of about thirty. He spoke English with only a slight accent, much like Joseph. His black trousers were the skinniest of skinnies and his gold top was almost a muscle vest. He also wore proper dance sneakers, like Rosa had in the UK.

Paige wanted to sit in the front row so they took places right in the middle. Youngsters began wandering in. Victor chatted in both Maltese and English. Rosa got the impression that he was known to some of the teens, especially when he was asked to demonstrate a couple of street dance moves. For her, those few steps proved his credentials as a dancer in fluid control of his body.

Finally, Joseph quieted everyone down and introduced Victor, who began to talk about the benefits of dance for exercise, fun and social events. He mentioned his competition successes and his studio in Msida. He ran through a few steps of various types of dance – 'But don't ask me to do ballet!' The teens laughed but he went on more seriously to explain how strong ballet dancers had to be and their 'crazy' flexibility.

Then he opened his arms in a welcoming gesture. 'Who can dance?'

From beside Rosa a small person erupted from her seat and shouted, 'Rosa can! Rosa can!'

Rosa laughed, expecting lots of people to have their hands in the air and for Victor to be beckoning them all onto the dance floor.

Instead, she realised with a sinking feeling, Victor was heading straight for her.

Zach watched as Victor led Rosa, blushing, into the middle of the dance floor. The way his eyes moved over her left Zach in little doubt that Victor was well pleased with his 'volunteer' as he joked that, despite the politically correct times, in dance it was still acceptable for the man to lead.

'For Latin dances,' he went on, 'we make a frame, create distance between us so we can move. We hold our arms forward.' He matched his actions to his words then batted his eyelids. 'We gaze into each other's eyes.'

The audience bellowed with laughter. Rosa looked self-conscious but accepted his hand beneath her shoulder, her arm along his, their other hands clasped.

Addressing the audience as if Rosa couldn't hear, Victor added with a wink, 'Of course if she was really trying she would hook her leg around my waist.'

Rosa's leg flew out with the speed of a striking snake and hooked itself over his hip. The hem of her duck-egg blue dress slithered upwards.

Victor's head shot round as he stared at her. Everyone

laughed. Paige clapped and laughed louder than anyone. Zach watched, understanding that Rosa probably just wanted to interrupt Victor's smarmy spiel by having a little joke at his expense but, still . . . wanting it to stop. Zach wanted that leg around his waist. Both of her legs would be even better.

Instead, he had to watch while Rosa returned her leg to its usual position and the polished Victor demonstrated simple Latin steps, forward, back, cha-cha-cha, back, forward, cha-cha-cha.

He released Rosa for a moment saying, 'Now, you should each choose a partner and try the same.' Zach murmured to Paige, 'Sit still, Sunshine,' and in a second had whisked Rosa away, making her give a squeak of surprise. Victor looked startled but, outmanoeuvred, set the music playing again and they and several other couples began the steps to the sultry Latin beat. Rosa's hand lay in Zach's, as warm as sunlight, and the other splayed over her shoulder blade. It made him want to pull her against him, bury his face in her hair and dance in a way that was altogether less for public consumption.

'Hey, Zachary! What about me?' an indignant little voice said beside him.

Rosa made to give way to Paige but Joseph came up and swept the four-year-old smoothly from her feet and twirled her off chanting solemnly, 'Forward, back, cha-cha-cha, little cousin,' while Paige squealed gleefully.

Rosa dipped her chin and put a curve in the small of her back then wheeled Zach around in a circle, her gaze locked with his. Obviously she hadn't taken on board the part about the man leading but wherever she wanted to lead him, Zach was there for this hot, earthy woman who'd got under his defences and, he was beginning to

189

suspect, was edging her way into his heart – a shock, given his track record with women.

When the dance ended they broke apart, as did the other couples. Zach gazed down into her sparkling eyes. 'You look as if you had fun.'

Rosa almost glowed. 'I did.'

Joseph appeared, puffing slightly, Paige hanging around his neck. 'Rosa, you dance well! We almost had no need for Victor. I think you could have led us.' He handed Paige back to Zach.

'I would love that but though I went to dance classes when I was a kid, now I just do Zumba. And I don't have certification or insurance to teach,' Rosa added, running her fingers through her hair to settle it after her exertions. A thoughtful look stole over her face, her brows curling slightly as she murmured almost to herself, 'But I could ask Mum to put me through my dance instructor training when I get back to the UK. It *could* be my new career.' Then realising Zach was listening, 'Does it sound mad?'

Something inside Zach flinched at her casual indication that she wouldn't be here forever but he answered, 'No, I think you'd be brilliant.'

Pleasure flashed across her face. In the Maltese sunshine she'd developed freckles that dusted her cheeks. 'I could maybe work at Blackthorn's part-time and dance part-time.'

In answer to Paige's insistent tugging, Zach bought them all Fanta from a stall manned by Maria and two teenagers. Zach made sure Paige had a good grip on her plastic bottle and popped a straw in the top for her. While she slurped like a broken drain, he listened to Rosa talk about becoming a dance instructor, her words tumbling over themselves as she explored her new idea. Infected by her enthusiasm he

190

felt a yearning to come up with a plan for his own life, to feel as she looked: brimming with excitement.

'It's so obvious,' she bubbled. 'I have no idea why I didn't think of it before! I literally could fill my life with dancing. I could take classes and join a drama group that puts on musicals and help with the choreography, be in the chorus line.'

'Where would you do all this?' he asked, because his feelings for her were too new and delicate for him to risk asking directly whether he could fit into her plans too.

Before she could answer, Joseph came up, still breathing hard from the dancing.

'Zach, could you do me a favour?' Joseph wiped a fine sheen of sweat from his brow. Nicholas Centre had no air conditioning. 'There are two bottles of wine in my office. They're a thank you to Victor. Would you mind running down for them while I stay with our guest?'

'Sure.' As a volunteer at Nicholas Centre Zach was used to making himself useful. He patted Paige's head. 'You stay with Rosa. I'll be back in a moment.'

Paige wasn't convinced. 'I could come with you to check you're OK.'

He laughed, crouching down to kiss her forehead. 'But then what about Rosa? Who will check she's OK? Here, you look after my Fanta and you and Rosa look after each other. I'll be quicker on my own.'

He was still grinning as he jogged downstairs to Joseph's office. There, he found the bottles of wine on the desk.

But most of the desk drawers, which were usually locked, standing open.

Chapter Fourteen

Zach gaped at the disordered desk.

'What the hell?' he said aloud.

Then suddenly a man lunged out of the gap between the door and the wall. 'Hey—!' Zach began but swallowed the exclamation as he was efficiently yanked round and stuffed into the space the man had come from.

He grunted as the door slammed into him, pinning him face first against the wall, the handle grinding painfully into his ribs. Someone began to fumble with the zipped pocket of his shorts. Cheek mashed against the cool plaster he tried to wriggle, to kick, to shove back, but in answer the door was slammed into him several times, beating the air out of him. Gasping as the pressure of the door slammed once more against his back he heard the sound of a zip, a tug at his pocket.

Then the pressure was relieved.

Dazed, he tried to drag air into his lungs, to shout, to pivot on his heel and confront his attacker. What he actually managed was to wheeze and stagger. Then he heard the door shut and the key turn.

'Fuck!' he gasped, massaging his elbow, which had taken a punishing knock. As his lungs inflated, he discovered that the hand that had been fumbling in his pocket had got away with his wallet but left his phone. It seemed pointless to try the door but he rattled the handle anyway, then, still panting for breath, telephoned Joseph.

After he was released from the room a couple of minutes later it was discovered that the secure cabinet on the kitchen wall, which held all spare keys, had been prised open, explaining how the desk drawers had come to be unlocked. The thief had obviously known where to look as the petty cash was missing. Joseph declared the centre closed for the day. Zach called Marci at the apartment to collect Paige as he felt the little girl would be better at home with her mum than listening while he went into the details of being attacked. Before long the police arrived – Joseph hadn't hesitated over calling them this time. The crime was clear-cut and not to be tolerated. Zach, battered and bruised, could feel his elbow pulsing more or less in time with his temper.

Rosa's earlier sparkle had been replaced by big-eyed apprehension. 'You're hurt,' she breathed.

'Just bruised,' he replied grimly but he was glad enough of the bag of ice she fetched from the kitchen for him to press against his arm.

An interview with the police followed, Joseph sitting down with them, frowning blackly. Maria and Rosa hovered in the background while others cleared the chairs away upstairs with much bumping and clattering. Joseph spoke of the petty thefts those connected with the centre had been experiencing. Zach gave an account of today's attack. The police officers, both male, asked about the contents of Zach's wallet.

'I'd just got a hundred euros out of the ATM,' he

groused. 'This is getting beyond a joke.' He and Joseph exchanged glances. The officers hadn't asked if they had any reason to suspect a particular person for the thefts. Zach was scared it was Luccio, scared the young man was going to end up in trouble with the police. And yet . . . was it better for him to learn a sharp lesson now, if indeed he was the thief, rather than get in deeper and deeper with the wrong crowd? Zach had decided to leave that decision to Joseph when he was assailed by a horrible thought.

'Shit. I had a valuable ring in my wallet!' Briefly, he outlined how the ring had come into his possession.

Joseph sucked in his breath. 'Why would you bring something like that here?'

'I was going to take it to the police station afterwards,' he responded testily. Then he had to endure the officers asking whether the ring was insured, making him wonder whether they suspected the whole thing of being a put-up job so that Zach could make a false claim. As the ring wasn't insured by him, at least, this point quickly passed.

Zach hadn't seen his attacker but concluded from the size, shape and strength that the person was male. It gave the police little to go on. Joseph didn't mention Luccio's name so neither did Zach. While his earlier brushes with the police had been entirely his own fault he was glad when they left.

Joseph was obviously upset. 'Zach, should you go to hospital?'

Zach shook his head. 'It's just a bruise. Sorry about the ring,' he added, knowing that the theft of that had complicated things.

Sadly, Joseph shook his head. 'How could you foresee?' He dug his hands moodily into his pockets, a cleft at the bridge of his nose. 'This is an uncomfortable episode.'

Zach agreed.

'When Luccio planted money on you he almost admitted his own guilt,' Joseph continued heavily. 'If you wish, I can telephone the officers and "remember" that. Say I was so troubled today that it skipped my mind.'

Zach rubbed his elbow. 'We don't *know* any of the thefts are down to him.'

'He hasn't been back to work, though I wrote to him.'

'He's a kid.' Zach knew what it felt like to be in trouble and still wished he could pull Luccio clear of the flames he was dancing with.

They said their farewells and Zach and Rosa went out to Dory's car, parked half on the pavement as was common in the narrow street.

'Good job Mum didn't want the car today. She's texted to say she's staying with Leslie. She'll come home tomorrow when he returns to the UK.' Rosa checked her mirrors and eased down the kerb. They didn't talk as she navigated her way to the seafront road, turning right to pass the formal flowerbeds, pine trees and palms of Gzira Gardens, and forking right at the 'Ir-Rampa' sign. She parked outside the basement garage doors and they trudged up to the lower terrace.

Zach was in no hurry to join Marci and Paige upstairs. Marci would be anxious and Paige bursting with questions. Rosa, on the other hand, was soothing. When she held open her apartment door invitingly, he stepped inside.

She fetched him more ice for his elbow and sat beside him on the sofa.

He sighed. 'I feel terrible about the ring. Whoever owns it could have had their valued possession returned.' He thought about joking that he should have had Rosa wear it but you didn't make jokes about putting a ring on a woman's finger.

'You didn't dob Luccio in,' she observed.

'I don't know who mugged me,' he replied. Then, when her eyebrows rose, insisted defensively, 'I don't.'

'I heard your conversation with Joseph,' she pointed out.

He slid down in his seat. 'Then you know we don't know it's him.'

She moved closer. 'How many chances does one young man get?'

He shrugged drearily. 'I've often wondered.'

She drew in her breath. 'That must have sounded as if I was talking about you. Sorry.'

'No problem.' They were silent for several seconds. It was beautifully cool in the apartment as the air con hummed. He noticed absently how comfortable the sofa was, a resilient smooth fabric in rust red and black leather. He'd chosen it for Nanna's holiday rental without thinking he'd ever occupy it.

Gently, she lifted his injured arm and kissed the red, swollen elbow. It was astonishingly erotic as he watched her hair slither forward, felt her warm lips brush his skin.

The coarse hair of his forearm prickled and stood on end. He became less conscious of the .pain. All he could think of were her eyes, her partly open mouth, her tongue tip as she licked her lips. Her slender body. Her delicate hands. He turned so he was facing her. 'You're beautiful,' he said, surprised to hear his voice coming out so hoarsely. 'I like looking at you. Like seeing you in the sun when your hair's down and your eyes are laughing. The sun makes you look golden. I like being in the same room as you. Watching you smile makes me happy.'

He saw her throat move as she swallowed but she didn't laugh or shut him down so he added, 'I like your body. A lot.' Still she said nothing. The silence made him nervous, doubtful. He forced a small laugh. 'Sorry. I'm being too direct. I like beautiful things.'

He made himself wait for her to reply, though the compulsion was to shove himself to his feet and mutter that she probably didn't want to hear all this and that he'd better go see if Marci was OK.

But then she breathed, 'Ohhhh. I don't quite . . . It's been so . . . Marcus . . .'

Heart sinking, he lifted a hand and touched her cheek. 'You're not over Marcus. I get it. I should have realised. I won't say any more.'

'I *am* over Marcus.' She slid her hand onto Zach's. All at once her eyes shone with tears. 'I'm not used to pretty words,' she whispered. 'Marcus . . . he wasn't that type.'

Spirits reviving abruptly, Zach leaned in and brushed a kiss on the end of her nose. 'He didn't tell you you're beautiful? The man's a moron. Or blind. But there must have been other men in your life.'

A tiny laugh shook through her. 'Not many. No one since Marcus.'

He slid his uninjured arm carefully around her. 'That can only have been your choice. Men look at you all the time.' He hoped they weren't going to get too deeply into sexual experience because his was definitely greater than she'd made hers sound. He brushed his lips against the crook of her neck and she shuddered with a tiny, sweet gasp that sent heat rocketing through him. He wanted to pull her down and go for it but bit down on the compulsion. If a woman shyly confided in you that she'd been choosy in her lovers, you didn't leap on her like a big randy dog.

At least, not the first time.

'I don't really know how this is going to go,' she whispered. But she tilted her head to give him access to her throat.

'There are no rules.' He nibbled his way up the side of her neck, inhaling the scent of lemons from her skin. 'I'm not expecting to go from kisses to an invitation into your bed.'

'Oh.' Her lips, warm and soft, inched along his jaw to his ear, making his skin shiver. Her fingers found their way to the back of his head, sliding into the short hair and caressing the sensitive hollow of his nape. Then her hot breath brushed his cheek as she moved her mouth to his. He felt as if she was hovering, exploring, deciding what to offer. Then her tongue tip slipped between his lips and desire flashed through him.

'But if I did invite you to my bed?' she gasped, when they came up for air.

'Yes,' he groaned, scraping one soft earlobe with his teeth. 'I'd say yes. Yes, please. Yes, let's. Ohhhh yesssss.'

A breathy giggle escaped her but then she pulled back to gaze into his face, searching his eyes. 'I don't want to be one of those women who talk about past men all the time but Marcus always thought he ought to be the one who set the pace. He used to say the man was "the engine".'

He snorted a laugh. 'What a prat.'

His reaction seemed to relax her. 'I would like to . . . make the running. A woman who takes things into her own hands.'

He strangled the urge to suggest exactly what he'd like her to take into her hands but amusement must have shown in his eyes because she snorted a laugh, then frowned severely. 'I didn't mean *that*.'

Nodding, he tried to compose his face into an expression that said, 'I know you didn't. I'm not laughing. I'm listening.'

Her golden eyes narrowed as if she wasn't buying it.

His amusement drained away. She really was the nicest, sweetest, least manipulative woman he'd met. Moron Marcus had made her unhappy so he could respect her wariness of men. He kissed one of her eyelids. 'I don't expect or assume or feel entitled.' He kissed the other, then the sweetness of her mouth, so she didn't construe his noble speech as 'not that bothered'.

A dimple appeared in her cheek. 'That's good. Thank you for respecting my feelings. Let's go to bed.' Then her eyes widened as if shocked to hear herself say it.

She laughed shakily, half inclined to retract when she saw heat flare in Zach's eyes. 'I said that out loud, didn't I?' She'd been telling herself not to get carried away by the shivers of desire chasing through her, not to rush, not to make herself vulnerable. She'd already let her inexperience show. Amazing she hadn't blurted out her entire sex CV: *My first wasn't till I was eighteen because I was scared about condom failure. His name was Flynn and he was almost as clueless as me. The next was a blazingly confident Dutch guy I met on holiday, Andert. He scared me by saying he was up for anything and setting out to prove the words 'curious' and 'explore' were large in his vocabulary. Then Marcus and I started seeing each other. Even when we weren't exclusive I didn't see other people . . . though I expect he did.*

'You did say it out loud.' He sounded strained, his hands stroking her back, yet he still gave her space and she realised he wouldn't push her if she wasn't sure.

The knowledge sent a wave of recklessness through her. She wanted this man. She'd barely noticed the lack of sex after Marcus but Zach made her hyper aware of him whenever they were together – a decent guy with an exciting edge. Caring but confident. Protective. She looked at him and her body said *I want you*. Slowly, she touched her mouth to his once more, accepting his tongue's caress as her hands stroked his strong forearms and biceps, following the hard lines of his collarbones before running her palms down over his chest and then up over his back.

Then she disengaged herself, slowly, gently.

She felt his regret but he let her pull back. Let his arms drop.

She rose and held out her hand. She was rewarded by his sensuous expression of pleasure as he realised she wasn't calling a halt but leading him to her room. She'd kicked off her flip-flops and the tiled floor was chill as they made their way down the hall.

Her room was cool and shady because she'd closed the blue shutters earlier. If she'd realised she was going to bring Zach back she might have chosen her sophisticated, smooth, white cotton sheets rather than the jolly yellow sunflower-splashed ones. Matching bra and knickers might have been confidence-boosting too.

Zach didn't seem as if he minded either of those things. His eyes burned into hers as he eased against her until she was touching him all the way down, breasts against chest, groin to groin.

He was hard. Boy, was he. She could feel the heat of him through her dress and her words caught in her throat as he came at her with a kiss so deep and carnal that she found herself rubbing against his hardness, dragging a deep, 'Mmmmm' from him. Then he seemed to collect himself, take it slower, pressing gentle, scalding kisses to her skin.

She slid her hands up inside his top, relishing the smooth, firm, hot flesh of his torso, feeling his ribs beneath her fingers. She pushed up the fabric and he pulled the T-shirt over his head, ruffling his hair. Eyes on fire, he watched as she fumbled with the snap of his shorts, breathing hard, one hand stroking a shoulder laid bare by her strappy summer dress, the other sliding down to cup her breast as if to tell her, *I'm in this. I'm letting you set the pace but I'm SO in this.* Once she'd unfastened him it was easy to shove his shorts until they slid down his legs.

For a moment she paused, drinking in his plain black boxers that moulded themselves around him, exhibiting his desire. Then she put out a hand and his breath hissed between his teeth as she touched him.

He brought his hands to the straps of her dress and eased them aside. The brush of them on her upper arms prompted a twin burst of pleasure. He stroked, he teased, his mouth on her collarbone while his fingers eased down the zip that ran along the back of her dress with such assurance she felt he must have already made a note of its location. The thought that he had perhaps made a mental plan of how to undress her made her tingle. Slowly, he pushed the fabric down her body.

When she stood before him in her underwear he whispered, 'So, sooooo beautiful,' unhooking her bra. The air trickled over her breasts, making her nipples peak as he made that back-of-the-throat 'Mmmmmm' again. They pulled off the last of their clothes, seeking the fastest path to skin, and sank down on the bed.

She heard noises that she dimly realised were issuing from her throat as his mouth worked its way around her breasts, licking, sucking, caressing, while his hand . . . 'Zach,' she gasped. Almost unable to bear the intensity she pressed her hands imperiously against his shoulders and he obligingly rolled onto his back while she explored the planes of his chest and the circles of his nipples. When she reached down to the silken hardness of him she said, 'Don't you dare remind me of what I said about taking things into my own hands.'

He groaned and gasped a laugh both at once. 'But I'm sure as hell not going to stop you doing it.' He settled back and let her lead. It made her feel powerful and in control. Groaning, she directed his hand, ready now for his touch, and he didn't seem to mind if she kissed him gently or bit him mindlessly as he caressed her, driving her on. When he gasped, 'Condom,' she nodded, because safe sex was sensible even though she was on the pill, not ever likely to leave anything as important as contraception to a man.

The only time her earlier diffidence touched her again was when she whispered, 'Can I . . . Do you mind if I go on top?'

'Go you,' he murmured, shoving pillows behind his shoulders, eyes dark and smouldering. 'I wonder if any man, ever, refused that request.' Then he gasped as she sank down on him. He stroked her, urged her and cupped her while she rocked herself to happiness and, finally, collapsed on him as he bucked and came inside her, their bodies so damp with sweat they slid over one another.

Later, after they'd come down, bodies tangled with the sunflower sheets, he murmured, 'My turn I think,' and proceeded to make love to her with such intensity that she thought she'd burst with pleasure. When he dragged the final orgasm out of her she closed her eyes and let her head flop back against his shoulder, saying, 'I definitely like you setting the pace too.'

She fell asleep with his gentle laughter shaking through her.

Chapter Fifteen

The next morning, when they were refuelling with omelettes and orange juice, Rosa spotted what looked like the bottom of a conference pear growing halfway up Zach's arm, bulbous and a dirty shade of green.

She paused, aghast. 'Oh, Zach, your elbow!'

He rubbed one of his bare legs hairily on hers and swallowed his mouthful of omelette. 'What elbow?' But he held his arm stiffly.

She clapped a hand to her mouth. 'I forgot you were hurt. We got . . . acrobatic.'

Amusement shimmered in his eyes but his voice was solemn as he assumed a long-suffering air. 'What did you think all the noise I made was about? Passion? It was stifled elbow pain.'

She snorted a laugh. 'I was going to suggest we shower together but not now I know I've been insensitive to your agony.'

'With you naked, all pain vanishes,' he promised her.

She pretended to ponder. 'Mum's seeing Leslie off about

eleven o'clock then she'll be home.' But she grinned at him and added, 'I think we have time.'

She felt a ballooning happiness at the promise in his answering smile as he polished off his breakfast. She couldn't remember ever being so comfortable with a man. It made her feel giddy, as if someone had pumped extra oxygen into her lungs.

It was some time later that Zach returned to his own apartment. They'd taken a while in the shower, probably because Zach asked her to show him how she could hook a leg over his hip, as she had with Victor the dancer, and then, despite her giggles and shrieks, he'd grabbed the leg and wouldn't let go while he explored the interesting possibilities afforded. When they'd finally dried and dressed and he'd taken a last kiss before stepping into the yellow light of morning, Rosa watched him make his way across the terrace towards the stairs, hugging the wall in case his sister were to glance out and see him coming out of Rosa's apartment.

She wondered what he'd tell Marci. Or maybe if your brother stayed out all night you didn't ask questions? Although she had no siblings, she could imagine that.

She tidied her room and changed her sheets, putting her music on and dancing as she worked. What had happened last night had been awesome, amazing and incredible. It could be a one-off, she supposed, or something more – the summer romance Dory had suggested? If summer romances made you feel as if you were floating on air, Rosa decided as she shoved the bedclothes into the washing machine and set it going, she could see why Dory had wanted it for her.

It was lunchtime when Dory finally trailed in – minus her usual smile.

Rosa had visited the nearby shops and was washing crisp green lettuce. She paused, chilly water splashing over her fingers. Her mum looked pink around the eyes. Had she actually shed tears over saying goodbye to Leslie? 'Are you OK?'

A weak smile lifted one corner of Dory's mouth. 'I've been stupid.'

Alarmed, Rosa hurriedly dried her hands so she could slide an arm around her mum's soft shoulders and usher her to a nearby bar stool. 'What? What's happened?'

Her mouth worked for an instant, then Dory gave a hiccupping sob. 'I've fallen in love.'

'Oh!' Relief coursed through her. With an uncertain laugh, she gave Dory a big hug. 'Shouldn't you be happy?' She thought of how the night with Zach had made her feel, though it was too early for her to acknowledge anything more than lust.

Helping herself to a piece of kitchen roll, Dory wiped her eyes and blew her nose. 'I am happy.' She let out a sob. 'I'd forgotten that this love lark removes a layer of skin. I've been standing at the airport waiting for Leslie's plane to take off so I could wave knowing he wouldn't even be able to see me! I wanted to shove people aside and follow him through security. I feel like an idiot.'

'Wow. It definitely sounds like something big.' A little rocked by a version of her mum she'd never met before, Rosa took a bottle of white from the fridge and poured them each a glass. The wine twinkled in the sunlight pouring through the window.

Dory took hers with a word of thanks, alternating sips with nose-blows, throwing in the occasional watery laugh and muttering, 'I'm happy really.'

They ate outside, tipping the parasol to shade them and

their repast of glowing red tomatoes, golden couscous, peppered Maltese cheese and, because they were English and had found a shop that sold it, pork pie and pickle. 'When are you going back to the UK?' Rosa asked when she judged Dory to be restored by food and wine.

'Not till Saturday week, the 25th of July.' Dory sighed mournfully. 'For the first three days of next week Leslie's going to be away in Scotland at his daughter's graduation. His ex-wife will be there of course and I don't want to create any awkwardness. Imagine how his daughter would feel! Grandpa's away with his golf club – Captain's weekend or something – and my editor's on holiday from tomorrow until the following Monday. I've set up a meeting with her and my agent on the Tuesday.'

Rosa began to say consolingly, 'Today's Thursday so it's only nine days until you fly—'

But Dory drained her wine, sitting up with a sudden flash of animation. 'We need to get lots done this week, Rosa! I don't know the deadline for this new vegan book or even how many recipes they want but if I keep busy the time will pass quickly.'

'OK, let's get at it,' agreed Rosa, glad to see her mum return to her usual self.

They bustled off to the supermarket. Rosa was beginning to feel the results of a busy night but Dory was bursting with energy, thinking aloud about a butternut squash and sage recipe as they drove. It felt like negative energy, though, stemming from unhappiness.

They were soon back in the car, their bags bursting with butternut squashes with waxy apricot-coloured skins, a new pot of peppery-smelling sage, bronze-skinned onions, papery heads of garlic, egg-free macaroni and vegan cheese. Rosa glanced at Dory's profile as they drove home. 'Have you booked your return flight from the UK?'

Dory checked both ways at a junction and then shot out into the traffic. 'I don't know how long I'll stay yet.'

'Didn't you say a week?'

Braking hard because the car in front did and earning herself a severe horn-tooting from the vehicle behind, Dory shrugged. 'My plans aren't set in stone.'

Rosa digested this, watching the boats in Sliema Creek tugging restlessly at their moorings. The sight was familiar now, though it had seemed so alien when she'd arrived a few weeks ago. 'Hopefully, you'll have sorted things out with your editor and eased your mind about Grandpa, so is that because Leslie will still be in the UK?' Surely her mum wasn't going to throw away her carefully planned Maltese summer for a man, after all these years of being emotionally independent?

Dory parked the car outside the green garage doors of Ta' Xbiex Terrace House. 'You can use the time to think about your own future. If you want to go to uni in the autumn you're behind the curve already.'

Noting that Dory had dodged her question, Rosa climbed from the car, hit by the heat after the air-conditioned vehicle as they hauled the shopping up the baking stone steps, over the lower terrace and into the kitchen. 'Actually, I've been wondering about training as an instructor in dance exercise. It's hardly storming the stage at Covent Garden but I'd love to be able to teach Zumba.'

Dory dropped her bags to give Rosa a beaming hug. 'That would be marvellous! You've always loved dancing.'

'It won't take much money to train.' Rosa responded to her mum's enthusiasm but suspected it was at least partly designed to take the spotlight off Dory's own plans.

207

'I could get my basic Zumba training for about two hundred and fifty pounds – but then there's an annual membership in addition and I'd need to find suitable halls or gyms. I'd want to offer an alternative, too, because Zumba still has a steady following but some people see it as too high-impact. Maybe FitStep because *Strictly*'s popular and people like dances based on Latin and Ballroom. I want the mortgage situation to be resolved so I know where I'm at financially.'

Dory washed her hands and took up her cook's knife to slice the ends off the first butternut squash and peel it. 'I said I'd help you financially. Don't scrimp or scrabble because I'm sure there's more to running your own classes than a couple of training courses and you'll need somewhere to live too. Or why not do a degree in dance? Can you do large pans of water for the squash and the macaroni, please?'

Rosa considered as she watched clear, cold water coursing into a pan, her heart executing odd little skips as she thought how fantastic it would be to totally immerse herself in dance for three years. Dare she? What would she do with that kind of degree at the end of it? 'I don't know what my UCAS points situation is,' she ventured, lightheaded at even having this conversation. 'I'm so out of touch. I might have to do a foundation year because I took my A Levels fourteen years ago, which would push me into four years rather than three. It's a long time since I got my gold medal in tap.'

'I don't see why four years should be a problem. You do what makes you happy.' Dory, having chopped the squash into even pieces, began to weigh out macaroni.

For the rest of the afternoon Rosa's fingers raced over the laptop keyboard and her mind raced around the idea of being a student. One moment she conjured up a vivid image of a fulfilling life of uni, the next she was convinced there was no way a thirty-two-year-old would be admitted as a novice, picturing the rest of the cohort as long-limbed, rubber-jointed eighteen-year-olds.

'Lovely,' Dory crooned when, later, she had produced bowls of golden sauce over vegan macaroni, with vegan cheese and without, with basil and without. 'Let's invite the Bentleys down to taste.'

Rosa's heart gave a tiny lurch as her mind abandoned the imaginary university life it had been inhabiting and flew to Zach but she said merely, 'Lovely idea.' Dory disappeared upstairs while Rosa took the usual pictures for the blog and social media, making use of the plentiful natural light from the window. Then she set the table outside with napkins, Maltese bread and blue china bowls.

Dory reappeared with Marci and Paige in tow.

'Uncle Zach's getting changed,' Paige informed Rosa, skipping straight into the kitchen, her eyes darting around, probably for signs of pudina or other goodies. 'He's been working on the roof and he's hot and smelly.'

Marci said, 'Uncle Zach won't thank you for broadcasting that,' but Dory and Rosa laughed and when Zach appeared five minutes later his hair was damp and he was fragrant with shower gel and shampoo. His dark eyes found Rosa. She sent him a smile and hoped her red cheeks would be put down to ladling out hot food.

Zach held two bottles of wine and he followed her into the kitchen with them.

His mouth said, 'I've brought red and white.' His eyes said *I want to be alone with you,* while his hand sneaked down and squeezed her left buttock, hidden from everyone else by the kitchen island.

'Oh!' she squeaked. Then, in a more usual tone, 'Could you reach down some glasses?' She waited until he was at full stretch then gave him a quick goose, hearing him catch a strangled breath as she sailed serenely outside clutching a handful of spoons and taking a seat beside Marci. She hadn't seen her for ages and though she was reserved at first, Marci did make an effort to join in the chatter. Rosa already knew from Zach that his sister had been struggling with anxiety again. His eyes became shadowed whenever he talked about it.

The still afternoon heat lay over the terrace like a blanket but nobody complained about eating a hot meal out there. It was just too lovely not to be enjoyed. Insects whirred lazily around the red heads of the geraniums and the spicy scent of Dory's herb pots rose up around them all. Snug between the house and the walls of the houses around, the terrace was an oasis of calm.

Dory dispensed the food with no sign of her earlier woe over missing Leslie and Rosa kept her laptop open to take down everyone's comments. At the end of the meal Dory asked about the dancing she'd missed at Nicholas Centre, which segued to the subject of Rosa entering the world of dance.

Zach's dark gaze dwelled on Rosa. 'You're seriously thinking of uni?'

She shrugged self-consciously. 'Maybe. I don't know whether it could be this year. It's coming up to the end of July already.' She wished her mum hadn't announced her possible plans. Dory didn't know about last night or the possibility, tangling confusingly with every other possibility, that it might lead to something.

Paige leapt up. 'I want to dance again! Rosa, can you put the music on?'

Rosa did and even Marci laughed and clapped at Paige diligently copying Rosa's steps. Zach took some persuading to get up, but finally he did, clapping and sidestepping with good humour, hamming up the wiggles. Paige dragged Dory and Marci up too but Dory soon sat down again, laughing and fanning her face. 'Not in this heat!'

Rosa grinned. 'This is only a warm-up, Mum. You want to see the high-impact stuff.'

'Yes, we do,' Zach agreed, taking the seat alongside Dory. 'Show us.'

Rosa protested but finally gave way to persuasion, put on 'Firehouse' and soon forgot to be self-conscious as she threw herself into the jumps and helicopters, crossing her arms and punching the air, jumping high, squatting low. Paige tried to copy her but was generally a beat or a phrase behind so that Rosa almost tripped over her and ended up laughing breathlessly, swinging Paige up in the air and making her squeal.

'I wish I could move like that,' Marci said admiringly. She checked her watch. 'I've set up a Skype session with my mum so we'll have to leave, Paige. Thank you for such a lovely meal, Dory.'

Almost as soon as she'd gone Dory received a call from Leslie and swiftly carried her phone off to her bedroom. Rosa and Zach were left alone on the terrace . . . but only for only a minute because Paige came back to the top of the stairs and shouted, 'Heyyy, Zachary! Granny wants to talk to you too.'

He rolled exasperated eyes but called back, 'One minute and I'll be there.' Then he gave Rosa a long, deep, silent kiss before murmuring, 'See you soon.' He ran lightly up the stone steps to play his part in the family chat.

Lips still tingling, Rosa cleared the table and tidied up

her notes about the reactions to Dory's macaroni. Everyone had enjoyed the additions of both cheese and basil. As she tapped at the laptop, half her mind was on Zach and when 'soon' might be. Then, to prove to herself she had plenty of things in her life other than a man, decided to ring Georgine at Blackthorn's to talk through her possibilities. If she went with her first idea of training as a Zumba instructor she'd be able to work longish part-time hours. On the other hand, were she to take the full-time degree course . . . well, then she wouldn't be able to work anything but weekends, if the uni were local. That was a scary prospect despite Dory's generous offers of support. Maybe a conversation with Georgine would keep her grounded. Stop her pinning too much on what seemed like an impossible dream of a dance degree . . . or one night and the man she'd spent it with.

She tapped her friend's name in her contact list, hoping that, bearing the time difference in mind, she'd catch Georgine before she left work for the day.

She did. And Georgine met her lovely new plans with prolonged silence.

Eventually she said carefully, 'As your friend, I can see how great and fun your options are. If you didn't work for Blackthorn's I'd tell you to go for one of them. But as your manager . . .' She blew out a breath. 'I want to support your wish to broaden your horizons and I want to adapt to staff needs, but you'd have to decide exactly how many hours a week you'd work. If you were an instructor offering Zumba classes on, say, a Saturday morning, that would be an inflexible commitment, wouldn't it? It would affect your ability to commit to weekend events at Blackthorn's. If you did the degree and could *only* work weekends or even just holidays . . . But I'd

212

only need you at busy times because we'd have our full-time staff.' She hesitated. 'Either way, I can't see anything but a zero-hours contract.'

'Oh,' Rosa replied, instinctively shying away from a contract that might offer flexibility but not stability. Trust Georgine to so unerringly put her finger on the snags. Weekends were busy at Blackthorn's. Kids were out of school. Blackthorn's needed staff that could be relied upon. Duh. She wished she hadn't given way to her impulse to make this call. Georgine was raising questions for which Rosa didn't have the answers.

'So you have decided that you're coming back from Malta, at least?' Georgine went on, as if to prove it.

Still thinking about the possibilities, including the hand-some man she'd unexpectedly started a thing with, Rosa hesitated. She gazed around the sunny terrace with the pots of herbs and geraniums. She enjoyed being in a country that made so much outdoor living possible. The sea was across the road and she loved putting on her mask and snorkel to immerse herself in the slow tempo of marine life. Even the cooler months, she understood, were significantly warmer than in the UK.

Georgine read Rosa's hesitation. 'Do I sense you're still not a hundred per cent on returning to the UK?'

'Um . . .' Once she told her employer she would return it would be an awkward position to adjust. She would have taken steps down one of the roads leading from her crossroads.

Confusion kept her silent.

Yes, she'd missed Blackthorn's at first but now options seemed to swoop towards her from the afternoon shadows. If she did her dance instructor training she could work anywhere. She could travel the world. Or stay right here

213

on a small rocky island in the centre of the sparkling blue Mediterranean Sea where her mum, aunt and grandparents had spent their daily lives before she was born. It was a different place now but she was a different generation. She was enjoying life here.

She tried to imagine herself resigning from Blackthorn's and Georgine getting someone else in her place. A new person schmoozing businesses for sponsorship and organising fundraising. Then she thought about staying here when her mum and most of the tourists had gone home. None of it felt that alarming.

Georgine sighed. 'OK. Let's not do anything irrevocable yet. Give it more thought. It's still only July.'

'Right. Thanks,' Rosa murmured, shaken by the clear potential to leave her old life behind when only a few short weeks ago she'd been mourning it. 'I'm sorry if I'm saying things you don't want to hear, Georgine. I was thoughtless to make the call before I was ready.'

'Being both your friend and your manager does make things tricky,' Georgine acknowledged with a small laugh.

Rosa ended the call no nearer a decision but maybe having learned some things about herself.

She wasn't as wedded to security as she'd thought.

Disappointing Georgine made her uncomfortable.

But she was feeling a definite urge to explore her options.

She glanced at her watch. It was five forty-five in Malta so four forty-five in the UK. She called Jeanine's direct line at her solicitor's office and enquired as to progress regarding Marcus taking sole responsibility for their old home and its mortgage. When she discovered no such progress had been made she rang off. Were Marcus's solicitors dragging their feet? Why would that be? Despite her earlier resolution not to, she pulled the laptop towards her and checked out Chellice's social media channels. If she expected to find: 'Guess what? I'm buying a house with my man!' she was disappointed. Chellice's Instagram feed was strictly business and her latest blog post was about the railway system in the UK – four stars for service and two for value. Marcus had always left the business social media to her. But . . .

She returned to the Instagram feed and analysed it more carefully. Every image for the past week was of Chellice's kintsugi, gold or silver veins standing out on green jugs or delicate iridescent bowls. She checked the Spun Gold website and online shop. None of Marcus's work. She frowned. What did that mean?

Marcus's number was still in her 'favourites', although it was definitely a misnomer now. She couldn't let this situation drift though. When she called he answered with a grumpy, 'Hello.'

She made her own voice pleasant. 'I'm hoping for an update. My solicitor hasn't heard from yours lately. I made the last mortgage payment so I'm hoping the changeover will happen before the next.'

'These things take time.' His voice was flat.

'Maybe you could gee your solicitor up so it takes less time?' she suggested lightly, trying to get a feel for what lay behind his terseness.

He sighed impatiently. 'Don't sweat it.'

Rosa felt her shoulders tense. Marcus not giving straight answers was never good. She cast about for a gambit to prompt a revealing reaction. 'So,' she said pleasantly, 'you and Chellice have parted ways?'

The silence was sudden. Her heart plunged. His voice, when it came again, was stiff. 'How in buggery do you know that? Yes, if you must know. We've parted ways both biz and personal so everything's in a state of flux. I've had to stop making things to create my own online presence and social media channels. It's become apparent to me that "together" in her language means "together until the first little problem and then I'm off".'

Rosa thought he'd probably taken Chellice doing all the social media work for granted and felt hard done by at having to do it himself but his sense of injury wasn't her focus. 'I'm sorry to hear it but I could have told you that Chellice likes people to be useful to her. Being useful to others is much less her thing. I suppose she was disenchanted when you lost all the money?'

'Mind your own frigging business,' he snapped.

Worry gripped her stomach in its prickly hands. She tried to keep her voice calm and agreeable because, even if Marcus had brought his troubles on himself, until the house was in his name alone her fortunes were tied to his. 'Sorry, but because of the mortgage it is my business if you're not earning money. If you're having to set up an online shop that will cost you, won't it? Shopping software, for example?'

'I can sell via Etsy and craft fairs,' he said sulkily.

She bit her lip, imagining how the scales might have fallen from Chellice's eyes when Marcus gambled away whatever had remained of his big win of four months ago. Separating her finances from his would have seemed the only sensible course and emotional disentanglement had inevitably followed. Rosa couldn't blame Chellice for that because she was trying to do much the same herself. 'Chellice won't be contributing to your household expenses. And you were already in difficulty . . .' She let the thought tail off on the air.

After several moments Marcus said gruffly, 'You're

wondering whether we should put the house on the market? Well, I think we should.'

Rosa screwed up her eyes and let her head tilt back, praying the conversation wasn't going to go the way she suspected it might. 'I wasn't wondering that. Why do you think we should sell? With the new road being built so close to our house and everything the price will be at an all-time low.'

He blew out a breath, sounding exasperated. 'You've just said yourself that I'm in a hiatus, financially speaking.' He didn't answer her point about the sale price.

'You must have stock of your woodcraft that will bring in money when you get it up on Etsy?' Rosa knew she was clutching at straws.

'Not much. We'd had some really good craft fares. Stock's low.' His tone was an uneasy mix of defensive and apprehensive.

'And you gambled all the income from those too,' she finished off for him disgustedly.

He didn't answer.

'I suppose you're seeing how useful it was to have a regular salary? And have a girlfriend with one too?' she snapped, her resolution to keep calm rapidly fading.

After another long, uncomfortable pause Marcus said, 'Look, I might as well be honest. Me taking over the house and mortgage isn't as straightforward as it seemed. The mortgage company would have been happier if I'd stayed in my old job. My self-employed income for the past three years was part-time so not sufficient for them to base a mortgage offer on. I told them Chellice had moved in as a lodger thinking that they'd be happy that I was getting income in the form of rent. Instead, they raised all kinds of petty objections about the terms of the mortgage and wanted that letter of consent from you. And they won't accept rent as income anyway, for some stupid reason.'

Her heart couldn't sink any lower. 'Because a lodger can take off at any time, as she has, I suppose. But, if we sell, we'll be lucky if there's any equity in the house at all. The construction of a dual carriageway more or less at the end of our garden made the estate too unpopular. And then there are the fees. Meanwhile, I'm tied to the house financially, having to make mortgage payments because you can't. It's a bit bloody much, Marcus!'

'I don't think we have much choice—' He halted. Then . . . he changed tack. 'Tell you what, let's give ourselves thinking time. We're going round in circles. Speak soon.' And the line went dead.

Rosa put the phone down on the table with a shaking hand. Had she just made it plain to Marcus that he could sit in the house for some time yet . . . because if he couldn't pay the mortgage then the rule was that she'd have to? 'Fantastic,' she said bitterly, into the air.

Snatching up her phone again she checked her bank balances. Cheap as it was to live with Dory, Rosa currently had no actual income other than pin money, and mortgage payments would swallow up her modest savings in less than a year.

The shadows lengthened as she sat on, elbows propped on the table while options whirled in her head.

Finally, she took up the laptop and began an email to her solicitor, laying out her uncomfortable situation. *I believe my best solution might lie in reversing the original plan*, she typed in conclusion. *If the house and mortgage are transferred to my name instead of Marcus's then at least I can rent the property out to cover a buy-to-let mortgage, as I don't want to live there myself. Or, as*

Marcus has suggested, we could sell the property. In many ways that's best but might leave us – i.e. me! – in a deficit position depending on what it fetches/fees etc, and also with the mortgage to be paid meantime. May I ask your views?

Even as she typed she knew that if she had to take over the mortgage then she'd have to return to Blackthorn's full-time because steady income was the mortgage company's god. No way would she accept help from Dory with the mortgage payments, as it would be tantamount to Dory supporting Marcus.

The prospect of a degree in dance receded somewhere in the vicinity of the moon.

One way or another, she thought, she had to sever this link with Marcus.

Chapter Sixteen

It was late on Thursday evening that Zach set out for Paceville. Though no one would blame him for washing his hands of Luccio after the attack at the Nicholas Centre almost a week ago, Zach's heart wouldn't let him give up on the younger man. Yes, he thought Luccio was his mugger, but they'd been friends.

That meant Luccio was desperate.

He could have called Luccio but it would have been too easy for the call to have been declined or even blocked. Then, alerted, he'd be on his guard for Zach trying to track him down.

He waited until Marci had gone to bed and didn't contact Rosa in case he got distracted. The thought of the pleasure he'd found in her bed caused him to suck in a quick breath as he trod quietly down the steps. Light from Rosa and Dory's apartment fell on the terrace as he glided silently by but he told his feet not to take him to their door.

He drove along by the black sea and then onto the busy regional road towards Paceville reflecting – even though it made him feel guilty – that living with a sister and a niece was seriously going to cramp his style with Rosa. Dory had told them earlier she was going back to the UK for a week so at least Rosa would have the lower apartment to herself for that length of time.

But he wasn't necessarily thinking temporary with her, it shocked him to realise. Last night had been equal parts instinct and lust, all his attention focused on being with her. Holding her. His libido had been screaming for more but if she'd wanted to do no more than kissing he'd have gone along with it.

In the past when he'd heard mates say of a woman 'we just clicked' he'd thought them soppy but it had felt exactly like that. Two things that came together because they went together.

He parked a couple of streets away from the bright lights of Paceville Pjazza, pulling himself out of his thoughts. When he got to the piazza on foot, hundreds of people filled it, as usual, gathering under neon lights in the hot Mediterranean night, drinking, laughing, dancing on the paving.

Zach didn't feel like partying. He knew Luccio was unlikely to hang his head and say, 'Sorry, I'll be good in future,' and return the wallet, especially if Beppe and his buddies were around. And he didn't know what Luccio might do when he had backup if he'd been prepared to inflict injury in Joseph's office. But, still, his elbow was throbbing as he threaded his way through jostling, warm summer bodies towards the steps of Triq Santa Rita, and Zach's gut was telling him reaching out to Luccio was the right thing to do.

The steps were thronged, a living carpet of people yammering, laughing and shrieking. Short summer dresses vied with body art for prominence. Music boomed from every bar, punctuated by the occasional whoop as some unwary tourist, usually in high heels, discovered that the steps were unequally distanced and uneven. A man in a T-shirt declaring that, *If it ain't happening here it ain't happening!* tripped and sprawled, smashing his cocktail glass and dropping his phone, swearing as he risked injury trying to grab back the phone from amongst broken glass and constantly shifting feet. Music pounded; voices shrieked.

Zach bought a beer then zigzagged from bar to bar. It was tedious, peering into dark corners, quartering the milling faces for Luccio's gangly figure and dark curls, like being in a living *Where's Wally?* puzzle.

Over an hour later he arrived at the foot of the steps without having caught a glimpse of Luccio or any of Beppe's crew. Smothering a sigh, he was about to resign himself to returning the next evening, Friday, when he stopped for one last perusal of the heaving revellers now tiered above him.

Then he saw it. A disturbance in the heaving throng. He narrowed his eyes and through pulsing pink neon light over bobbing heads, he caught Luccio's profile, surrounded by Beppe's buddies. Beppe at the rear, they moved in a body, parting the sea of people with their bulk. Zach stepped aside, trying to be inconspicuous as he watched them halt outside Spirit bar.

He hovered, giving them quarter of an hour to be served and to stake their claim on an area of the steps. Then he began to make his way up again, making his gaze unfocused, his route meandering.

When he got close enough, he made a production of pretending to notice Luccio. 'Hey, how are you doing?' he called, ensuring he sounded casually pleased to see the younger man rather than as if he'd been looking for him.

He held his beer bottle, though it was empty, to enhance the impression of being in Paceville only to socialise.

Luccio started, his eyes widening when he saw Zach, probably wondering why Zach sounded so friendly when, at the least, even if Luccio was innocent of mugging Zach, he'd falsely accused him of stealing.

Zach nodded to Beppe and the guys standing around him, all of whom gazed unsmilingly back, then he returned to Luccio. 'Got a moment?' Casually, he ushered Luccio a little further along the step on which they both stood.

'What?' Luccio demanded sulkily.

'Did you know I got mugged at Nicholas Centre yesterday?' Zach dropped his voice so Beppe and crew couldn't hear, stepping aside to let four women thread their way past, using it to edge Luccio still further from the crowd he seemed caught up with. He studied Luccio carefully, pretty sure he could see fear lurking in his eyes, though he'd twisted his lips in an expression of scorn.

Luccio gave a great, overdone shrug. 'How should I? Why tell me this? I don' know.'

Zach wasted no time in argument. He lowered his voice. 'Don't be used by Beppe, Luccio. I've seen his type before.'

Luccio let his gaze lock with Zach's and his eyes shone as if with tears before he looked away. 'I don' know why you tell me this,' he repeated dully. Then he flicked a glance back over his shoulder. Beppe's gaze was fixed on them, eyes dark and unreadable beneath his broad forehead.

Zach kept most of his attention on the young guy he'd considered his friend. 'The shit that's going on, it's not really you, Luccio. Planting money on me – why would you do that? Running off then ignoring Joseph's request to talk?'

Luccio gazed blankly over Zach's shoulder.

'OK.' Zach clapped him on the arm. 'But if you need help, come to me. Or why don't you go back to Sicily? I know you still have family there. Start a new life.'

Naked longing flashed into Luccio's eyes but then he slapped away Zach's hand and snarled something Zach didn't understand – probably Sicilian and pithy. Or pissy.

But as Luccio turned away, Zach tried a last appeal to his better nature. 'That ring, Luccio? It belonged to someone who cherished it.' Though he didn't know that for certain he felt pretty sure most people would value something that cost thousands of euros.

Luccio stumbled, sending Zach a frightened look at this proof that Zach connected him to the mugging. Then he straightened and swaggered his way back to his coterie, tossing off a remark that made the rest laugh as they flicked unfriendly glances Zach's way.

Wearily, Zach climbed the rest of the steps and made his way back to his car. He'd tried to do the right thing by Luccio but had little to show for his efforts. He wished he'd taken Rosa out somewhere instead. It made his heart lighten just to think of her. He checked his phone but it was after one a.m. Perhaps he could set something up for tomorrow night. There was a restaurant in Valletta he liked, one that looked over the City Gate and was reached via an old armoury magazine within the city walls.

He could share his knowledge of the city's history and maybe impress her a little.

Friday morning had hardly got going, however, when Zach received a phone call.

He stared at *Dad* on the screen with surprise before picking up. 'Is everything all right?' He and taciturn Steve generally just exchanged a text every three or four weeks, otherwise keeping up with each other via Zach's mum, Amanda. Steve's main preoccupations were his wife, his parents and his job, and he gave the impression his children were more of a headache than a joy.

Steve sounded more than usually impatient. 'Depends upon your interpretation of "all right".'

Zach replied cautiously, 'Oh?' He'd just come out of the shower. He frowned into the mirror and raked his fingertips through his wet hair.

'It's time you came back to England,' Steve said baldly. 'I'm trying to cope with a lot here: Mum needs help with everything and Nanna can't manage alone now Grandad has dementia. Surely you've frittered enough time away in Malta?'

Zach ignored the note of condemnation. Water off a duck's back. Steve always considered himself in the right; Zach was wrong and nothing Zach did would ever be good enough. It was best to try and dig down and discover what was behind his words. 'What's the matter?' Swiftly, he corrected himself. 'I mean, I know what's the matter with each of them but is there something new?'

'Nothing unexpected,' Steve admitted grudgingly. 'But you are part of this family and that comes with responsibilities. Marci's got her hands full with Paige and Electra's gallivanted off to the ends of the bloody earth.'

Zach gave himself permission to semi-switch off while Steve enumerated his complaints. He'd never imagined Zach would stay away so long. Steve was working full-time. Zach's mum Amanda needed help and there was only him to give it. Grandad Harry needed help and Nanna Rebekah wasn't so young.

Zach did feel guilty. Maybe he hadn't stayed away so much as run away. If Mum and his grandparents needed him . . .

Steve switched to Zach's shortcomings. 'You're thirty-two, Zachary. You've stepped off the career ladder. You've never even found a girl to settle down with.'

Zach wondered how that would feel and whether the girl would have hair that jiggled around her face and shone in the sunshine. Until Rosa Hammond wandered into his life he'd assumed he wasn't the kind for deep relationships. Kelly, Mel and Amelia had convinced him women were unreliable. But Rosa wasn't particularly trustful of men either. Could they somehow learn together how to rely on another person?

'It hints at immaturity!' Steve rounded off.

Zach hated being called immature. 'I hear you, Dad,' he interrupted smoothly. 'Aunt Giusi's apartment isn't finished yet but I'll definitely think about what you said.'

'Why isn't Aunt Giusi's apartment finished? What have you been doing all this time?' Steve demanded.

Zach smothered a sigh, not bothering to reiterate that Aunt Giusi hadn't decided whether to move in herself or rent it out to holidaymakers. Steve knew all this. He chose to forget it when he felt like a rant.

Steve went on through his list of grievances: his kids weren't around, the National Health Service was under-funded, his grotty boss, his inadequate pay, the typically awful bloody British summer and, finally, the pain of watching his dad fade.

All of his woes were genuine. But the way he expressed them didn't invite sympathy.

Still, Zach conceded, for his dad to have called him, even if in a typically confrontational manner, meant there was a reason. Maybe Steve was genuinely reaching breaking point and the only way he knew to ask for help was to issue orders and instigate guilt trips?

Wandering to the window as he listened, Zach drank in the view over The Ramp, over the seafront road, the rocky beach and up Lazaretto Creek to Valletta. Blue sky. Blue sea. White yachts. Golden fortifications constructed centuries ago to protect Valletta. Spires and domes and lookouts. The enchantment of the island settled around him. He did not want to leave, not one bit.

Then Steve vented a great sigh and said in a long-suffering voice, 'I don't suppose you'll come. You never fail to let me down. It started with that business at eighteen and you repeated all the same mistakes at thirty. You're a taker, Zachary.'

With an effort, Zach kept his temper. 'I haven't taken a penny from you since I was eighteen.' But if you took Steve's unfortunate manner and dogmatism out of the equation, his life wasn't easy. Was he frightened of the future? 'I do understand you've made sacrifices for Mum and Grandad,' he said. 'Nanna asked me to come out here—'

'And now I'm asking you to come back.'

Zach half-laughed. 'I didn't hear you ask. I heard you tell.'

Steve sucked in an audible breath. 'Still having anger management issues? When you got in that fight—'

'One loss of control in thirty years doesn't warrant that remark,' Zach cut in. He could have retorted that his dad had been angry ever since Zach could remember but he took yet another breath and tried to de-escalate the quarrel. 'I need time to think, Dad. I'll get back to you.' But he came off the phone furious with himself for handling his father so badly. He was never going to be a 'Yes, Dad' son but they'd been like two bulls, blindly clashing skulls and achieving nothing but fresh wounds. Zach should remember he was living a comfortable life in sunny Malta while Steve struggled to care for Zach's mum and grandparents and hold down a full-time job.

Taking several deep breaths, he tried to recall himself to his day. It was Friday. His intention had been to see Rosa, check everything was OK with Marci and read through a long circular from the agency through which he got work. There were a list of assignments on offer but also notice of a new bid system, one he felt wouldn't benefit him when he started work for them again.

He was down to assist at football coaching at Nicholas Centre from two o'clock, when he planned to tell Joseph about his fruitless encounter with Luccio last night.

After breakfast, though, he'd call his mother. Steve would have left for work and Zach could get a realistic feel for whether he was genuinely needed at home in Cornwall. Amanda could be relied upon for a calm view. As he headed for the kitchen and the coffee maker, glad Marci and Paige were in the bathroom judging by Paige's piping voice floating through the door, he acknowledged an irony. His mother and grandmother were the ones he trusted and went to; his sisters and niece he protected – yet none of his romantic relationships with women had ended well.

He took cereal and coffee up onto the roof and, when it had gone, rang his mum.

'Hi,' he said, glad to hear her soft voice. 'How are you today?'

'OK,' Amanda replied. 'OK' if 'OK' was in constant pain, Zach thought.

After they'd chatted for several minutes, Zach describing his view from the roof in the early sunshine, he mentioned the call from his dad. He thought he'd been delicate about trying to get a feel for whether Amanda needed more help than Steve was able to provide when she broke in.

'I really hope,' she said, tone steely, 'that your father hasn't tried to get you to come home to help. He has, hasn't he? I told him not to! Why doesn't he ever listen? Zach, you absolutely must not come home. I keep telling him I don't need the amount of coddling he foists on me.'

Astonished by this outburst from his usually mild-mannered mother, Zach said, 'Mum, if you need me home, I'll come.'

'I don't!' she said in as near to a snap as she ever got. 'I need people to stop treating me like—' She paused and took an audible breath. When she spoke again it was more moderately. 'You're happy in Malta. I'm no worse and I don't know why Dad's got this particular bee in his bonnet. Just forget it ever happened, darling.'

But Zach couldn't.

After the call ended, he paced the roof terrace, fighting a heavy feeling that something was wrong at home; more wrong than his parents were admitting. After a while, he telephoned his grandmother Rebekah. 'How's Grandad?' he asked after a few minutes of telling her what he'd been doing in Malta.

Rebekah sighed. 'Deteriorating slowly, I'm afraid.'

'Are you coping?' he asked, treading carefully. He didn't want to give any hint that Steve was finding Harry burdensome. He could imagine her dismay and hurt.

'For now,' she said, then moved the conversation on. 'How's Aunt Giusi? Has she moved in yet? Are Lance McCoy's daughter and granddaughter still in the lower apartment?' Zach talked to her for almost an hour. She loved to hear about Malta even if caring for Harry tied her to Cornwall.

229

Finally, when Nanna had gone off to get Harry up and ready to face the day, Zach texted Rosa. *Hello, beautiful. Don't suppose you're free for a morning walk by the sea? xx*

Her reply came promptly. *Definitely but only until about 10.30 then on duty in Mum's kitchen. xx*

His heart lifted.

Rosa was already waiting on the lower terrace when Zach ran down to join her. His shorts were cut-offs and his white top simple and sleeveless but it hugged his chest and shoulders. The smile that flashed across his face at seeing her made her temporarily forget that she'd lain awake for much of last night with her mind circling all the issues around Marcus and the house. Without apparently worrying whether they'd be seen, he cupped her head and found her mouth gently with his.

The tingling touch of his parted lips somehow relaxed her. Placing her hand on his chest seemed to connect her to the life she was living in Malta more than the ground beneath her feet. When the kiss finally ended he took her hand and they ran down the steps to street level.

'Mum's driving me crazy,' she said, as they turned right towards Msida Marina. Reaching the end of The Ramp, they crossed the road, passing The Black Pearl – the pirate ship restaurant – deserted at this time of day and looking as if it had been carelessly parked on the pavement. In the marina the boats were crammed along the pontoons in rows like so many cars in a car park, gleaming white on a sparkling sea.

Still holding hands, they walked on a narrow way between the yachts and burger vans and fishermen. 'Mum's shoehorned in all kinds of recipe trials this week to write

230

up from my notes while she's back in the UK,' Rosa explained. 'Her editor wants a different book from the one she's been working on and it's put her in a mega tizz. It's hard to get her to stop for so much as a cup of coffee.'

Zach listened, dark eyes attentive, as they reached the end of Msida Creek where the pavement broadened into a promenade. 'I've talked to both my parents this morning. Dad seems to want me to go home but Mum says I shouldn't.'

Rosa's step faltered. 'Go home for good?'

He didn't look as if the thought filled him with joy. He paused and stared up Msida creek towards the golden stone ramparts of Valletta and she followed his gaze, remembering how he'd promised to show her the historic capital city and take a tour of the tunnels that ran beneath it. Had they run out of time?

He answered, 'For good? I suppose it depends on what I find there. Dad and I don't always see situations in the same way but I've begun to wonder if I'm using my sense of grievance to dodge my responsibilities. Mum sounded odd . . . not desperate, precisely, but not far off it, even as she was refusing to agree that she needed me home. And then there's Nanna and Grandad. Nanna says she's coping but what if she's not?' He squinted against the sunlight bouncing off the sea. 'Just because Dad's always complaining doesn't mean there's nothing to complain about.'

It was already almost thirty degrees, though it wasn't ten o'clock yet, and there was no shade where they stood. The heat seemed to bounce off the paving and creep up their bare legs.

'I can see why you're worried.' Wisps of hair clung damply to her forehead and she brushed them back as she leaned on the marina railings beside him. She almost told him that bloody Marcus had managed to lose all his money and she might have to go back to her job to afford mortgage payments because he wasn't able to. But thinking about the property that had dropped well below its original value and an ex who'd dropped just as drastically in her estimation filled her tummy with ice. They were each being pulled into their old lives and she hated the idea of acknowledging out loud that none of her dreams were going to be realised. The degree. Even a part-time career as a Zumba instructor might be slow to establish if she was also working full-time at Blackthorn's.

And as for their relationship . . . She found herself frowning in exactly the same strained manner he was as their arms touched, skin hot from the sun. If they both went home they would be in the same country but not this one. She'd checked Google maps and found Redruth and Liggers Moor to be over four hundred miles apart.

It felt as if they were over before they'd really begun.

They trailed back to the apartments, each lost in their own thoughts.

At the foot of the stairs up from the street, Zach gently pulled her around to face him. 'I haven't gone anywhere yet. Any chance you could manage a swim at the end of the afternoon?' Then, with a wink, 'Paige asked me to ask you.'

She managed a smile, pretty sure he'd made that up. 'Tell her I'll do my best.' Then she let go of his hand to climb the stairs to the next level because she'd rather their families didn't know there was anything between them but friendship. There was no point.

In the kitchen, mind still three-quarters on Zach, she found Dory chewing a pen as she frowned at a shopping list.

'Let's be organised,' she said briskly, glancing up as Rosa slipped in. 'We'll shop this morning for the next three days. I want to work on different risottos, both rice and barley. They're great for vegans because you can chuck so much in them. We'll need vegan butter and cheese.' She added them to the list. 'We'll go to the supermarket and also that fruit and veg van on The Strand. If he's got nice figs I'll work on fig desserts. I'm thinking of something with cheese and marmalade.' She grabbed up her bag. 'The thing with trying out so many recipes in a few days is that we're going to have way too much food. We'll have to invite the Bentleys for lots of meals.'

Feeling cheered at this prospect, Rosa gathered up the shopping bags and followed Dory out. It wasn't until they were in the supermarket with a laden trolley that she realised she hadn't asked Zach when he'd return to the UK, if he did. In eight days, when Dory flew home and Rosa would have sole possession of their apartment, Zach could already have gone.

The first batch of risotto – barley, so Dory said it should be called 'orzotto' but most people called it 'barley risotto' – was full of pumpkin and asparagus. She tried it with and without white wine and one version with minced mushrooms, experimenting with varying levels of rosemary, garlic and pepper. The final tasting provided lunch for them, Marci and Paige, Zach having gone to Nicholas Centre. Marci didn't mention anything about the possibility of her brother heading back to England so Rosa didn't either.

Pumpkin and asparagus orzotto tasting (vegan) Rosa typed at the top of a fresh document, watching the words appear on the laptop screen. She'd already taken photos indoors where she could make the light even. Each dish was in a bowl of a different colour. She peered at them, lined up on the table. 'I'm not sure the one with minced mushrooms should have gone in the yellow bowl. It looks muddy.'

Marci put some on her plate, which was white. 'Does it look better on here?'

Dory and Rosa inspected it. Dory said, 'No. It's the minced mushrooms.'

Rosa made the appropriate note while Dory mused, 'I could try it with button mushrooms because they'd stay whole. Flavour without mud.'

Paige helped herself to slices of fresh bread, buttered them thickly and used them like edible spoons with which to scoop the orzotto up and stuff it into her mouth. 'I like them all best,' she pronounced eventually, and Rosa noted the comment gravely in her document.

It wasn't until after lunch, when Dory was slicing red peppers, green beans, onions and broccoli for a vegan risotto with rice that Rosa checked her email and saw a message from Jeanine at her solicitor's practice. It proved disappointing. Jeanine stated she could only advise on the legal processes involved and suggested Rosa seek information from an estate agent and/or financial adviser. She would await her further instructions.

Rosa broke off to take pictures of the beautifully chopped veg while Dory sautéed shallots. Then she returned to the laptop and searched online for estate agents in Liggers Moor. Selecting three, she looked at their listings for semis on the Roman Way Estate where she and Marcus had lived together.

It looked as if half the estate was trying to move out.

Prices were lower than she'd hoped. Red corner flags on images tried to tempt buyers with *Recently reduced!*

and *Unmissable!* but precious few sported a smug *SOLD*. End terraces in Kiln Road, like theirs, she saw with a slither of horror, were listed at thirty thousand pounds less than she and Marcus had paid.

Thirty thousand!

It was much worse than she'd thought. Since February, when she'd been fighting her way through the turmoil of the relationship ending, she'd obviously failed to register a mass exodus from the estate. Work on the nearby dual carriageway surely couldn't have had such a drastic effect, could it? Certainly, being awoken at six a.m. by the roar of earthmoving equipment seven days a week was unpleasant. But could it prompt such plunging market values?

Even supposing they were able to sell, where the hell would they find the funds to make up that kind of deficit as well as paying fees?

Fingers shaking, Rosa emailed two of her old neighbours, Vix who lived further up Kiln Road and Angeline who lived in Quarry Close, nearby. She began with a couple of chatty paragraphs then went on to say how taken aback she was to see prices so low. *What's been going on? It would be great to have your local insight, if you don't mind,* she finished.

Rosa wrestled silently with the temptation to place the negative equity situation before her mum but she could imagine Dory offering to pay off the thirty thousand and Rosa couldn't stomach the idea. The idea of asking for *thirty thousand pounds* or more that would vanish, just to get Rosa out of an uncomfortable situation, was repugnant. Rosa and Marcus splitting up wasn't Dory's fault and neither was Marcus being a knob about gambling.

She finished her notes, her worries making her feel

slightly nauseous, and when Zach showed up, Paige bouncing beside him, it was all she could do not to throw herself on him and demand a hug.

'I got my shnorkel!' Paige shouted, waving her mint-green mask and snorkel. 'C'mon, Rosa, we're going swimming in the sea.'

Dory glanced at the clock over her glasses and exclaimed, 'Look at the time! I'll clear up, Rosa.' She beamed at Paige. 'I'll make fig tartlets for when you get back. Would you like that?'

Paige, obviously having caught on that Dory and food were a positive combination, shouted, 'Yeah!' When Zach raised his eyebrows at her she added, 'Please.' Then, 'What are figs?'

Rosa left Dory showing Paige figs with purple skins while she whizzed to her room to change. On an impulse, to give Zach something to remember if he was to disappear from her life, she wriggled into a black bikini with slender gold chains forming the sides. She'd bought it for a hen party spa weekend and, glancing in the mirror, she saw with satisfaction that it was every bit as revealing as she remembered. The top cupped her breasts, the chains over her hips lengthened her legs. She threw over it a plain white cover-up that in no way would hint at the brief, sexy ensemble beneath.

After the air-conditioned comfort of the kitchen, stepping out into the sun, even late in the afternoon, was so like stepping into an oven that Rosa thought she knew how the fig tartlets were about to feel. 'Phew, can't wait to get into the sea.' Swinging her fins from her fingers, her mask and snorkel in her backpack, she smiled down at Paige. 'Do you think you'll remember how to swim?'

Paige trotted on her tippy-toes. 'Yes! Uncle Zach will

put on my armbands for me and I'll stay up. We're going to shnorkel, aren't we? See fishes?'

'That's it.' Zach winked at his little niece. His eyes were tired and troubled, Rosa thought, but when Rosa asked whether he'd booked a flight home he said, 'Not yet.' Then he teased Paige gently, as always, holding her hand until they were safely on the rocky beach. While he was busy inflating armbands and cleaning Paige's little green mask, Rosa took out her own gear then slipped the practical white towelling cover-up off and waited.

When Paige was ready to go Zach straightened and yanked off his T-shirt before glancing at Rosa. He made a noise as if he'd swallowed his tongue.

Enjoying his pole-axed expression, Rosa smiled sweetly. 'Ready?'

His gaze roamed over her, over the brief triangles of fabric, lingering on her breasts, the curve of her waist. He cleared his throat. 'I think I have to get in that cold water.'

Satisfied with the effect she'd had, Rosa followed him to the edge of the rocks, self-conscious at several other looks she received while they forced bare feet into fins. Holding hands – and Rosa holding on to her bikini top – the three leapt into the relief of cool waves. They trod water while they adjusted their masks and positioned salty-tasting snorkels in their mouths, then dipped their heads and let their legs float out behind them as they watched shoals of fish cruising the seabed, pausing to nibble at some treat before flitting away.

Paige kept lifting her head, spitting out her snorkel and crying, 'I can see silver fishies! And rainbow ones!' then repositioning the snorkel to put her head down again. As if they were a little family, the three of them drifted slowly. When Paige tried to make some pronouncement and got a mouthful of seawater instead, Zach hooked an arm around her to support her while she coughed and spluttered. As if it were the most natural thing in the world he hooked his other arm around Rosa, drawing her close, and they bobbed together.

'What are you doing later?' he murmured, his hand tightening on Rosa's waist.

'We're going to eat fig tartlets!' Paige boomed, evidently assuming his question was for her.

Zach smiled, the affection in his eyes evident even through the glass of his mask. 'We are, aren't we?' Then, to Rosa, 'And even after that?'

'Not bedtime!' Paige wailed.

Zach arched an eyebrow at his niece. 'Don't you like bedtime? There are times that I like it a lot.' He sent Rosa a look that brought colour to her cheeks.

'I don't have plans for later . . . yet,' she murmured and then they returned to their snorkelling until it was time to get out and dry themselves.

They returned to find Marci ensconced on the lower terrace with Dory, a bottle of wine open between them and flip-flops kicked off. 'I've been talking to Steve on the Barracks Brats Facebook group,' Dory called as Zach came into view, waving her wine glass.

Zach let go of Paige so she could run across the terrace and throw herself on Marci, babbling about rainbow fish and the sea tasting horrible. 'Oh?' he commented neutrally.

Dory was pink-cheeked, which suggested this wasn't her first glass of wine. 'Marci said I could take pictures from your roof terrace and I put one up in Barracks Brats. He came on and asked how we were liking the apartment and if his kids were behaving themselves.'

Rosa caught Marci glancing at Zach over Paige's head.

'I said you were both lovely and he must be proud of you!' Dory went on.

'Nice of you,' Zach said with a smile but Rosa knew from what Zach had told her that Steve wasn't the kind of parent to advertise pride in his children.

Expansively, Dory invited the Bentleys to dinner. 'We still have a ton of risotto – rice this time – which heats up beautifully.'

Once Paige had established that fig tartlets were still on the menu too, everyone accepted. Rosa didn't look at Zach but there was a decided 'unfinished business' vibe between them. When Paige went to bed, Marci would stay in with her. Dory would probably go to her room to FaceTime Leslie and then Rosa and Zach would be left alone. She couldn't wait.

By nine, Paige and Marci had departed and Dory was showing signs of doing the same. Rosa had just exchanged a smile with Zach when his phone began to ring.

He answered, 'Hi, Joseph.' He listened, then, 'Yes. Yes, I can come . . . Is she? I can imagine. Just give me time to drive over.' When he'd ended the call he glanced ruefully at Rosa. 'Luccio's aunt Teresa, who he's been living with, contacted Joseph. She's worried about Luccio and Joseph's asked me to join them all at his and Maria's house. He thinks I might have more insight than he has.'

Disappointment trickled through Rosa but she could say little other than, 'Poor lady. You must go.'

Zach thanked Dory for the meal, said goodnight and went for his car keys.

Rosa and Dory loaded the dishwasher, hand-washing the wine glasses and throwing out the remains of the risotto because they were completely risottoed out. Dory said, 'Pea guacamole toast tomorrow,' and disappeared in the direction of her room.

Rosa showered and dried her hair, wondering whether Zach would return in time for a nightcap – or something. Checking her phone as she wandered back out to enjoy the cooler air of evening she spotted notifications that both Vix and Angeline had now returned her emails.

She read them with a plummeting heart. *It's pants*, wailed Angeline. *It was bad enough they decided to build the frigging new road right next to us but now there are rumours of subsidence and people are panicking. Prices have dropped through the floor.*

Vix offered additional information. *Of course, nobody ACTUALLY knows an ACTUAL person with ACTUAL subsidence in their ACTUAL house but still the rumours fly. There are more sale boards than I can count. Jonno and me are going to sit tight and be glad we don't have to sell.*

Rosa groaned and let her head tip back against the sun lounger, the wood still holding something of the day's heat. Then she forced herself to return to the screen.

First she consulted a financial advice site that suggested options for vendors of difficult-to-sell houses. The companies that guaranteed to buy any house, apparently, typically paid seventy-five to eighty per cent of the market value. That was rubbish.

Companies that took over mortgages needed equity in the property – and even then the deal was only for the desperate. That was rubbish too.

She was trapped.

With a heart like lead she looked again at the journey between Liggers Moor and Redruth where Zach lived. Six and a half hours. If Zach went back to help his family they would not exactly be on each other's doorsteps.

Chapter Seventeen

Luccio hadn't been home for days and wasn't answering his phone. Zach agreed to go and look for him. He messaged Rosa to explain that instead of trying to spend time with her he was going on a Luccio hunt. *He's gone missing before but not for so long. His aunt's worried and so are Joseph and I,* he added.

Her reply, *Understand. Hope he's OK xx,* was genial enough but not much in the way of engagement.

He parked his car then wandered around every bar in Triq Santa Rita and even gave up an unreasonable number of euros to enter a couple of clubs. He saw no sign of Luccio or Beppe and his buddies in the partying hordes. He widened his search into Triq San Ġorġ and Triq Santu Wistin before he gave up. There were literally hundreds of nightspots, thousands of people, and Luccio could be tucked up in bed with a girl somewhere and not giving his aunt's peace of mind a thought.

It was three when Zach crawled into bed, wishing he'd had better luck. Even a tetchy meeting such as their last would have been better than coming up blank.

Though exhausted, he found it hard to sleep. Where was Luccio?

At six, Paige flung herself on top of him shouting, 'Heyyyy, Zachary! Can we go shnorkelling?'

With a groan, Zach buried his head under the covers while Marci retrieved her errant daughter, scolding her for bursting into her uncle's room and apologising in a whisper to Zach. He spent the next hour seeking much-needed sleep but it was obvious from the number of times Marci raised her voice that either Paige had woken up in pain-in-the-arse mode or Marci was feeling tense. Or both.

Finally, his phone screen flashed and he couldn't resist checking to see whether it was a text from Rosa. It wasn't – just a notification from a podcast to which he subscribed.

Yawning, he gave up and rolled out of bed and into the shower, wondering whether the budding thing between them was going to have the opportunity to flower.

Rosa, when he texted her, replied: *In the kitchen with Mum this morning.*

Zach spent time chatting to Marci while Paige did some colouring, reading aloud an email he'd received from Electra. *Glad to hear you're all OK in Malta. Would love to be there myself.*

'Not exactly informative.' Marci grinned. 'She seems to be living life to the full in Thailand.'

Then, because he was more than half convinced he'd need to go home, at least for a week or two, Zach looked at flights. A single traveller, even in July, could get on a flight without much notice. He had the funds. All he needed was to overcome his reluctance.

Marci propped her chin on her hand, reading over his shoulder. 'I suppose I'll have to go too if you go, or when this doctor's note runs out.'

He studied her. Though there had been times when she'd seemed brighter, right now she didn't seem any happier than when she'd arrived. 'You're feeling well enough to return to work?'

She shrugged.

'If you're not, then you need to see the doctor again.' He sounded brotherly, he recognised.

'Or get a new life.' She sighed.

'In many ways it's worked for me,' he observed. He loved his life in Malta. Even the winter wasn't really winter. There were wind and storms but not snow and frost and you also got balmy days when the thermometer read eighteen or twenty.

Then his phone rang and *Mum* appeared on the screen. Although he was usually happy to hear from her she'd obviously been upset by his dad summoning Zach home and apprehension prickled through him. He greeted her smoothly, however. 'How's everything?'

'I'm outside,' she declared unexpectedly. 'The taxi driver's very nice but he says he can't carry my cases up all those stairs because he's got a bad back. Are you in the apartment? Can you come down and help?'

Zach had trouble processing her words. 'You're in Malta?' he asked stupidly.

She gave an uncertain laugh. 'Surpri-ise!'

He scrambled to his feet. Marci, obviously hearing his side of the conversation, followed suit, her eyes wide. With Paige crying, 'What happened? Where are we going?' they hurried down the two flights of steps to the street – where they found their mother leaning on two sticks, suitcases and a backpack at her feet. A white taxi was leaving.

Amanda's blonde fluffy hair lifted in the breeze, her cheeks rosy in the heat. Her body, cushiony from medication and lack of meaningful exercise, was covered by a loose cotton dress. Her blue eyes looked both weary and apprehensive and the shifting of her feet told Zach that her rheumatoid arthritis was giving her pain. Nevertheless, the instant she saw her children and granddaughter she produced a blazing smile.

'How lovely to see you!' she cried, switching both sticks into one hand so she could hug Paige, who reached her first. 'Paige, I think you've grown in the weeks you've been here. Are you having a lovely time?'

Paige chattered loudly about the sea, the pirate ship, it being too hot and ice cream while Marci hugged Amanda too.

Zach was last to step into his mother's embrace, his mind racing. What did this mean? Why had Amanda arrived without any notice, especially when his dad had insisted she was too incapacitated to travel? There was no upside to keeping her standing in the street while he demanded answers so he said, 'How about I get you upstairs while Marci waits with the cases down here? I'll come back for them.'

'What about me?' demanded Paige.

'You go first to make sure there's nothing on the stairs to trip Granny,' he suggested, judging that condemning Paige to guard the suitcases with Marci would only lead to grumbles and wails. He smiled down at his mother, ensuring his face wasn't betraying: 'How the hell are you going to manage those stairs?' while his voice said: 'Shall I take one of your sticks?' Amanda's favoured method of climbing steps was to divide her weight between a stick and the handrail. Going up was easier than going down and he didn't even want to think how that was to be achieved. However, she knew the property and the steps and yet she'd arrived alone and couldn't have hoped that a lift would miraculously have been installed. Neither could he imagine external stone staircases lending themselves to stairlifts, even if the planning authority could be made to accept the necessity in a 'house of character', as these stone houses were often termed.

The progress up the steps was accomplished excruciatingly slowly and with sharp intakes of breath from Amanda. Zach positioned his hand beneath her arm to take some of her weight but was of limited assistance, judging by the lines of pain on her face. He wished she'd been one of the sufferers from whom rheumatoid arthritis stripped weight because then he could have carried her.

When they reached the lower terrace he suggested, 'Take a break here, Mum. Paige, you wait with Granny.' When Amanda had gladly lowered herself into a chair and Paige dropped onto a lounger he glanced into the kitchen, saw Dory and Rosa, tapped on the glass and opened the door. 'Sorry to intrude. I hope it's OK for Mum to take a break on your terrace. She's not all that mobile.'

'Your mum's here?' cried Dory. Without hesitation she switched the heat off beneath whatever she'd been stirring and came out to introduce herself with, 'You probably know already but I went to school in Malta with your husband,' and she offered Amanda a cold drink while Rosa moved the parasol to give her shade.

He watched his mum smile in gratitude for these small kindnesses then he ran back down, grabbed the suitcases and toiled back up, Marci behind him hissing, 'I thought she was supposed to be too ill to travel at all, never mind travel solo!'

'Me, too,' he panted, heaving suitcases that felt as if they each contained the proverbial kitchen sink. He hauled them as far as the flat area outside the upper apartment's front door then sped down to rejoin everyone else on the lower terrace, sweating in the late morning heat.

Amanda rested for long enough to drink a glass of iced lime and soda, chatting to Dory and Rosa who offered round yesterday's fig tartlets as if they'd fully expected to pause their kitchen activities and extend hospitality. Amanda asked how they were enjoying their summer in Malta so far and they waxed enthusiastic. 'Though I have to fly back next week,' Dory added.

Zach tried to contain his impatience as Dory asked about Amanda's journey and Amanda explained how she'd been helped through both airports. He was delighted that his mum had had airport assistance but why was she here at all? Why just show up? Why not ask him to meet her at the airport?

Finally, Amanda said she was ready to move on. Zach helped her up to the top apartment, wincing along with her at the pain of climbing the steps. While he delivered her to the sofa, watching her sink into it with evident relief, Marci dragged the cases into the hall and settled Paige to watch kids' programmes on the TV in Marci's room.

Then they both sat down and gazed at their mother.

She gave a half-laugh. 'Sorry to land myself on you.'

Zach patted her plump arm. 'You're as entitled to be here as any of the rest of the family.' He tried not to think that what he'd once considered his bachelor pad was getting seriously overcrowded. 'You took us by surprise, though. We could have been out and you would have been stuck with your luggage on the pavement and nowhere to even sit down.'

'I know,' she confessed. 'I took a chance. I was pretty

certain that if I'd told you my plans you'd have tried to dissuade me.'

'We probably would,' Marci agreed gently. 'It's the steps, Mum. They're not going to go away.'

'No. They're an issue.' Amanda sighed. Then she reached for their hands. 'I have something to tell you . . . I'm afraid I've left Dad. I need somewhere to think what to do next.'

Silence. Even the noise of the traffic on the seafront road on the level below The Ramp faded as Amanda's children gaped at her. Zach was the first to recover sufficiently to speak. 'I thought you were the only one—' He halted, unsure whether saying his mother was the only one his father could show love to would be helpful. Moreover, it would be unfair as Steve showed love to his parents too.

Marci's response was more considered. She squeezed Amanda's hand. 'Can you tell us what happened?'

Amanda wiped sweat from her forehead and Zach got up to turn up the air conditioning. 'I'm sorry if you're upset,' she said huskily. 'Dad's so . . . I get frustrated to hear him endlessly telling people how much he has to do for me. I can do more than he'll admit if I have enough time. I've joined an RA support group and it's helped me to see that being supported to care for myself is the way forward, not Dad dictating my routines to suit his working day. I know Nanna Rebekah's feeling steamrollered by Dad too.' A tear welled over the rim of one eye and she dashed it away. 'Us not coming here for the service kids' reunion was typical. He made the decision on his own. When I said I wanted to come he said, "Getting you through airports would be a nightmare."'

Marci looked tearful too. 'I'm sorry it's come to this, Mum.'

247

'Yeah,' said Zach, inadequately. What he heard through his mum's fairly diplomatic explanation was that Steve was controlling. Yes, well, Steve *was* controlling.

'Everything came to a head when he tried to guilt you into coming home, Zach, though I'd asked him not to.' Amanda sniffed. 'I challenged him and he snapped, "If everything's left to me then you have to put up with the way I do things." So I said we were over.' She took a tissue from the pocket of her dress and blew her nose.

'How did he take it?' Zach tried to imagine. His customarily mild-mannered mother could stand up for herself but his dad often met a challenge with an explosion.

Amanda wiped the corner of her eye. 'He sneered at the idea of me being able to live alone then stomped off to spend the night in the spare room. He wasn't open to discussion so I began packing. He went to work without saying a word yesterday so I booked in a Gatwick hotel and went taxi-train-taxi there. I've hardly slept because of getting the taxi for the six-twenty flight this morning. I'm sorry—' she stopped and wiped away more tears trickling down her cheeks '—I had to get away. But now I'm here you both look horrified.'

Zach knelt and slid his arms around his mother, knowing how badly she must have wanted to get to Malta if she'd subject her poor painful body to the rigours of the journey from Cornwall. 'It's fantastic to see you. We're just shocked at what's happened.' But what about those frigging stairs? Without ground-level accommodation Amanda would have problems if Zach wasn't there to help her. Marci would be willing, he knew, but Amanda was heavy and Marci had Paige. Paige took the stairs like a gazelle but four-year-olds needed supervision.

Amanda obviously intended to grit her teeth and struggle

but Zach wasn't convinced that teeth gritting would counteract unstable knees and racking pain.

'I think the first thing is to get you settled in a room,' he said, thinking rapidly. 'Maybe Marci would get you a cup of tea while I change a bed.' He didn't say it would be his because it had a double bed and an en suite shower complete with grab rail. Paige could maybe go in with Marci so he could have Paige's room but he'd worry about that later. He left Marci with Amanda while he changed sheets, freed up wardrobe space, conducted a lightning-fast clean-up in the bathroom and grabbed a pile of clean shorts, T-shirts, underwear and toiletries.

He rejoined his mum and sister as Paige began asking about lunch and what they were going to do today. Leaving Marci to deal with her daughter, he grabbed Amanda's suitcases and showed her to what was now her room. Standing in the middle of it, balancing on her sticks and edging from foot to foot, she burst into tears. Dismayed, he inched her around until she could perch on the edge of the bed, then hugged her while she cried in slow sobs.

'It's OK,' he murmured – senselessly because it obviously wasn't all that OK to end your marriage and be exhausted. 'You'll be OK here.' Apart from there being thirty-two steep steps to negotiate whenever Amanda wanted to go anywhere. He had no idea how they were going to make this work but if his mum needed refuge so much that she'd go to the lengths she'd gone to, he wasn't going to discourage her.

Chapter Eighteen

Rosa read the message from her dad and sighed. *Your mums not answering my messages now please ask her to.* Nearby, Dory studied Monday afternoon's recipe trial of chocolate hazelnut brownies with dairy-free dark chocolate and flax ground in water in place of an egg. 'OK,' Dory said. 'They're ready.'

'Let's get some pics before and after you cut it into squares,' Rosa suggested. The phone was on the tripod ready. 'They smell delicious. I'm looking forward to this tasting.'

She waited until the photos had been taken and notes made before she decided to read out Glenn's text to Dory.

Popping a square of brownie into her mouth, Dory snorted. 'I'm not giving him money. I told him not to contact me again on the subject so yes, I'm ignoring his messages until he hits on a new topic.'

The reaction wasn't unexpected or unreasonable but it made Rosa feel uncomfortable, not because she felt sorry for Glenn but because he was her father. Glenn had given her life, it was true. He'd also given her the distrust of men that had made her jump to conclusions with Marcus, hastening the relationship's end – although that had proved a good thing. All she felt for Marcus now was irritation and injury over the spot he'd put her in.

It was with Zach she felt a connection. They'd known each other only a few weeks and shared that one night yet she felt he'd never disappoint her.

She wondered what he was doing. She'd scarcely seen him since Amanda had arrived two days ago. She knew the story behind Amanda's unexpected appearance from late-night phone conversations. It had been hard to meet up because Zach was spending a lot of time with his family. Amanda, leaving Steve to come to Malta despite her severe mobility issues, felt relieved to have reached a sanctuary but was upset and worried.

'I helped her down all the stairs yesterday to take her for a drive, and up again later, but the effort and pain was almost too much for her,' he'd said on the phone, sounding anxious. 'I hate to see her in pain and I'm frightened she'll stumble. Whatever her support group says I think it's going to be hard for her, with her physical limitations, to start a life alone. Marci's worried about her too, and the more Marci worries the more Marci worries, if you see what I mean.'

'I do,' Rosa had assured him but had had nothing more useful to offer than a listening ear. She'd been about to suggest they meet up on The Ramp and go for a moonlit walk when Paige had woken in the throes of a nightmare and Zach had gone to help soothe her.

Rosa hadn't seen anything of him today but she'd been busy in the kitchen with Dory and probably an entire army could have trudged across the edge of the terrace and Rosa wouldn't have been aware. Dory was squeezing a couple of weeks' work into one and wasn't to be turned from cooking every day. 'When I've gone you can have a lovely week off,' she promised.

Rosa replied wryly. 'Apart from updating the Cafeteria Cook's blog, scheduling posts, sorting and labelling pics?' But she winked so Dory would know she was joking. Dory was worried about meeting her editor next week in case she discovered there was a sinister reason behind the Mediterranean book being so abruptly halted and wanted to be able to report the vegan book to be underway.

Dory greeted the joke with only a quiet smile so Rosa gave her a hug. 'Are you still worried about Grandpa?' She'd phoned him a couple of times herself but he always seemed much as usual to her.

Dory sighed. 'He's going to miss his friend who's relocating. And now two of his usual golfing society friends are having operations that will keep them off the course for a few months. I'm worried he's more lonely than he's letting on.'

'He'll be glad to see you,' Rosa said consolingly. 'And you'll be glad to see Leslie, too.'

At least Dory's face lit up at that. 'Can't wait!' She glanced at her watch. 'In fact, I'm due to FaceTime him. You stay and have a lovely relax.' She patted Rosa's hand.

Dory had left her the clearing up along with her kind words so 'a lovely relax' wasn't on the cards yet, but Rosa didn't mind loading the dishwasher. She just reflected that the more worried Dory got, the more determined Rosa became not to add to her anxieties by confessing the tight spot she found herself in regarding hers and Marcus's house.

Finally, she carried a mug of coffee onto the terrace, enjoying the scent of pine on the night air, and decided that if she didn't know the answer to her own problems she might have it in her power to resolve one of her mum's. She drew out her phone and telephoned Glenn.

'Is that you, Rosa?' Glenn's voice asked cautiously in her ear.

It had been several years since they'd actually spoken rather than just exchanging occasional texts. 'Yes. I got your message.' She waited in vain for his voice to spark off a feeling of affection . . . or of anything.

'She hasn't answered.' Glenn sounded discontented.

'No?' she replied neutrally. Then, as diplomatically as she could, 'Can you explain why you feel she owes you something?'

'She's my wife,' he expostulated. 'It's all right when the man gets a windfall, isn't it? The woman soon sticks her hand out. I don't see this is any different. I haven't got a job and you'd think she'd be sympathetic.'

Rosa felt her eyebrows rise and instead of saying, 'Wife? Ha!' said persuasively, 'You split up when I was a baby. Do people really get new settlements after all that time?'

'She expected spousal maintenance and child support,' he returned obstinately. 'So it's fair.'

She answered him firmly. 'But you didn't pay your maintenance or child support very often, did you? You were hardly ever in work. I remember Mum doing all kinds of jobs at home from addressing envelopes to making toy parts to make ends meet. When I got older we used to deliver leaflets together in the school holidays and at weekends.'

'She managed,' he scoffed.

'Yes, because all that was in addition to her work in school kitchens. I'm shocked you feel entitled, to be honest.' She lay back on the lounger in the shade of the parasol.

253

Why was she even bothering to try and rationalise with her dad? It was like dancing with smoke.

Glenn said bitterly. 'Your mother went in for a baby. Why should I spend my life paying for her decision?'

She tried not to recoil from that. '*Your* decisions were selfish and unsupportive so why should she pay for that? I really think that if you pursue this all you'll end up with is a solicitor's bill. And PS, thanks for reminding me you never wanted me, Dad. That really got me onside.'

He muttered something that might have been an excuse but Rosa had lost patience. Dory was right to ignore Glenn's preposterous demands and there had been nothing to gain in Rosa trying to mediate. 'Don't keep messaging Mum or me about this,' she suggested. 'It's a waste of everyone's time.' She ended the call feeling hollow, regretful that she'd probably severed the threads, weak as they were, between them. If she was ever a parent she'd definitely try to be a Dory rather than a Glenn. Dory might chivvy Rosa about sometimes but her heart was big and her intentions everlastingly good. Rosa vowed not to mind about being tied to the kitchen this week. Dory had offered her a fabulous opportunity to come out here and when you compared that with the lack of anything from Glenn . . .

Moving her lounger into the sun, she wondered what it would be like if Dory actually settled down with someone. With Leslie. After being the focus of Dory's love for so long it would be an adjustment for Rosa but she was in her early thirties for goodness' sake and Dory totally deserved it.

When her phone bleeped on a text she rolled her eyes, thinking it might be her father again. Instead it was Zach. *You dating yet? xx*

She laughed softly as she replied: *If the right man asks.* xx

Until he does, fancy going out with me? A walk to a nice bar this evening? xx

Smile widening she texted back, *Sounds lovely.*

Meet me at nine, he ended.

On The Ramp, she agreed. They weren't exactly a secret but, by tacit consent, neither had they advertised whatever was going on between them. With so much uncertainty in their lives discretion felt best.

As nine drew near, the low sound of Dory's voice on the phone in her room telling Rosa that her mum was well occupied, she let herself out and was waiting at the foot of the stairs when Zach jogged down them.

'Hey, beautiful,' he murmured, and kissed her, slow and long, his caressing tongue sending tingles to all her most sensitive areas. He held her against him as if needing the hug and she felt aware of his blood pulsing through his veins, the air flowing in and out of his lungs, his heart pumping. Everything that was him.

Then they walked out to the seafront road, watching the lights scribbling in gold on the black water between the yachts. On Manoel Island stood the pale bulk of long-deserted buildings. One had been the hospital for infectious diseases in the seventeenth century, Dory had told her. Now its empty windows were as black as the night but its stone as pale as the moonlight.

Zach's hand was hot around hers. There was not a breath of breeze and the warm air seemed to settle around them as they strolled. 'So we finally broke out,' she joked gently. 'Has your mum settled in?'

He heaved a sigh. 'Slightly. She's been playing I-Spy with Paige through the window of the apartment today but she must feel restricted. Those steps are a nightmare for her. It's got so I feel guilty for running up and down them so easily.'

She squeezed his fingers sympathetically. 'Any news from your dad?'

'They've talked several times. She doesn't go into detail but I get the impression he gets cross and she puts the phone down. As usual, he cuts off his nose to spite his face. If he wants a reconciliation he should shut up and listen to her. Take notice.' His short laugh was without humour.

They made their way to Ta' Xbiex yacht marina and into Gżira gardens where palms and pines had become elegant silhouettes in the lights that flanked the pathways. Although there was chatter and laughter from a nearby bar, the gardens were occupied only by the shadowy presences of strolling couples and a group of teens perching on the back of a bench.

Rosa and Zach found an isolated seat under a twisted pine, pine needles rustling beneath their feet. Zach slid his arms around her and kissed her forehead. She leaned into him. 'Families, huh?' she said. 'You're obviously worried about yours.'

'It's a tricky time. Mum needs my support and who the hell knows what Dad needs.' He laughed. 'I thought I'd coped with having my sister and my niece to consider but now I'm living with my mum.'

She laughed too. It was too warm for cuddles but she didn't want to move away from the firmness of his body. 'I'm living with my mum as well.'

He sobered. 'I don't want you to think I've done a hit-and-run on you after our night together. Not by choice. I want to spend more time with you but it's so weird. I'm not even sure if I should hold your hand in front of anyone from our families. We've had no opportunity to agree boundaries.'

'It's an unusual situation, with you and me here temporarily,' she agreed softly. She made herself say the next words, though they weighed her down with sadness. 'Those crossroads we both stood at . . . some of the roads seem less accessible now.'

He nodded.

His top was sleeveless and she rested her cheek on the flesh of his shoulder. 'Let's pack our backpacks and take off down one of the roads before it closes altogether,' she murmured. When he met the comment with silence she glanced up at him. 'That was a joke. I know it's impossible. Your mum's reliant on you right now. I've seen how much help she needs on the stairs.' And Rosa couldn't afford to consider setting off on her travels now Marcus had failed to take over the mortgage. She hadn't told Zach that it looked as if she'd have to go home and return to her job. Instead, clutching at straws, she'd sent an email to two of the local estate agents asking for their views on whether hers and Marcus's house would sell or perhaps rent out. Neither had answered yet. Until she absolutely knew there was no choice but for her to give up on her summer in Malta, she was reluctant to let stark reality spoil what time she had left.

It was ironic when she remembered how unsettled she'd been when she first arrived on this Mediterranean island baking in the sun. Now all she wanted was to stay here.

They left the bench and headed for a bar, finding a table amongst the tourists outside, drinking wine and talking until closing time at midnight. It was like a proper date. They wandered home, the roads quiet now, the millions of stars brightening in the black velvet sky as households put out their lights.

On the first flight of stairs they paused before the lower terrace to share long, unhurried kisses. Rosa could feel Zach's arousal against her but he murmured, 'I want you – but not like a couple of teenagers up against the wall while their parents wait for them to come home. If it was a choice it would be hot but I'm not feeling much love for it as a necessity.'

She slid her hands inside his top and stroked his back. 'There must be hotel rooms available on the island. But Mum will be flying off on Saturday . . .'

He kissed her again, his hand on the nape of her neck as if frightened she'd float away if he didn't nestle as close to her as he could. 'That sounds worth waiting for.'

He kissed her again and again and things got pretty steamy up against that wall after all.

'I think my bubble's burst,' Dory declared dramatically the next morning.

They'd been shopping for cannellini beans because Dory wanted to make a vegan Italian ribollita. Somewhere between a stew and a soup, though traditionally making use of leftovers, ribollita wouldn't be ribollita without the beans. Rosa had already recounted her unsatisfactory telephone conversation with Glenn, met by angry head-shaking from Dory, and now Dory was glaring at her phone as Rosa drove. 'I've got another email from my editor, Defne. She's asking to put next week's meeting back to Wednesday as she "still needs a few things to come together".'

Rosa, who found some Maltese drivers believed in travelling from A to B faster than she would herself, kept her eyes firmly on the junction she was crossing. 'That doesn't sound too terrible,' she ventured, squinting against the sun. She hoped not, anyway. Life was holding altogether too many surprises for comfort at the moment.

'Doesn't sound encouraging either,' her mother almost snapped. 'People only keep news to themselves if they know it needs breaking gently. I'm sure Defne's hiding something. I bet they're not going to offer a new contract. *The Cafeteria Cook Does the Plant-Based Diet* will be my last with them.'

Rosa couldn't shift her from this gloomy view, though she tried. 'Are you going to ask what Nita thinks?' Dory usually got straight onto her agent to discuss career matters.

'Doing it now.' Dory tapped on her phone the rest of the way home. She was still at it when Zach appeared at the kitchen door and she only looked up with an absent smile when Rosa let him in, her heart tripping over itself at the sight of him, hair combed diagonally back, shorts and top clean and fresh, feet bare.

She greeted him, hoping she didn't sound too breathless.

He sent her a long slow smile. 'Do you mind if I put a chair for Mum on the side of the terrace? It makes a big difference if she can stop for a break halfway downstairs.'

'Of course!' Rosa and Dory chorused, Dory adding, 'You don't have to bring a chair down. There are plenty out there.'

He looked pleased as he thanked her. 'Also, do you fancy coming up for lunch? Mum would like to get to know you better. She says it will be salad so she doesn't have to compete with a famous cook.'

Dory laughed off this description but accepted the invitation. But she was visibly dispirited again once Zach had left and said, 'We won't begin work till after lunch.'

259

Rosa was startled at this departure from the pace of the past few days. 'What shall I do?'

'Chill,' Dory threw back over her shoulder as she headed for her room.

So Rosa grabbed a chocolate brownie and took a book out under the parasol on the terrace until lunchtime rolled around and Dory reappeared.

They took the stone steps to the upper apartment, panting in the noonday temperatures in the mid-thirties. They were welcomed at the door by Marci, Paige hopping at her side. 'Hello, hello!' bellowed Paige. 'We're all having lunch together. Granny's here! We've been cooking chicken and sardines.'

'Not together,' Marci put in, dark eyes smiling. Rosa hadn't seen her for several days and Zach had mentioned her anxiety a couple of times so she was pleased to see her looking composed. Maybe, she thought as they followed her into the hall and then into the open kitchen-dining area, having her mother near was having a positive effect on Marci, no matter how style-cramping Zach was finding the current living arrangements.

Amanda, now they had this chance to get to know her better, proved to be a lovely woman, a little nervous in her manner, moving her large body slowly and breathlessly from task to task. 'Thanks for coming,' she said. 'The stairs make it hard for me to get out. I do need to make myself tackle them sometimes, though.' She carried to the table an olivewood board stacked with crusty bread. 'It's important to keep as healthy as I can so I need to walk.'

Rosa felt sorry for her. She seemed so sweet and Zach, Marci and Paige obviously held her in great affection. If she winced when lifting something too heavy for her swollen wrists, Zach or Marci automatically put a hand beneath hers to help with the weight. The strategy of helping rather than taking over was how she'd like to be treated if she found herself in similar straits, she decided.

They gathered around the table and Rosa was conscious of Zach's presence, feeling his gaze like a caress. Once or twice his hand brushed her bare leg beneath the table, which was . . . well, delicious. She was sorry when after lunch Dory sighed and said though she wasn't in the mood they'd better go and work. Rosa agreed to a late afternoon 'shnorkel' with Paige and Zach though and, with that to look forward to, followed her mother down for another afternoon of note taking and clearing up.

Dory was uncharacteristically gloomy as she assembled celery, onion, carrot, kale and garlic. 'Am I wasting my time even writing this bloody book?'

'It's contracted,' Rosa protested.

'*A* book's contracted,' Dory responded. 'They could change their minds again about what they want.'

Dory was so down that when Rosa checked her emails between washing veg and taking notes to discover a message from one of the estate agents she'd approached, she kept the contents to herself, though she read it with a silently sinking heart. Market conditions on the Roman Way estate, it said, were 'extremely challenging'. The property *could* be valued for her if she wished to list it but perhaps it would make sense for her first to examine listings of similar properties and see whether she wished to proceed to market. It also gave a ballpark rental figure for properties like hers, supposing tenants could be found.

She stared at the figure in dismay. That level of rent would cover the mortgage but leave little for maintenance or periods when the property might be empty. There was a link to information on their website, from which she gathered that only the biggest of numpty landlords would base financial decisions on the property never being empty between tenants. And if the numpty landlord did so, the mortgage company would not.

Her lunch felt like a belly full of lead.

Then Dory gave a yelp that snatched Rosa's attention from her own woes. 'That arse!' Dory snapped, glaring at her phone. 'That *arse*! Oh, I'd like to kick him in the nuts.'

Shocked, because she never remembered hearing her mum offer anybody violence, even hypothetically, Rosa gasped. 'What now?'

Before replying, Dory grabbed wine from the fridge and poured two glasses, thrusting one into Rosa's hands and downing half of hers. 'Your father!' she gasped. 'He's actually had the utter cocking cheek to get a solicitor onto me! John Hector of Hector, Charles and Charles has requested I share details of my earnings since the date we separated as their client is "suffering a long period of unemployment" and my circumstances have changed significantly.'

'No!' Rosa breathed, craning her neck to read along with her mother. Dory almost blew a gasket over the phrase 'with reference to a number of factors including the assets available for distribution'.

'They're my assets and they're not available!' she raged. 'There's no mention that Glenn never fulfilled his spousal maintenance and child maintenance obligations and we separated over thirty years ago.' And she went off into a such a long stream of swearwords that Rosa was secretly impressed.

'I'll ring him,' she declared, reaching for her phone.

Dory stayed her hand. 'Don't muddy the water. I'll see a solicitor while I'm in the UK next week. This is nothing more than a bloody try-on.'

Sinking onto a bar stool, Rosa sipped her wine thoughtfully. 'It doesn't make sense, Mum. You can't claim post-divorce, can you? There must have been a settlement at the time – if you had anything to divide when you split up.'

'We divided things all right,' Dory snorted, polishing off her wine as if it were water. 'Like he got the car and I got the car *loan*.' Then she groaned and put down her empty glass in favour of clutching her head. 'Damn, blast and buggeration. We never actually got divorced.'

'Whaaaat?' Rosa's ears began to buzz. 'You and Dad *didn't get divorced*? Of course you did, when I was a baby. *Didn't you?*'

Dory topped up both wine glasses and plumped down on the bar stool next to Rosa's wearing an expression of guilty misery. 'Sorry. I should have told you this before.'

'Yes.' Rosa noticed her wine glass shook when she picked it up. Her mind searched through a fog of memories, trying to recall occasions when Dory might have used the word, 'divorced'. No, it had always been, 'I'm single' or 'when we split up'.

'But you've never corrected me when I said you were divorced,' she pointed out.

Dory wiped tears from both cheeks. 'Sorry, but it never seemed important. I *felt* divorced. When we first split up I was advised to go for legal separation with an enforceable agreement as to maintenance and support. Glenn's response was to get himself fired so he didn't have to pay it. I suspect he lived off cash-in-hand jobs and being someone's unofficial lodger. He was a free spirit like that. And for "free spirit" read "shady character",' she added bitterly.

Hardly able to believe her ears, Rosa demanded, 'But you never took the next logical step – divorce?'

'Logical?' Dory picked up her glass and put it down again as if wondering where the wine had gone. 'It actually seemed *il*logical. It would mean a bill if a solicitor handled it as well as time I didn't have to do it DIY. I was too busy fighting to stay afloat. In the early days, still being married was protection against other men who tried to get too close and later I pushed it to the back of my mind. I wasn't surprised that Glenn didn't start proceedings either. He didn't want to remarry any more than I did. Being tied down didn't exactly suit him. And I never dreamed that I'd make a few quid and he'd have the gall to suggest he was due a share.'

Rosa sighed, reading to the end of the email from John Hector of Hector, Charles and Charles. 'It says here that English courts have the option to award ongoing maintenance payments to the financially weaker spouse. They suggest it might be better to make a clean break and a lump sum payment now.'

'I'll give all my money to a donkey's home first,' Dory vowed.

After Dory had gone out 'to cool down', she said, although storming off into the afternoon heat seemed an unlikely way of doing that, Rosa stowed unused ingredients in the fridge, thinking hard.

Her mum was in such a fix that Rosa was more determined than ever not to share her increasingly bad news about the Roman Way house, saying, 'How about giving me a large sum to throw down a black hole of negative equity?' And if the claims of Hector, Charles and Charles had any merit, Dory might need her money.

How on earth had they got here? Two weeks ago they'd been enjoying Malta with Dory riding high in her career and Marcus fast fading into Rosa's background. She resolved to focus on the week (or whatever) of Dory's absence when she'd be able to spend time with Zach. Take a breath.

Afterwards . . . well, that would be decision time.

For now, she'd cheer herself up with a dance. Her phone was already connected to the kitchen's smart TV and she found her playlist on YouTube and scrolled down until she found Taylor Swift's 'Shake it Off'. In her imagination, as she danced, she shook off Marcus, the house, the mortgage, negative equity, the bastards who had decided that right beside the estate was a good place for a dual carriageway and the exceedingly odd behaviour of her parents.

Then the door burst open and Paige flew in crying, 'Can we dance with you?' Zach was on her heels and soon they were all thrashing their arms around to Taylor Swift, singing lustily and not caring if they got the steps wrong. Rosa threw back her head to laugh at Zach flopping his arms like an orangutan. Marcus would never have fooled about like that. Soon she really did begin to feel better.

Dory returned when the dancing was over and Rosa had changed ready to go snorkelling. 'I've found a solicitor in Liggers Moor and made an appointment for Monday,' she said grimly, wiping sweat from her forehead and pulling a bottle of cold water from the fridge.

Zach edged towards the door. 'If you two have something you need to talk about, Paige and I can swim on our own.'

'Awwwwww, nooooooo,' Paige moaned, deflating with disappointment.

'It's nothing secret.' Dory told Zach about Glenn's perfidy and the email from the solicitor.

He listened as she quickly gave him a run-down of the

afternoon's events, frowning. 'But where did the solicitor get your email address?'

Dory shrugged. 'Glenn had it so I suppose he passed it on.'

Zach's eyebrows became dark slashes above his eyes. 'I'm not an expert, but do you think a solicitor would use an email address they don't have permission to use?'

'Well, they've done it.' Dory called the email up to show Zach.

Zach read it then muttered, 'Give me a moment.' He began tapping and swiping at the phone screen. In about ten seconds he passed the phone back to Dory. 'I can't find a law company by the name of Hector, Charles and Charles. Nor their address.'

Eyes widening, Dory slowly took the phone back. 'That utter ratbag. He's made this up to scare me into settling with him, hasn't he?'

'That would be my guess.' Zach grinned. 'He probably made the logo and stuff on Canva and created what sounds like officialese by picking up phrases from some lawyer's website. The email address would probably lead back to him if you had the computer science to follow it through. You can probably forget it.'

'Forget it?' Dory said dangerously. 'I do *not* think so. I have an appointment with a solicitor on Monday. I'm going to make Glenn regret this.' Then she obviously remembered Rosa and said with compunction, 'Sorry. I don't want to do anything you'll find upsetting. What do you think?'

Rosa hoisted her snorkelling gear over her shoulder, thinking longingly of plunging into the cool ocean less than a hundred yards from where she stood. 'I think you should get a divorce.'

Chapter Nineteen

From the bathroom, Zach heard his mother scream.

He'd been musing on whether he should have another go at finding Luccio but now he threw open the shower cubicle door and, grabbing a towel, sprinted out into the hall with water streaming down his body, stubbing his toe on the hall table as his feet slithered on the tiles.

Then Amanda laughed and said, 'I honestly can't believe it. I can't believe my eyes! Why on earth didn't you tell us?'

From this Zach deduced that whatever had made Amanda scream, she wasn't in danger. He slowed his pace, limping into the kitchen-diner to see Amanda hugging someone awkwardly at the same time as looking down and saying, 'Isn't he a darling? Oh dear, I think I ought to sit down.'

Zach, clutching his towel with one hand, shoved a bar stool up to Amanda's behind. 'There you go.' Then his gaze fell on a slight woman with spiky black hair grinning at him, a huge backpack towering higher than her head.

And a baby in a carrier on her front.

'Electra?' he said in astonishment.

'Hey,' she said laconically. 'Didn't realise Mum was here.' Her hand rose to cup the back of the baby's head protectively. 'This is Huxley. Your nephew. I call him Hux.'

Astounded, Zach said, 'Holy shit!' Then he glanced around to check Paige wasn't within earshot. He took in Electra's air of wary defensiveness and the exhaustion around her eyes. Then he stepped in for a one-armed hug, at the same time inspecting the little boy who was fast asleep in the papoose. He wasn't a tiny infant – probably as much as a year old, Zach estimated – with a headful of hair as thick and black as Zach's own. 'He's beautiful but he must be heavy,' he said, not betraying his shock and astonishment at Electra not only being here but, apparently, having become a mother without mentioning a word to her family, which was a step up on even her level of free-spiritedness. 'Give me ten seconds to jump into a pair of shorts and I'll help you with your stuff.'

When he returned, Marci and Paige had arrived on the scene and Electra was looking more exhausted by the moment. Zach decided to take charge. 'Marci, could you hold Huxley? Paige, you could sit next to Mummy and Huxley, couldn't you? Electra, let me have that backpack. It looks enough to pull you over.'

Relieved of baby sling and backpack, Electra almost fell into a chair. Her legs and arms, protruding from cut-offs and T-shirt, were thinner than he remembered. She wore the staleness of a long journey. Her hair still spiked but her skin, which was usually fairer than Zach's and Marci's, had darkened, presumably from the Thai sun.

Amanda got her a drink and a sandwich she only picked at while she gazed around at them all, saying bluntly, 'Shall I save you a load of questions and give you the bullet points? I decided to move on from Thailand because everything's twice as expensive there for foreigners than for nationals and thought I'd call in here to see Zach and Marci. Hux's dad is Thai and was only casual. He doesn't know about the baby because I didn't realise until I'd moved on from Panan Krabi to Bangkok that I was even pregnant and I wouldn't know how to contact him.' She smiled faintly around at the astounded faces of her family. 'I'm sorry I didn't tell you but—' Then the smile faded. 'Where's Dad?'

Instantly Zach understood. Steve would be difficult about Huxley in the same way he'd been difficult about Paige. He approved of babies born to two parents who were married to one another, preferably in a church, before the infant's arrival. 'In the UK,' he said reassuringly. They could explain the parlous state of their parents' marriage presently.

Electra heaved a relieved sigh. 'Huxley's lovely but he's hard work.' Her lip wobbled and, as if in sympathy, Huxley squirmed on Marci's lap and let out a long whinge. 'I'm shattered,' she whispered.

Amanda, looking distressed, struggled to her feet and laid her hands on Electra's shoulders. 'You're here now, darling. Don't worry.' Her voice was comforting but her face was pink and her lips shook.

Zach opted to play to his strength: pragmatism. 'I'll change sheets and stuff then you can go to bed.' Leaving Marci to deal with the fast-waking Huxley and see to changing and feeding him, he vanished into the room that had been Paige's, then his – and was now about to become Electra and Huxley's. He gathered up his things then changed the bed he'd used and put the mattress of the other on the floor for Huxley. He knew Huxley was too small for a normal height bed but he didn't have a cot in his back pocket.

Within five minutes his youngest sister was fast asleep while the other members of the family looked after Huxley who, nappy clean and tummy full of scrambled egg and bread and butter, toddled and laughed, his black eyes sparkling. Whenever he saw something he wanted he extended his hand towards it, opening and closing his fingers and saying, 'Utts!' They decided that he was saying 'Hux' in the hopes that the object in question might be given to him.

'Gosh, a grandson,' Amanda kept marvelling, eying this unexpected and lively addition to the family, trying to keep Huxley from crashing into her legs. Then, her eyes shadowing, 'I hope Electra's OK.'

It was evening before Electra emerged to answer the question. Rested, showered and in clean clothes she looked much more the sparky little sister Zach had always known as she sat down at the dinner table. 'I had a pretty rough time at the birth and the hospital bills took up a big chunk of my reserve,' she said between mouthfuls. 'Help with Hux cost a lot too. The kindergartens are great but not free.'

Zach wasn't shy about asking what he wanted to know. 'Did anyone hurt you, Electra?'

She rolled her eyes. 'Put away your sword of protectiveness, big brother. Of course not.'

'Then why all the secrecy?'

She sat back with a sigh, her eyes flicking to her mother as she appeared to debate her reply. Finally, she said, 'I couldn't face the aggro with Dad. You know what he was like about Paige.'

'Oh, dear.' Amanda's eyes filled with tears. 'That's why you came here instead of home to England.'

Electra gave her an apologetic look at the same time as cutting up bread and butter for Huxley, who was making his meal vanish like a human food disposal unit. The family apartment hadn't been equipped with a high chair but the one in Aunt Giusi's holiday let next door hadn't been in use so Zach had borrowed it. 'If I told you but didn't tell Dad it would have put you in a difficult situation, Mum. But now I've made a decision and I'm en route to England because I think it will be easier for me to handle the work/childcare balance there. I have to support my son and give him a settled childhood.' She reached out and gently stroked Amanda's hand. 'I'm pathetically glad to see you. Just give me a while to work up to telling Dad, OK? Trying to be a traveller and a single mum proved a bit much. I need to gather my strength before I face him.'

Marci gave her a sympathetic hug. 'Don't worry. Dad's in England and you're here with us. You gather all the strength you want.'

Zach, though, put forward another view. 'Why not get the worst of Dad's rant over by phone before he meets Huxley? He's difficult but not an ogre. You have to tell him sometime.'

With a shrug Electra, changed the subject. 'There are only three bedrooms here. How's it going to work? Have you given up your own room to Hux and me, Zach? That's not fair on you.'

'I can take the sofa,' he said, refusing to acknowledge that with four adults and two small children the apartment felt full to bursting. The stairs were going to be a pain for Electra with Huxley as well as for Amanda. The outside space was on the roof or in the garden a floor below. Huxley was obviously bursting with energy and, as Zach had discovered while Electra slept, not shy about letting his feelings known when things didn't suit him.

As if to reinforce Zach's thoughts, Huxley tired of his meal and began to shout, straining against the restriction of the high chair straps. When Electra set him free he toddled off to investigate the kitchen cupboards. In the course of the afternoon Marci had already moved everything to higher cupboards that could harm him or break.

Now Huxley busied himself pulling saucepans out from a shelf and dropping them. Zach hastily got up to intercede before the tiles cracked. 'I'll fit childproof latches on the cupboards tomorrow,' he promised, as Huxley began to bellow with rage at having his saucepans put out of his reach.

Perhaps catching Huxley's mood, Paige demanded to be allowed to leave the table and play with 'the baby'. Marci couldn't persuade her to show Huxley how nicely she could eat and gave up, complaining that Paige was always up at the crack of dawn when she hadn't eaten enough dinner the evening before.

Zach knew what that would mean for him, sleeping on the sofa. His thoughts strayed to getting a camp bed and mosquito net and sleeping on the roof terrace.

It wasn't until the children ran out of steam and were both asleep that the adults were able to talk. Amanda gently told Electra about her and Steve; Electra, listening round-eyed, gave her mum an impulsive hug and cried, 'I never thought it would happen but you've got to do what's best for you.'

Apart from that, Amanda was unusually quiet.

While Electra and Marci talked about their futures Zach texted Rosa. She agreed to meet him on the lower terrace and he slipped away with a casual farewell, stepping out into the soft summer evening.

It felt as if he were leaving all the stress behind.

A shadowy figure jogged down the stone steps and advanced towards Rosa with a quick stride. Then she was lifted off her feet and fitted against the firmness of Zach's body while they kissed. It felt right to melt against him, to wrap her arms around his shoulders and her legs about his hips as they fastened hungrily upon each other.

The night was close and sweat beaded on her back but in a day of bad things, this, at least, was good. So good.

Eventually, Zach restored her to her feet, breathing fast. He took her hand and they headed off to a small bar Zach knew in Msida. Several of the boats in the marina showed lights as they wandered past. 'People living on board,' Zach commented. 'Imagine spending weeks on a boat, sailing from country to country. Malta, Cyprus, Greece—'

'You sound as if you're ready to try it.'

He laughed, pulling her closer as they walked. 'Sounds pretty appetising right now.' Then, as they found a table outside the bar and ordered drinks, he told her that his other sister, Electra, had turned up, 'complete with a toddler none of us knew about, a little boy called Huxley'.

Rosa stared. His hair wasn't as neatly combed as usual, falling over his forehead as if wilting in the heat. 'Why didn't she tell you?'

He shook his head. 'Because she knew Dad would be difficult,' she said. She does take her free-spiritedness to extremes.' He drank deeply of his beer before adding ruefully, 'She's hurt Mum's feelings. She said she couldn't tell Mum because it would be expecting her to keep a secret from Dad but it's a weak explanation. They Skype regularly. I found myself wanting to tell her to grow up. There's maybe more of Dad in me than I like to admit.' He rolled his eyes and laughed.

Then he asked whether Dory had calmed down about the trick Glenn had tried to play and the conversation moved on.

Rosa had meant to tell him that she'd probably have to go home soon. The second estate agent had replied with a brief message saying sorry but they could not currently accept her property on their books. They didn't say it was because it was on the Roman Way estate and they couldn't sell what they already had listed from that area, but it was logical to suppose it.

With a feeling of clutching at straws she'd telephoned Chellice, trying to keep her own tone neutral in the face of Chellice's obvious wariness at hearing from her out of the blue after so many months. 'I was wondering if you could give Marcus a message for me.' The message was imaginary but she hoped that by sounding ignorant of what Marcus had told her she'd discover whether or not it was true.

Chellice cut across her impatiently. 'We've split up and we're not working together either,' she snapped with no trace of awkwardness, which a lot of people would have felt in the circumstances of her having moved on to Rosa's turf only to abandon it when she found the grass not particularly sweet.

What had Rosa hoped to hear? That Marcus had lied, that Chellice was still living with him and could somehow be obligated to cover the mortgage?

She was acting like an ostrich, she told herself, as she wandered hand-in-hand with Zach. Unless Zach was going to not only move back to the UK but also make it somewhere close to Liggers Moor they were only ever going to have a long-distance thing – one that didn't have much of a chance. His family. Her family. Her ex's stupidity. She hadn't told him about the negative equity trap closing over her head and it would be so much nicer to pretend the rubbish stuff wasn't happening while Dory was away and she and Zach would have privacy in the apartment. Nothing, she told herself firmly, was going to interfere with that.

So she ordered another glass of wine and got Zach talking about where he'd go on his imaginary Mediterranean yacht journey of sunny skies and starry nights, pretending she would be going with him and arguing as to which of the Greek islands to visit as if it really was going to happen. One day.

Chapter Twenty

If there was anything more exhausting and stressful than manoeuvring down thirty-two steep steps with an adult with limited mobility, a toddler plus buggy, a small child and two bickering sisters, Zach had yet to meet it. And never wanted to. He zipped his lips when Paige suggested he 'just carry Granny' or pointed out that the weather was boiling and the baby screaming.

Amanda's smile kept wavering towards a grimace of pain, though Zach took as much of her weight as possible because it was Friday and she'd been stuck inside the apartment almost continuously since she arrived last Saturday. His car was inadequate to carry all of them so Zach had ordered a seven-seater cab to take them to Tigné Pjazza where there were strolls to be had on level ground.

Once down the dreaded steps, the plan did prove successful. Everyone enjoyed the drive of a couple of miles beside Lazaretto Creek and then Sliema Creek. It didn't matter if the traffic was slow because there were yachts and fishing boats to gaze at and a few people on paddle-boards – even one with a Labrador dog perched majestically on the front. Once at the piazza, Amanda, beaming beneath her white sunhat, was able to get along on her sticks between the blocks of apartments to see the rocks of Tigné Point and the wonderful view of Marsamxett Harbour, Valletta and Fort Manoel. Boats came and went busily on the brilliant blue sea while Amanda watched happily. Relaxing, Zach began to think of accessible areas for other trips out.

His sisters and their children continued along the walkway that looped back to the piazza but Zach knew stairs that lay that way and escorted his mum back along the path they'd come by, not sorry to have time alone with her. They rambled around the periphery of the piazza and gazed down at the old military buildings, reminders of Tigné Barracks. He was able to point out where the ack-ack guns had stood, guarding Tigné Point from marauding aircraft, and which block of offices had incorporated part of Tigné Barracks School, which Dory, her sister Lizzy and his dad had all attended. 'I remember it when all the barracks buildings still stood,' she said quietly.

'Was that when you brought me, before the girls were born?' Zach was familiar with this bit of family history.

'That's right. By the time we could afford to come again with all three of you this was all a massive building site.' Amanda turned. 'Here are your sisters and the children. I'm ready for lunch.'

Eating in the shade was pleasant. It was safe for the children as the piazza was pedestrian-only. Huxley had napped in his buggy and awoken full of smiles, especially when food was set before him. Amanda patted his foot where it dangled from the highchair and received a four-toothed smile in return.

Zach's sisters and his mum talked about the children

and Zach was able to think about the – much anticipated, on his part – scheduled departure of Dory tomorrow, and the luxury of privacy with Rosa. Yesterday evening Electra had asked him to take her to wherever Malta's clubland was and Marci had volunteered to babysit Hux. Zach had complied, feeling that Electra needed an evening off but Rosa, though invited, said she was shattered after a day in the kitchen and would leave him to show his sister the bright lights.

Feeling a prickle of guilt as he thought about Paceville, Zach had searched his memory and realised that it had been the early hours of Saturday when he'd last tried to check Luccio was OK. He fired off a text to Joseph asking if he'd heard anything from Luccio or his aunt. When Joseph replied to report that Teresa said she still hadn't seen Luccio but had received a text saying he was fine and staying with a friend Zach had replied: *Relieved!*

However, he wasn't naive enough to think that one vague text meant everything was OK in Luccio's life and had kept a sharp eye out for him in Paceville. It had been without result.

Now, lunch over, Zach's family sought the air-conditioned comfort of The Point shopping centre, which went down several levels below the one at which they entered. Again the party split in two and Zach was happy to stick with his mum, finding seats for her to rest on and helping her in and out of lifts. By the end of the afternoon Amanda was tired enough to want to return to the apartment and Paige asked about 'shnorkelling' so they once again called a cab.

The climb up the stairs was another torrid adventure in full sun, Electra and Marci following as Zach gave

Amanda his arm. He'd rather they'd gone ahead and left him to it but they seemed to think they were doing something helpful by edging along behind. It was he and Amanda who – finally – stepped into the hallway of the apartment first.

The sound of footsteps alerted Zach to a presence in what should have been an empty apartment. 'Who's there?' he called sharply.

A man stepped into the hall from the living area, sleeves rolled up, hands jammed truculently in his pockets.

'Dad?' said Zach disbelievingly.

'Steve?' gasped Amanda at the same time.

Steve scowled, hunching his shoulders. 'How the hell are you getting up and down those stairs?' he demanded.

'With difficulty – but I'm managing it.' Amanda trod past him with the halting, rocking gait that told Zach her knees were killing her and slowly lowered herself onto the sofa. The smiles that had wreathed her face all afternoon were gone. She met Steve's scowl calmly. 'I didn't expect to see you here.'

'I'm entitled to be. This apartment belongs to my mother.' Steve's gaze flicked to the others, who, unfreezing, followed Amanda into the living area.

Electra brought up the rear, eyes wary and defensive.

Steve's eyebrows abandoned their habitual position low over his eyes and shot up when his gaze fell on Huxley. 'Who's *this*?'

Huxley screwed up his nose in a toddler grin, apparently not minding the snap to Steve's tone. Electra dropped a kiss on her son's head. 'Huxley. My son. Your grandson.' With no warmth in her voice, she reeled off a bullet-point list of how Huxley came to be, similar to the one she'd given the others a couple of days ago then, declaring that

Huxley needed changing, headed for her room without waiting for her father's comment.

'Don't go after her,' Amanda cut in, before Steve, looking stunned, could do no more than stare down the hall in the direction in which Electra had vanished.

'Grampy, do you want to see my bedroom?' asked Paige, evidently not picking up on the tension. 'I sleep with Mummy now and Auntie Electra and Hux sleep in my room.'

'Maybe later,' Steve promised, managing a smile for her. 'I need to talk to Granny.'

Zach said, 'Hi, Dad,' noticing that Steve hadn't actually greeted any of them properly, then took a seat beside Amanda. 'What would you like to happen here?' he asked her. He ignored an exclamation of annoyance from Steve at his words.

Amanda gave a disbelieving shake of her head. 'I've no idea.' Her words were choked with tears.

'I'll get you a hotel room, if you don't want to stay here now.' It would be better for Steve to get a room but Zach knew that if he suggested it Steve would point out again that the apartment belonged to *his* mother. Zach patted her hand, anger at his father rising up inside him.

Steve had plenty of anger of his own. 'For goodness' sake, what next? I have to chase my wife across Europe and now you're trying to persuade her to go to a hotel?'

Zach's attention remained on his mother. 'Your call,' he told her seeing, from the corner of his eye, Marci taking Paige's hand and ushering her in the direction of their bedroom.

Amanda sighed. 'A hotel would be a waste of money and I can hardly hoof him out. I suppose I'll have to talk.' Then she added, 'But would you stay?'

It sounded like his idea of a nightmare but Zach nodded before saying to his father, 'Why didn't you sit down? Would you like a drink?'

'Thank you so much,' Steve said, his tone dripping sarcasm. It was a common tactic with him to get snotty and leave others to try and guess why. Zach had long since decided not to bother. He busied himself in the kitchen, opening cold bottles of Cisk beer and shoving biscuits on a plate in case his father hadn't eaten. It was a reflection of Amanda's state of mind that she, too, took a biscuit, although she didn't usually eat refined sugar because of her weight.

'I'm surprised to see you,' Zach heard Amanda begin with a hint of antagonism in her voice. 'When Zach invited us out here to have a holiday around the reunion, leaving aside the fact that *you* decided *I* couldn't travel, you said you couldn't get away from work and your mum needed help with your dad.'

'Those stairs are too much for you,' Steve began.

Amanda was having none of it. 'Answer my point.'

A quick glance over his shoulder rewarded Zach with a glimpse of Steve looking taken aback. He said, stiffly, 'Naturally, when I told work about you leaving me they gave me time off. And Mum has put other help in place for her and Dad. She says she has the money with the income from the apartment downstairs and coping with him between us has become too much.'

Whether it was Harry or Steve who'd become too much for Rebekah, Zach could only guess.

'So I'm here to sort things out,' Steve pronounced with the note of finality his family knew so well.

'You're not coming in with me,' Amanda muttered angrily. 'I'd sleep on the floor first.'

'You're not going to sleep on the floor,' Zach said gently before his father could respond.

'So where's he going to go?' Amanda challenged Zach. Her eyes shone with tears, her cheeks flushed.

'He'd better have the sofa.' Zach tried to sound soothing.

'But where will you sleep?' Amanda sniffed.

'I *am* here!' Steve broke in icily.

'Yes, that's the problem.' Amanda heaved herself to her feet and stumbled blindly to her room.

Silence followed her exit. Zach checked the time and saw it was nearly six. The family was supposed to be having supper on the lower terrace tonight to eat up the results of Dory's latest recipe tasting. He might have to make their excuses at this rate.

'I don't see what I've done wrong,' Steve grumbled bitterly. Zach thought it wisest not to comment but he did try and put himself in his dad's place. First Amanda had rejected his care and said most of it was never necessary and now Rebekah had made other arrangements for Harry. Was his dad feeling adrift? Unneeded?

Steve spoke again, his voice hard. 'I don't know what your sister thinks she's playing at.'

'Which one?' Zach dropped down in a chair and took in the permanent angry furrows on his dad's forehead, the once-dark hair that had been frosted both by years and cares.

'Electra! As if we didn't have enough with Paige—'

'Paige is a wonderful child and she loves you,' Zach retorted.

Steve had the grace to look abashed and even glanced about as if it had only just occurred to him that his granddaughter was no longer in the room. Then his appraising eye returned to Zach. 'I see there's a new tattoo.'

Zach glanced down at his forearm, at the open cage

282

that had felt so significant when he'd first come here. His skin, his ink, his business.

When he didn't respond Steve returned to his earlier complaint. 'I don't know what I've done wrong.'

Zach's patience snapped with a noise he almost heard. 'I could give you a list, if you truly want to know.'

Steve's eyes glittered. 'Then do go on,' he said, once again employing his unpleasant sarcasm.

Zach, in contrast, made sure to keep his own voice polite. 'I'm afraid you're negative. Let's take the immediate situation. You could have asked Mum how she was instead of telling her she couldn't climb the stairs, even though she'd patently just done it. You could have been less angry. Said hello to your children and Paige and given out a hug or two. You haven't seen Electra for two years yet you focused on something that, in your eyes, is wrong – having Huxley. You could have asked his name or said he was a lovely-looking kid. You could—' he paused to question his wisdom but then said it anyway '—have respected Mum's wishes and not come chasing after her.'

His face like thunder, Steve stormed to his feet. 'How dare you!'

Zach got up too. 'Easily. She's my mother. I love her. She needs someone to stick up for her.'

'Against me?' Steve spluttered.

'Against you,' Zach confirmed.

For several seconds Steve glared at Zach, eyes black with fury. Then he turned and charged out of the apartment with a resounding slam of the door.

Zach was left alone. 'So, that went well,' he said to the empty room. 'Good job, Zach.' And he went to tell his mum and sisters that he'd committed the cardinal sin of criticising Dad and Dad hadn't taken to it.

283

Amanda and Marci sighed and shook their heads and shrugged off this not-unusual state of affairs.

Electra, on the other hand, seemed to be taking savage satisfaction in Steve's reaction to meeting Huxley for the first time. 'Just as I expected!' she fizzed. 'Makes it all about him. Don't worry about upsetting him, Zach, because he never worries about upsetting us.'

Perhaps it was because he was regretting having been too direct, Zach found himself speaking sharply. 'I expect he was hurt that you hadn't told him about Hux. I expect we all are, to be honest.'

Electra halted, her eyes stricken. 'Don't you turn on me or I'll clear off again.'

Zach, exhausted by the tension in his family, sank on to the edge of the bed. With a crow of delight Huxley capered forward and tried to climb his legs like a bear cub on a tree. Zach grasped the stocky little body and swung him into the air. 'How about staying to let your family get to know your son and your son get to know his family?' he said to Electra. 'Do you think Mum needs more stress right now?'

Electra's face grew even more stormy. 'You're sounding like Dad!'

'I did see the stubborn look on his face and recognise it from my mirror,' he owned up. 'But you're acting like him too – making it all about you.'

'Oh, clear off!' Electra snapped, throwing her hands in the air.

With a last tickle of Huxley's portly little belly, Zach prepared to do so. But he paused long enough to say softly, 'We're all in tricky situations right now, Electra. Let's try not to fall out.'

*

The terrace was already in shadow when Rosa and Dory made it home, exhausted by an afternoon where, according to their phones, temperatures had reached thirty-seven degrees Celsius. Dory had decreed that on the day before her return to the UK they'd earned an easy afternoon taking photos at Ta' Qali farmers' market, but the sun had been merciless. 'We should have relaxed here in the shade,' Dory said as she turned the key in the lock and threw open the door.

Rosa followed her inside, feeling limp in the heat. 'Let's get that air con going! I have to nip to the loo.' She made her way through the kitchen diner.

No sooner had she set foot in the hall when a flurry of movement erupted in the corner of her vision. 'What—?' she cried, trying to turn, heart leaping with the shock of realising that someone was in the apartment. Then a heavy body crashed into hers, bouncing her off her feet, her shoulder connecting powerfully with the wall. 'Oof!' The floor rushed up to hit her and feet in trainers scuffed uncomfortably close to her face. She lay on the cold floor tiles, trying to make her lungs work.

What had just happened?

Air finally entered Rosa's body at the same moment as, from the kitchen, Dory screamed.

The sound galvanised her. She rolled over, disregarding her bruises, and staggered to her feet. 'Mum?'

'Who was that?' Dory roared, sounding panicky. 'Some young man's just flown out of here. Are you OK? Rosa? *Rosa*!'

'Just about,' Rosa managed, still crowing for breath. They stumbled into each other where the hall opened into the kitchen and clung together while Rosa told her mum about being bowled over like a skittle. Her shoulder stung and she knew she'd have an egg on the back of her head.

'Oh, darling!' Dory pressed kisses on Rosa's forehead and hugged her tighter.

They gazed around warily, ready to jump at the least thing. 'What if there's someone else here?' Rosa demanded, a chill trickling down her spine.

Dory reached into the kitchen for a saucepan and grasped it like a bat.

With visions of her crippling someone, Rosa said hastily, 'I'll ring Zach and see if he's upstairs. Maybe he'll look with us.'

They retreated to the terrace, which felt safer than in the apartment. Rosa made the call, shocked to see her fingers shaking. 'There was someone in the apartment when we arrived home,' she explained breathlessly. 'We're not keen on checking out the rest of the rooms on our own. We wondered whether—'

Zach vented a shocked expletive. 'I'm on my way.'

In seconds they heard the sound of running feet and then he was beside them, breathing hard. His eyes were concerned as they ran over Rosa. 'Are you OK?'

'The ratbag knocked her down,' Dory exclaimed, hugging Rosa again and making her wince as she squeezed her sore shoulder.

'But I'm fine,' Rosa put in hastily, seeing Zach's eyes darken.

Once Zach had satisfied himself that Rosa wasn't badly hurt he vanished inside the apartment. Rosa hurried after, heart thumping. 'You can't go on your own! What if there's someone with a weapon?'

Then she halted. 'Oh!'

Zach had flung open Rosa's door and it looked as if

someone had snatched the room up and given it a good shake. Drawers had been dumped on the floor and clothes sprawled drunkenly from the open wardrobe. She gazed around with dismay. 'Glad I had my laptop with me.' She picked up a small box. 'I had a few bits of costume jewellery in here. It's empty but he won't get rich on my trinkets.'

Zach's jaw was set, his brows dark slashes above stormy eyes. Dory's door stood ajar and, with her agreement, Zach shoved it all the way open. 'Looks like this is where the intruder was when you surprised him.' Half the room was as tumbled as Rosa's but the rest looked untouched.

'I suppose we'll have to call the police,' Dory said unhappily.

Zach turned to Rosa. 'Did you get a look at the guy?'

'Barely.' She rubbed her shoulder again because it was really beginning to burn. 'I just got an impression of a man.'

Her mum was more helpful. 'I got a better look as he ran past. Early twenties, Mediterranean appearance, dark curly hair, lots of stubble, a bit gangly.'

'Shit,' Zach muttered.

Rosa didn't need to see the dismay written on his face to know what he was thinking. 'Luccio?' she asked softly.

'I hope not.' He delved in his pocket for his phone and in a few moments had pulled up an image to show Dory of Luccio at Nicholas Centre, laughing, a white football balanced on his hand. 'That him?'

Dory shrugged. 'It could be but I only saw him for a second. The man in your photo's clean-shaven and the hair's shorter so it's difficult to be sure.'

Zach stuffed the phone back in his pocket, frowning. 'I wonder if I could have prompted it?' he murmured half to himself.

'How?' Rosa couldn't imagine.

He sighed. 'When I went looking for Luccio after being relieved of my wallet at Nicholas Centre I tried to prick his conscience and said something about someone cherishing the ring that was in it. *If* it was him who mugged me, he could have thought that meant the ring belonged to one of you and come along to see if you had any more expensive stuff.'

'*If* and *could*,' Rosa comforted him optimistically. 'It could also have been a random crime by a stranger. There must be loads of people who fit the description.'

Dory got in touch with the police to report the crime. They wanted to send an officer along so the mess had to be left, even the glass in the bath from the broken bathroom window, presumably the point of entry.

It was a good time for Zach to contact Joseph. Briefly, he explained what had happened. 'I take it you haven't seen Luccio? Can you check with Luccio's aunt Teresa?'

Joseph did so then Zach reported heavily, 'Joseph says Teresa still hasn't heard from Luccio since she got that one text saying he was with a friend.'

Before Rosa could repeat that the intruder could have been anybody Marci and Paige arrived, shouting, 'Knock, knock!' at the open kitchen door and stepping inside. In the shock of discovering the intruder, Rosa had more or less forgotten Zach's family was supposed to be coming to supper to eat up some baked rice dishes Dory had tried this morning.

Dory instantly motored into action, refusing to cancel their plans. 'What, because of some bad lad's misbehaviour? There's a fridge full of food to be eaten.'

Zach went to help Amanda down to the lower terrace and Rosa, shoulder and head aching, served drinks while

Dory chopped salad. Zach returned with Amanda and also his younger sister Electra and her adorable toddler Huxley. The evening was busy but surprisingly fun given the earlier events. A couple of times Zach attempted to talk to Rosa but always someone joined them in the kitchen, hunting for a clean fork or a top-up to their drink.

There was a peculiar tension about him and she was touched to think it might be caused by worry over her being freaked out by the intruder. When he'd begun, 'There's something—' and been interrupted three times, Rosa suggested quietly, 'Let's talk later,' and Zach subsided.

It was an informal gathering on the terrace. Dory and Rosa began to get to know Electra and Huxley while Paige ricocheted about asking when dinner would be ready. Rosa put out the salad and bread and Dory brought out four dishes of baked rice. Rosa's laptop came out so she could make notes of the feedback, her typing deteriorating as the wine in her glass went down. Marci had been quiet but eventually clucked her tongue and took both laptop and note-making over, proving herself quick and competent. 'Getting some practice in for your return to work?' Rosa asked as she took the computer back with thanks.

Marci smiled back ruefully. 'I suppose I ought to do exactly that.' She said no more, though, so Rosa didn't press her.

Everyone was shocked by the news that a thief had been in the lower apartment and when they weren't talking about food the conversation was all about that.

Two male police officers arrived and Dory took them indoors while Rosa asked the others, 'Who's for chocolate mousse? There's only two of them to compare.'

The mousse tasting was well underway by the time Dory called Rosa into the lounge to recount her side of things to the police officers. Rosa explained, 'It was over in a split second so I couldn't identify anyone.' Dory said she wasn't sure whether she could either. They'd already decided that the resemblance to Luccio was so uncertain that it would be wrong to mention his name. Their statements were brief and soon they were out on the terrace again, shaking hands with the police officers as a man appeared up the steps from the street.

Her experience with an intruder so fresh in her mind, Rosa jumped and clutched her chest.

Zach's family stopped talking.

The man's eyes landed on the police officers, his frown deepening. 'What's this?'

Rosa opened her mouth to ask who he was and what it had to do with him but Zach touched her hand. 'This is my dad. He arrived today. It's what I was trying to tell you in the kitchen.'

Rosa closed her mouth again, dumbfounded.

'Steve!' said Dory in a glad voice. 'I had no idea! Why didn't anybody tell me you were here? How great to see you again. It's only fifty years since we were at school together, isn't it? I'm glad we met up again on Barracks Brats at least because we love the apartment and wouldn't have known about it if you hadn't mentioned it in the Facebook group.' As the police officers said goodnight and left, Dory ushered Steve over to join the others.

Rosa turned to Zach. 'Your dad's here?' she whispered, conscious of an odd atmosphere.

'He's come to talk to Mum,' he murmured back.

'But, Mum's right, not a single one of your family mentioned him!' She glanced around. Huxley had fallen asleep in Electra's arms and she was gazing into his face. Amanda was looking remote and Marci was showing

Paige something on her phone. Nobody was smiling apart from Dory who was chatting easily to Steve, not betraying an instant's awkwardness although she knew full well that Amanda had come to Ta' Xbiex Terrace House to get away from him. Rosa admired her aplomb.

'It's been tense.' His voice was flat.

Out of sight of the others she found his hand with hers, stroking the inner part of his wrist.

'Rosa!' Dory called. 'Come and meet Steve.'

Rosa had to disengage from Zach and move closer to shake hands. Having a Maltese mother, Steve's colouring was generally dark. His hair was thickly streaked with silver, he was shorter than Zach and the smile that usually lurked in Zach's eyes was absent. 'Pleased to meet you,' he said politely.

'I was explaining why the police were here,' Dory said. Then her hand flew to her cheek. 'Rosa! I've just realised that if I go home tomorrow you'll be here alone. Zach, what about that window? Oh, dear, Rosa, perhaps I ought to cancel. Will you be frightened?'

Zach smiled at Dory. 'I won't let her be frightened. I'll sort the window tomorrow and stay with her while you're away.'

Dory looked arrested. 'Oh, will you?' After a tiny pause she continued, 'Well, we do have a spare room and the apartment upstairs must be crowded so if you're sure you don't mind, that would put my mind at rest.'

Rosa flushed as she detected a flicker of comprehension and amusement in her mother's eyes. One person, at least, seemed to have worked out how the land lay between her and Zach.

The party began to break up. Children needed their beds and Amanda was yawning too. Zach helped her up the stairs, Steve following silently behind. Rosa realised she'd never made notes about the chocolate mousses but both dishes had been emptied so maybe they were equally delicious.

When their guests had departed Rosa closed the apartment doors saying to Dory, 'Steve wasn't terribly chatty, was he? He's going through a tricky time, of course, but I found him forbidding.'

Dory snorted a laugh. 'Never mind Steve! I think you're a lot more interested in Steve's son. Has this been going on under my nose? When he told me he'd stay here while I was away you looked like a child caught with both hands in the cookie jar. Rosy-cheeked Rosa!'

Rosa giggled, flushing all over again. 'We've been seeing each other,' she acknowledged. 'We agreed to fly under the radar because—' She halted, a chill sweeping over her that had nothing to do with the air conditioning. In a week or two she'd probably have to go back to real life, which she'd decided not to explain yet to Dory for a lot of good reasons. 'Because he might have to go home and be near his family in Cornwall,' she ended.

Dory eyed her speculatively but said, 'Your business is your business.' Then she added with a wicked twinkle, 'But wasn't I right about a summer romance? Just what you needed!'

It took them an hour to put their rooms to rights then Zach returned and cleared the glass out of the bath. He frowned at the empty window aperture. 'I've looked in the garage but don't have a board to cover it tonight. I'll look online and see if I can find someone to come out and do it.'

Dory gave him a sweet smile. 'Why don't you stay here tonight and protect us? I haven't packed yet and my plane leaves at about eleven tomorrow so I'll go get on. 'Night!' She wafted away in the direction of her own room.

Once she was out of earshot Zach turned slowly to Rosa, one eyebrow cocked. 'Did your mum just suggest I stay the night?'

Happiness simmered inside her. 'I think it was more of an order.' Pushing the bathroom door shut she stepped into his arms and kissed his neck, something she'd noticed always made his eyes close. 'So your dad just turned up?' she said against his skin.

He settled her a little closer. 'Mum doesn't know what to make of it. She hasn't got big reserves of money for a hotel and the apartment belongs to his mum, which makes it tricky. I suppose they're going to have to work something out, whatever the "something" is. He's not in a sunny mood and everyone's on pins.' His eyes smiled. 'It'll be a relief to be down here.'

She teased him gently. 'I'll be fine if you'd prefer to spend time with your dad.'

Groaning, he buried his face in her hair. 'There's no one I'd rather be with than you.'

Chapter Twenty-One

On Saturday Rosa awoke to the agreeable sensation of a male body spooning hers. It took resolution to peel away Zach's caressing hands when her alarm went off. 'I have to take Mum to the airport.'

Zach complained like a disappointed teenager. 'Awwwww . . .'

She smothered a laugh, conscious of her mother on the other side of the bedroom wall. 'Later,' she promised.

With her usual efficiency, Dory was packed and ready to leave the apartment in time for her 11.05 flight to Leeds Bradford Airport, suitcase at her feet and laptop bag on her shoulder. With a beaming smile she brandished her phone. 'Leslie's messaged. Naturally, as it's the last Saturday in July, it's raining in England. He's meeting me at the airport and driving me home.'

Rosa, fizzing at the prospect of a glorious week or so with Zach, gave her mum a big hug. 'And where does he live? Norfolk? Not exactly next door to Leeds Bradford Airport.'

Dory was unabashed by the teasing. 'So he'll have to stay the rest of the weekend, won't he?'

After waving her mum off at the airport with an easy mind, Rosa drove home past new roads and flyovers under construction. The flat-roofed buildings were familiar to her now, the prickly pears lolling over walls in less built-up areas and capers growing wild beside the dusty roads. Outside Ta' Xbiex Terrace House she left the air-conditioned comfort of her mum's little white hatchback with a 'Phew!' at the midday heat but it didn't stop her racing up the stone steps to the apartment. Zach, who'd been spending time with his family, arrived within minutes, his smile broad and hot.

'I heard your car.' He swooped, pulling her in for a long, deep kiss. When they emerged, both breathless, Rosa could feel his heart beating *boom, bah-boom* against her. She more than half-expected that they'd spend the afternoon in bed but Zach had other plans.

'I got an emergency glazier to fix the bathroom window. Joseph's been in touch,' he went on. 'There's a lunch for the kids at Nicholas Centre and he's invited us all. I've been too busy to volunteer this week and he wants to see the cousins he hasn't caught up with for a while – Dad, Mum and Electra – and to meet Hux. Do you mind if we go?'

'Not at all.' Rosa took Amanda, Electra and Huxley in Dory's car – Marci having shown Electra where to hire a child car seat – and Zach drove Steve, Marci and Paige. They parked with the usual difficulty in the narrow street next to the centre and let themselves in through the door in the wall.

Young lads were messing around with a football in the

courtyard and a fair-haired boy plonked himself in Zach's path as soon as he saw him. 'Want to play keepy-uppy?'

'Maybe later, Oliver. I'm here for the lunch with my family and you always beat me.' Zach intercepted the ball Oliver flicked his way and headed it niftily back. Then he turned to offer Amanda his arm up two steps and soon they were in the coolness of the old building. Lunch was about to begin in the big salon upstairs and, while Zach stayed with his family, Rosa helped Maria and others ferry plates of food up to the large buffet table.

Bread with oil and dips or piled with a tuna mixture jostled with cheese or pea-filled pastizzi – flaky pastry delights Rosa had already learned to love. Maria tried to teach her how to say 'qaghaq', the Maltese name for honey rings, but, after a couple of attempts, she felt she might be better sticking to the English. She did better with 'imqaret', fried pastry stuffed with dates. Rosa suspected these luscious pastries and sweets would vanish before the bite-sized salad stuffs and raw vegetables.

Plates were rapidly filled with delicious-smelling treats and carried gleefully to the tables ranged around the room. Happy young voices rose to the ceiling and the open windows let in the noise of cars in the street below. Zach's family had seated themselves at one round table but Steve and Amanda were on opposite sides. Even Steve couldn't remain glum when Joseph, beaming all over his face, wrung his hand and pulled him into a hug roaring, 'My cousin! I began to think Malta would never see you again.'

Amanda appeared hot and fatigued despite the open windows and Rosa noticed each of the Bentley children checking on her at one time or another. It contrasted with the indifference with which they all seemed to regard their father. Steve's gaze strayed often to Amanda but Amanda rarely glanced his way.

Always happy to help out with young people Rosa mingled, chatting, fetching and carrying, taking photos for social media so Joseph could tag in the sponsor, a company that made medical equipment. It made her feel nostalgic for Blackthorn's. She pushed the thought away. She'd be back there soon enough. She'd soon need to confirm to Georgine that she'd be returning to her previous role full-time.

It was nearly five by the time the gathering was over. Amanda had been found a quiet spot in the kitchen with a cup of tea while everyone else helped carry chairs or stack tables, though Huxley's contribution mainly consisted of stretching his arms towards anything he wanted and shouting, 'Utts!' Zach managed to get to the courtyard for a couple of the requested games of keepy-uppy. Steve, saturnine face set in the severe expression that seemed his default, assisted with the breaking down of the buffet table into six smaller tables.

Rosa tried to strike up a friendly conversation as they took an end each of a table to stack it. 'How does it feel to be back in Malta, Steve? Do you love it like Mum does? She's a real Maltaphile, if there is such a word.'

Steve shrugged. 'Haven't had time to feel anything, to be honest. Too much family stuff happening.' He thought for a moment, then tacked on, 'Great to see Joseph. Been years.'

'What will you do while you're here?' she persisted, hoping to encourage him to thaw a little as they added their table to a stack. 'Visit old stamping grounds? Swim? Find nice restaurants?'

Steve grunted. 'Don't know.'

'Zach's not much like you,' she blurted out, unwisely voicing her thoughts as she couldn't help but compare Zach's kindness and humour to this gloomy, abrupt man.

His laugh was short and bitter. He paused at the next table, fixing his eyes on her. 'Suppose he's told you about his past? His bits of bother?'

His words lit a flame of anger inside Rosa. She let her end of the table drop, half-hoping it would bump his fingers. 'Just as well, or you'd have let the cat out of the bag, wouldn't you?' Slightly mollified to see by his expression that she'd discomfited him, she made an excuse and left him to stack tables on his own. Hadn't anyone ever told him that parents were meant to be onside with their kids? He'd almost looked as if he'd enjoyed the potential opportunity to diss his son.

She went to find Zach in the courtyard and volunteered to be the official counter in a fierce keepy-uppy tournament being refereed by Axel. The walled courtyard was in shade now but still the gladiators sweltered as each got three opportunities to keep the ball bouncing off some part of their body. Zach came second with a score of twenty-seven. The winner was Oliver with forty, who beamed, flicking the ball high in the air in triumph.

Rosa gave Zach a consolatory hug.

'I'm sweaty.' He laughed in protest.

'Never mind.' She stood on tiptoe to whisper in his ear. 'I know where there's a nice big shower.' She was rewarded by him instantly rounding up his family for the drive home.

Once there, Zach helped Amanda slowly, painfully up the steps to the upper apartment. Steve began to say something but Amanda gave him a ferocious glare. 'I *know*, Steve, all right? I know stairs are hard for me but *I'm doing it anyway.* Right?'

Steve subsided. Rosa went into her apartment as her phone beeped with a text message from her mum.

Safely home! Called on Grandpa en route and he seemed touchingly glad to see me so think he's missed me, even if he wouldn't admit it before. Going to take him for dinner tomorrow after he's played golf. Are you OK? Is the window fixed? x

Dory's message reassured her. She was still holding the phone when it began to ring and *Marcus* scrolled across the screen. Zach burst in from the terrace at that moment, laughter in his eyes as he mock-growled, 'I hope you're going to make good that shower promise, sweetheart. Oh – or do you want to take that call?'

'Nope.' Firmly, Rosa pressed *decline*. 'Let's check out your shower gel.' She wouldn't let Marcus spoil her time with Zach. The house was going to force her back to Liggers Moor. But not yet.

Zach swept her up and bundled her along the hall to the bathroom and she let her head fall back as she laughed with joy.

Rosa was pretty sure that the next week was the happiest of her life.

On Sunday they walked to Sliema to catch the Marsamxett ferry to Valletta because Zach wanted her to see the Fortifications Interpretation Centre, which told the story of how the ramparted city had come into being. She was particularly struck by the models of the sunken forts. 'I can show you two in Sliema,' he offered. 'Fort Tigné and Fort Cambridge.' He linked his fingers with hers, obviously relaxed and happy. 'Shall we have lunch in a restaurant actually inside the ramparts? Last time I went there I was on my own but I'd love to show it to you.'

She leaned in to his warmth. 'This is like a tour of hidden Malta.' The restaurant proved to be fascinating, situated in a sloping, arch-roofed tunnel, but she preferred its terrace, a big balcony looking out over Valletta city gate. Sheltered from the midday sun by a cream parasol, Rosa asked how his family had been when he'd visited the upper apartment this morning.

Zach's eyes clouded. 'Dad's sleeping on the couch. Mum's asked him to go home but he's too stubborn.'

Rosa felt a moment's guilt at sitting here in these beautiful surroundings, floating with happiness and holding Zach's hand. 'Should you be with them?'

He shook his head. 'She said no, she needs to decide what to do next. Dad's obviously not going to make leaving him easy.'

'And how's Marci?' Rosa asked.

Zach's gaze became distant. 'Not great. She knows she has decisions to make about when or if to go home and her job. I think first Electra and then Dad turning up has destabilised her, made her think that if determined people like them are struggling with life then what chance does Marci have? And Paige says she doesn't like Malta any more and I'm sure it's because the apartment's so crowded and she's picking up on Marci's anxiety.'

'We could take her snorkelling later,' Rosa suggested, sorry to think that sunny little Paige might be unhappy.

'Let's do that.' He squeezed her hand across the table and gave her the slow, hot smile that made her tummy flip like a pancake.

Monday morning passed in them making love slooooowly, enjoying having the apartment to themselves. After a shower then brunch on the terrace, Rosa's hair springing around her face as it dried, Zach met his mum upstairs to help her torturously down, pausing on the terrace to chat to Rosa while Amanda gathered her strength for the second flight. 'It's nice of Zach to take me for a drive,' she puffed when they'd got her settled on a chair. 'I hope you don't mind me taking him away.' Her eyes twinkled as if she was well aware that there was more keeping her son at Rosa's apartment than ensuring she wasn't home alone.

Realising that the more time she spent with Zach the more obvious their relationship became, Rosa just smiled, gesturing to her laptop on the table in the shade. 'I have stuff to do for Mum and of course he wants to spend time with you.' Zach had shown no sign of wanting to spend time with Steve, but she didn't say that. Although she'd tried to make allowances for Steve being hurt by his wife's defection, he was the spectre at the feast as far as she could see. Zach was often quiet and reflective after contact with him.

Still, her own dad was no asset. She wondered how Dory would fare today when she discussed Glenn's bogus dash-for-cash claim with her solicitor.

After Zach and Amanda left, her only company was the insects buzzing around the pots of herbs and geraniums. Although she found herself remembering the intruder and keeping one eye on the steps to the terrace, Rosa got on with scheduling posts for the Cafeteria Cook blog.

A couple of hours passed and she was ready to move on to the Facebook page when Dory rang, beginning without ceremony, 'How he thought I'd fall for his crap after all this time—'

'Who? Dad?' Rosa had to pull her head out of a Top Tips for Choosing Fresh Fruit post and concentrate.

'Who else?' Dory paused and drew in an audible breath.

'Zach was right. That firm of solicitors who "emailed" me don't exist. My solicitor says there's no chance of a court action succeeding after this length of time. I'm going for divorce straight away. Glenn's lucky I don't try and bring a deception case against him.'

'Wow,' said Rosa, slowly, shocked how her stomach churned at this news. 'I supposed a part of me had hoped Dad wouldn't sink that low. It was better knowing almost nothing of him than having proof he's so unscrupulous.'

Dory's tone became contrite. 'Sorry. That was awful of me to give you the benefit of my victory rant. I almost forget he's your dad sometimes.'

But Rosa sighed and reminded herself of her resolve that this week was for only happy things. 'Don't worry,' she said. 'I'm just glad there was no substance to his claims.' By the time she rang off, Zach had reappeared and she was able to throw herself in his arms for a big comforting hug.

'Hey, hey,' he murmured, squeezing her comfortingly. 'What's up?'

Face buried against his chest, Rosa explained. Then, 'It's not that it's a shock precisely. It's more that it's highlighted the truth. My dad's a grubby man who'd lie and cheat to get money from a woman he only ever let down.'

He comforted her with kisses then spirited her indoors and made such tender love to her that it drove the whole distasteful episode out of her mind. Later, deciding now was a good time to let their relationship become more public, they ate up on the roof, staring up Lazaretto Creek and the lights that danced amongst the boats on its dark waters beneath the star-spangled sky. Sipping wine, Zach told her about the Great Siege in the sixteenth century when the Maltese used Turkish heads as cannonballs.

302

Rosa watched his eyes light up as he talked of Ottoman invaders, corsairs, galleys and land forces, thinking how happy she was to have this time together. To wake with him in the mornings and fall asleep with him at night.

Tuesday was a languid day when they joined Zach's family – even Steve – on the rocky beach across the road. Not seeming to notice that her grandparents rarely spoke to one another Paige told them about the ring she'd found and showed them the crack in the rock. Zach was rueful about his part in the ring never making it back to its rightful owner.

Tuesday whizzed past and on Wednesday, Rosa awoke early. She hadn't wanted to worry about her return to England this week but, unfortunately, the worries hadn't got the memo and they poured over her, preventing her from dropping off again. Zach slept, his chest moving gently, stubble darkening his jaw, his expression as peaceful as a child's. *I think I love you,* she told him silently, *but I don't know how we could make a relationship work. Would you exchange Malta for Yorkshire? Or if you return to the UK at all would you have to be in Cornwall to support your mum? Would you want me to clear up all my business in Liggers Moor to join you there . . . ?*

Today was the day when Dory was scheduled to travel to London to meet her editor and agent so she texted her: *Hope it all goes OK. Let me know! xx*

Then, because she was a pragmatic woman and didn't know how much longer she'd have this man in her bed, she touched Zach and he jumped awake to pull her close and replace her anxious thoughts with happy ones.

Later, Zach joined his family for lunch while Rosa edited Cafeteria Cook photos for Instagram. *The Cafeteria Cook Does Stealthy Eating* was on promotion so she scheduled a stream of social media posts about that and linked a couple of YouTube videos to the Facebook page. Then she shut her laptop with a snap. Dory had told her to take plenty of time off this week, she told herself, so took her e-reader onto the terrace to await Zach's return.

When he finally arrived, her e-reader had switched itself off and she was dozing as Zach stooped to drop a kiss on her mouth before throwing himself onto the adjacent lounger. 'My family!' he said with feeling. 'My sisters have wisely gone out and I wouldn't dare strike a match upstairs in case the air between my parents explodes.' He passed his hands over his face. 'Mum says Dad should go home and get used to being single. Dad says he's not going unless Mum goes with him. I wish he'd give her some space. I suppose I'm going to have to talk to him again. And that never ends well,' he added gloomily.

Rosa took his hand sympathetically but was saved from having to think of something to say by a FaceTime call from Dory, whose face loomed on the screen, pink and sparkling with excitement.

'Rosa! Oh, hello, Zach, how are you doing?' Dory cried, obviously catching sight of him but plunging on without awaiting his answer. 'It wasn't bad news at all! My editor wanted to talk to me about *a TV tie-in*! Woohooooooo! The TV company wanted vegan, hence the sudden change of title, but she couldn't say anything until she was sure. And Grandpa's here to say hello, too, look!'

The image slid sideways until Rosa could see a dear and familiar face, lined with age and lots of smiles. 'Hello, darling,' her grandfather Lance said in his rusty voice. 'I'm afraid your mother's been celebrating. She's had a long boozy lunch with her editor and then she turned up at my house with a bottle of champagne.'

'Grandpa!' Rosa exclaimed gladly. 'How are you?'

'I'm fine,' he declared reassuringly and told her about his latest golf game. Then the image switched dizzyingly back to Dory.

She gabbled, 'Rosie-posy, I am sozzled but lovely, lovely Leslie, love of my life, has arrived to take me out to dinner to soak up the bubbles. But isn't it fantastic news? I can hardly believe it. I'm going to be back on telly and in my own show! Phew, eh? And my editor's really pleased with all the fabby-do-dah social media biz you've been doing. Oh, by the way, are you OK? Yes? Hooray! I'm staying in England a bit longer because I've got a vid thing to do for a YouTube channel and because of Leslie. See you soon! Bye!'

Rosa was laughing as the call ended. 'I think my mother's pretty tipsy! But, wow, what fantastic news for her.'

Zach grinned. 'Rosie-posy, eh?'

She rolled her eyes. 'She used to call me that when I was a kid. I wish she hadn't dragged it up in front of you.' But only the hardest heart could be proof against Dory's ebullience and complain about a childhood name slipping out.

He took her hand and lifted it to his lips. 'I won't tell anyone, Rosie-posy, honest.' Then his phone began to ring and he hunted for it in his pocket, still laughing as he answered, 'Hey, Joseph.' Then the smile was whipped from his face and replaced by a frown. 'Do you know what happened? No? Of course I'll ring him back. Can you text me the number?'

He ended the call frowning. 'Luccio's telephoned Nicholas Centre. Apparently he's in Mater Dei hospital's orthopaedic ward. He's somehow been parted from his phone but another patient says I can ring him on his.'

There was a grim set to Zach's jaw as his phone beeped. 'Joseph's just sent me the number.' He tapped the screen then put the call on speaker so that Rosa could listen.

'Yes?' said Luccio's voice.

'Hey, Luccio,' said Zach in an easy, friendly voice. 'You OK? What are you doing in hospital?'

'You said call you if I need.' Luccio's voice wavered.

Brows snapping down, Zach nodded. 'Yes. What's happened?'

'Beppe,' Luccio hissed, as if trying not to be overheard, and began to speak rapidly, his English suffering with his obvious emotion. 'He breaks my ankle. He takes my phone and passport. I keep giving him things, Zach, but always he demands more.'

Rosa listened in horror to Luccio explain that Beppe, the leader of Luccio's group, had been coercing Luccio to steal for him with a mixture of threats and faux friendship. Luccio had tried to break away and been shoved down the Santa Rita steps for his pains. Beppe had dropped all pretence of being his friend. 'He has my phone and passport,' Luccio reported miserably. 'My ankle needed a pin so I had operation. Beppe, he says he'll pick me up from hospital on Friday.'

Zach's face was tight with fury but his voice remained kind and calm. 'Is Friday the day you expect to be discharged? What about your aunt Teresa?'

'Don' involve her,' Luccio hurried in. 'Beppe, he don' treat women well.'

'I understand.' Zach's voice was low and easy and Rosa could see why Luccio had felt he could turn to him. He inspired confidence and didn't waste time on voicing opinions or exclamations. Luccio had stolen from Zach, set him up and even injured him but Zach understood that ringleaders could be intimidating and manipulative. He'd been in the same tight spot.

Rather than feel troubled by the reminder, it made Rosa respect Zach more as she listened to him question Luccio and discover that Luccio had been miserably sleeping on Beppe's floor because Beppe had threatened to smash all of aunt Teresa's windows if Luccio returned home.

Zach ended the call with, 'Let me think what to do. Today's only Wednesday so I think we can be confident you won't see Beppe for another couple of days. And don't worry, Luccio. You did right to contact me. At the very least I'll get another phone to you tomorrow.' He gave more reassurances but his mouth was a grim line as he ended the call.

'The scales have definitely fallen from Luccio's eyes,' he observed, putting away his phone. He was perched on the edge of the lounger now as if ready to plunge into action. 'At long last he sees Beppe for the petty tyrant he is.'

Tentatively, she took his hand. 'I know you want to help him, but what can you do?'

He stared down at her hand in his as if not really seeing it. 'Luccio stands in more danger than I ever did. Nastier ringleader. Weaker Luccio.' He screwed up his forehead in thought. 'I'll wander along to Paceville tonight and see what I can find out.'

Instantly, Rosa's admiration for Zach's support of Luccio was replaced by alarm. 'Can't you go to the police? Don't get involved in anything!'

Slowly, Zach's gaze lifted to hers. Seconds passed then he said deliberately, 'The kind of courage it takes to risk retribution by blowing the whistle . . . I don't believe Luccio has it. If I go to the police it will get him in trouble and Beppe-types, they know how to vanish like smoke when police turn up. Luccio needs my help.'

He rose, wiping his palms on his shorts, his gaze never leaving Rosa's though it had become distant. The brief Maltese dusk was arriving, making his face a place of shadows.

Rosa scrambled up from the lounger as he strode into the apartment. 'I didn't mean to sound—'

He paused to interrupt gently, 'I'm already involved because I can't let Luccio down.' He looked almost a stranger. 'But I won't involve you.'

Chapter Twenty-Two

He hadn't dealt with Rosa well. The knowledge rolled in Zach's guts. Her eyes followed him unhappily as he threw on clean clothes, probably not knowing how to react to this street-wise side of him.

She instinctively shied from Luccio's situation. He didn't blame her but it wasn't in him to float on in the happy bubble he'd occupied for the past few days and abandon Luccio to misery. He tried to reassure her. 'I'm going to check on Mum first. I won't be long. Don't worry.' He gave her a brief peck goodbye then ran up the steps two at a time to the upper apartment with a lightness he wasn't feeling.

Steve was seated on the sofa watching TV. He gave Zach one of his cooler looks. Zach said hello then went to tap on his mother's bedroom door. He found her lying on her bed, also watching TV. Zach thought it was a bitter indictment on their marriage that they were watching the same programme in different places. 'How are you doing?' he asked softly.

Amanda managed to summon a smile. 'Surviving.'

'I'm going out. I guess Electra and Marci will be back soon but do you want anything first?'

'No, thank you. You go out and have a lovely time.' Amanda's smile grew wider and Zach could imagine she had a vision of he and Rosa going out for a romantic evening. He wouldn't sully the vision with the truth. Neither of his parents would appreciate his errand.

He strolled back into the living area and sat down beside his father thinking he might as well get all unpleasant tasks over with at once. Steve kept his eyes on the TV as he snapped, 'Is your mother all right?'

Zach wondered how to answer. Eventually he tried, 'I'm not sure she's being made better by the situation.'

'All those bloody stairs?' Steve leapt in. 'I tried to tell her—'

'But she didn't want to listen,' Zach finished for him, wearily. 'That's because she's entitled to make up her own mind.' He hesitated. 'I always thought you could show Mum love but she doesn't seem to be feeling it right now. You've got the opportunity to build bridges with your wife and kids here. You've taken time off work. Nanna's arranged care for Grandad. Why not take advantage?'

Steve turned to him, eyes and mouth wide in shock. 'Build bridges? I've always done my best for my family—'

'Really?' Zach sighed. 'Dad, what you see as "doing your best" we see as you throwing your weight about. Either that's alienating your family or we're a uniformly ungrateful lot, aren't we? Ask yourself why Electra travels and Marci and me came out here? Why would Mum come when the apartment is so manifestly unsuitable for her medical condition?'

After several seconds of silence Steve rasped, 'That's told me, hasn't it?'

Zach sighed again. Today had begun wonderfully well, Rosa waking him in a way any straight male would appreciate, but it had gone rapidly downhill. 'I'm not saying it to hurt you. I think it's time for plain speaking. Believe it or not, I love you.'

'You've got a funny way of showing it!'

'It seems a family trait,' Zach said softly. Steve turned his face once again to the TV screen as Zach got up and left. He'd made an attempt with his father. He could do little more.

He jogged down both flights of stairs, resolutely not pausing at the lower apartment to see Rosa. She was not on board with him checking out Beppe and he could neither blame her nor reassure her and he didn't want to see more wariness in her eyes.

He drove to Paceville, parking then walking to the area that was bouncing with tourists, ringing with music, laughter and chatter. Considering how much time he'd spent here on his eighteen months on the island he felt curiously disassociated from the women in short, tight dresses, the men in skinny shorts. He headed for the hub, the familiar Triq Santa Rita, buffeted by hot bodies, almost asphyxiated by fumes from alcohol and whatever was being smoked.

He stopped to buy a drink. The guy behind the bar laughed aloud and shook his head when Zach tried to order alcohol-free beer so he bought a real one.

A long, tedious evening ensued. With no game plan other than to play it by ear if he spotted Beppe, Zach wandered up and down the steps trying to keep his mind on Luccio instead of Rosa.

Finally, he spotted the largest of Beppe's buddies and then, after several minutes, Beppe himself slid out of the

311

darkness of a bar and leaned his arms on a tall table, a shot glass in his hand. Judging by the bloodshot whites to his eyes it wasn't the first shot of the evening.

Zach made a beeline for him, unwilling to let him vanish. 'Hey,' he called as he got closer. 'Do you know where Luccio is? His aunt keeps ringing me. Says he hasn't been home.' He drank deeply from the beer he'd barely touched, hoping he looked harmlessly tipsy.

Beppe looked slyly pleased. 'Maybe.'

Gazing around, Zach asked, 'Where? His aunt's doing my head in.'

A couple of Beppe's buddies smirked. Beppe tossed off his shot. 'Tell auntie that Luccio won't be home for a while.' Then he roared with laughter.

Zach assumed a pugnacious expression. 'No, you tell him to contact her, right?'

Judging by Beppe's scowl, he didn't appreciate being given orders. 'He can't,' he snapped.

Zach stuck out his jaw, gambling on a ringleader's hatred of being confronted or doubted. 'Just tell him. Or don't you know where he is?' he added on a moment of inspiration. 'I bet he's left Malta. You just don't know it.'

A sneer stole over Beppe's face. 'He tried to.'

Zach drank from his beer while he pretended to consider this, putting in a theatrical little weave as if tipsy. Then, 'How do you know? Bet Luccio's hooked up with some girl. Left your little gang and left the island.'

With an irritated curse Beppe delved into his pocket. 'I know!' he snarled. And held up a phone and passport.

'They Luccio's?' Zach shook his head as if to try and clear alcohol fumes. 'Why have you got them?'

As Beppe opened his sneering mouth to answer, Zach

wove back up a step then stumbled rapidly forward, staggering bang into Beppe.

'Hey!' protested Beppe, teetering on the edge of a step. Zach snatched the phone and passport, shoved Beppe with all his strength and, pausing only to grab a glimpse of Beppe and his buddies falling down the steps like dominoes, turned and legged it. Ignoring the shouts, screams and the crash of glasses shattering behind him he sprinted up the steps, using knowledge gained on past hook-ups to fly into the hotel at the top and jump into an elevator. On the fifth floor he paused to get his breath, hoping to confuse any pursuers by lying low. He spent the time having a low-voiced telephone conversation with Luccio, who sounded on the edge of tears to know Zach now held his passport. After half an hour, Zach ordered a cab then went coolly down to Reception by another elevator and jumped into the back of the black vehicle, locking the door and asking the driver to take him to the street in which he'd parked.

His heart pumped hard. It wasn't his personal demon Fitzmo who'd been bested tonight but he felt an epic sense of satisfaction.

Zach paid the cab fare, picked up his car and drove to the hospital. As it was the middle of the night he was able to park close to the main doors. They swished open at his approach and he strode along the corridors. He'd only experienced hospitals second-hand when a friend, parent or grandparent had a stay but he'd formed the opinion that nobody questioned you if you looked as if you were going about your lawful business. When he saw a neat row of wheelchairs in an alcove he liberated one and parked it outside the orthopaedic ward. Then he rang the number of the phone Luccio was able to use. By arrangement it would be on silent and only buzz.

Thirty seconds later, Luccio appeared, moving carefully on crutches. His hair was a mess and he looked as if he hadn't shaved for days. 'I discharge already,' he murmured as he dropped into the wheelchair. Apart from the hiss of the wheels they were silent as they glided back to the elevator and down to the ground floor.

A large woman emerged from a door behind the small reception desk and said, 'May I *help* you?' in the way people did when they meant, 'What are you doing?'

Zach kept on going, tossing back over his shoulder, 'I'll bring the wheelchair back in two minutes.' At the car, he helped Luccio swing into the back seat and passed in the crutches. Then he dumped the wheelchair near the front door and ran back to the car.

After he'd parked on The Ramp he kept close company with Luccio up the first flight of steps as the younger man went cautiously on his crutches. It wasn't until they neared the top that he saw their way was barred by a sun lounger . . . and Rosa on it, her face illuminated by the screen of her e-reader. Evidently, she had no intention of him visiting Ta' Xbiex Terrace House without her knowledge. Wondering what that meant, he watched her expression relax at the sight of him then her eyebrows fly up as she took in Luccio.

Her bare feet dropped to the floor either side of the lounger and she jumped up. 'Are you OK?' she whispered, carefully moving aside the sun lounger so that it made no noise. There were no lights on in the upper apartment. He hadn't checked the time for a while but felt sure it was well into the early hours of the morning.

'All good.' He escorted Luccio into her apartment and, when Rosa had stepped inside, closed the door. Belatedly, he thought of possible consequences of his impulsive

314

shoving of Beppe down Santa Rita steps. 'Sorry to bring him here, but I need to get him some clothes and pick up my passport. We're booked on the six-thirty ferry to Sicily.'

She stared at him for several moments. Then, 'Tell me what happened.'

A glance at the kitchen clock showed him they had over two hours before the ferry sailed so he complied, trying to depict the encounter with Beppe like a scene from a sitcom rather than a tawdry moment in the middle of Malta's most notorious night spot. He wound up, 'You have to remember I've had several years more experience of life than he has and he's not as clever as he thinks.'

He thought he saw the tension leave her body at his ingenuous explanation. 'I could drive you to the ferry. Parking might be difficult.'

Zach was about to refuse when he remembered Beppe's threat to smash aunt Teresa's windows. 'Does Beppe know where I live?' he asked Luccio, anxiety spring to the fore.

Luccio shrugged. 'I don't know. Maybe.'

Zach glanced at Rosa, thinking about the downsides of leaving her here on her own. 'Maybe you should come too.'

'I get seasick.' She looked rueful.

'OK. Drive us to the ferry and then get breakfast somewhere till Dad's up and about, on the off-chance Beppe comes round asking questions. I'll be back late this afternoon.'

'OK,' she said slowly. But she looked away and, after a few words with Luccio, she vanished into her bedroom.

Zach got Luccio a couple of pairs of shorts and two T-shirts then installed him in the bathroom to wash and dress as best he could with a cast on his ankle. Then Zach followed Rosa. He found her dressing, a backpack on the bed. He drew her gently into his arms. 'I'm really, really sorry. I said I wouldn't involve you but I simply didn't think about my passport and I don't want Luccio to have to go alone. He's had too much of a scare. I don't think Beppe will turn up but I'm going to ring Joseph from the ferry and get him to find some reason to come here and be visible. Beppe won't smash windows while there are people about.'

'It's OK,' she said, but her smile didn't reach her eyes.

He felt worse and worse. 'Have you had any sleep at all?'

'A bit,' she hedged.

He sighed, leaning his forehead on hers. 'I've dragged you into this shitty little episode. I just couldn't leave Luccio to be bullied and used by Beppe.'

'I know.' She squeezed him. 'And I know why, don't worry.'

Her manner was determinedly breezy as she drove them to the Virtu Ferry Terminal at Marsa in the inner part of Grand Harbour. Luccio swung off on his crutches after saying goodbye to Rosa and refusing Zach's offer to try and find a wheelchair. It was still dark but Zach could see enough of Rosa to tell that her eyes were huge with tiredness.

'Sorry,' he whispered again. 'He's going to live with his cousin in a quiet part of Sicily till he gets on his feet – no pun intended. He won't come back to Malta.' Then he set off after Luccio.

As they lingered in the waiting room and the minutes ticked down to boarding time, Luccio looked at Zach. 'Thank you. I couldn't have done this without you.'

Jolted out of his thoughts, Zach smiled at the young man in his borrowed clothes. 'You probably could but I know how it is to feel as if you can't. You were young and vulnerable when your parents passed away and you didn't know how to take charge of your life.'

Luccio nodded but didn't look encouraged. 'I have been stealing for Beppe because he threaten me.'

'Yes,' Zach said gently.

'And I steal from you. I hurt you in Joseph's office.' A tear leaked from the corner of his eye.

'I know.' Zach made eye contact with Luccio. 'I *know*, Luccio. I told you. I had someone in my life like Beppe. But you're free of him now and I know you won't do these things in the future.'

'Beppe can catch the ferry easy—'

Zach clapped him on the shoulder. 'I doubt he'd bother to travel to Sicily on the off-chance you've gone back there and he could locate you. But anyway,' he tagged on, 'I'll see what I can do to discourage him.'

Chapter Twenty-Three

Rosa found a café in which to eat breakfast. Zach texted her to tell her they were on board. The next message, a couple of hours later, told her they'd docked in Pozzallo and Luccio's cousin – an older cousin, so maybe he'd keep him on the straight and narrow – had picked him up.

Hardly able to keep her eyes open she managed to get herself home at about ten and ensured the doors were locked before falling into bed. Her sleep was fragmented and she kept waking, heart racing, dreaming of Zach being in trouble. After a few fitful hours she was glad to escape to the land of the waking.

Outside on The Ramp Joseph and Axel were sorting recycling into boxes, she discovered, when she went down to street level. Joseph had pretended they needed a quiet area in which to do this and had checked with Steve it was OK for them to use the apron outside the garages for this purpose. Beppe had so far not been seen.

Marci and Paige visited her on the lower terrace and Rosa gave them cold drinks and biscuits. 'Where's Uncle Zachary?' Paige demanded, jumping along a crack in the paving.

'He's gone somewhere.' Rosa thought it best not to go into detail but offered Paige a biscuit instead. She'd never been mixed up in anything like the Luccio/Beppe situation before and it felt unreal and unsettling.

Finally, it was time to pick Zach up from the ferry terminal. He emerged looking dazed with fatigue but managed a grin when he saw her, falling into the passenger seat, shutting his eyes, groping for her hand and lifting it to his lips. 'Nearly over.'

'Only nearly?'

She'd meant it to sound like a joke but knew her misgivings had come through when he sighed and sat up, freeing her hand and answering indirectly. 'I need to pick up my car.' He wasn't forthcoming with further details of his plans and the moment Rosa pulled out of the car park he appeared to drop off to sleep. She addressed him softly a couple of times but he continued to breathe slowly and evenly.

However, he awoke the moment they pulled up outside the house, had a quiet word with Joseph, kissed a surprised Rosa goodbye and hopped into his car, apparently deaf to enquiries about his destination.

It wasn't until three hours later that he returned.

Joseph and Axel were still grimly sorting recycling that must have been sorted twelve times already. Rosa had told them she was fine twice but they'd just smiled and carried on. Rosa flew down the stairs when she saw Zach's car pull up and reached him as he was shaking hands with the two men and they were packing up to go.

His feet dragged on the stairs to the lower terrace, his hand on her waist. 'I'm desperate for sleep,' he said but he held her hand, towing her along with him to the bed. Once there, he dragged off his shorts, kicked off his flip-flops and dropped onto the covers like a falling tree.

'What have you been doing?' She crawled onto the bed beside him.

He gave a snort of grim laughter. 'Laying information with the police about Beppe. Beppe's been using Luccio as a cat's-paw so that if anything went wrong it was Luccio who copped it, not him. Like that night he was chased up here onto your terrace? Beppe had tried to cheat some nasty people out of something and sent Luccio along as the messenger. And the ring Paige found and I lost when I was mugged? It was Luccio who stole it. He passed the ring to Beppe and the pictures we took of it are such good evidence the police have gone to pick him up in the hopes it's at his place. I have to make an official statement tomorrow but the police are delighted because they knew there was a mini crimewave going on but not who was at the centre of it. Luccio gave me so much information to pass to them that Beppe should be good and screwed.'

His eyes were closed, his lips barely moving as he talked. Rosa nudged him. 'But Luccio was involved, wasn't he? How's he going to keep out of trouble?'

Zach smiled faintly. 'He's going to stay in Sicily. He called his aunt Teresa from the ferry and she's going to send on his stuff. I doubt the police will trouble to pursue him. It's worth the risk, anyway, to get Beppe out of circulation.'

Then he went to sleep. Rosa lay beside him sifting through her thoughts, realising, with dawning relief, that this uncomfortable episode was on the way to being behind them. Eventually, she slept too.

As Rosa showered, she heard the shower cubicle door open and close again. 'Hey, you forgot me,' a sleepy male voice complained.

Blinking shampoo from her eyes she found herself plastered against Zach's body. 'You were out for the count,' she pointed out, her spirits soaring at seeing the return of the warm and smiling Zach she knew.

'I'm not now,' he said, rubbing against her to let her know he was very awake indeed. His hands glided over her, creating tingling paths of pleasure over her breasts, down to circle the swell of her stomach and down further to make her gasp. 'You're beautiful,' he murmured in her ear.

Rosa's reply was a slow, 'Mmmmmmmmmmm,' coherent sentences feeling too difficult.

It was some time before they made it out of the shower and by then Rosa felt as if her legs had turned to boiled spaghetti. Luckily, both she and Zach were dressed by the time they heard a thumping on the French doors to the terrace.

'Zachary!' a man's voice roared.

Zach's head snapped around, a frown puckering his brow. 'That's Dad. What the hell is up with him?'

They hurried to unlock the door and slide it open to find Steve, his face twisted with fury, waiting with two blue-clad police officers, a man and a woman. 'Must you always be wrong side of the law?' Steve all but howled.

The officers gazed at him, astonishment written plainly in their expressions. After a pause the female officer addressed Zach. 'Mr Zachary Bentley?'

Zach, after directing a blistering glare at Steve, told them he was. 'Is this about the report I made last night?'

'Perhaps we can speak to you privately?' the male officer broke in, a wary eye on Steve, who had snapped into silence.

321

Zach took the officers indoors. Rosa stared out on the terrace and glared at Steve. 'What the hell's your problem?'

Steve glared back. 'It's always the bloody police with Zach.'

Fury erupted inside her and she found herself yelling. 'He's helping the police sort out some seriously bad people. He's helped a younger guy out of a crap situation. He's working *with* the police!' When Steve looked taken aback, Rosa took a step towards him. 'You automatically thought the worst of him.'

'You fly with the crows, you get shot at,' Steve muttered, but looking a lot less sure of himself.

Rosa snorted. 'Only by people who shoot first and ask questions later.'

Then she turned at the sound of the French door opening once again. Zach and the police officers strode out. Zach addressed Rosa but he was wearing that closed, remote look again. 'They picked up Beppe last night so they need my statement as a matter of priority. My phone's run out of charge, which is why they came to fetch me. Sorry about the bullshit with Dad.' He turned to Steve. 'Sorry you were bothered. They asked for my address in Malta so, obviously, I gave Nanna's apartment rather than Rosa and Dory's.' Then he stalked to the head of the steps, the police officers close behind.

After a moment to gather her thoughts, Rosa flew down the steps after them. The silver and blue car with *Pulizija* on the side waited at the kerb. 'Do you want me to come with you?' she called.

Discomfiture flashed over Zach's face. Then he shook his head and climbed into the back of the car.

Rosa watched it drive away. She took several deep breaths, gazing over the railings, over the seafront road, over the rocks, giving herself a minute to be calmed by the deep blue of the sea and sky.

When she got back up to the terrace Steve had vanished.

Good. She didn't trust herself to speak to him civilly and Zach should be the one to have the satisfaction of telling him the whole story of his involvement with the police.

She ate croissants, sorry Zach wasn't there to enjoy them with her, then busied herself with household tasks while she waited for him to return. The dishwasher was rumbling and the washing machine spinning when she received a FaceTime call from Dory. She carried her phone outside and seated herself under the shade of the terrace parasol as she answered teasingly, 'Are you sober yet?'

Dory, looking less pink-faced than last time they'd spoken, chuckled. 'Perfectly! Now we need to catch up on how everything's going with you.'

'Fine,' Rosa replied.

'Now tell me the truth,' Dory interpolated.

Rosa hesitated, wrong-footed.

On screen Dory lifted two reproving eyebrows. 'I happened to meet Marcus, Rosa. He seemed to think I'd know all about you having to take over the mortgage payments. You should have heard him making excuses! None of it's his fault, apparently. Now, how about you come clean and tell me the whole thing?'

Feeling caught out, Rosa sighed. 'Not all of it is his fault. Not the glut of properties on the market, at least. The rest though . . .' She spent the next fifteen minutes explaining how Marcus had lost his money and failed in his undertakings. 'So I'm in a negative equity trap,' she ended on a sigh. 'Or we both are but I'm the only one with any money.'

Dory had listened in silence but now she said, 'And how are things going with Zach?'

'Pretty well.' Rosa felt a smile break across her face at the memory of this morning's adventures in the shower. Then the smile faded. 'I think I'm going to have to go home though. The only way I can see to get out of this financial situation is to take up my job again full-time. Nothing else makes sense.'

Dory snorted. 'What part of "let me help you" didn't you understand when we discussed it before?'

But Rosa cut across her. 'I can't let you help me pay off the shortfall if we could sell the property, Mum. It would be like flushing the money down the toilet. That's not the same as supporting me through uni.'

Dory closed her eyes and groaned. 'Rosa, I am going to get *serious* money for this TV show. *Serious*. I'll buy the frigging place for what you owe on it and rent it out.'

Rosa paused, wondering how much money *serious* money was but not able to believe the situation was going to be resolved this easily. 'It's a nice idea but you can't rely on getting tenants, from what the estate agents have said to me.'

'You can always get tenants if you price it low enough. In a couple of years the road will be finished and people looking for affordable property will forget that there used to be a pretty view. Prices will come back up and I'll sell it. Next problem?'

Head spinning, Rosa stammered out her thanks, tears burning in the corners of her eyes. 'I don't suppose there is a next problem,' she sniffed. 'If you're sure . . . ? You're the best mum in the world! When are you coming back to Malta? I owe you a slap-up dinner with champagne to celebrate your TV show.'

Dory looked coy. 'I'm going to stay with Leslie for a while. He's got a month's consultancy work here, then we might come back. You can stay on that lovely sunny island and have a lovely time with your lovely man, OK? You can give me lots of help working remotely,' she added quickly, as Rosa opened her mouth. 'So stop looking for problems and enjoy your summer and take your time deciding what to do next, as we agreed.'

'I intend to,' Rosa said, squeezing in a few more thank yous before ending the call. Heart soaring, she watered the plants on the terrace, noticing, guiltily, that the herbs were looking desiccated without Dory bestowing TLC. She wiped the table ready for lunch, wondering when Zach would return and executing a few happy dance steps, light as air without the house problem on her shoulders. She was pretty sure she knew what she was going to do next. She needed to talk to Zach first though.

A prickle ran up her neck and she swung around to find him standing at the top of the steps, watching her. She giggled, feeling her face heat up, but it wasn't the first time he'd seen her dance. She started to burst out with her good news. 'Guess what?' But he looked so odd that she changed direction. 'All finished with the police? Everything go OK?'

'Pretty much,' he said. 'You know what it's like. A lot of talking. Repeating. Form filling.'

'Not really,' she said, wrinkling her nose and grinning. Then, when he remained where he was, black vest top billowing in the breeze, 'What's up?'

Slowly, Zach came towards her, the expression in his eyes bleak. He took her hand and led her indoors.

'What is it?' she asked, suddenly frightened.

He led her to the sofa. 'I've been having a word with

myself. Being realistic. Rosa—' he took both of her hands, looking straight into her eyes '—I'm calling it a day.'

She stared at him, at his unsmiling mouth and ruffled hair, unwilling to believe that he meant what she thought he meant.

'Between us,' he clarified, his eyes full of pain. 'I'm a trouble magnet and I don't want to involve you in stuff like the Luccio situation.'

She protested. 'You were helping Luccio. Doing good.'

'Maybe,' he admitted. 'But I could see how anxious you were about me getting mixed up with Luccio, about the way these things seem to seek me out. And you're—' he paused as he hunted for words '—so nice.'

'You were disappointed when I asked you not to get involved,' she said in a small voice, disregarding the 'nice' comment. 'That was a mistake. Luccio reached out to you.'

Gently, he squeezed her fingers. 'I'm not disappointed. I can see why, after Marcus, that you like right and wrong to have clean dividing lines. But I don't always see things that way.'

Slowly, his eyes closed. When they reopened they held the same remote, bleak look that had unsettled her before. 'This morning – Rosa, I could have curled up and died when you defended me against Dad. I felt low and slimy that *I'd* put you in that position. I hated it. Defending me . . . it's so close to having to apologise for me.' He swallowed. 'If we were to carry on together you might be put in that position over and over. You see, when I heard what had happened to Luccio I didn't think of you, or you and me. I just acted. I might not mean to get involved in something similar in the future but I can't guarantee that I won't.'

'But it's because you protect the underdog,' she protested, cold dread settling in her stomach.

He didn't argue. Instead, he lifted a hand and pressed his fingertip to her lips. 'I mean it.'

He held her hands for a long moment more then, as Rosa watched in shock, packed his stuff and moved back upstairs.

Chapter Twenty-Four

Zach trudged into the family apartment, backpack over his shoulder and snorkelling gear hanging from his hands.

Amanda was seated on the sofa with a book, which she closed as soon as she saw him. 'Dad told me what happened. I think he feels bad.' She hesitated. 'But, darling, must you always involve yourself in the problems of others? It always seems to rebound on you.'

If anything was needed to reassure him that he'd made the right decision concerning Rosa, his mother's words did the job. Misery churned inside him as black as boiling tar and for once he didn't care if his mum was upset. 'I'm going to buy an airbed and pitch camp on the roof. If you see Dad, ask him to stay away from me, will you?'

She inched to the edge of the sofa, face lined with concern. 'Have you and Rosa argued? Dad might explain to her why he jumped to conclusions if it will help—'

He heard the bitterness in his laugh. 'I don't need his kind of help, thanks very much.' Then he stopped, feeling a cold hard lump jump to his throat. 'It's over with Rosa,' he muttered. 'I need leaving alone.'

He tossed his things in the corner then left the apartment, head averted as he passed the lower terrace in case Rosa was there. This morning he'd walked all the way back from the police station hating himself. He'd let Rosa get involved in driving him and Luccio to the ferry. Luccio had broken into her apartment, for fuck's sake! He'd shoved Rosa over, invaded her privacy, scared and upset her. Then, not thinking that his actions might later impact on Rosa, Zach had pissed off Beppe. Beppe might go to jail eventually but he'd be around once he'd been charged, possibly stirring up trouble. What if he made trouble for Rosa? Luccio had said Beppe didn't treat women well. What if he was violent with Rosa? Or worse . . . ?

And Rosa's defending him to his dad had been humiliating. Today she'd been on his side but what if one day she saw him differently? What was the word she'd used about her own dad? 'Grubby'? His breath caught. He wouldn't be able to bear it if she thought of him like that. He remembered when he'd done his community service, aware of people talking. Whispers that followed him like the breeze through leaves. He couldn't risk hurting her.

Wouldn't.

He'd skimmed across the surface of life since his eighteen-year-old self had committed that first transgression.

But now . . . he was feeling everything deeply. Every . . . thing.

Jaw set, he bought an airbed and foot pump then carried them home, threw them on the roof terrace and went out again to drink beer and detest himself.

When he returned home it was past midnight and he had to cling on to the stone handrail to make his feet follow the steps. Once on the roof he found, to his surprise, the airbed inflated and laid under the canopy, made up

329

with a pillow and a couple of sheets. Water, crisps and sandwiches were set out beside it. Water was a good idea, he thought. If he drank the contents of one of the bottles he'd have something to pee in.

Luckily, he'd lain down without actioning this plan when he heard footsteps and his sisters appeared, seating themselves cross-legged on the floor beside his bed. 'I'm smashed,' he warned them.

'Thought you would be.' Electra patted his hand.

Marci followed suit.

'What?' he said suspiciously, pulling himself up on an elbow – with difficulty – to glare at them.

'Nothing,' they chorused.

He fell back on his pillows. 'Thanks to whoever made up the bed,' he said gruffly.

'We waited till the kids were asleep or you'd probably have found them in it.' Electra laughed. Then she sobered. 'Mum told us . . . about Rosa.'

'Yeah.' He closed his eyes again.

They remained silent. But when Zach felt the first swimminess of drunken sleep he heard Marci sigh. 'You always stuck up for us, Zach. We wish there was something we could do. Dad's sorry if he messed things up. We could talk to Rosa—'

'I messed things up with Rosa. I mess everything up. She'll be better off without me.' He didn't open his eyes. 'Let me go to sleep.' It came out as a grumble but he knew his sisters wouldn't take offence.

'You're one of the good guys,' Marci protested. 'You've been great while I've been out here, putting up with me moping about. Looking after Paige.'

'And I came to you instead of Mum and Dad,' Electra said, her voice low. 'There's a reason for that, Zach. I

330

needed time to think and someone to talk to and I knew you'd be great.'

He turned on one side. 'We've hardly had a chance to talk.' But he opened his eyes again. 'But now you've stopped me passing out, why don't you both tell me what you're going to do next?'

Silence. The girls exchanged glances. 'Make good homes for our kids?' Electra said, after some thought.

Marci nodded. 'Best place to start. Now all we have to do is decide how.'

'Be as happy as you can?' Zach suggested.

Both sisters seemed struck by this and they talked it over for a while, sharing one of Zach's bags of crisps. He flitted uncomfortably in and out of sleep, the roof seeming to tilt alarmingly as his body punished him for drinking too much.

Finally, Marci patted his elbow, saying, 'Don't let Dad spoil things.' Electra ruffled his hair, then they got up and left him to his drunken dreams.

In the morning he had to let himself into the apartment to use the bathroom and be ill. That hadn't happened for years and it didn't make him feel any better about himself. He cleaned his teeth, which improved things microscopically, and he wished himself a million years away from this hangover.

When he emerged he found Steve waiting, his hair tumbled. 'Your mother said I have to apologise,' he said gruffly.

'Don't bother, if that's the only reason you're doing it.' Zach went to the kitchen sink, filled a pint glass with water and sank it. He waited to see whether it would make a reappearance. When he was sure it wouldn't he turned to find his dad still lingering.

'OK,' Steve said with an obvious effort. 'I'm sorry because I'm sorry. That girl of yours gave me what for and she was right.'

Pain lanced through Zach's head and heart simultaneously. 'You admitting you're wrong? That's a first! Anyway, she's not my girl now.' She wouldn't have to worry about him getting mixed up with bad people or shoving bullies down stairs any more.

He refilled his water glass and made to brush past, wondering if he could sleep again, sleep off his pounding head and queasy stomach.

'Zach!' Steve called.

Sighing, Zach turned back.

Steve ran his hand through his greying hair. 'I'm sorry if I spoiled things with you and her. I had been thinking about what you said about me alienating people. But when I opened the door to two coppers asking for you—' He passed a hand across his eyes. 'I saw red.'

Zach wanted to snap, 'And red's your favourite colour, right?' but he brought himself up short, hoping it was real remorse he saw in his dad's eyes and having to acknowledge that Zach's history with the police was a factor in Steve's snap reaction. 'Thanks for the apology but you've probably done Rosa a favour.' And somehow he made it out of the door.

Zach did manage a couple of hours more sleep, waking only when the sun angled under the canopy to bathe his face. His hangover had abated a little but his leaden guts reminded him that the greater ill was emotional.

He lay on the airbed, which was beginning to make him unpleasantly sweaty in the rising heat of the first day of August, and forced himself not to run down the steps to Rosa and tell her he didn't mean it. Didn't want it. But nothing had changed. He was still him. Instead, he break-fasted on the crisps his sisters had left him then went downstairs intending to shower away the last of the stale alcohol.

He halted just inside the apartment. Suitcases littered the hallway. Paige, better than any guard dog when she heard the sound of the door, bounded out of her room. 'We're going on an aeroplane tomorrow! Me and Mummy and Granny are going to sit together and Auntie Electra, Hux and Grampy are going to sit together! Mummy says on the plane I can have a box of chips to eat.'

'Wow, that's amazing,' Zach answered automatically. He raised his eyebrows as Marci hovered into view. 'You're going?'

She looked pale but managed a smile. 'I think Granny needs help putting things in her bag, Paige.'

'I'll do it!' Paige turned and raced down the hall, arms extended like aeroplane wings.

'You're going?' Zach repeated softly. He'd lived with his sister and his niece for weeks before the rest of the family had descended on them and was taken by surprise at her sudden decision.

'We all are.' She drew him into the kitchen area and set the kettle to boiling. 'Electra's made me see that a good first step is to stick with the job I have and I'm good at, in the short term. I'm going to see if I can get behavioural therapy to help with anxiety. I've arranged an HR interview to talk about a phased return to work. What I think will help me cope is that Electra and Huxley are going to live with Paige and me, at least while she looks for a job. I won't be alone. In fact, I feel pretty optimistic about living with Electra. We'll shore each other up.'

333

'It sounds like a great plan.' Impulsively, he hugged Marci. It *did* sound like a great plan. Marci would steady Electra; Electra would buoy Marci up; the sisters would babysit for each other. He realised Marci was speaking again.

She lowered her voice. 'Mum and Dad are going to "talk".' She made air quotes with her fingers and flipped her eyebrows expressively.

'How do you think that's going to work out?' One side of his mouth quirked.

She blew out her cheeks. 'We can only leave that to them. Maybe it's a step in the right direction that Dad has admitted he's approached Mum's disability like his problem instead of her problem. And I think he's genuinely horrified to have put a spoke in between you and Rosa. It's made him take a hard look at himself.'

Zach didn't – couldn't – answer.

She smiled tentatively, sliding a hand onto his shoulder. 'However successful or unsuccessful we are in sorting ourselves out it's time we all went home and stopped letting our problems impact on you. We've crowded you for too long. We all love you and want the best for you, Zach. Don't be too hard on yourself.'

Patting her hand, he tried to say, 'Thanks,' but the lump in his throat blocked the word from coming out.

Chapter Twenty-Five

The seven-day weather forecast said, 'Hot and sunny'. So did the ten-day and fourteen-day. Rosa closed her laptop with a sigh. August in Malta was sweltering. So here she was in the middle of all this hot-and-sunny on a nugget of gold in the middle of a sapphire ocean and she felt as if the bottom had dropped out of her world.

Since packing his things yesterday, Zach had stayed away from her.

She'd caught up on everything she'd promised to do for her mum for now. What should she do next? Malta had something for everyone – wasn't that what the tourism sites said? Swimming, snorkelling, diving, restaurants, cafés, bars, history, bus rides . . .

As she pondered all these options, she wandered outside, fighting the urge to look up and see if a hot man was gazing down at her from the roof terrace. She quelled it. But she jumped when she realised someone was coming down the steps. Squaring her shoulders she turned.

It was Marci, smiling.

Rosa's shoulders relaxed, even as disappointment bit

into her that it wasn't Zach. She arranged her features in an answering smile. 'Hiya.'

'Hiya.' Slowly, Marci approached. 'We're all leaving tomorrow. I'm sure everyone will want to say goodbye but I wanted to take a moment to say thanks for the time you spent with Paige.'

Rosa was surprised Marci felt such a small service deserved a particular mention. 'You're welcome.' Then her heart tipped over as she realised what Marci had said. 'You're all leaving?' she queried. All?

Marci shrugged. 'Well, not Zach. I don't know what his plans are.'

Something like relief coursed through Rosa but she hid it behind a cool, 'I see.'

An uncertain expression crossed Marci's face. She hesitated, before saying in a rush, 'It's just a shell. Zach's not such a tough guy underneath. It's a pity Dad turned up. I think Zach was beginning to believe in himself but then Dad managed to overlay that with his own distorted views. Dad doesn't even realise he's doing it. He's a negative person. Minor faults are blown up in his mind to become major issues. Zach's not a gangster, Electra's not a selfish waster and I'm a single mum with anxiety, not the burdensome embarrassment Dad seems to see. But when you're told something often enough you begin to believe it.'

Unsure that she should comment, Rosa joined in the hug Marci offered. 'Thanks. I'll miss you,' she muttered.

Marci blinked reddening eyes. 'Try not to give up on him.' She turned and headed back the way she'd come.

After staring sightlessly at the geraniums and herbs around the patio, Rosa fetched her bag, locked up the apartment and set out, following the sea creek past the bridge to Manoel Island, hardly aware of the multitude of vendors touting boat and bus trips as she reached Sliema or the press of sweaty tourists. She cut across until she reached the slightly quieter promenade at Għar id-Dud. There she found a table at one of the kiosks and bought a pint of Cisk. Enjoying the shade from the canopy, her back to the other customers, she watched the waves rolling onto the rocks and families laughing and calling as they enjoyed the rippling sea.

Until this summer her life had been ordinary. Then she'd come here and before long had begun to understand how narrow her horizons had been, living in Liggers Moor, the town where she'd been brought up, with a guy she'd been to school with. Life could be less ordinary, she realised. In fact, this summer had been pretty extraordinary.

A conviction grew in her. She might not yet know what she was going to do with her life but she knew what she wasn't going to do.

Wasn't that just as important?

She picked up her phone. Marcus answered her call, sounding apprehensive. 'I was going to call you. There's a problem.'

'Always is,' she replied philosophically. 'What is it this time?'

Marcus cleared his throat. 'The electricity bill,' he said gruffly. 'I can't pay it. I've got my website sorted now and stuff to sell so I'll be earning soon though,' he added hurriedly.

Rosa took a couple of sips of her cold beer and sank lower in her chair. 'We put all the bills in your name when I left so how does this concern me?'

The silence lasted a good ten seconds. At last Marcus, sounding thunderstruck, said, 'I thought . . . that is, I can't pay . . . obviously it's got to *be* paid, so I hoped—'

337

'I'll leave you to figure that out,' she said calmly. 'Meanwhile, Mum's prepared to buy the house for what it will take to cover the mortgage, freeing us from the negative equity trap. I can rely on you to vacate without being forced out, can I?'

Another of those long, thunderstruck silences. Then, 'Hey, hey, hey, you're moving quickly aren't you?' Marcus spluttered. 'Where am I supposed to live?'

'I'm afraid I'll have to leave you to figure that out too,' Rosa said. 'Unless you have an alternative way of buying me out? Maybe another big win?' she asked.

Marcus said nothing.

'Thought not. So I'll tell Mum you'll move out and ask her to get the ball rolling, shall I?'

'I suppose I have no choice.' Marcus sounded dazed.

'I don't think you have,' Rosa said softly. 'Bye, Marcus.' Ending the call, she ordered another pint of beer and watched pigeons perching on the stone posts between the railings that guarded the drop to the sea.

She'd drunk her second pint and was halfway down her third when she telephoned Georgine.

'Hey, you!' Georgine sounded upbeat. 'I hope you're calling with good news. I have my fingers and toes crossed. We're having a fab summer here but we need our super-schmoozer back pouring her energy into the place.'

Rosa laughed but tears pricked the corners of her eyes. 'About that,' she said awkwardly.

'Oh.' Georgine sighed. 'This isn't good news?'

'I've decided not to return to Liggers Moor yet,' Rosa admitted. 'Sorry. You were fantastic, letting me take a leave of absence, but I look at all the amazing things Mum's doing with her life and I want to change direction too. Not to be a bestselling writer but . . . well, something.'

338

After another sigh, Georgine said, 'I suspected you'd make this decision. As much as I'm gutted to hear this news, I want you to be happy. There will always be a place for you at Blackthorn's though. Don't forget that. And I expect an invitation to visit you in Malta.'

'Absolutely!' Rosa responded. 'Malta – or wherever I end up.' They dealt with the formalities of Rosa resigning without working her notice and she ended the call feeling a crazy, whirling combination of sadness, happiness, anticipation and apprehension. 'You've done it now,' she told herself aloud, making a woman at the next table grin and give her a thumbs-up.

She ordered lunch, feeling the three pints of lager sloshing a little in her empty stomach, then picked up her phone again, selecting *Dad* in her contacts, then *message*.

Mum told me what happened, she typed as a conversation opener, then she paid her bill and set off walking again while she waited to see if she'd get a reaction, jogging down steep steps onto the rocky foreshore at Font Ghadir, peering into rock pools where children were plying fishing nets.

Her phone buzzed.

I shouldn't have done it but she's got so much more and I haven't had a job for a long time, Glenn wrote. He continued with blame, regrets and excuses in equal measure, then: *I am sorry I wasn't a better dad too because you seem a very good person like your mum.*

Rosa actually smiled as she read it, though she shook her head at the same time. It was nice to receive a compliment from him for once but Glenn would never change. Like Zach's dad, he didn't like to attach blame to himself. Marcus was much the same.

Only Zach was a big enough man to take responsibility for everything he was. And look where that had got them.

339

She tucked her phone away and scrambling on over the rocks, watching jet skis and boats plunging through the waves fifty yards out, still thinking about her dad and how he'd never had much because he'd never worked for it.

A thought hit her so hard that she actually stopped, one foot on one rock and one on another.

Glenn had brought influence to bear on her for probably the first time in her life.

All he had to look back on was regrets. She wasn't going to do the same.

Chapter Twenty-Six

Zach had got the apartment back how he liked it, more than three weeks since his family had left. The fridge was full of beer, bread rolls, ready-prepared salad, burgers and chops. Only one bed wore bedclothes and that was his.

From phone calls, he knew Marci and Electra were doing OK sharing Marci's home and Paige had almost stopped mourning opportunities to 'shnorkel'. Huxley had graduated to saying 'Utts WANT!' when he desired something. Amanda and Steve were 'living apart together' in their home while they decided whether they could find a new way for their relationship to exist. Harry now had daily carers and Rebekah was managing well. Nobody had suggested there was now a need for Zach to go home to Cornwall.

Aunt Giusi had finally decided not to live in the so-far empty apartment in Ta' Xbiex Terrace House because of the steps and would remain in Lija. Zach was fitting the kitchen and bathroom and furnishing the place as a holiday let. The work would last about four weeks, which would take them to the third week in September, so he'd advertised it from 1st October. It had been booked for half-term week within the hour and was now taken for most of October and November.

It was a pain in his backside that Aunt Giusi's apartment was on the lower floor. There was a wall between the lower terraces but Zach could often hear Rosa's music or her voice on the phone. It sucker punched him every time.

With plenty of time on his hands, Zach had dusted off his laptop and was teaching himself fiction writing from a book, trying to understand the value of resolving conflict and achieving goals – at least on behalf of his characters. He wasn't sure he'd ever make that headway himself. In fact, being stuck after the first few chapters, unable to develop his story but enjoying the occasional erotic scene felt like a metaphor for his life.

He continued to volunteer at Nicholas Centre. He missed Luccio. Joseph had taken on a school leaver called Carmen in his place.

From time to time his path crossed Rosa's, as she was still living in the lower apartment. She was politely friendly but never initiated a conversation. Daily, he wrestled with his feelings for her versus his decision not to drag her into his messes.

Now, Saturday afternoon, he was back to where he'd been when she arrived in June: on the roof terrace pretending to work and watching her. She'd watered the plants and eaten lunch on one of the loungers while she did something on her phone. Then she'd swivelled round and perched on the edge of the lounger, becoming very still.

Deep in thought?

Feeling ill?

Finally, she turned and looked straight at him. Caught

staring, he wanted to retract his head like a tortoise. Instead he watched her rise and pad barefoot across the terrace towards the stairs.

Tensely, he waited.

Then, just when he thought she must have gone down the stairs not up, she appeared, strolling across the roof terrace in a short orange and yellow ethnic print dress. She helped herself to one of the chairs that he'd neatly stacked and sat at an angle to him, hair writhing in the breeze. It was longer now but still curled at the ends like a host of inverted question marks. 'I've come to tell you I'm leaving,' she said. 'Mum might be back in a week or two but, anyway, she'll pay the rent to the end of October as agreed.'

He'd almost stopped listening at 'I'm leaving.'

'Oh,' he croaked. He had to swallow. 'Where are you going?' His heart took up a slow, panicked rhythm. She was leaving. Going. Nearly gone.

Her gold eyes remained fixed on him. 'I almost had to return to Yorkshire. Marcus couldn't make the house payments so I thought I'd have to take them over and maybe even live in the house because it's deep in negative equity. But Mum put on her white hat and galloped to my rescue.'

Astonishment made him say, unguardedly, 'All this happened in the last three weeks?'

She tucked her hair behind her ears. 'In July. I didn't tell you because I wanted to enjoy that week together without wasting it worrying about the inevitable.' Her gaze didn't waver. 'It was a real threat to us being together. If your family had needed you at home, that would have been another real threat.'

As Zach watched dumbly, her eyes shut for a couple

of seconds and then flipped open. 'Those were the things I thought would end us. Not your bullshit. It's not what you call being a trouble magnet that's keeping us apart. It's how you've chosen to see yourself.'

She rose, smoothing her dress. 'I've given you three weeks to get over yourself but it hasn't happened. Do you remember our conversation about being at our crossroads? Well, I'm going down one of those new avenues. I'm not going back and I'm not going to spin my wheels any longer. You've made a decision and we're both stuck with it.'

He licked his lips, which had gone suddenly dry. 'Where are you going?'

'Italy.'

'Italy?' he repeated blankly.

'To start with. Mum's funding my travel so I've bought a ticket to Milan. My plan's to head east from there – see places like Croatia and Montenegro. After that—' She shrugged. 'Who knows?'

Speechless, his heart wrenching around inside his chest, he watched her turn and walk away.

Then she paused.

Retraced her steps.

Her eyes were angry now. 'I'm going to say something else. I suppose I thought it was obvious but maybe it's not. Zach, I believe in you. I was right beside you getting Luccio out of Malta. None of the *trouble* you've been in has been that troublesome, in my view. You're a good guy. Steve's just undermined you. If there had been a stink when you shoved Beppe down those stairs, I wouldn't have vanished like your old girlfriends. You could have trusted me.'

She planted her hands on her hips, her voice rising.

'And, by the way, do you envisage that because you've rejected me with the excuse that it's for my own good I'll find a better kind of happiness with someone else? That this miraculous man is waiting for me and I'll one day be grateful to you for saving me from myself? That's breathtaking arrogance.'

Her small bare feet carried her a step closer to him, her eyes narrowing. 'You say you're protecting me by ending things but I think you're protecting yourself – from me disappointing you if things go wrong again. At least own it!' She dashed the back of her hand across fast-reddening eyes and choked, 'Good luck, Zach. Don't stay at the crossroads forever hiding behind "I am not worthy". It'll be lonely.'

Smarting, but also fighting the urge to smile at being the target of her speaking up for herself, Zach watched her stalk down the stairs.

He had a grandstand view then as she took garbage out to the collection point on the street, straightened loungers, swept the terrace and carried cushions inside. Despite the heat of the day, he shivered. Was she preparing to leave *straight away*?

A couple of hours later, Rosa dropped her phone in her pocket, swung her backpack onto her shoulders and checked the lock on her suitcase.

Her eyes burned as she stepped out onto the terrace for probably the last time and locked the door. She loved Malta but she couldn't bear to be so near Zach without hope. Without touching him. Loving him. Seeing nothing but wariness in his eyes when they met. She could live without a man, obviously, and had been brought up knowing exactly how to. Nevertheless, her heart felt like a rock. A big, heavy, lined with lead, rolled in crap, rock.

She looked up at the sound of voices and two male uniformed police officers arrived on the terrace. They paused at the top of the stairs and nodded hello, then began up the stairs to the Bentley family apartment.

She paused. The doorbell sounded and after a few moments she heard Zach speak, then the rumble of the police officers' voices. She strained to listen.

Then voices came closer and the police officers passed down the stairs to the street.

Rosa stood frozen. Her phone beeped and she thought it was probably her cab driver to tell her he was waiting in the street below but still she couldn't make herself leave. What if Zach needed help?

Then, Zach came down the steps. Slowly, warily, he halted, clearing his throat. 'My car's been found on Dingli Cliffs.'

Her eyebrows flew up. Dingli Cliffs were on the other side of the island. 'What was it doing there?'

He shrugged. 'Presumably joyridden. I haven't been out today and hadn't noticed it had gone. Someone's tried to set fire to it, but it didn't take hold. The police came for the key. They've towed it and now they want to get in and have a look around.'

'Beppe's revenge?' she asked. 'I suppose he's out, awaiting his court date.'

He shrugged again. 'Maybe.' His eyes slid away from hers. 'I'm telling you in case you thought . . .'

She watched him fight with himself, knowing very well what conclusion he thought she might have leapt to when the police officers arrived. 'I trust you,' she told him softly. 'I *trust* you, Zach. And I don't believe I've ever truly trusted a man before.'

His gaze returned to her, burning with something . . . Was it hope?

He drifted closer and, slowly, reached for her hands. 'But if it is Beppe's revenge – do you see what I meant about attracting trouble?'

Her fingers tightened on his. 'If it is then you've annoyed a criminal by getting Luccio safely away. Just like you were trying to help your friend Stuart in that pub, and just like you got caught in stupid teenaged high jinks because you were busy saving Stuart's life. You stand up to be counted when it matters, when most people take the safe option.' She paused before repeating deliberately, 'I *trust* you.'

His eyes searched hers. Dark. Intense. He cleared his throat again. 'Enough to stay?'

Her heart leaped and a smile took control of Rosa's mouth but she suppressed the urge to jump into his embrace. He was asking her for a commitment but it felt important that he make a choice too. 'Definitely. I want to be with you, Zach. In Malta, in England or halfway around the world. But,' she added, holding his gaze, 'only if you can trust me too.'

Then he was dragging her into his arms, crushing her to him. 'I do. And I sure as hell don't want to live without you.'

In her pocket, Rosa's phone began to ring. After several moments of hot, urgent kisses, she freed herself to answer.

'This is Aaron, your taxi driver,' the voice in her ear said politely. 'I am outside your building.'

'Sorry,' she said breathlessly, her heart soaring up into the blue Maltese sky. 'I'll run down and pay your fare – but I'm not going to the airport today after all.'

Epilogue

Nineteen months later

Zach jumped out of the cab and hurried up the broad, swept path of the palazzo in the centre of Malta. March was a good month for a wedding, before the hot weather set in. If it had been August he was pretty sure he would have had to wear ice packs inside his dark blue suit.

He was late, though he'd called ahead to explain.

Joseph, waiting with the wedding planner, beamed when Zach hove into view. 'You're late, cousin,' he said reprovingly, waving him past like a marshal at a race.

The wedding planner, a tall man with a shaven head, smiled and fell into step beside Zach. 'Don't worry. I got the photographer to take a few extra minutes with the bride inside the palazzo.'

'Thanks.' Zach slowed as they rounded the corner of the building to see the flower-decked awning and rows of people sitting either side of the central aisle on beribboned chairs. The gardens stretched around them, formal hedges beautifully clipped and daisies, lilies, freesias and orange blossom like lacy edging.

Zach flushed as everyone craned round to watch him approach, most of them grinning. A silver-haired man at the front rose with an expression of exasperation. Zach took the seat beside him. 'Sorry, Dad. Bit of a crisis report from . . . well, I can't say where from. All OK, though.' Zach was working now not just with Nicholas Centre but also other institutions who supported kids trying to get out of bad situations. Rosa had helped secure the funding for his position. He still looked after the apartments and Rosa was now a fully fledged instructor in Zumba and other dance-exercise disciplines, whizzing around the island's gyms and hotels in her silver car.

He turned to smile at his mother, Nanna Rebekah and Aunt Giusi in the row behind. Grandad Harry wasn't well enough for the journey back to Malta but they had him in their hearts.

Amanda, her sticks propped beside her, leaned forward to whisper. 'Your sisters are trying to control Hux and Paige. They started hurling rose petals around without waiting for the bride.'

Zach couldn't stop grinning, his heart pounding with excitement beneath his expensive suit. 'Good job we didn't get them handing out baskets of strawberries.' He carried on a low-voiced conversation with his parents, who still shared a house. Steve had been given early retirement and now he had a pension and didn't have to work he was less stressed. After coming so close to losing his wife he'd agreed to couples counselling. Amanda, in response, was attempting to do something she called 'including him in my independence'. What it boiled down to was that Steve

349

was learning to offer help rather than force it upon Amanda and Amanda was accepting help when she needed it – but only when she did. According to Marci, Steve must have 'swallowed an anti-negativity pill' and had made progress towards accepting other people's points of view, which made him criticise his children a lot less.

Shockwaves had rippled through the family when Zach, via Skype, had asked Steve to be his best man and Steve, after a moment's jaw-dropping shock, had audibly swallowed and said, 'I'd like that.' Perhaps the shockwaves had not so much rippled as exploded, causing astonishment and even amusement, but the gesture had been applauded by all. Electra had called it a nine-carat gold, jewel-encrusted olive branch. Rosa had shrugged and said, 'Zach wants to be friends with his dad.'

Zach looked over to the other side of the congregation and nodded at Dory's boyfriend Leslie, who looked chipper in a grey suit. Dory and Leslie divided their time between the UK, where Dory could easily service her publishing and TV obligations, and an apartment in Valletta with a view of Grand Harbour that meant their visitors spent a lot of time at the windows.

The wedding celebrant appeared at Zach's side, her suit black and blouse white, greeted him and asked, 'Ready?'

On a sudden flutter of nerves, Zach bounded to his feet. 'Dad, have you got the ring? Is my tie straight?' He tried simultaneously to check his tie, jacket and hair.

Steve rose, fishing the small box out of his pocket to brandish it reassuringly. 'You look fine.'

Then the music began and Zach turned to see Rosa walking towards him, hand-in-hand with Dory, who was resplendent in a dress and hat of buttercup yellow. Rosa's hair glowed in the sun, white flowers threaded through it. Her dress flowed around and behind her, cream satin and lace, her bouquet a mass of daisies and fern.

Zach caught his breath. She was beautiful. And she was his.

Rosa had had no intention of asking a man to 'give her away' and it felt absolutely right to drift up the aisle holding hands with her mum, the person who'd loved and cared for her. 'Zach looks amazing,' she whispered, taking in the tall, chiselled handsomeness of her husband-to-be in his well-cut suit as they processed up the swept path in the proscribed stately manner.

'You'd better marry him,' Dory whispered back.

Rosa suppressed a giggle. 'Maybe I will.'

As they drew level with the groom, Rosa exchanged Dory's hand for Zach's, smiling into his eyes as Dory took Rosa's flowers and fell a step behind. Zach's hair was dark and glossy, his jaw cleanly shaved. He made her heart lurch as, together, they took another step and met the celebrant beneath the wedding arch.

He whispered, 'You're beautiful. Sorry I was late. A supervisor at one of the houses found what she thought were pills on the floor of a young guy's bedroom. Turns out they were cinnamon Tic Tacs.' He grinned, but his fingers squeezed hers apologetically.

Rosa smiled. 'I wasn't worried.' She returned the pressure of his fingers before the celebrant cleared her throat and began the service. They'd written it together, all about trust and love, the things important to them. Rosa repeated the words that made Zach her husband, her steady voice not betraying for an instant that her heart was swooping and twirling.

Zach made his vows with the same steady certainty.

And then they were kissing and the guests applauding and beaming, Paige strewing their way with rose petals and Hux spinning around on the spot because his basket was already empty.

Zach's strong hand clasped Rosa's as if he'd never let go. Amanda dabbed her eyes and so did Dory, laughing through their tears. Rosa couldn't imagine how anyone could cry at weddings because all she felt was a dizzy, beaming joy.

Then Steve stepped forward. He cleared his throat and stuck his hand out to Zach, looking him straight in the eye. 'Proud of you, son,' he said. Rosa turned to catch Zach's stunned reaction, the smile that blazed across his face.

And she found she was crying at a wedding too, though beaming through her tears. The rose petals flew on the wind, the photographer's camera clicked, and Zach touched his lips to hers.

He looked down at her. 'Happy?'

She didn't hesitate. 'Always.'

Loved

Summer on a Sunny Island?

Then why not try one of Sue's
other sizzling summer reads
or cosy Christmas stories?

The perfect way to escape
the every day.

Come and spend summer by the sea!

Make this a summer to remember
with blue skies, beachside walks
and the man of your dreams...

What could be better than a summer spent basking in the French sunshine?

Grab your sun hat, a cool glass of wine, and escape to France with this gloriously escapist summer read!

In a sleepy village in Italy, Sophia is about to discover a host of family secrets . . .

Lose yourself in this uplifting
summer romance from the
Sunday Times bestseller.

This Christmas, the villagers of Middledip are off on a very Swiss adventure . . .

Escape to a winter wonderland in this heartwarming romance from the *Sunday Times* bestseller.

One Christmas can change everything . . .

Curl up with this feel-good festive romance, perfect for fans of Carole Matthews and Trisha Ashley.

It's time to deck the halls . . .

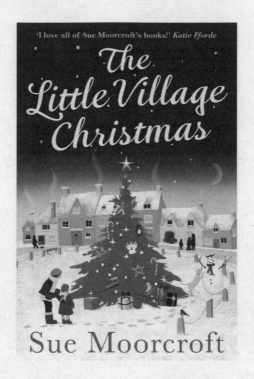

Return to the little village of Middledip with this *Sunday Times* bestselling Christmas read.

*For Ava Blissham,
it's going to be a
Christmas to remember . . .*

'I love all of Sue Moorcroft's books!' Katie Fforde

The
*Christmas
Promise*

Sue Moorcroft

Countdown to Christmas as you step into
the wonderful world of Sue Moorcroft.